NUFF SED

A NOVEL OF DESERT STEVE

MARKUS MCDOWELL

RIVERSONG
BOOKS

An Imprint of Sulis Internationa Press
Los Angeles | Dallas | London

Cover photo of desert near Gruendike's Well by Markus McDowell
Cover photo of Steve Ragsdale, July 4, 1942, by Fred Johnson. Fred Johnson Collection, Sierra Club-Angeles Chapter Archives.
Cover Design by Sulis International Press

ISBN (print): 978-1-958139-51-6
ISBN (eBook): 978-1-958139-52-3

Published by Riversong Books
An Imprint of Sulis International
Los Angeles | Dallas | London

www.sulisinternational.com

Fiction By
Markus McDowell

Nuff Sed: A Novel of Desert Steve
So Deep in Shadow
Mortals As They Walk
The Sky Over Chaos
Onesimus: A Novel of Christianity in the Roman Empire
To and Fro Upon the Earth: A Novel

Contents

For James Oban McDowell,
one of the most inquisitive and delightful boys
I have ever met.

July 15, 1921
~Blythe, California~

"'Nuff sed."

"Excuse me?" The tax collector seemed confused and not a little irritated.

"What's so difficult to understand, Mr. Jessup? I can't pay my farm tax. Acts of God and the Devil have conspired to make it impossible. Acts of God? Bad growing season and the Spanish flu pandemic. Satan? That's the government's Great War causing low cotton prices. I need an extension."

"I find it troublesome that you equate the government with the Devil, Mr. Ragsdale. These are difficult times for everyone." Jessup took off his eyeglasses and laid them atop the open file on his desk. "Even in the best of times, we rarely offer more than two extensions. You've had two."

"Don't think you understand basic economics. If I pay *you* now, I can't buy seeds and supplies for this year. I'll have no crop to sell, and you will get *nothing*. Or, I can give you twenty-five percent *now*. That enables me to buy supplies, plant a crop, and pay the rest after harvest, plus what is due for that year."

"I cannot give you another extension."

"You'd rather have nothing than twenty-five percent now and the rest later?"

Mr. Jessup looked out the window. A minute stretched out. He sighed. "I might be able to take half now and half in a month, but I will have to check with my superior."

Steve recalled that Lydia had asked him not to lose his temper. He took a breath. "Blood from a turnip, Mr. Jessup."

Jessup shook his head. "I've made my offer."

He held his tongue again. *We elect these incompetents and pay their salaries, and in return, they charge us for living on our own land.* "Do you know what a farmer is, Mr. Jessup?"

"Of course I—"

"A farmer is a human being who gets farmed to death by politicians."

"Mr. Ragsdale—"

"I have a wife and four children. You're offering me a Hobson's Choice: pay now and have no money to plant a crop. We starve. I don't pay you, you take my farm. We starve. That 'bout right?"

Jessup sighed. "I am not going to debate with you." He held Steve's gaze.

Steve nodded. "Guess it's good to be a fat ass on the government teat rather than a cotton farmer in your jurisdiction."

"Now, Mr. Ragsdale, there is no call for vulgarity. We are done. Good day."

Steve nodded and pulled out a sheet of paper. "One last thing. May I borrow your pen?"

Jessup, frowning, slid a pen and inkwell across the desk. Steve dipped the tip in the ink, signed the document, and slid it back.

Jessup looked at it and frowned. "What's this?"

Steve stood up. "You now own a cotton farm in the Palo Verde Valley. In four weeks, when we have vacated our belongings, it's all yours."

Jessup opened his mouth and then closed it.

Finally got him to shut up, Steve said to himself. "Enjoy, but beware. The government bureaucrats are the Devil's ass." He turned to leave.

"Gonna go change the world, Mr. Jessup. Or at least the part of it between here and Indio."

The tax collector found his voice. "A hundred miles of empty desert?"

"Quite true." He tipped his hat. "Farewell. I have to pay a visit to old prospector about his well."

Coffeyville, Kansas
(1882-1908)

The Old Boy Himself
~1882~

James Ragsdale stepped off the back porch and looked around his farm in the bright sun. He cupped his hands around his mouth.

"Alice! *Sarah Alice!*"

The little girl came running out from behind the barn, a dog chasing after, its long ears flapping. She screeched to a halt as she arrived, head tilted back to look up at her father. Her calico sundress was dingy and a bit ragged.

"Yes, Father?"

"I need you to watch your brother—I'm going into town to get Doc Johannsen."

"Is the new baby here?!" She did a little dance.

He smiled, his rough features softening. "It has begun."

He didn't tell her that the contractions were unusually painful, along with other discomforts. Not like the births of Alice or Charlie. James had delivered Charlie himself, in the middle of the night. A midwife had been present for Alice. This time, they needed a doctor. James thought it would be fine— some births are harder than others—but better to be safe.

"Now run along. I'll be right back. Leave your mother alone. Beatrice is with her."

He watched her disappear into the house, the screen door slamming behind, trapping the puppy outside, who began to squeal and dance about the door. James knew Alice would do as he said—for seven years old, she was remarkably mature and responsible. Not like Charlie, who was as stubborn as a mule and less smart.

James' horse was tied at the post, already saddled and bridled. He'd had a premonition the baby might come today, even though it was early.

The Ragsdale farm was only about a mile outside of town. As he galloped down the dirt road, dust kicking up behind, he wondered about this new child. Phebe was sure it was a boy. Women's intuition or something. James hoped she was right. Girls go off and get married into some other family. He needed ranch hands.

Life was rough in this frontier town, and James liked it that way. Coffeyville was a place where a man could be a man, where politicians were scarce, and the officials were concerned about practical life-and-death matters, not newfangled ideas from the big east coast cities.

He prodded his horse a little faster and scowled up at the sky. It was going to be a hot day for the new one to enter the world.

The doctor called James back. Phebe was resting, newborn in her arms, nursing. She gave her husband a weary smile.

Doc Johannsen was packing up his bag. "Well, that was a rip-snorter, James. You got one obstinate boy there."

James glanced at the newborn, quiet at his mother's breast. "But everything is well?"

"Healthy cry, which they probably heard back in town. Phebe and the baby are well. Never seen anything like this boy. Maybe it was the hailstones."

James frowned. "Hailstones?" The Doc had always been a bit quirky.

"You didn't hear? Seventeen-inch hailstones in Dubuque. Lots of damage, livestock dead, three people killed. You know, sometimes seemingly unconnected events are actually connected."

"Not sure I believe seventeen-inch hailstones."

He rummaged in his medical bag. "Swear on my Bible. Came over the telegraph just before you showed up at my office. Now…" He pulled out some papers. "Need to fill out the birth certificate." He sat down at a table and prepared his pen and ink.

"Government paperwork. Why they need all this?"

The Doc was used to James' views about politics, so he ignored him. "Name?"

Steve recited the name that he and Phebe had decided on, spelling the first one for the doctor. The doctor carefully inscribed the full name on the form, squinting through his spectacles. "Middle name Albert?"

"My father."

"Ah, good, good. Nice strong name. Parents' full names and ages?"

"James Albert Ragsdale. Phebe Ann Ragsdale. We're both twenty-nine."

The doctor filled out a few more lines, then pulled another form out of his bag and painstakingly copied the information from the first card. Once it was completed, he laid the copy aside and put the paper, pen, and inkwell back in his bag.

"Thank you, Doc, I'll render payment tomorrow."

"No hurry, James, I'll just repossess if you don't pay." He cackled. James smiled politely—Doc repeated that joke every chance he got. "No need to walk me out."

James went to Phebe. The baby was sleeping soundly now, although the expression on his face seemed like he was a bit unsure about this life.

It's not an easy life, little one, James thought to himself. *But it's a good one, blessed by the Lord with land, three children, good work to do with one's hands.*

Phebe's eyes fluttered open, and she gave James another smile.

"How are you feeling, my dear?"

"Tired, but fine."

"Quite an ordeal, the doc said."

"That just means he's gonna be strong and opinionated."

"Does it?"

"Yes." She took a breath and looked down at the sleeping child. "Would you call Alice and Charlie in?"

James went and retrieved the two, who were sitting with Beatrice in the main room. Alice had seen one newborn—Charles—when she was five. She made her way over to the bed, touching the little cheek. Charles stood waiting in the doorway, twisting his hands together and fidgeting.

"Go on over, Charlie. Say hello to your new brother."

"What's his name, Father?"

"Steven Albert Ragsdale."

"Oh, you are so stubborn!" came an exclamation from kitchen.

"Who are you talking to?" James shouted, getting up from the chair where he was cleaning his pipe.

"Your new son!" She laughed as James entered. He looked down at the infant, struggling in her lap as she tried to get him to latch on to her breast. "He's a few weeks old, and just has to have things *just so*. He wants to be on his left, not his right. Has to have this blanket around him—and he *knows* when it isn't his blanket!"

James smiled. "Smart boy. Like his sister."

"He knows what he wants, that's for sure."

"That's a Ragsdale trait. He'll do just fine." He approached the chair where she was sitting with Steve in her lap. "I'm going into town. They've started new services on the LL&G line from Chicago and Philadelphia. Gonna be lots of new businesses coming in."

"You thinking of taking a new job?" She smiled. They'd been married for eight years, but she'd known him since they were children. He was a clever and excellent provider. Always thinking.

"Amusing. But where there is growth, there is opportunity. I'm going to see if I can offer some of my services to the crews once they start working within about twenty miles of here."

"Good idea."

"With the railroad, this town is going to change a lot. Joe Parsons was complaining—said he voted against the rail coming here. Now he tells anyone who will listen that things are out of control."

"I haven't heard anything bad. The general market and clothing stores are excited."

"Eh. Growth brings both good and bad. Does no good to kick against the goads. Accept what you can't change, turn it to your advantage. Maybe someday..." he reached down and placed his large, rough hand on Steve's head. The boy stopped his struggling and crying. "...maybe someday Steve here will run one of the business ideas I got."

"Let him grow up a little bit first, my dear?"

The baby had been silent and still until now, as if he were listening to the discussion. When has father removed his hand, he stretched up and latched on to his mother's breast.

"Look at that. You have the magic touch, my dear."

"God's blessings is all." He leaned down to give her a peck on the cheek. "Be back in a couple of hours."

At the motion, little Steve pulled way and turned to look, then resumed his meal.

A Human Being Farmed to Death

~1887–1892~

Steve's first five years showed him to be an active and curious child. He was always taking things apart, he loved the outdoors. Often his parents weren't sure of his whereabouts on the farm.

"Steve! Where are you? Get in here. Your uncle will be here soon and your mother wants you cleaned up!"

Steve looked up from where he had been panning for gold in the little irrigation ditch beside the wheat fields. He knew it was unlikely to have gold in it, but it was fun to pretend. On the other hand, the discovery of gold in the Yukon last April surprised everyone, so you never knew. He had wanted to build a screening contraption across the gulley, but his father said no. Would trap too much brush, he said.

Steve would rather be outside, especially if Uncle Robert was visiting. But he knew better than to argue with Father. He put the tools away, as he'd been taught, brushed off his trousers and shirt, and headed inside.

"Steven!" his mother exclaimed as he came in the door. She waddled a bit, as she was going to have another baby in about five months. Steve hoped it was a brother—but nicer than Charlie. The last one, Rosa, was only one and a half now, and

Steve wasn't sure about her. "Your brothers and sisters are already cleaned up. Go out back and wash up, and then change into clean clothes. Uncle Robert will be here in less than thirty minutes."

Steve never understood why they had to get "cleaned up" when Uncle Robert visited. *He* never cleaned up. He was loud, he enjoyed embarrassing Steve for some reason, and he was usually drunk. Even during the day. When he was around, Steve's father often got drunk, too. Steve thought that made him what adults called "a bad influence," but his parents seemed to see nothing wrong with the man.

As he came back into the house, freshly scrubbed—though probably not to his mother's standards—he heard his uncle's horse clippity-clapping up the dirt drive. He ducked back into the room he shared with Charlie and changed clothes. He took his time, waiting for his mother or father to yell for him. He didn't wait long.

"Steve! Your uncle is here. He has something for you!"

Great. What was it? A mousetrap hidden in a newspaper? A live raccoon in a bag? The latter was the worst prank his uncle had pulled on him. The poor thing was half-starved and frightened, but not as scared as Steve when he opened the bag and the raccoon flew out, scratching and clawing. Even his father seemed irritated by that one, although Charlie couldn't stop laughing.

When he came out of the room, his uncle was standing with his back to him, speaking with his father. Charlie was sitting on the couch next to Sarah, who was holding Rosa. She was allowed to do that even when Mother wasn't in the room because she was twelve.

"You're not kiddin', brother," his father was saying. "I knew Cleveland would make a terrible president. What a waste, that giant statue from France! Governments shouldn't be spending money on such useless trifles."

"Yup, gonna be some big dedication in October with a ticker tape parade." As Uncle Robert spoke, he turned and saw Steve, who was trying to work his way over beside the couch where he might not be noticed. "Hey, little podner, there you are! I brought you something special. You heard of Coca-Cola?"

Of course he had! *Everyone* had heard of Coca-Cola since it came out last year. He had never tried it, though one kid at school said he had one on a trip to Independence. He said it was like drinking candy syrup, but it tickled your mouth.

"I've heard of it." He was both excited and suspicious.

His uncle smiled. "But ya haven't had one, right? Wait right here." He disappeared into the kitchen.

Steve looked at his siblings. "How come you guys don't get any?"

"We already got ours," Charlie said, smothering a grin. An obvious lie, and besides, there were no drinking vessels nearby. Steve might only be five, but he wasn't stupid.

Robert came back. "Here ya go, little guy. Taste the nectar of the gods!" He handed Steve a small wooden cup filled with a dark liquid. Steve took the cup and looked inside. It did not look appetizing. It smelled syrupy sweet—like he'd heard—but with some other smell he didn't recognize.

"Go on, take a gulp!"

Steve took a tentative sip. It *was* sweet, but something else

—

"Aw, go on, ya can't have that experience everyone is talking about without taking a gulp. You'll feel it going down!"

Steve took a deep breath and upended the little cup. As soon as it began flowing down his throat, he knew he'd made a mistake. Not only did his throat burn like fire, but there was a terrible taste mixed in with the sweetness. Like kerosene.

He gagged, and his stomach roiled. Robert was bent over laughing. Steve could hear Charlie cackling. As he flew out onto the porch, he heard Robert say, "I put some of my whisky in it. The look on his face!"

Steve heard his mother say, "Oh, Robert, that's not—" before he vomited over the side of the porch.

A few years later, his father felt he was old enough to learn how to hunt.

"Hold still," his father whispered. "If you make a sound or motion, you'll spook him."

He wanted to say, "I know! I'm eight!" But his father was right. He tried not to move a muscle. His arms began to ache, holding his Marlin 1881 rifle. He continued to look down the barrel at the white-tailed deer.

"Don't hold your breath like that," his father whispered in his ear. "Slow, long breaths. If you don't, then you'll have to take a big breath, and he'll hear you. Only hold your breath when you squeeze the trigger."

The deer jerked its head up, looking in their direction. Steve didn't move a muscle—not even his eyeballs. The deer kept looking for a bit, then relaxed and resumed eating the grass below.

"See?" His father whispered. "You've now learned a lesson without any consequences. Lessons are better *with* consequences—the worse the consequence, the more effective the lesson. So you'll have to work to remember this one."

Steve had practiced enough back at the ranch. He didn't need his father's reminders. But if he was honest, he was glad he was here the first time doing real hunting.

The whispered comments continued, which seemed to violate his father's own words. "You know how to sight. Line up his heart—not the head. Head is a better shot, but harder to make."

The deer had his head forward and down, grazing. An eight-pointer. Steve could see the front ribcage from the side, but it was slightly obstructed by some branches. He had a clear view of the top of its head.

He slowly moved the rifle sight over the deer's forehead. Right in the center, just above the eyes. He took a breath, let it out, and held it. He squeezed the trigger just as his father spoke. "Now, when you are—"

The forest echoed with the blast. The deer jerked, back legs splayed out, then he convulsed and collapsed in a heap.

His father stood up. "Welp. Not what I told you to do—risky head shot. But can't complain when it's dead on. Let's go take a look."

"Steve, what a wonderful specimen!" his mother exclaimed when she saw his kill. Alice, Charlie, and Rosa trailed along. "We'll have some fine venison in the coming weeks."

Steve beamed.

"Ha, Mother, what do you know about shooting deer?" Charlie said. "I been shooting since I was younger than Steve."

James turned on the boy. "Pipe down. Steve did a fine job—better than your first. And by the way, your mother is an excellent marksman."

Steve grinned to himself. He loved it when Charlie got cut down to size. He got away with so much because he was thirteen. Steve couldn't wait to be thirteen.

"Gotta say, I never seen a boy so young with such a feel for a rifle. Just like his grandfather." He looked at Steve. "He'd have been proud of you—using his rifle. Next week…" he leaned down into Steve's face, "we'll hunt for some black-tail or cotton-tail. Much more difficult. Traps work better, but you need to learn to hit small targets." He stood up straight. "Now, go dress the beast. You earned that right."

Charlie made a rude sound.

"When you're done," James continued, looking at Charlie, "have Charlie to help you wrap and store it in the ice box." Steve enjoyed the scowl on his brother's face. "I'm gonna go read today's *Journal* and see what else Harrison has messed up this week. Damn Democrats."

"Language!" Phebe said.

James ducked his head. "Sorry, Mother. But they just made Wyoming a state. There's nothing there but Indians and squatters! President's an empire-builder, I tell you, and nothin' good ever came of that."

"I know, dear. But don't use bad language in front of the children." She turned to Steve. "Go dress your deer and clean yourself up. I made apple pie for dessert."

"Apple pie?! Do we get some too?" Rosa said, jumping up and down.

Her mother laughed. "Yes, there is enough for everyone."

Steve headed out the door, full of pride. And not a little of it was for showing up Charlie.

In the ensuing year, Steve began experimenting with building things. His parents encouraged him, his dad was quite proud of his cleverness.

He had just finished his most ambitious project. Having installed it, he stood in the doorway, watching his new little brother sleeping in the bassinet. Such a tiny little thing. But boy, could he wail. They should have named him Wailer instead of William.

"Standing guard over your brother?" Steve jumped as his mother entered the room. "That contraption you built is quite helpful, Steve."

Steve beamed. "Father helped me with it at the end." He was working on being more humble—his father often said he was "too full of himself—be a proper gentleman."

She put her hand on Steve's shoulder. "Father said you thought of the whole thing. *Invented* it, he said."

Steve shrugged. "It wasn't that hard. I knew you were busier now that Alice got married, so I thought of this. A little bell on gears and levers so it only rings if he moves *a lot*, not just turns over or wiggles. So you don't have to keep checking on him."

She looked at the bassinet. "What about this other part?" She pointed to a line that ran from the bassinet's side, through some pulleys, and out an upper vent.

"Well," Steve said, falling into the role of teacher, "I know babies like to be rocked. So, that line there goes out and onto the roof. This is the part Father helped me with. We put up a wind vane with a ratchet gear and a stopgap, and as the wind turns it, it pulls the line and rocks William. There's a set of cogs on the roof that keep it from rocking too much if the wind is strong. And you can disconnect it right here." He pointed.

His mother was still smiling, but had a strange expression as she looked at him.

"What is it, Mother?"

She shook her head. "Nothing. Just thankful for you."

They heard footsteps on the porch and the door slam. "Phebe?!"

19

His father never called her "Phebe." As soon as his father entered the room, he knew something was wrong. He glanced at Alice, who also seemed spooked.

"James? What is it?" Phebe said, as she went to him.

James let out a big breath. His face contorted, and he turned away for a moment, looking out the window. Steve felt his heart pounding. The other three arrived at the door with Minnie holding Rosa's hand, Charlie behind.

"What's going on?" Charlie said.

James spoke. "Your Uncle Robert..." He stopped again. Steve had never seen his father this emotional.

Phebe put her hand on his arm. "What about Robert?"

"He's dead."

He Who Makes a Crooked Trail...

~1892~

"What happened?" Phebe said.

Dead? Uncle Robert was dead? Steve felt a pang of guilt as he realized he felt elation, not sadness.

James shook his head. "I'm not exactly sure. The Sheriff found me as I was leaving town. He said Robert was outside Ginger's Saloon, dead on the planks. Needed me to come get the body."

No one said anything for a moment. Phebe led James into the kitchen and set him at the table. The rest followed.

"Do they know what happened?" She asked.

"Yeah," he sighed. "He was drunk. He'd been thrown out of Poppy's, so he went down to Ginger's. They said he picked a fight with the Fallington boys, who ganged up on him. Robert was either shoved or just fell through the doorway. Must've hit his head or something. The doc pronounced him dead right there."

"Those Fallington boys are liars, father," Charlie said, anger in his voice. "I gotten in fights with 'em, too. Prolly killed uncle and then made up the story that he started the fight."

Steve doubted that. He'd also had run-ins with the Fallingtons, but Uncle Robert hung out with them all the time. They wouldn't kill him on purpose. And with Uncle's penchant for—

"There was other eyewitnesses, son."

Steve glanced at Charlie—he could see he didn't believe Father. Charlie always liked Uncle, probably because he was friendly to Charlie and mean to Steve. And ignored the girls.

There was silence. Rosa's eyes were big. Minnie, only five, was looking from her mother to her father and back, unsure of what it all meant.

Phebe took James' hand in hers. "God have mercy. I am so sorry, my darling."

"They gotta arrest them Fallington boys, right, Father? String 'em up for murder!" Charles said. "Don't matter if'n they meant to or not! He's dead." *Always the hothead*, Steve thought. *Was that tears in Charlie's eyes?*

"I don't…think…so," James said. Steve had never heard his father sound so sad. "They said Robert had been drinking all day. He was trying to start a fight in Poppy's, that's why they kicked him out. Sheriff says they was just defending themselves."

No one knew what to say. Rosa went over behind her father and put her hands on his shoulders. "I am so sorry, Father."

Steve was afraid if he said anything, his voice might betray relief rather than sympathy. He still felt guilty, but you couldn't argue that Uncle didn't have it coming. Like his mom said, alcohol is the devil's brew.

James nodded. "Thank you, children." He took another deep sigh. "I guess he loved his liquor too much."

"Steve! Where are you?"

Steve's lanky frame appeared from behind two bales of hay stacked on top of each other. "Yes, Father?"

"Your mother has dinner ready—what are you wearing?" James frowned at his nine-year-old son. He had on one of his father's old vests, a makeshift gun holster, and his cowboy hat. In his hand was a small stick, which he was holding like a pistol.

"Oh, just some stuff."

"What stuff?"

"I'm playing train robbery."

"Train robbery? Like the ones who robbed the train station in Red Rock a few weeks ago? How do you know about them?"

"Heard you talking about them with Mother. Read the paper you brought home. One of 'em escaped from prison last September after the rest robbed a station in Waggoner."

"Ah, well. Yes. That's all true." Steve was observant and clever, if a little odd. "I'm not sure pretending to be thieves and murderers is the best—"

"Oh, no, Father, I'm not the gang! I'm the head of the posse chasing 'em down! That there chicken coop is the train. We're sneaking up on them from behind the train so they won't see us. We ain't making the same mistakes the marshals made in Red Rock. They'd never come back to the caboose—only the engine and the bank car. Right?"

James smiled. "I would imagine that's right, my boy." He stepped over and rubbed the boy's mop of a head. He was surely the smartest of the bunch. "Maybe you'll be a lawman someday. However, apprehending the gang will have to come later, because all good posse leaders must eat dinner when their mother calls."

Steve pouted. "But we were 'bout to storm the train!"

"They'll wait."

Steve nodded and followed his father into the house, head down.

Four months later, in October, the family was walking down Main Street, as they often did on Thursdays. Phebe liked to go shopping on the day many of the stores got in shipments, and James enjoyed bantering with other citizens, as well as buying the latest *Coffeyville Journal*.

They had finished the shopping and other errands and we're walking leisurely back to the wagon. Phebe was holding one-year-old William as they walked. Rosa and Minnie walked just behind, holding hands. Alice had joined them from nearby Labette with her two boys, as her husband was helping raise a barn. Thankfully, Charlie had gone off to go find his friends as soon as they arrived in town.

They finished shopping and were strolling down the street. James called out to a man walking in the other direction.

"Preacher! Good to see you."

It was Reverend Blailock, who came over and shook James's hand and bowed to Phebe.

"Ah, the Ragsdale family and Mrs. Alice Thomas and the boys. And where is young Charles?"

"He's around somewhere, with John and Wilbur."

Steve caught up and shook the preachers hand firmly, as his father had taught him. "Thank you, Reverend, for the lesson last Sunday."

Steve meant it. Bold and confident, the preacher stood behind the pulpit with a thunderous voice, explaining and urging everyone how to live a godly life. It all made sense to Steve, those lessons on what to avoid, how to work hard, and how to treat others.

The man smiled. "You are most welcome, Steve. The Lord's Word is a balm to all, from farmers to the president himself."

"Well," James drawled, "thank the Lord for Harrison. Cleveland needed more of that Word." He glanced at Phebe. "In my opinion."

"Can't we all. Good day, folks."

Once he was out of earshot, Phebe leaned over. "James, you don't need to bring up how much you disliked Cleveland all the time. He's gone."

"Mark my words, woman, Cleveland's going to run again next year, and it will be a disaster if he wins."

Phebe opened her mouth to speak, but at that moment James was saved by Charlie arriving.

"Charlie, just the man I wanted to see," James said. "Would you take your mother and everyone back in the buggy? I need to go order some supplies from the farm store, and it may take a while because I need to look through some catalogs. I can walk back."

"Can I go with you, Father?" Steve asked. Not only did he *hate* when Charlie drove the buggy, but he liked Coffeyville. Sure, he enjoyed the farm—the land, the rocks, the animals, and insects, the hills in the distance (which he had explored many times). But towns—the streets, building, a microcosm of humanity, all living and working together to form a community. Stores, hotels, banks, other services. How did one plan a town? Did someone own it? Were there rules about how to lay out streets? Which buildings go where? It seemed quite interesting—and even fun—to Steve.

"I think that's fine if your mother doesn't need you for anything at the farm."

"If I need anything, Charlie can help." Phebe said. They took their leave of the others, Charlie giving Steve a sneer behind his father's back.

The two walked down to the farm store.

"Steve, I'm going to be spending some time looking over catalogs and talking to Mr. Orson. You can come with me if you want and look around, or stay out here and wait. If you come in you gotta be quiet."

"I'll stay here. I like watching the horses and buggies go by."

The main street was slightly muddy from the rains last night, and he wandered down a few blocks closer to the center of town. He watched as buggies, horses, and pedestrians went about their business. He wondered why they couldn't pave the roads with bricks or stones. Surely it couldn't be that difficult. You could design little ruts for the water to flow through when it rained. He'd read about just such a thing in ancient Roman roads. If they could do it, surely modern men could.

A commotion down the road caught his attention. In front of the First National Bank, a couple of men were yelling as they ran. Three other men ran into the Condon Bank on the other side of the street. Steve peered closely. Something wasn't right...

Down a bit further, Steve saw another group of men with guns approaching stealthily along the wooden sidewalk. Someone yelled, "someone's robbin' the banks!" Scanning the street, he saw other citizens with guns taking up positions. Another shout: "The Marshal's on his way!"

Steve scanned nearby and saw a horse with a rifle in a holster hanging from the saddle. He ran and pulled out the gun, grabbing a bag of shot hanging from the holster. He loosened the tie as he ran, crouching, to a row of barrels in front of the clothing store. Loading the gun, he took up a position that made himself as small a target as possible, while still able to see, between two barrels, the front doors of both banks. He carefully checked the gun, and then positioned his hands and lined up the barrel with his eyes at the front of the Condon Bank door.

There was a commotion, and three men burst out carrying bags and rifles. One jerked backwards with a spray of blood from his head and fell to the ground. The rest scrambled to find cover and return fire.

Steve heard screaming, yelling, and gunfire as if it were in the background. He was focused, just like he was taught and had done many times. One of the men was behind a barrel on the sidewalk, but from here, Steve had a clear shot. He squeezed the trigger, felt the recoil, and watched the man jerk and fall back.

"Nice shot, boy!"

Steve turned and saw a man squatting beside him. He must have taken cover beside him when the shooting started. Steve hadn't noticed, he was so focused on the bank entrance. His father would be disappointed. True, focus is required when shooting, but one must still be aware of the surroundings. In a different situation, he could have been easily ambushed. A lesson without consequences. He thanked God.

Steve peered back over a barrel and saw two men exiting the National Bank, firing their weapons as they ran for the alley. As he lined up to try to hit the moving target—not that different from hunting deer with his father and brothers—both men fell to the ground, writhing and screaming.

Steve turned and sat down, back against the barrels. He breathed deeply, calming himself as his father had shown him.

"Here comes the Marshal! But we took care of them, huh, buddy?!" shouted his companion. "We showed that Dalton Gang!"

Steve's head whipped around to the man. "Dalton Gang?!"

God Alone Can Understand

~1892–1901~

"My word, look at this," James Ragsdale said, sitting down at the dinner table, waving a newspaper over his head. "A Ragsdale helped take down the Dalton Gang!"

Steve was grinning from ear to ear. His father was a strict disciplinarian, and he doled out praise sparingly.

"Let me see!" Rosa said. He handed her the paper. It was folded to the story about the failed robbery. He pointed to a paragraph. She read it aloud.

> ...One brave teller declares to the robbers that the vault has a time lock and can't be opened for another 10 minutes (this was untrue.) The robbers decide to wait, however their plan is interrupted as the townspeople open fire, including George Cubine, Henry Yamamoto, Silas Brighton, J.B. Holland, and young Stephen Ragsdale.

Little Minnie turned her big eyes to Steve. "Are you a hero? Are you gonna go and fight bad guys?" She looked a bit sad at this prospect.

"No, silly, he's only ten," Rosa said.

"I heard that all four of the gang were killed, including Bill Dalton," Alice asked. "Is that true? It doesn't say here."

"It's true. We saw the bodies ourselves after I retrieved Steve," James answered.

"Did you shoot Dalton himself, Steve?" Alice asked. Steve noted that Charlie was quiet, with an unreadable expression.

Steve tried to adopt a nonchalant and humble attitude, as he had seen his father do when praised. "I just did what anyone would. I got one of them, don't know who, or even if it killed him."

"I heard Eighth Street was blocked because they were working on it, so the gang couldn't put their horses in front of the bank."

"That's what the marshal told me," James said. "They were attempting a double bank robbery. Bob wanted them to be the first to ever pull one off. Didn't end well, thanks to the citizens of Coffeyville. Including Steve."

Steve's mother entered from the other room, carrying a pot, which she placed in the middle of the table. "First of all, I do not understand all of this exuberance. Yes, the gang was killed, but citizens *died*, too! We are fortunate that Steve wasn't one of them!"

"Fair point," her husband replied. "I saw the bodies of George and Lucius. The Marshal told me there were two others. But five of the Daltons are dead."

Phoebe gave a stern look to him. "And *secondly*, the supper table is not the place for this sort of talk."

"Steve learned well. He knew how to take cover, remain calm, do what you gotta do." The look from his wife became more intense. James nodded. "But, yes, Mother is right. Let us give thanks for the food, and may God comfort our deceased citizens and their families."

After a prayer, they discussed their day as they ate. When finished, the children helped clean up the table and dishes.

Charlie walked by and leaned down close to Steve. "Good job, little brother. You did good. Maybe you *can* be a lawman some day." He gave him a little punch and went into the kitchen with a load of plates.

Steve was taken aback. That felt better than shooting one of the Dalton gang.

But he wasn't gonna be a lawman. He knew what he wanted to do.

A year later, the Dalton Gang event was forgotten, and life had returned to normal. Steve rather missed the attention he got at school because of his small part in the takedown of the gang. But the farm, schoolwork, church, and his own pursuits made him happy.

He had always loved reading, and that led him to begin writing. Mostly little snippets of poetry, at first. Occasionally, he'd try writing an article about Coffeyville, imagining that someday, perhaps, the *Journal* would publish one of his pieces.

School ended for the year as harvest season began. On their last day of school, Steve came home and went to the room he shared with Charlie. His brother was sitting on his bed looking at a piece of paper.

Charlie never read unless forced by his teachers or parents.

"What are you reading?" Steve asked.

Charlie looked up with a sinister smile. "Seems to be bad poetry."

Steve's heart sank as his brother began to read.

"Among them rolling plains and golden fields, and the sun beats down and the earth yields, are the farms of Coffeyville, proud and strong, farmers work hard all—"

Steve stepped forward and tried to grab the paper, but Charlie swung it out of the way and stood up.

"Give it *back*, Charlie!" Steve shouted.

"And though the work is tough and the days are long, their spirits remain high, their hearts are strong, for they are the backbone—"

Steve lunged at his paper. Charles twisted away and held the paper above his head. Steve jumped for it, but Charles' sixteen years made him much taller than Steve's eleven.

Charles laughed. "Hey, let a guy take a look!"

"No! It's *private*!"

Charles shoved Steve, and he fell back against the bed. He held the paper in front of him and read out loud.

"Among them rolling plains and golden fields, And the sun beats down and the earth yields—"

Steve jumped up again and swung at Charles' face with a fist. Charles moved away and the blow landed ineffectively on his upper arm.

Charles laughed. "No need for violence, little brother! Oh, this is even better!

"Lydia, the love of my life, with her brown hair and brown eyes, shining brighter than the morning light, she makes the world a paradise."

Steve knew he would never hear the end of it. "That's personal, and you have no business!"

"What is going on in here?" James was standing in the doorway. "You two stop roughhousing."

"Steve is writing poetry!" Charlie exclaimed, as he pushed Steve down again. "Listen to this! 'She is the missing piece, that I've been searching for—'"

Steve's mother appeared beside James. "Charles, you stop that right now and give it back to Steve." She looked at her husband. "Make him stop, James."

"Aw, but Mother, this is such hilarious stuff. Didn't know you was a comedy writer. 'Lydia, the love of my life,
With her brown hair and brown eyes—"

James stepped into the room. "Charles, return the paper to your brother. Go outside and clean up the horse stable like I asked an hour ago."

"But, father—"

"*Now*, Charles. Or there will be hell to pay." The swear word earned James the evil eye from Phebe, but she said nothing.

Charles tossed the paper at Steve, who grabbed after it and clutched it against his chest, dropping to sit on the floor. Charlie squeezed past his mother, muttering something about how he couldn't wait to tell the guys at church.

James sighed. "You're writing poetry?"

Steve did not look up. "Yes, sir."

James pursed his lips and gave Phebe a stern look back. "Waste of time, boy. Did you finish your chores in the barn?"

"Yes, sir."

"Cleared out that planting bed your mother wanted?"

"Yes, sir."

His father pursed his lips and said something to Phebe as he left. His mother came and sat on the floor next to him.

"Don't you mind, Charlie. He's an ornery young man, not quite an adult yet. That age is mean, but he will grow up to be a fine brother. Besides—" she ruffled Steve's hair, "I heard the last thing he read. It sounded wonderful to me. Romantic. You keep up writing. Maybe someday, you'll get published in a magazine or a book!"

Steve looked up at her. "You reckon?" He appreciated that she did not ask about Lydia.

"Indeed. I've read worse in some of my women's magazines." She took his chin in one of her hands and tilted it up towards her. "If you like writing poetry, don't you worry what anyone says. Not Charlie, not your father. Not even me."

"Father doesn't like me writing poetry."

She sighed. "Your father has worked hard all his life, scratching out a living. He never had time to read much. He doesn't understand. Sometimes, when people don't understand something, they don't like it."

"He thinks it's sissy."

She paused. "He wants you to do what he did in life, like most fathers. But each person should decide. Do you want to be a writer?"

He shrugged. "I like putting my thoughts on paper. But I like other things. I like making things—the new feed trough, the bassinet rocker, but also poetry, inventing things...I don't know. I guess I like thinking about something and then making something."

"You keep exploring whatever you want—including poetry. Charlie is just jealous."

Steve looked up at her. "You think so?"

"I know so. He is jealous of your mind and your creativity."

They were silent for a moment.

"Mother, there *is* one thing I might like to do with my life. But...I think I want to keep it to myself for now."

She stood up and ruffled his hair. "That's fine. It's a wise man who keeps his own counsel."

Steve wondered how she would react when he told her that it was not farming, or being a lawman, or *any* of the other things anyone in their family did.

He was *sure* his father would not approve.

The next few years went by quickly. The best thing Steve recalled about the time was that Charlie got married and left. He and his bride—her name was Coral Alice, but everyone called her "Isabel"—had moved into a small farm outside of town that had belonged to her grandparents, who had recently passed away.

Steve, approaching twenty years old, struggled with his life. He had finished school, and missed the reading, learning, and writing. As much as he enjoyed the farm, he would rather not work it all his life. He wanted to do something bigger—more meaningful. For many years, he had known what that was, but was unsure of the reaction he would get from his family.

One Saturday evening, he walked into the kitchen. His father was standing at the table looking at a letter while his mother was chopping vegetables.

"I want to be a preacher," he blurted out. He immediately cursed himself. That was not how he intended to bring it up.

"Oh!" His mother said, putting down the knife and turning towards him. "I think that's wonderful."

"A preacher?!" James said, dropping the letter on the table. "Why on God's green earth would you want to do that?"

"James!" Phebe said.

James turned his attention to her. "It ain't a proper man's job." He paused. "I know it's a worthy profession. But…"

"Why don't we let him tell us about it? Let's all sit down."

Steve regretted his spontaneous confession. He was keenly aware that his brothers and sisters were in another part of the home and might overhear. Rosa and Minnie, now seventeen and fifteen, would be supportive, but he wasn't sure how

35

William or Daniel would respond. And he didn't need them getting involved. At least Charlie was gone.

Steve took a seat and fidgeted with his hands. "I want to do something that makes a difference. People get caught up in all sorts of vices that make their lives and others' miserable. I like teaching and telling other people the truths."

"I think it's a noble calling," Phebe said.

James cleared his throat. "It may be a noble calling. But it ain't proper work for a Ragsdale. Preachers are soft. Dependent on the congregation for pay. Not to mention the thankless work it is. Remember Pastor Killian!"

Steve remembered. Killian had preached for a year, having graduated from seminary in Philadelphia and been sent to the pastorate in Coffeyville. He immediately garnered criticism, mainly because of his of his less-than-conservative lifestyle and what many called "big city" ideas in his sermons. There was much consternation and debate all over the town. Then, Pastor Killian was seen at Tucker's Pub, drinking whisky with some saloon girls, and that was the end. He was tarnished as a hypocrite and a blasphemer, and he resigned and left town.

"I'm not Pastor Killian. Killian was wrong and a hypocrite. I would never drink or even visit a saloon."

"It ain't about drinking. It's about the people. If a preacher tells the truth, you're either going to starve or get shot. And you are a young man who speaks his mind. Enough said."

This was just what Steve feared. His father saw the pulpit as a weak profession—like writing. He didn't understand.

Phebe lay a hand on his arm. "How long have you been thinking about this, Steve?"

"Years. A few months ago, I talked to Pastor Blailock about it. He suggested I go to the Methodist Seminary in Evanston, Illinois."

Now it was his mother's turn to look concerned. "Illinois! That's so far away!"

"It's not that far, mom. Only a day and a half journey. And it's only two years from September to March. I'll be home at Christmas for three weeks in all summer to help with the farm."

His mother looked conflicted.

James attempted to soften his tone. "Son, you're clever, and I'm sure you'll be good at whatever you wanna do. But you're meant for real work. To be shut up in a church, wearing robes, not working outside—"

"Not everybody has to work outside, Father."

"I know that! We're not talking about anybody, we're talking about you!" He stood up from the table, knocking the chair back. "Never thought a son of mine, especially the smartest one, would want to waste his life on some namby-pamby—"

"You want me to waste my time on a farm?!" Steve joined him in standing. "Doing the same thing that everybody does? Live my whole life by the crop seasons and then die with nothing to show for it?"

James' eyes flared. "Listen to me, young master, don't you *dare* talk to me in my house like—"

"Both of you, *stop it.*" Now Phebe was standing. "First of all," she said, facing Steve, "your father has worked hard all of his life to give us a good life. All with his hands. Don't you dare criticize that. And you," turning her attention to her husband. "You're not worried about how Steve will be treated. He's tough. You just have a bad attitude towards anything that's not what you do. Because you don't understand it."

Just then, William and Daniel entered. "What's happening?" William said, worry on his face. Daniel, who was seven but rarely spoke, stood beside him, watching.

"Your brother is about to ruin his life." James said, then turned and left the room.

Phebe squatted down before the two boys. "He's not ruining his life. We were just talking about how he might become a preacher."

"He ain't gonna stay here and help with chores?" William said.

Now Steve was burning inside. "Not everybody works on a farm, William!" Steve said.

He saw Daniel looking at him with a smirk. "And what's your problem, Dan? You have no friends and you hardly talk to anybody!"

"Steve! What is wrong with you? Apologize to your brother right now!"

Steve smacked the table. "You'll all be apologizing to me when you see the difference I'm gonna make!" He turned and stormed out of the room, ignoring his mother's pleas to come back.

If Our Ignorance is Bliss…

~1902~

He dismounted, tied his horse to a post, took off his spurs and placed them in the saddlebag, along with the pistol his father had given him for his 16th birthday.

The thought of his father's disappointment about his decision still stung. But he was leaving in a few weeks, and this was his last Saturday night dance before embarking on what felt like true adulthood.

The dances were held on the first Saturday of the month, weather permitting. The town leaders cleared out an area behind city hall, built a puncheon floor, and set up a few tents, tables, and chairs. The dance floor was a new addition. In the past, they simply spread straw on a hard dirt floor.

There was always a local band—usually with guitar, upright bass, fiddle, and percussion. They played some of the popular music of the day, though Steve rarely recognized any of the songs. His family was not musical, being more interested in books, magazines, and newspapers. His only exposure to music, besides these dances, were the hymns they sang in church.

"Hey, Steve! Come with me to get a drink."

It was his best friend, Roman, part of the Smithson clan who had ranches on the east side of town, out towards the Cherokee lowlands. They'd been in school together since they were old enough to attend. Steve did not approve of his drinking, of course, and they often argued about it. Roman would ask him to drink with him, as a way to dig it him, and Steve always responded the same way.

"You don't have to drink to have fun you know."

"You wouldn't know fun if it bit you on the ass." They headed towards the makeshift bar.

"I saw Lydia," Roman said. "She was dancing with Clint."

Steve felt a pang of jealously. "No concern of mine."

Roman laughed. "Just thought you might like to know. If you're gonna punch him in the face, lemme know, I wanna watch."

"We're not courting. She can dance with whoever she wants."

"Yeah, but I know you wanna punch him."

Steve didn't reply. Roman was right, he'd been sweet on Lydia since they were children. They were friends, but hadn't moved beyond that. Since he was headed to seminary, there probably was no reason.

Roman ordered a glass of whiskey for himself and a sarsaparilla for Steve. They found a table and sat down where they could watch the dance floor. Steve scanned the area but didn't see Lydia or Clint. Wait. There was Clint, over at another table, chatting up a woman. It was not Lydia, to Steve's relief.

"You ready for seminary?"

Steve looked at him. "Yup."

Roman shook his head. "Still don't understand why you wanna go off and do that."

"We've had this talk. Charlie's going to inherit the farm someday, which means I'd always be under his thumb. I'd have to eventually do something else. I'm going to go to seminary. I'm gonna make a mark on the world."

"Yeah but what kind of life would that be? Always thought you'd end up a lawman if not a farmer."

Steve shrugged. "Both are noble. Decided on this one."

Steve didn't want to discuss it. He suspected that Roman was jealous. Roman was the only son among four sisters. He'd be stuck at his father's farm, helping him out, and then taking over once his father was too old. He had no other path.

Steve loved the idea of the unknown. Uncharted territory.

"Where are you going to preach when you're done? Here?"

"Maybe. I know preacher Blailock wants to retire. Or Texas. They say there's lots of new towns, and new churches are springing up everywhere. Colorado, too."

"Hello, boys!" A voice said from behind them. Steve jumped. It was Lydia. She looked down at Steve, standing beside him. "Evening, Steve."

Her smile was beautiful. He doffed his hat. "Good evening, Lydia."

Roman spoke up. "Lydia, Steve was just telling me he wanted to dance with you."

Steve whipped his head around at Roman to give him a steely stare. Damn him.

"Did he now?" She looked into Steve's eyes. "I would be amenable." She held out her hand.

NowSteve was both irritated and pleased. He stood and took Lydia's hand. The band was playing "Twilight Thoughts" by Mazurka, a popular dancing tune for couples. Steve was nervous dancing with Lydia—because of his interest in her, not because of his dancing ability. His mother taught all her children how to dance.

They stepped up onto the rough-hewn log dance floor. "I don't like this new puncheon floor," Lydia said. "It wears out my dancing shoes too quickly."

"You like dancing?"

Her eyes sparkled. "Oh, I love dancing! Almost as much as I love cooking!"

"I remember the stew you made for Antonio's birthday. Right after President McKinley died. I know it was a sad time for all, but I still noticed how excellent your cooking was."

"Much obliged." She sat a moment. "That was a terrible time. Can't believe someone shot the president." They sat a few moments in silence, and then Lydia spoke again. "You are off to seminary soon?"

Steve was pleased she remembered. "Yes."

"I think that's wonderful. A man in the pulpit, making the world better." The smile left her face. "When do you leave?"

"Three weeks. To Evanston, Illinois."

"Oh, that's wonderful! I have never been farther than Independence! But I want to travel. I don't want to stay in here my whole life."

Steve smiled. He felt the same. "Where would you like to go?"

"Oh, pretty much anywhere." She tossed her head, and Steve admired her lovely brown hair, piled high with curls dropping down the back of her neck. "I would like to go west. Maybe Arizona or California."

"How will you decide?"

"Well, I suppose that depends on who I marry." She gave a little awkward laugh. "Not that I have any suitors."

An awkward silence ensued.

The song stopped and Lydia pulled away from him slightly, still holding his hand with her arm on his side. "If it is not too bold of me, I would ask you to write me while you are gone."

His heart fluttered a little. "I'd be honored. And I'll be back before Christmas and during summer. The whole program is only two years."

"Good. I will write in return. We should stay in touch, do you agree?" The band started playing a polka—Steve thought it was "Redowa," but he wasn't sure.

"I love polkas! Do you know how to dance to polkas? I can teach you!"

"I know how to polka."

Steve could not keep the grin from his face.

Six months later, Steve was sitting in a class studying the Pentateuch. He was not particularly fond of the teacher, Mr. Robertson. He mostly lectured, and when he did offer time for questions, he responded with more lecture, as if he was there to spit out information, and they were there to spit it back out at examination time. Steve preferred the teachers who challenged students to think.

Steve's orientation to seminary during last semester had been interesting. Some of his fellow students, also from small western towns, felt overwhelmed by the "big city" of Evanston. Not Steve. He enjoyed challenges, and he liked exploring new ideas and places.

He'd known for a while that he saw things differently than most. However, it became more significant in seminary. That didn't bother him. He knew he had a keen mind. He knew he saw things others missed, and he felt it gave him an advantage. Often, he would ask questions in class that did not occur to the other young men. Occasionally, it even garnered praise from his teachers.

Unfortunately, he also learned that questions were considered a threat by some.

Today, the class was examining the book of Genesis. When he had listened to sermons or read the Bible, he just thought about the words and what they meant. But at seminary, it was different. There was history, languages, theology, and doctrine—background to understand scripture. Doctrine was emphasized, and Steve understood that it was *Methodist* doctrine, and not necessarily what another denomination might profess. This bothered Steve, because truth should be truth. If the truth couldn't be discerned, then it was opinion or theory. Nothing wrong with those, but they should be distinguished from "truth."

He enjoyed the study of ancient history, languages, and even some of the theology, but he discovered that some doctrines contradicted what he had learning, and sometimes even contradicted what scripture itself said! Where was infant baptism in scripture? Or tithing at ten percent? Perhaps there was nothing wrong with those things, but to suggest that they were biblical doctrine seemed disingenuous.

Robertson had just begun lecturing about the first couple of chapters of Genesis. When he invited questions, Steve spoke up.

"When Genesis says creation took seven days, how are we supposed to understand that? After all, we know the earth took more time than that to develop, and we know the earth is older than that. Is it an analogy of sorts?"

Robertson was a small, balding man with a spectacle, who had gotten his degree from Princeton, but had preached for many decades in a Methodist church here in Evanston. Steve had noticed that when a question was raised that the professor did not like, he paused, leaned back against his desk, and folded his arms.

He did so now. The class waited.

"Mr. Ragsdale, the question you have posed is one that has been raised any many times by those who refuse to take scripture at face value. It says what it says. Many people, misled by human constructs, believing they have all the answers, have said that if the Bible contradicts science, the Bible must be wrong. But it is the opposite."

He strode to the chalkboard and drew a large circle, and inside it wrote "God." He drew another circle beside it, and wrote, "Science."

"Now, men, which one shall be your Diety? The one who created the universe? Or theories put forth by man? Does salvation come from God or from scientists?"

This appeared as a straw man argument to Steve. Of *course* salvation was not found in science—that wasn't its purpose. The purpose of science was to try to understand creation. The purpose of scripture was to teach humans how to live properly. When the two contradicted each other, either science was wrong, or we misunderstand scripture. Surely, it could not *always* be that science was wrong.

"There is no question it is God," Steve said. "But I know a lot about geology and animals from growing up in Kansas. Is it possible we could be reading scripture incorrectly?"

"You are not a geologist, and you grew up in a backwater place in—where was it—Coffeyville? God's word is always correct."

Steve was fuming. Not only did he insult his home, but mischaracterized what Steve said. wasn't suggesting that scripture was incorrect. was wrong, he asked if they could be misinterpreting it. Could this man not see the difference?

"Perhaps not, sir, but there weren't even *days* until God created the earth and the sun and the moon. Might this not mean it's an analogy?"

Mr. Robertson pointed at Steve. "And so we see the arrogance of youth. You learn a little bit, and you think you know better than all the people who have studied for far longer than you've been alive. Take a lesson, men!"

This was not the first time something like this had happened. His father had taught him to question everything, to think and explore. Steve had assumed that the study of scripture and faith would be the same.

It was not.

He recalled a bit of doggerel he had written:

If our ignorance is bliss, then as fools we'll be missed.

Robertson continued. "When you get your pulpit, you will find people will ask foolish questions like Mr. Ragsdale. It is crucial to know how to answer properly."

Steve eventually realized it did no good to debate with such people. They could become outraged just for asking a question. Since they held his graduation in their hands, he learned to nod and keep his curiosity to himself.

Once he got his own pulpit, it wouldn't matter. He would preach and teach as he understood it. And if he wasn't sure about something, he would tell his parishioners that.

A Hundred Million Bellyaching Fools

~1904-1907~

By the end of his two years at seminary, Steve was more than ready to complete his training. If he didn't have a predilection for never giving up, he would have dropped out after the first year. He enjoyed learning, but the hardheaded doctrinal stances continued to infuriate him. Why did people become so attached to traditions when they contradicted plain facts?

During that last year, Pastor Blailock announced his retirement, and recommended Steve as his replacement. The bishop agreed. Steve did not attend the graduation, since it wasn't required for the certification and the diploma. The Coffeyville Methodists welcomed him warmly as a local boy. Even his father softened his stance somewhat, but never mentioned his position or preaching, even though he attended services with the rest of the family.

Steve enjoyed preparing his reading, studying, writing, and delivering his weekly sermons. He found dealing with his flock a more of a mixed bag, however. Many listened and learned, and were appreciative, but others whined and complained at every turn. The word around town was that he was a "firebrand in the pulpit," which he took as a compliment. He was not sure everyone meant it as such.

He often chose as his topic vices and virtues, and he would stand tall in the pulpit and deliver his exhortations.

> "It is our duty to follow the Lord's ways—lest we find ourselves in eternal damnation at the end of our life. There is no other path. If the righteous are *barely* saved —what of us? Drinking and gambling and prostitution? What hope do we have?"
>
> "Even if you don't engage in those vices—are you any better? Lying. Gossiping. If scripture tells us the most righteous people are barely saved, what hope have the rest of us?" Another dramatic pause. "Change your ways, sinner! Follow the Lord's commands, and have hope in salvation!"

He went on like this every Sunday, selecting passages from various places of scripture to support the topic for the day. On some Sundays, he would go for two hours. No one complained.

At first, that is.

They sat in the bleachers, side-by-side, as the Fourth of July parade went by on Main Street. Steve looked appreciatively at Lydia's sundress and hat. She squealed and clapped her hands as one of the wagons set off a firework, sizzling upward and exploding in the sky high above.

"Oh, I just love this. What a great country."

"It *is* a great country. It could be far better if our politicians weren't so incompetent."

Lydia remain silent. While she seemed to agree, she never said much about politics. Steve, like his father, was frustrated with both local and national authorities. Roosevelt was okay, but he had to deal with the idiots in Congress and a hundred million bellyaching fools. Steve didn't have a hundred million fools, but he had a couple of hundred in his flock who seemed just as incapable of clear thinking.

Today, however, he had something more important on his mind. Once the parade was over, they made their way down the boardwalk. As soon as they were far enough away from the crowds, he stopped and took Lydia by the hands.

"Lydia, I have become quite fond of you. And I believe you are fond of me. A preacher should have a wife. Will you marry me?"

She put her hands to her mouth. "I reckoned this was coming, but I didn't expect it tonight! Oh, Steve, of course I will. I want to spend forever with you. Wherever it leads us."

Steve smiled and gave her a light kiss on the cheek. "Wherever it leads us."

A year later, as he sat in his office at the church, there came a knock on his door. He did not get many visitors, unless they were to complain or ask for help. That was fine with Steve, except for the few that seemed to have nothing to do but complain and criticize.

The weekday mornings were slow at the church building, and his office was a place of refuge. He would read and study for the next Sunday's sermon, go over the list of prayer requests, and make visits to the infirm and elderly of his congregation. He did not work at the church on Fridays and Saturdays, both to take a break before Sunday, and to help out around the farm.

Saturday nights, however, found him back at his study, going over the sermon for the next day.

"Come in!" He called out.

The door opened to reveal the substantial bulk of Poppy McKinnon, the proprietor of Poppy's Saloon. Steve was surprised to see him—he did not recall ever seeing him at the church. Since he was the man who served the most alcohol in town, Steve was not particularly happy that he was standing before him.

"Preacher Ragsdale, do you have a moment?"

Poppy seemed nervous and Steve noted that he did not take his hat off. Uncouth.

"Mr. McKinnon, good morning. Please, have a seat." He indicated one of two chairs placed in front of his desk.

"Thank you." Poppy sat down and finally removed his hat, placing in on his lap. "You can call me Poppy. Everyone does."

"Very well, Poppy. What can I do for you?"

"Well, sir, it is a bit of a delicate matter, and I hope you can hear me out—"

"—Of course—"

"—and understand my concern. I...I..." He paused and wriggled in his seat as if he could not get comfortable.

Steve affected a smile. "I am here to listen and understand and serve our community."

Poppy nodded. "Thank you, sir...uh...Preacher. Thank you." He took a deep breath. "I own the saloon on Main Street, perhaps you know of it?"

"I've lived here all my life. I know it."

"Well, yes, of course. I've been running the place for nigh on thirty years—when we was just an outpost. As you might know, I make money from the food I serve and the liquor I sell."

"And, as I recall, prostitution a few years ago before the sheriff shut you down for some illegalities along those lines."

Poppy reddened. "Yes, an unfortunate miscalculation by me, succumbing to the pressure from a...ah...a certain constituency. Just tryin' to make a livin'. Ain't easy with that Roosevelt takin' over for good ol' McKinley, God rest his soul."

Steve had to fight with himself not to respond to that ridiculous statement. Roosevelt was far better than that idiot McKinley. God rest *his* soul.

"And it was over ten years ago."

Steve didn't respond. Poppy didn't seem recalcitrant.

"Anyways, alcohol is where I make the most money. And... well, I don't wanna tell you how to do your job..."

Steve thought he knew where this was going. He waited.

"Well, preacher, shucks, I'm just gonna say it. Your sermons on the evils of alcohol cost me money. I know you're new here —"

"I grew up here, Poppy."

"Yes. But as a *preacher* here, you are new. And I don't know what they larned you in seminary school, and wouldn't presume—"

"Say your say, Mr. McKinnon."

Poppy took a deep breath. "I came to ask you to stop talking so much about alcohol. I understand that our town drunks—and we both know who I'm talking about—might need to hear your words. But they aren't sitting in the pews. Sir." He seemed relieved he had gotten it out.

Steve worked to keep his anger under control. It would not do for the town's preacher to act out of control. "Appreciate you coming to talk to me. But alcohol is a blight on society. Leads to arguments, loss of self-control, sexual sins—all acts that are against the fruits of the Spirit. Find other ways to make money that don't do the Devil's work."

"But…but not everyone acts like that. Most of my customers just have a drink or two after work and head home to families! They's good people."

Steve shook his head. "Evil and unnecessary vice. Ain't no one worse off from *not* drinking. 'Be not drunk with wine, wherein is excess, but be filled with the Spirit.'"

Poppy leaned forward. "Most people don't drink too much, if I understand what that means." He sat back, embarrassed. "I can't say I knows much about the scriptures, though my momma read 'em to me when I was young. But you just quoted—"

"I've walked past your place at night—seems like most are quite drunk!"

"What about that passage 'bout Jesus making wine? I don't know where it is, but someone told me it was there!" Poppy was starting to get a little worked up.

Steve nodded, slightly impressed that Poppy knew any passages from the Holy Scriptures. "The Apostle Paul told Timothy to drink a little wine for his stomach. As *medicine*—they didn't have medicines like we do now. And you ain't selling wine, anyhow." He tried to soften his voice. "Look, Poppy. It ain't your fault you're in this spot. Previous pastors did not preach as they should have—"

"—Pastor Killian understood!"

"Pastor Killian was a hypocrite and got run out of town."

Poppy's face turned red, and he gritted his teeth. "Look, pastor, it ain't just me. Others are upset, too. And you always going on about—"

Steve sighed. "Keep to the topic, Mr. McKinnon."

Poppy set his jaw, the nervousness dissipated by his fury. "Your job is to preach and run the church for the people who care about that sort of thing. It isn't to put people out of business for selling something that is legal!"

"God doesn't care whether it's illegal or not. Sin is sin."

Poppy looked down, then back up at Steve, shaking his head. "I think you've lost your way and yer position has gone to your head." He stood up. "I tried to talk civil, but you are stubborn!"

"It's called integrity, Mr. McKinnon. Your motivation, on the other hand, is money—another root of sin!" He stood to face Poppy. "Choose mammon and alcohol if you wish, but I'll never stop preaching against it."

Poppy held Steve's eyes for a moment, then rose and headed for the door. "You have not heard the last of me. It's not right!" He slammed the door behind him.

If He Tells the Truth He Would Starve

~1907-1908~

A few months later, Steve and Lydia had their first child. A boy, who they named Thurman Carl. It was an uneventful birth, and the first human birth Steve had performed, though he had helped deliver many calves, colts, and lambs since he was a boy.

Lydia had asked Steve to call the doctor to come and examine the baby. Steve didn't see the point, but she told him that more and more women were having doctors perform examinations on newborns. Back east, many were even having doctors perform all births, not just the difficult ones.

For Steve, this sounded merely like a way for doctors to make more money. Birth was natural, and if there were no issues, why do you need some stranger involved? You didn't call a horse doctor for a birth unless there was a problem. And midwives were readily available if necessary.

But Lydia was insistent, and pointed out that she wanted to make sure he was healthy, and also they required a birth certificate, which the doctor could provide. Steve didn't see the point of that either, and blamed all this on the women's magazines that Lydia read. But she was his wife, and he wanted to make her happy. Besides, giving birth was what women did, so if that's what she wanted, so be it.

Two days after birth, Steve retrieved the doctor, who did an examination on both the boy and his mother. As the doctor was packing up his bag, he called Steve into the bedroom. "Everything looks good, Steve. You got a healthy, strong son. Congratulations. And Lydia is recovering quite well."

"Good to hear. Already knew that, though."

The doctor ignored the slight and finished packing up. "That'l be five dollars. You planning on having more soon?"

"That's the plan, God willing." They both looked at Lydia.

"I would also like a girl." She looked at Steve. "*We* would like a girl."

"Yep. But also more boys. Follow me, doc. Got a gold coin for you."

"Appreciate quick payment. I'm headed to San Francisco soon. May not come back."

"San Francisco? I hear it's a mess there."

The doctor shook his head. "Over four thousand killed, so they say. Most of the city destroyed. Lots of needs for doctors."

"Still? The earthquake was—what—four or five months ago?"

"April. I seen pictures. Like a thousand sticks of dynamite went off."

"God help them. Good luck to you, Doc, if I don't see you before you scoot off. That's the Lord's work you're doing." *Not delivering or checking babies unnecessarily,* he thought to himself. He opened a drawer in the sidebar and pulled out a bag. He extracted a three-dollar and two-dollar coin and placed them on the table.

"Thank you kindly." The doctor set his bag down and retrieved a paper from his coat pocket. "Birth certificate. Need to fill this out before I leave. I'll make a copy for you and have it delivered." He leaned over the dining room table. "Boy's name?"

"Thurman Carl."

"Good, strong name," the doctor said as he wrote.

Once finished, Steve saw the doctor to the door and returned to his Lydia.

"Should you go 'round and tell our families they have a grandson?"

"I sent Rob over to the farm to tell mother and father, and told him to go to yours after. I'm sure mother will be here momentarily, even with all Rose's wedding plans going on. Mother must be in seventh heaven: a daughter getting married *and* a new grandchild."

"I still can't believe Rose is marrying Roy." She sighed as she looked at little Thurman, then back up at Steve. "He's not going to be a preacher, is he?"

Steve shrugged.

"I know you're unhappy, husband."

He gave her a tight smile. "Difficult times make for a strong will. I'll figure it out or do something else. Don't you worry your pretty little head."

She smiled weakly. "I'm not worried. Whatever it is, I know you'll take care of us." She looked down at Thurman again. "All three of us."

Steve stood in the doorway of the church after the service and greeted his parishioners. Lydia used to stand with him, but now, with Thurman over a year old, she waited in the buggy with him. He could be a handful.

Most of his parishioners were kind, if only offering trite or perfunctory comments. A few always took a moment to express criticisms—usually the same few. Steve wished that they would choose a more conducive time for a constructive discussion. He didn't mind critiques. But these "negative nellies of the nave," as he called them, were not serious. They had nothing constructive to offer, so they spent their time complaining.

"So…Preacher Ragsdale…gots a question for you." This was Johann Silberstein, the town's deputy sheriff.

Steve nodded. "Of course, officer."

"Perhaps a bit unusual, but mebbe others have mentioned it. The World Series is coming up…and…"

Steve sighed inwardly. He enjoyed baseball as much as the next person, but he felt he delivered a powerful sermon today, and this chap wanted to talk sports.

"I think it's going to be Tiger and Cubs, and, as you know, my father was a huge Cubs fan."

"I'm pretty sure the Lord does not choose sides in baseball, Johann."

He flinched. "Oh, no, that wasn't my question. I wondered if…well…on that first Sunday, if perhaps…you're a baseball fan……maybe the sermon—er, the service—could be a little shorter that day. I've heard you say God wants us to enjoy the good things in life, too…and, well…"

Steve forced a smile. "I'll see what I can do, Officer."

In the first year or so that he was in the pulpit here, he would've engaged the sheriff. He would've explained to him that yes, God *does* want us to enjoy the good things of life, but not to the exclusion of Him. That is the way to vice and even idolatry.

But after six years, he felt like he was fighting a losing battle. He was not a quitter. But wisdom required knowing when to cut your losses.

He had some ideas…

In September 1908, Steve received a telegram that Bishop Shaun of the Kansas Conference South was coming to visit with him. While it was not u usual for bishops to travel occasionally to visit the congregations under their authority, it made Steve nervous. He wasn't quite sure why.

The afternoon of the visit he sat in his office fidgeting, almost relieved when he heard the door open at the appointed time. He rushed out into the sanctuary.

"Good afternoon, Bishop. Hope your journey was well. Good to have you here."

Steve was lying. It was *not* good.

"Thank you, Minister Ragsdale, it was a fine trip, though we got out of Columbia late. Apparently, they were effecting repairs to the trustle."

"Coffee?"

"No, thank you. Never touch the stuff. I enjoy fine sherry in the evening, apart from that, it's water for me."

Steve took note but said nothing, as he conducted the Bishop down the aisle of the old church and into the pastors' study to the right of the sanctuary. He indicated a chair to the bishop, and Steve took the one next to it.

The bishop took a deep breath. "There is no easy way to begin, so I will jump in. There have been numerous complaints sent to the Conference office about you, Minister Ragsdale. There are serious concerns about your doctrinal stances."

Steve was a bit taken aback. He thought there might be complaints about the length of his sermon or his constant preaching against alcohol. "Doctrinal stances? I adhere to all the primary doctrines of the church. I preach weekly from scripture."

"Perhaps I was too broad. There is really only one issue of concern. While it is true that we have had complaints about your bold preaching on drinking, that is a doctrinal issue as much as a moral one, and you *do* preach sound scripture. Furthermore, our investigation has shown that your work in the pulpit and in the community are satisfactory."

Steve's curiosity was piqued. Though Poppy was the first one to complain to his face about his stance on drinking, there had been others—always those with a stake in profiting from the sale of alcohol. He was happy the Conference backed him up, but if it wasn't that...

"Well, then, to the point," Bishop Shaun said. "Do you believe a literal seven days of creation?"

Ah. That old bug-a-boo. "I don't think they are literal, but that does not change the meaning of—"

"The seven days of creation are seven days of twenty-four hours. Otherwise, scripture would not have said so."

"I have never preached a sermon about whether the days were literal or not. I preach the doctrine that God created the world—"

"Nevertheless, a number of your flock suggest to us that you do not believe it, and you have just confirmed it. How they learned of it is of no concern of mine nor the Conference. I must say I am dismayed to find out the reports are true."

"But... Bishop Shaun, surely this is not an issue of doctrine. How many days it took is irrelevant to the *meaning* of the passages.Jesus told parables that were not literal had an important meaning behind them. Besides, you can't have a first day if God hadn't created the sun yet."

"Minister! I did not come here to have you attempt to teach *me* about the Holy Scriptures. I am your elder and represent the authority of the Church. Here is what we shall do. You will write a letter describing your previous erroneous thoughts, and how further study has led you to recant. Through careful study and prayer, you affirm the seven literal days of creation. You will read this letter to your congregation this Sunday, and then post it to me the next day, at the Columbia office. And then things will calm down and go back to normal. There need not be further action.'

This is outrageous! Steve thought, his blood boiling. *Highfalutin' fancy-dressed religious authorities dictating to the masses. Didn't Jesus critique that very thing? Careful prayer and study? He wanted Steve to lie to his congregation.*

"Sir, I grew up in this town. My father taught me all about the lands around here. Even a brief study of the rock formations and geography this area...not to mention the flora and fauna—"

"Stop! Are you suggesting that your own unsophisticated upbringing supersedes God's word?! Perhaps you should not even be in the pulpit." He fixed a strong stare upon him.

You may be right about that, thought Steve.

Bishop Shaun sighed and visibly softened. "Mr. Ragsdale. Steve. I am not here to harangue you into submission. Certainly, we can have discussion. There are some passages that are more difficult to understand than others. But *my* concern is our flock. We must stand firm and united on everything we profess as the Church, or they will not know when to believe us. Leave it to the theologians and the professors to debate the thornier subjects. We must speak with the United voice to the tender sheep who look to us for guidance."

Steve knew this was a losing battle. Just like seminary.

He knew that the bishop was using the tactic of berating someone, then pivoting to being kind and conciliatory. It put a person on the defensive, then made them feel as if they were being understood.

It galled him to play this game.

"Yes, I understand."

"Good." The Bishop stood up and smooth his smock. "I shall be dining tonight with Bishop Adams in independence. So I must be on my way."

Steve could play games too. "I'm disappointed, Bishop. I was going to offer a tour of the church, and dinner with my wife and I tonight. But I understand how important your duties are."

Steve hoped the bishop would not detect the insincerity in his statements.

"I'll find my way out."

Steve listened as the footsteps echoed out in the church. He sat for a few moments looking at the desk, then stood up suddenly.

"So shall I. 'Nuff sed."

"He *reprimanded* you?" Lydia's eyes were wide. "I've a mind to go have a word with him myself!"

"It wasn't just a reprimand. He demanded I recant publicly, then send a letter to him saying the same!"

"This isn't right. I know you to be a faithful man. One who does not twist his words or scripture."

"And I'll pay five bucks to the man who could find out that I've ever done otherwise!" He had been pacing back-and-forth in the kitchen. Finally, he sat down. "He is small-minded. Most of them are."

They both sat in silence. Steve was leaning forward in his chair, Lydia was staring down at the table.

"Did you write the letter yet?"

"If I do, I will be writing a lie just to keep a job. Writing something I don't believe because arrogant men in fancy robes told me to."

Lydia nodded.

"A man without integrity is a man with nothing, even if he owns the whole world."

"If you are anything, dear Steve, it is a man of integrity. One of the reasons I married you. I will support you in whatever manner is required."

He reached over and took her hand. "My dearest Lydia, you used to say that you wanted to get out of this town. Do you still want that?"

She nodded, her eyes growing big.

"And you used to say you wanted to go to California. Do you still want to?"

"I do." She offered a puzzled smile.

He squeezed her hands. "I have been thinking about this for a while. I enjoyed my studies at the seminary, and many things about the pulpit. But preaching, church leaders, and the pew-sitters, are not what I thought them to be. I was eager to work for the Lord, but I am doing the work of men who tell me what to say instead."

"You're smarter than all of them."

"True or not, this visit has told me that this is not my calling. I *am* going to write a letter to the bishop and announce it on Sunday. But it will not be a recantation, it will be a resignation."

Lydia nodded. She already suspected as much.

Steve thought, as he had many times, that she was a strong, loyal woman. Perhaps overly opinionated and stubborn at times, but he preferred that over mousey and passive.

He stood up and straightened his coat. "No reason to delay writing."

"Good." She stood with him and laid a hand on his arm. "But what are we going to do?"

He smiled again. "We are going to farm cotton in California."

The Palo Verde Valley
(1908-1921)

The Palo Verde Valley

The Palo Verde Valley lies on the border of California with Arizona, along the Colorado River. While it is part of the Colorado Desert, which is part of the larger Sonoran Desert. It is a rich and fertile area, with agriculture being its largest industry. Melons, alfalfa, vegetables, and cotton are the primary crops.

In 1877, Thomas Henry created the Palo Verde Irrigation District (PVID) to provide and control irrigation from the Palo Verde Diversion Dam to the farms in the valley. Blythe City (later shortened to simply "Blythe"), sits at the center of the valley, founded by a San Francisco businessman, Thomas Henry Blythe, also in 1877.

By the early 1900s, the land was booming. Cattle farming had become important, thanks to Frank Murphy and Ed Williams of Arizona. The Hobson brothers came out from Ventura County and formed the Palo Verde Land and Water Company, resulting in further growth. Advances in clothing and cloth manufacturing made cotton a much-needed commodity, and cotton farming boomed after 1900, along with the other agricultural products. The town gained a newspaper, The Blythe Herald, in 1911.

In 1916, the California Southern Railroad line was extended to Blythe from Rice, causing massive growth in the region. The city was incorporated on July 21 of the same year.

California, Twixt the River and the Sea

~ 1908 ~

"California?" Her eyes were shining. She always wanted to move to California. He was not sure if she knew just how big it was.

He gave her a big smile. "There is a valley about one hundred and fifty miles west of Phoenix: the Palo Verde Valley. South of a town called Blythe City. Homesteads for sale all through the valley. Big demand for cotton. They've run canals for irrigation from the Colorado River through the valley—been working on it for thirty years."

She peered at him in admiration. "How do you know all this?"

"I've been researching for a while. Blythe City got a post office recently, so I posted a letter to the land office."

"But...but...really?" Sobered, she put her hand on his arm. "We just pick up and leave?"

"Well, not quite that simple. I need to take a trip out there and see what's available, then purchase the land."

"Just you? Leave us here?"

"From Phoenix to Blythe City and beyond, there are no roads. Just wagon ruts in the desert. Won't be an easy trip. I'll take my horse. Or maybe a stagecoach. Once I've bought a farm, we'll pack up and go."

She sat, staring at the table for a few moments. She looked up. "Let's do it! I know you are not happy here, and I have always wanted to go to California."

Steve smiled. She was such a trooper. "We're at the end of September. I say go as soon as possible—good time to travel the desert. Maybe we could plan on moving, God willing, in November."

"The baby is due in January." She looked at him with raised eyebrows. Their second child.

"Yes. Do you prefer to wait until after the baby is birthed?"

She shook her head and laughed. "No! I'm saying the sooner, the better."

He took a deep breath. "Very well, I shall begin working on a plan. Let's see…" His eyes became distant. "Will talk to Elmer at the stagecoach office, see what he knows about the route. He'll have good advice. Gotta figure up how much money I can free up."

He stood up, mind elsewhere, and walked out of the room, still talking. "Once I have a travel plan, I'll send a post to the land office again to make an appointment, once that's done, I can…" His voice trailed off.

Lydia smiled. She loved it when Steve began working on a new idea.

He reigned his horse at the top of a small ridge, overlooking an empty land. His companion rode up beside him.

"As you can see, Mr. Ragsdale, we are only a couple of miles from the Colorado River." The man pointed to the east, where a ribbon of water flowed lazily through the desert landscape. "Over there is the main branch of the Powas canal that you can tap into. All set up for you through the PVID! If you decide to take advantage of this great offer!"

Steve was a little tired of Mr. Popovic's sales talk. He never stopped talking about the PVID. Not to suggest it wasn't impressive. It had turned a dry desert into a fertile valley.

Steve had already decided to buy the land. It was a prime location. He was mapping out in his mind where the house would go, the barn and work sheds, and that long flat area, closest to the canal, where he would grow cotton.

Steve pointed across the river to the brown mountains. "Looks like there are two washes there—one about forty degrees to the north, another about the same to the south. What are those? Any water there?"

Popovic squinted through his spectacles. "Sir, your eyes are better than mine. But if I remember a-right, the one on the left is the Trigo Wash, on the right is the Mohave wash. Seasonal. That's some pretty inhospitable land over there."

"What about hunting?"

"More than you could ever want! We got mule deer, bobcats, jackrabbits, quail."

Steve nodded. Mr. Popovic had informed him—also more than once—that a train station would be built in Blythe in the coming years, when the tracks reached here from Los Angeles and Phoenix. That would make it easy to move the harvested cotton. Until then, he could use a co-op, or just haul the cotton to Phoenix or Los Angeles himself after selling as much locally as he could. One hundred and fifty miles from Phoenix, two hundred from Los Angeles. Indio was about 110 miles to the west. Other than Blythe, the closest town was Calexico, on the border with Mexico—supposedly an up-and-coming town that had just been incorporated. There were no roads, just ruts through the desert sands, which were travelled enough to keep them visible—most of the time. The government had recently begun to put up signs directing travelers to water sources.

"Mr. Ragsdale, I hope you see the benefit of buying this land. Irrigation in place. Friendly people. Train station coming. Blythe is becoming a central hub between the cities to the west and those to the east. And the price is unmatched!"

Steve nodded. "Yes, you've told me." He scanned the land from his far left to his far right. He had never spent much time in desert areas, but there was something about it that drew him in. As if he *belonged*. He was intrigued with the idea of scratching out an existence here, carving out a niche in what might seem like barren lands. But Steve's research and exploration over the last weeks told him that the desert was rich with life, flora, and fauna—with or without canals. His heart was full with the idea of the challenge.

"Mr. Popovic, let's go back to your office and sign those papers."

The land office man beamed. "Oh, excellent. You won't regret it, Mr. Ragsdale!"

Steve reckoned he was right. No more pulpit. No more working inside a building all day. Here, he could use his mind *and* his body to create a home and a farm for his growing family (with a soon-to-be second child). It was empty land now, but he would create his own little empire.

Steve checked the last tie-down on the buggy, then stood back and took it all in. Two horses (both belonging to him). Two buggies, one his, one borrowed. Both were loaded with all their earthly belongings.

"You 'bout ready, son?" His father seemed a bit more pleasant now that Steve had given up preaching.

Steve brushed off his hands on his duster. "Yup. Guess I better round up the crew. Where's William?"

"He's off saying a private goodbye to Laura, I reckon."

"Alright. Well, there's no use puttin' it off."

"No. Listen, son…"

Steve turned. He didn't want some drawn-out parting. He knew his father was uncomfortable with such things, too, but for some reason, James always felt the need to give a speech at important events.

"California's a long way from Coffeyville. But my money says you doing the right thing. Never thought you's cut out for pulpit work. Not that you ain't smart, but you got better things to do then mess with people stuck in their ways. They want someone who tells them what they already believe. Truth is—" he looked around, "—you's the best thinker in the family."

Steve nodded. "Thank you, Father."

"Well," the tall, gray-haired man drawled, "a person deserves to plot their own path and larn it all themselves." James clapped Steve on the back. "You got a good start on a family, Lydia's a good woman, and a fine boy you got there and another on the way! Truth is, I'm kinda jealous—would love to head out west and farmstead m'self."

"Still plenty of land out there, father."

James laughed. "Welp, maybe someday, if'n I can get your mother to go along." A moment of awkwardness was removed with a change of subject. "So, what's the travel plan?"

"Gonna try to make Oklahoma City by sundown, camp out somewhere if we can't find a night house. Albuquerque the next day, Flagstaff an easier leg beyond that, then a short trip into Blythe and the farmstead. I'll send a telegram when we get to Blythe."

"Your mother will appreciate that. She gonna miss that little baby of yours." He grunted. "And you and Lydia, of course."

"She'll miss her grandchild more, and she ain't even met him yet."

They both chuckled as they headed back into the house.

"But it's so *far*!" His mother said with teary eyes.

Steve hugged her again. "It's not like we can't travel to see each other on occasion. And there'll be a train going into Blythe soon."

She pulled away and wiped her eyes with a kerchief she was holding. "I know." Steve could see she was trying to be strong. "And I know you will do well out there." She reached over and squeezed Lydia's hand.

Lydia moved in and hugged her. "We'll write often, Mother Ragsdale." She shifted little Thurman to her other hip, off to the side of her six-month bulge.

Steve went to his other siblings standing nearby. Rosa and her new husband, William, were first. Steve thought William was a good guy, though a little full of himself.

"Rosa, you and William take care of yourselves."

"You, too, Steve." She hugged him.

Next was Minnie. She took his hands. "I'm a-following you out there in a few months," she said.

Steve nodded. "You keep saying that. Shouldn't you find a husband first?"

"They ain't nobody here. I'll find me a man out there."

"Maybe so. California is big." Steve looked around. "Where's Daniel?"

The youngest brother had been a black sheep since he was born. Always off by himself, didn't seem to connect to the rest.

James often said the boy was born into the wrong family—though he never said so in Daniel's hearing.

"Dunno," Minnie said. "Saw him headed out into the woods early this morn."

"Well." Steve looked at his father. "We talked last night, so guess that's all the goodbye he needs." He glanced at his mother and saw a pained expression.

Steve turned to Laura, William's bride-to-be. "Sorry for taking your fiancé away. But I'm so thankful for his help getting out there."

"You're welcome, dear Steve. With the wedding next month, I'll be plenty busy."

"And when I get back," William said, "I'll be finalizing the purchase of *our* farm in Noel!"

"All right, everyone!" Steve shouted. "No point puttin' this off. Let's get on the trail." He looked back at William. "You ready?"

William hugged Laura and kissed her cheek. "I'm ready, big brother!"

"A Ragsdale caravan, heading west," his father announced. "You're going to set the place on fire!"

William laughed. "Not literally, I hope! Remember when you burned down the shed, Steve?"

"Sure do," he replied, as he helped Lydia up into the carriage, then took Thurman from his Mother and handed him up. He patted the horse on the neck and then climbed onto the seat at the front of the carriage. Unwinding the reigns from the pommel, he raised his hand to the family assembled in front of the old house. "Goodbye, everyone! God be with you all."

A mishmash of responses sounded forth as Steve flicked the reigns. William did the same with his horse and wagon, and the two beasts put their heads down and strained forward until they built up momentum, settling into a steady walk.

The Ragsdales were on their way to California.

Put-put-putting and Take Me to L.A.

~ 1908–1909 ~

Steve and Lydia stood on the slight rise, gazing at their farmstead. To the left, on a flat area about 100 yards from the dirt road, Steve had already laid the foundation and finished most of the framing for their home.

"It's going to be such a lovely house! I can already imagine it. How long?" Lydia exclaimed. Thurman, in her arms, squirmed. She set him down between them.

"As soon as we finish Billy and Beatrice's roof, they'll all come over and help me finish. I can do the rest myself. Maybe another month?"

He chewed on his lower lip as he scanned their new land. "But I got to get the land ready for planting before March. Can't seed any later than April or we won't make this growing season."

"I wish I could do more to help. The land sure looks good and fertile."

Steve smiled and placed his hand on her belly. "You're doing plenty by growing this little one. Leave the building of homes and the growing of cotton to me."

"Still, I wish I could do more. I'm getting to where I can't walk and explore the land. Have you seen some of the rock formations beyond the river?"

Steve laughed. "Of course I have. There will be plenty for you to do after the baby is born and the house is finished. Pete at the farm store told me that a lot of the Indians in the area are looking for work. They know a lot about growing cotton and other crops in this area."

"Can we afford hired hands?"

"I'll figure it out. When I was talking to Pete, he was needing some work done on his automobile, and Gerald has to put in a new pumping system for a new field. There aren't a lot of mechanics in the area, so it's good opportunities for me."

She put her hand on his arm. "You are such a hardworking man."

"You know how much I love working with my hands. As soon as I resigned the pulpit, I felt lighter. This is the kind of thing I should have done. It's like making something out of nothing. With God's help, of course."

They stood for a bit, gazing out in the cool dusk of the California desert. Lydia turned to find where Thurman had wandered off to. He was about twenty feet down the slope, sitting in the dirt playing with something. "Thurman! Show me what you have in your hand!"

The little boy jumped at the shout, and then held up a small, chubby arm, clutching something in his hand.

"What is that?" She leaned over to Steve.

Steve peered at the little boy. "Looks like a rock." He grinned. "Or maybe a scorpion."

As Lydia jumped up with a shriek, he laughed. "Just joshing!"

"Oh, Steve! Don't do that! You know that's my worst fear!"

"Eh, he's fine. I got bit by a scorpion when I first came out here. Not a lot of fun. But a good lesson."

"You weren't a year old!"

"Fair point. Let's get back to the tent." As they headed down the slope, Steve scooped up Thurman, who emitted squeals of delight.

"It will be nice when we have the house finished, and I can get out of that tent. Not to complain, it's serviceable."

"It's fine for now, but we'll need a more insulated house and flow vents once the weather turns hot in May or June. This ain't Coffeyville."

"A new life for us, on the frontier, with our second child on the way."

Steve smiled down at Thurman, "You are going to have a brother. And five or six more!"

"Hey!" Shouted Lydia from behind. "I have a say in this, husband!"

"Father!" Thurman came bursting out of the house, running on his small legs. Steve dismounted his horse wearily and picked up the two-year-old with a sigh. It was not far to Blythe City, but it made for a long day.

Lydia came out of the tent cabin. "Steve, I'm glad you're back. Was it helpful?"

Steve sighed. "Not really." He looked her up and down. "Bless me, woman, you look ready to give birth any moment now!"

She slapped his arm playfully. "Come sit down and tell me about it."

She took Thurman from him and went to pour him some water from a jug, then joined him at the crude table they used for meals, work, and anything else that needed a large flat surface. The tent was a large room, divided into two by a hanging tarpaulin. Bedroom on one side, living areas on the other.

Thurman sat on the floor playing with a little toy horse Steve had carved for him.

"The Farm Bureau was not much help. Practically every question I asked, they said I should go to Los Angeles and talk to people there."

"Los Angeles! How far is that? Hundreds of miles?"

"Three hundred and fifty, to be exact. That's where all the buyers, major equipment suppliers, and other infrastructure for the cotton industry. Guess it makes sense."

"So we have to go to Los Angeles?"

He looked at her with a smile. "Us? I ain't gonna travel across the desert with my young son and my wife with child."

"Oh, pshaw. I'm the toughest woman you ever met. Besides, I am tired of being here alone when you go on the errands to Blythe and Calexico. *Especially* being with child. I'm going with you."

Steve frowned. "Need to go post-haste. I don't know, Lydia…" he stared off, thinking. He was torn. Leaving his wife and toddler for a week wasn't good. But the journey—

"I've talked to a lot of people about the journey from here to Los Angeles, borrowed a magazine that some automobile group publishes once a month about traveling the desert."

"Automobile? Across the desert?"

"Apparently these new Model-T's are better than horses and buckboards. The route from here to Mecca can take nine hours to go ninety miles. Two ruts through the sand, which sometimes shift or disappear with the winds. Little to no water, of course. No habitation between here and there except perhaps a few solitary cabins."

"Why would anyone build a cabin in the middle of the desert?"

"Prospecting. Some have hit it big, but what a life. In the summer it can hit 110, 120 degrees. No water unless you dig a well, scant wildlife or edible plants."

"What about after Mecca?"

"We wouldn't go to Mecca—too far south. Indio is the next place, then San Bernardino, the first proper town. More towns after that until you reach Los Angeles."

"We can do that. Coming from Coffeyville was much further, and some of that Arizona desert—"

"I know. But not ninety miles of empty desert." He took a deep breath. "If we can make Indio, we're fine. It's Indian Village, but a town has sprung up, including Happy's Ranch. In an emergency, we could find a place to stay." He looked at her belly.

"You worry too much. We women been giving birth in deserts and mountains and huts and caves since the beginning. Like I said, probably gonna be about two weeks if I figure correctly. If we go today or tomorrow, that is plenty of time."

He snorted. "And babies always come on the day the mother says."

"I'll have you know that my mother and grandmother predicted the exact day of each of their children's birth."

"Very well." He scratched his beard. "I concur. I don't like leaving you two for that long."

The doctor came out of his surgery into the waiting room. Steve stood and picked up Thurman, where he was playing with a wooden soldier. "She's healthy, Mr. Ragsdale. A fine birth. Congratulations."

Steve nodded. "She?"

"Indeed."

Steve nodded. "Thank you, Doc. Sure glad you were open and willing to see us. We didn't expect her to come this early. Glad we were here in San Bernardino and not in the middle of the desert."

"Your wife told me you were returning from Los Angeles to Blythe. Pretty bold of you to travel across the desert with her so close to giving birth. But she's a strong woman. Easy birth. You'd have been able to deliver if you had to."

"I've delivered animals, I could do it. But I ain't married to them." He laughed. "More important, all we had was our carriage. If we were home it'd be a different story."

"She'll be fine to travel tomorrow. How far is it? I've never been that direction."

Steve shrugged. "Ten or eleven hours. Depends on whether we lose the tracks in the sand between here and Blythe City. Been rough on the horses." Steve had brought both horses to pull the buckboard—just in case.

"I hear people are driving automobiles across the desert nowadays."

"Apparently they are pretty tough—better than horses, they say. Simple machinery, and easy to fix if they break down. Might buy one myself. Easier to fix a machine than a horse."

The doctor laughed. "I'll stick with my horses. Your wife should rest overnight. You and the little boy can sleep on the couch in the waiting room, if you'd like, then get on the road before first light. She'll be fine riding in the buckboard. It's covered, I assume?"

"It is. Mighty kind of you, doc. I got blankets we can bring in."

"Good. Now, let's fill out this birth certificate. Full name of you and your wife?"

"Steve Albert Ragsdale and Lydia Isabelle Ragsdale."

"And the little girl's name?"

"Thelma Isabelle Ragsdale."

The doctor scribbled on the paper in front of him, then took out a second form and copied the information. "Now, Mr. Ragsdale, when you get back home, you should have a doctor there do an exam on little Thelma. In around two months."

"I thought you said everything was fine?"

"It's just to keep tabs on new births. We've discovered we can prevent a lot of later problems with some preventative care."

Steve grinned. "Or a good way to make more money."

The doctor laughed. "Not the first time I've heard that. But it is true that regular examinations *do* catch problems before they get worse. Important for newborns and the elderly."

"Just joshing you, doc. I'll allow that it makes sense. I do that with my animals on the farm."

"Indeed. Now, I have one more patient to see here in my office. Make yourself at home."

"Thank you. I'll go see my wife and then into town to get some vittles for us. How much do I owe you?"

They settled up, and Steve looked at the little boy in his arms. "Come on, Thurman, let's go see your new sister."

Steve straightened up and stretched his back. He had just finished planting a row of cotton—the eleventh row so far. Hardly a dent.

It had only taken him a couple of weeks to prepare the soil, having located a cheap source of used straw from a rancher down south. He had furrowed the field and ran irrigation pipes and trenches to supply water.

He was a little pushed for time because everything needed to be planted no later than April. Cotton required almost two hundred days from planting to harvest.

He looked over at the three Indians he had employed to help. They knew the crop well, and he had learned much from them. Still, they were uneducated in the ways of technology, and he had some ideas about how to improve irrigation and even make planting and harvesting easier next year. For example, a modified Model T could replace horses for furrowing and digging trenches. He was intrigued.

He heard his name, and turned around to see Lydia making her way carefully through the field. She was carrying a basket, with two-month-old Thelma in a sling against her chest.

"Hello, my dear Lydia. What's in the basket?"

"I brought you lunch."

"You are a fine wife. I'm not sure what I would do without you." He looked around. "Thurman sleeping?"

"He is. And without me, you'd waste away without sustenance, I am certain. I have to keep that wiry body fed!" She set the basket down and pulled out a blanket.

"Are you going to eat with me? Let's move over here, where I haven't planted any seeds yet."

He spread out the blanket, and Lydia set out bread, sheep mutton, and cheese.

As they ate, he told her about the progress they were making and his concern about having to wait two hundred days before he could sell any of his crop. He was making extra money or trading labor by doing work for neighbors, especially machine and welding repairs. He had even begun to work on some local

Model T's, which had a double benefit: money, and learning about the automobiles.

It made for long days, working on their house, preparing fields and planting the land, and the odd jobs. He fell into bed each night not long after sundown, fast asleep. It made life difficult for them, but he reminded Lydia it would not be forever. It would get easier once the house was finished, and more so when the crop came in.

"Oh! I brought some extra food for the Indians. Maybe I'll take them some of this bread and butter, too."

"They always bring their own food. I've tried some of it. They find ways to use a lot of plants and roots native here that many might not think edible. They said their wives know a lot of tricks. You'd enjoy talking with them if I can get them to come visit. They are quite shy."

"I would love to learn from the Indian women. I know they use cotton to make garments. I'd like to see how they do that."

Steve finished eating and took a long draught of water from a jug.

"I'm going to offer some of our greens to the Indians to see if they will help out with finishing our house. If all three will work, we should be able to finish the interior walls and ceiling over the weekend. Then I could finish the flooring myself. We could start moving in, even though there would still be a lot to do."

"That would be wonderful. So exciting to think—"

Steve wasn't listening, staring intently where the house and the tent sat. Lydia stood and turned around to see a buggy coming down the road. It stopped in front of their house, and a man and a woman got out.

"Who is it?"

"If I'm not mistaken, it's Minnie and a man I do not recognize."

"What is she doing *here*?"

They made their way back down the slope. Minnie and her companion spotted them and waited patiently.

"Minnie! How good to see you. What an unexpected surprise!"

Minnie hugged her brother and Lydia. "Hello, dears." She turned to the man beside her, waiting. "Allow me to introduce you to Robert Moore, a kind friend who offered to help me move from Coffeyville."

Steve and Lydia exchanged brief glances and greeted the young man.

"I thought you were moving out to Taft," Steve said.

Minnie laughed. "Yes, but when you are traveling a thousand miles, two hundred is not much of a detour. I so wanted to see you all and the new little one." She gazed at the baby with a smile.

"We are delighted you made the trip," Lydia replied as she clapped her hands. "You can stay for dinner, and we can make room for you to sleep—though our home isn't finished yet, as you can see."

"Thank you. And that will be fine. We came to see you, of course, but also to bring news." She turned somberly to Steve. "Daniel is…gone."

"Gone?" Steve said.

"He disappeared about a year ago. We waited, then Father hired a tracker. He discovered that he left Coffeyville on a train to Texas."

"He just ran away from home? Didn't tell anyone? What is he, sixteen?" Steve, being so much older than Daniel, never really felt close to him. But Daniel wasn't close to anyone. "Guess it's not much of a surprise."

"Fifteen. It's worse. The tracker never found him, but he did find out that he got caught up with some bad characters. His trail ended. Tracker said he's probably dead."

"Oh, no," Lydia cried.

Steve shook his head. "Grifters. He who makes a crooked trail will get caught by the tail."

"I know you were never close to him, but thought you would want to know."

"How is Mother?"

Minnie shook her head. "Not well. She always worried about him, and now the worst has happened. But William is marrying Laura this December, and I am hoping that will distract her. She's hoping you all will make the trip back."

"Alice wrote us not long ago. We're—"

"Let's not stand out here in the sun," Lydia interrupted. "Come on inside and I'll get us some cool water."

Three years later, Steve was on his way to Blythe for some supplies and to pick up some shipments. As he rode along, he considered how well everything had gone. He had finished the house, and had two years of growing cotton under his belt. The first year was a bit rough—but a good learning experience. Last year was much smoother, and he made a good profit, and this year he really felt like he knew what he was doing. Lydia gave birth to a third child, another boy (Steve's delight), whom they named Herbert.

He dismounted in front of the General Store, on the south part of Main Street..

Steve had walked into the Blythe General Store, where the proprietor, Harold Small, was beckoning to him from behind the counter.

"Steve, just the man I was hoping to see. Got someone I want you to meet."

In front of the counter was a slim man about Steve's age. From his clothes, hair, hat, and physique, Steve estimated he was not a laborer. Probably worked in an office.

"Randall," Small said, "this is the man I was telling you about—Steve Ragsdale. Cotton farmer down south, a well-read man. Always has interesting things to say about articles in the *Herald*. Especially if they're political in nature."

A genuine smile accompanied a firm handshake. "Randall Henderson. Pleasure to meet you, Mr. Ragsdale."

Steve in Randall shook hands. "Are you the Randall Henderson who was recently hired as editor at the *Herald*?"

Randall smiled again. "One and the same. I was hired about six months ago."

"Read every issue. Don't care for some of them syndicated columns from those writers back east, but you gotta present all sides."

"True," Randall laughed. "Can't be educated if you don't hear other views."

Steve nodded appreciatively. "Couldn't have said it better myself."

"Knew you two would hit it off," Harold interrupted. "Be back. Gotta get some stock from the back."

"You been here all your life, Steve?"

"Naw. Grew up in Coffeyville, Kansas. Was a preacher-man for a while, got fed up with small-minded parishioners, heard about cotton, came out to build a farm with my wife and one child. Got three of 'em now—five, three, and a new one just a few months old. How's about you?"

"From Iowa. Came out to Los Angeles when I was nineteen, went to the University of Southern California, then became a sportswriter for the *Los Angeles Times*. Worked at the *Post* in Parker, Arizona, for a bit, then got this job here."

"Well, that sounds like a mighty adventurous life. What exactly do you do as editor?"

Randall laughed. "You name it. Write news articles, presswork, sell advertising, and even some Linotype composition. I do some commercial printing on the side to help meet bills."

"Sounds like a one-man operation."

"I enjoy it. How long you been farming cotton?"

"Just starting my third year. Took a bit to get going, but I'm a quick study."

"You met any of the characters out and around here?"

"Characters?"

"I'm thinking specifically about the desert rats, as people call 'em. These men—and some women—who love the Colorado Desert. Live in shacks, use burros, scratch out a living from sand and rocks. Many prospect for gold or gems. Thinking of writing a book about them."

"I've heard tell. Back last year in Indio, met some man said he planned on moving out to the desert to prospect. Name was Gus, I think."

"Might be Gus Lederer. Travels through here and Arizona a good bit."

"Also met an interesting man named Edmund Jaegar. Don't think he's one of your desert rats, though. Teaches in Palm Springs. Storehouse of knowledge about the biology of the desert."

"Yes, I know Jaegar. Published some work on the condor in *American Geographic*."

"You married, Mr. Henderson?"

"Tied the knot last year. Vera is her name."

"Like to invite you and Vera for dinner sometime."

"That's mighty kind of you. I'm sure that Vera would love meeting your wife, especially us being fairly new to Blythe."

"I'll speak to my wife and we'll find a time. By the way, I fancy myself a bit of a writer—essays on various topics. Some poetry as well. Only thing published is letters to the editor, though. So far."

"I'd like us to start publishing local writers and local interest essays. Love to hear your ideas." He reached out his hand again to shake. "Must take your leave, though, and get back to the paper."

Steve nodded and shook Randall's hand. "Mighty fine. I'll come by or leave a message at the *Herald* about dinner."

Steve sat at the table, looking through mail and preparing to read the paper. He heard the door bang and looked around to see Lydia coming in, holding baby Herbert, trailed by three-year-old Thelma and five-year-old Thurman.

"Good evening, my dear," she said, as she deposited Herbert in a new little bassinet that Steve had built. "I did not hear your horse."

"Walked him the last mile or so. Pushed 'em pretty hard coming back."

She took a seat and gave him a smile. "Why is that?"

"Can't stand being away from my best girl."

She laughed and kissed him on the forehead. She nodded at the envelope in his hand. "What's that?"

"Letter from Minnie. Getting married in a few weeks."

"She is? Who's the lucky suitor?"

"Robert—the one we met."

"Shall we be attending?"

Steve shook his head. "Can't. It's 350 miles from here to there, and the roads are worse than between here and Los Angeles. And no direct route. Can't be gone from the farm that long this time of year. Someday, when we have more help, we'll have more time."

Steve could tell she was disappointed. She looked down and saw the paper folded open to an advertisement. She pointed at it. "What's that?"

"Advertisement for Henry Ford's new Model T."

"I know what it is," Lydia said. "And I know what you are thinking. Aren't they expensive and unreliable?"

"No, that's all changed over the years. That's what's so exciting. Ford said he wanted to make an automobile for everyone. Solid, easy to repair, and low price, so anyone with a decent income can buy one."

"I didn't know that. Do we really need one?"

Steve nodded. "An automobile will make our lives easier. Not only for trips to Blythe, San Bernardino, or Los Angeles, but it can be modified to use on the farm for many of the jobs we use horse or cows for."

She looked surprised. "It can?"

"Oh, yes, that was Ford's idea. It can do things cheaper and easy than animals. 'Course, we won't do away with all our horses. Always need one at least, I reckon."

"It's exciting to think of us owning a mechanical buggy." She frowned. "But can we afford it?"

"I think I can swing it. Saving up a little for a while now. They run about $350."

Lydia raised her eyebrow. "That's a good bit of money, but lower than I guessed. I remember Old Pete back in Coffeyville had one, heard he paid *fifteen hundred* for it! That's outrageous."

"Ford has changed everything. It was the innovation of what Ford called an 'assembly line' that has made it inexpensive to produce."

"You know best, husband. There are *four* of us now." She nodded at the crib, youngest, Stanley, slept.

"True. Though I'm thinking we might oughta make it five."

She cocked her head at him, eyes twinkling. "Is that right? Are you planning on starting an empire?"

Steve laughed. "Maybe I will."

After the fifth growing season, Steve took one of his horses to Phoenix. He sold the horse and bought a new Ford Model T.

As he rolled to a stop in front of the porch of the farmhouse, he honked the horn. Thurman was the first to come running from around the side of the house as fast as his legs would carry him.

"Father! Father! You bought me an automobile!"

Steve laughed. "It's for all of us, son. Gonna make working the farm and trips a lot easier."

"And to visit our families back in Coffeyville!" Lydia said, appearing on the front porch, holding Stanley. Trailing her was Thelma, almost four years old, and hardly leaving her mother's side.

Steve shut off the engine and opened the door, stepping out. "What do you think?"

She looked the automobile up and down, as if she were examining vegetables at the market. "More room than the coach version you showed me." She shook her head. "I am still leery of machinery over a living animal." She turned to look at him, reaching up on her tip-toes to give him a peck on the cheek. "But the best thing is looking at your shining eyes."

He smiled. "Indeed. I'm usually suspicious of newfangled things that become all the rage, but what Ford has done is historic." He looked around. "Where's Herbert?"

"He's inside, looking at his books."

Steve shook his head. "He's only three. That boy will not be a farmer, will he?"

"I doubt it." She smiled. "Got your brains and love of learning, but not your love of the outdoors or working with his hands."

He shrugged. "The world needs people who aren't farmers." He looked over at Thurman, who was running his hand along the running board. "Thurman, go get your brother." Steve moved to the back of the vehicle and patted the cover, which was folded back. "See this? Folds up and over to turn it into an enclosed buggy, protected from the sun and weather. And look at these seats!"

She peered inside, running a hand along the back of the front seat. "Leather?"

"Yes. And look at this…" He ran to the front and folded up the hood. "Beautiful," he said, pointing to the seventy-seven-cubic-inch four-cylinder engine. "It can go as fast as forty miles an hour."

"Ok, but what about fuel? Horses don't use fuel."

"Oh, but they do. Oats and water. And they need shelter, medical care, and more. But with fuel at twenty-one cents per gallon, and the distance you can go on a full tank, it's about the same as owning a horse. It won't come up lame, however, or get diseases, or old and unable to work."

"Or die!" Thelma cried. Her favorite dog had died last summer. Lydia patted her head.

Steve continued. "Engine can use gasoline, kerosene, or ethanol. Uses about a gallon to go eighteen miles. But for you, my dear, here is what matters. Come along!"

He led her to the other side, opened the door, and took her hand to help her slide into the passenger seat.

"Oh, quite comfortable!" she coo'd.

Thurman arrived with Herbert in tow, the latter making excited noises as he saw the contraption.

Steve shut the door and stood back, gazing at his wife. "Yup, just as I thought. You give the Lizzie a whole new beauty. Henry Ford should take a picture of you in it for advertising."

She dimpled and reached out to grab his hand. "You are a darling. Shall we go for a…a…?"

He smiled. "Drive. Thought you would never ask." He turned to the children. "Everybody in! We're going for a ride in a horseless carriage!"

What a Hell of a Fix
We Are In
~ 1918 ~

The ensuing years saw even better crops and another boy—Stanley, who turned out to be a more portly version of Steve. When the boy was able to walk, he was constantly at has father's side. He loved the sand and the sun.

The Great War was still raging, but seemed to be moving towards an end, maybe by the end of the year according to government officials. The economy was good on its war footing. Steve was able to hire several Indian farmhands, which made it easier for the Ragsdale family to travel to Phoenix or Los Angeles together. They decided to take a trip to Los Angeles in July of 1918 for Steve to make some new contacts for his cotton and examine some new machinery.

They had been driving for what seemed like many hours, but Steve's pocket watch said it had only been eighty minutes. Though he had done this route a few of times before, he had forgotten how difficult it was.

The road between Blythe and Los Angeles was over desert sand. There were no signs, except a few the government had put up where there might be water (often there was not). From the outskirts of Blyth, until one reached the Indian village of

Indio in the Coachella Valley, there were no towns or outposts of any kind.

Steve knew of three wells they would pass along the way a little off the path: Patterson, Ford, and Hopkins. Wells were almost always named after the prospectors who dug them.

Beyond Indio was Palm Springs—about 120 miles from Blythe. It was not much of a town except as a fashionable resort, mainly known for its healthy climate and the *Desert Inn*— a hotel and sanatorium. Steve had no use for such a place, but Indio, twenty or thirty miles before that, was a fine little town. From there, it was an easier trip to Los Angeles on paved, or at least maintained, roads.

Presently, though, the Ragsdales were about halfway along the most deserted stretch of the journey. Since it was one of the hottest months of the year, they had not seen one horse, wagon, or automobile since they left Blythe.

"What was that?" Lydia asked.

"Don't know." Steve's brow furrowed. Something didn't feel right about the automobile. He hoped it was a tire problem— easy to fix. But he had a feeling it was something mechanical.

"Could it be the rocks kickin' up?" Thurman said from the back seat. Steve glanced back. The vibration and sound had woken Thurman, but Thelma or Herbert were dozing undisturbed.

"Maybe." He eased off the throttle a bit, listening closely. Sort of knocking or rattling sound. And was that an intermittent grinding? "Nope."

He pushed down on the throttle and the engine made a groaning sound and coughed. He eased off, and the engine went silent.

Stanley stirred and began to cry. Lydia shushed him. "Did we run out of fuel?" she said.

"No." It sounded like the engine had no fuel, but they should have plenty. He had extra fuel in containers.

Herbert woke up and looked around. "What's happening? Are we gonna die in the desert?"

"No, ya loon," Thurman replied. "Father can fix anything."

Herbert began to cry. Lydia turned and reached back to touch the seven-year-old. "We're fine, Herbert. Just relax."

Steve put the automobile in park with the hand lever, then shifted the spark advance all the way up. "Let's try to re-start."

He got out. Lydia woke Thelma and handed Stanley to her, then moved to the driver's seat.

Steve, in front of the vehicle, said, "Make sure the ignition is set to battery, not magneto. Advance the throttle a little."

Lydia did as he asked. Steve pulled out the choke lever and turned the crank three times with his right hand to prime the engine.

"Ok, turn the ignition on."

She did so. "Done."

He cranked again, this time with his left hand in case the engine kicked back. The engine tried to turn over, but would not catch. He folded open the bonnet and opened the fuel tank. At least half full.

After waiting a few minutes, they tried again. Same result. Raising up, he took off his hat and wiped his brow. It was still early morning, but getting hotter by the minute. He estimated it was around ninety-five at the moment.

He let out a sigh as he walked around the automobile, squatting down to scan the ground underneath. He walked to the rear. Turning slowly, he leaned down and touched the ground, bringing his hand up to his face to take a whiff. "Hm."

Thurman appeared beside him. "Did you figure it out?"

Steve looked as if seeing him for the first time. "Get back in the car." He walked in the direction they had come, crouched over, still scanning the ground between the ruts in the sand. *Gotta be a fuel leak. But if there's fuel in the tank, then that means...*

Thurman walked back to the right rear door, but did not get in. Steve returned to the front of the vehicle. Thurman crept quietly along the side, so he could peer inside the engine. Steve leaned down and slid a hand and arm carefully down between the machinery, turned his head and followed the fuel line from the engine. He grunted and pulled his hand back up, wincing as it brushed some hot metal.

He spotted Thurman. "I told you to get back in the automobile, Thurman."

Thurman backed up, but kept watching with big eyes as Steve placed his hat on the ground, laid on his back, and slid under the automobile on the hot sand and gravel. After a few moments, he squirmed out and brushed himself off while walking to the driver's side. Lydia searched her husband's eyes.

"Not good," he said with a faraway look. "Fuel line. One of the tires is punctured as well, but I can patch that." He smacked his lips. "Need to think a bit."

He walked about twenty yards away and sat on a boulder, staring at the sand. The leak was in the line itself, not at a connection. It was a nasty rip, twisting the line and leaving a three-inch-long gash with ragged sides. Probably had snagged a sharp rock when they were coming down the roughest part of the hill, just after Hopkins Well. The good news was that the rip was at an upward bend in the line, higher than where it left the tank, so it only leaked fuel when the engine was running.

He did not have a replacement line, of course. He thought through what he did have. Some tools. Extra fuel. Not much else. What could he use to fashion as a repair?

He looked back in the direction they had come and pulled out his pocket watch. They left out of Blythe City—called just Blythe, now—almost four hours ago, which meant they had travelled about fifty and had fifty or more to go to reach the nearest town of Indio. They were in the desert's center. Couldn't be a worse spot.

If he could not figure a way to repair it, they had two options. Hope another automobile or horse or carriage came along, but in July, that could be days. He could probably catch some rattlesnakes and cook them. But water would run out quickly with five people. The other option was to walk back to Blythe (a trip of about eight hours or more on foot.) The younger children couldn't do it, so he'd have to leave them all here with Lydia.

"What a hell of a fix we're in," Steve said to the sand.

If the wind isn't blowing, the desert is eerily quiet. Almost unnatural. Though, of course, there is little more "natural" than an empty desert. Unfortunately, Steve couldn't enjoy its beauty at the moment.

He had gone through everything in the automobile, trying to find something to repair the line. He had even wandered about the area—though not out of sight of the automobile—hoping there might be something he could use. Walked up and down the trail both ways—maybe someone dropped something.

There was nothing. By the time he returned to the automobile, the youngest were whining and crying and Lydia was doing her best to calm them. He looked again at the engine, feeling the gash in the line. As he walked around the Lizzy one more time, he gave the front tire a swift kick.

He leaned against the front of the automobile and sighed. Guess there was no other choice. Soon as it cooled enough during the night, he'd head back. He'd leave the rifle and his pistol with Lydia and Thurman—both were good shots. Take the minimal amount of water with him, he could leave the family with the rest.

He knew Lydia would argue with him. But what other solution was there? Wait and hope for the best?

A distant sound caught his attention. He looked up, along the rough trail in the direction they had been headed. An object, far away, but moving slightly. No. Two objects. More than one person or beast. Not an automobile. He looked at his family in the car. Lydia was sitting with her head back, resting. The three in the back seat were talking or arguing. Thurman was sitting on the ground, leaning against the back tire.

Steve stood and walked slowly to the back of the automobile. Keeping his eyes on the figures approaching, he opened the boot and took out his shotgun. Most people were fine, but had seen enough—and been through enough—to know to be prepared for the worst. Especially in the middle of the desert.

He walked to the front of the automobile. Thurman jumped up when he saw the gun. "What is it, Father?"

Steve reached down and took the boy's arm, then leaned towards him. "For the last time, Thurman, get in the automobile."

Thurman knew when it was time to give in and obey his father. He ducked his head. "Yes, sir." He went around to the other side and got in beside his siblings.

Steve walked to the front of the vehicle. As he passed Lydia, saw the gun. "Steve? What's going on?"

"Probably nothing," he said, without looking away from the figure ahead. "In fact, maybe what we need. Just wanna be cautious."

He took up a position against the side of the automobile, where the open bonnet gave him a bit of cover. The rest were protected in the car. For the moment.

As the shape drew closer, it resolved into a man riding one burro and pulling another. He had on a large-brimmed hat, and Steve could see a long, gray beard down the man's chest. Long strings of similarly gray hair flowed down from under the hat on either side of his face—a face dark and weathered. The burro had two old saddlebags on either side; the other beast was loaded with sacks full of something. A shotgun was stuck through one of the straps of the saddlebags.

Steve relaxed, dropped his gun to his side, and walked towards the man.

"Steve?" Lydia called out.

"Seems to be a prospector," he called back. "Think we're fine."

The man drew up and stopped. "Howdy, traveller. Not a good place to stop. Your contraption broke?"

"Broken fuel line."

The man nodded, reached down and took a swig of water from a canteen at his side, replaced the cap.

"Don't get many people through here. Peter Gruendike's the name."

"Steve Ragsdale. We're headed to Los Angeles from Blythe. Done it before, never had a problem. You live around here?"

Gruendike nodded, and gestured towards the automobile. "Got a cabin nearby. Just there." He motioned to the north. "Reckon I can help you fix it."

Definitely a prospector, and perhaps one of the "desert rats" Randall Henderson had been speaking about. Scratched out a life in the desert, hoping to prove up and live a life of luxury. "My wife and four children in the automobile. Would appreciate the help."

"Gotta help here. Life or death." He spat to the side onto the sand. "Reckon ol' Pedro—" he nodded at the burro "—can pull that contraption over if'n some others come spiriting by."

As they hitched up the burro to the automobile, Steve asked the old man about himself. Gruendike had come out here with his brother, Wilbur, about ten years ago, and settled near the old well dug by someone named Brown. After cleaning out the well, about three hundred feet deep, his brother had enough of desert life and left for more civilized areas.

Gruendike was a strange character—probably because he spent so much of his time alone. His social skills were lacking. Laconic, with long pauses between words and sentences. He had apparently decided personal hygiene was optional, along with pronouns, conjunctions, and even verbs on occasion.

After Steve and Gruendike, with the help of the Pedro the burro, pulled the automobile off into the sand beside the ruts, he led the Ragsdales a short distance to his cabin. The well was close by, and there was a paddock beyond that, where Gruendike stabled his two burros.

"Blythe City?" Gruendike asked, as he heated stew in a big pot over the fireplace, which was in the middle of the room. Steve looked up to see a hole in the center of the roof for the smoke. The cabin was small: one room, a bed in the corner, a table, a few chairs, and a workbench. Truly a sparse living— only what he needed. It was rather intriguing. The smell inside was a mixture of body odor, burnt meat, tallow, and dirty clothes. Steve was glad this was the desert—in a more humid climate, the odors might be overwhelming.

"We have a cotton farm south of Blythe."

Long silence. "Why you out here?"

"Headed to Los Angeles for some meetings." Steve thought he had already told him that as they were pulling the automobile.

Gruendike made a grunting noise as he dumped another jar of stew into the pot. The jars were old, and Steve assumed the meat inside was from some animal the old prospector had shot and stored, with spices or maybe just salt. Steve didn't ask what the animal was.

The old prospector sat down in a chair covered with blankets. "Not many people come by." He looked at his fingernails and picked at something. "Busy day if two or three. Weeks go by—no one." He looked up at Steve. "You ain't the first I pulled out. Once found a whole family dead in their contraption when I came back from Mecca.

Steve glanced at Lydia and the children and changed the subject. "You about halfway between Blythe City and Indio here?"

Gruendike frowned. "Yep. Me and my burros." He sat for a moment, staring up into a corner of the cabin. "Couple others at Corn Springs, 'bout ten miles south in the hills. Gus and Little Tommy."

"You should set up a little outpost." Steve said, wondering if Gus was the same Gus that he had met in Indio. "Fuel, automobile repair, perhaps some food and water. Make some money."

"Nah," he drawled. "Gonna prove up on my 'stead, move down to Calexico in a proper house. Found a vein that's promising. Take a couple years."

Steve nodded, still thinking. Lydia spoke up. "How do you survive out here, Mr. Gruendike?" Lydia said. "You got your well, but what about food?" She reached over to pull Stanley's arm, who was inspecting a set of jars on a shelf with what looked like dried fruit.

"Deer, bobcat, jackrabbits, snake. Gotta know how to track. Not easy. Tried growing plants, not much luck. Cactus fruit okay, and pine and juniper gives some flavor. Get supplies from the Indians in Indio."

Herbert's eyes grew big. "You eat rattlesnakes?"

Gruendike looked at the boy as if seeing him for the first time. "Good meat, boy." He got up and went over to a rough cupboard. "Got some."

Thurman, who had been standing by, listening, grew a large smile. He was the more adventurous one, which worried Lydia but made Steve proud. Gruendike offered some to all, but only Thurman and Steve partook. Thurman declared it "some pumpkin!"

A meager dinner of some sort of stew was ladled into four pots (all that Gruendike had), and the seven ate in relative silence, the youngest sharing bowls. Thelma laid down on the floor by her mother's feet and yawned loudly.

"You all can sleep here. Not much space, but cozy and holds the cool in the morn."

"Mighty hospitable of you, Gruendike. Thurman, go get our blankets."

"We get your leak fixed to tomorrow. Got an idea 'bout that. You can get on your way in the morn."

And with that, the grizzled old man went over and fell into his little cot, snoring almost immediately.

Can't Get By on Six-Cent Cotton

~ 1921 ~

Lydia looked up from the book she was reading to Stanley as Steve entered the house. She knew immediately something was wrong.

"What is it?"

Steve sat down in his favorite chair. He took a deep breath and let it out in a big whoosh. Pulling his pipe and a pouch of tobacco out of his pocket, he filled the bowl and lit it.

Stanley wriggled off the bench and toddled to his father, who carefully set down the pipe and picked him up to set him on his lap. "Good afternoon, Stanley. Good day?"

The little boy nodded and played with his fingers. Steve looked over at wife. "The prices are worse than I thought. A man can't get by on six-cent cotton. And the irrigation problems with the flooding last season didn't help."

"But the pandemic is over. And Mildred told me that she and Bill are recovering—not as much profit, but getting by."

"They're better off than us because Bill has more acreage than we do. He makes up for the lower prices in quantity. Costs don't rise per hectare commiserate with the crop yield. But he told me yesterday he's close to margins."

She waited. She trusted Steve to figure things out. He always did. Even if it was unconventional.

Steve set Stanley on the floor, picked up his pipe, and stood. "I need to go over the numbers again. We're ready to plant, but it isn't looking good. Got no money to buy enough seed to plant the whole farm. The Spanish Flu is over, but buyers are still being cautious. We're not on a war economy any longer. Hope Wilson gets thrown out of office next year. Only thing he's done right was enacting Prohibition." He shook his head. "I wanted to expand by now. This'll be our tenth season."

"But the Great War ended over two years ago."

"That's the seductive thing about war. War economies are good. But when they end, everything drops like a rock. A war and a pandemic are a double punch. If we'd been here twenty years, maybe we'd have made enough to get through lean years."

Steve could hold forth for hours on the greed and incompetence of politicians. Lydia didn't disagree with her husband—he read a lot of newspapers and talked to a lot of people. But she had four children to raise, a husband to care for, and a large household to manage. She couldn't see how someone in far-away Washington or Europe could affect her. And she couldn't do anything about it, anyway.

"The pressing issue is that the farm tax is due. I gotta go up and see the collector in Blythe. And unless I can figure something out, we can't pay."

A bit of anxiety stirred in her stomach. "What will they do if you can't?"

Steve shrugged. "Maybe they will offer an extension. But the economic problems ain't ending any time soon. This season's crop—even if we get it planted, will put us further behind. Eventually, if I can't pay, they'll repossess."

"What?!"

"Yup. Take our farm. Welcome to the new America." He looked at her as he took his pipe out of his pocket and fiddled with it. "We made an agreement and I ain't living up to my end. That's how they see it, and it ain't wrong. Don't matter that it was a devil's agreement, and the Devil's causing the problems, I agreed to it. Not that I had a choice."

Lydia thought for a moment. "If they won't give an extension, we could always go back to Coffeyville and stay with our family 'till we get back on our feet."

Steve pointed the stem of his pipe at her. "I ain't goin' back, crawling like some beaten dog, tail between my legs."

"Steve, if we—"

"Not going back, Lydia. There's always options. Just gotta think of them. 'Nuff sed."

Steve wiped his brow with his hat as he stood outside the office. He knocked on the plain, wooden door. The black letters on the frosted glass window of the door read:

Joseph J. Jellup
Tax Collector
Blythe, Riverside County

"Enter!" a voice called out.

Steve opened the door. "Good afternoon, Mr. Jellup."

Jellup was hooking a mask on his face, despite the government's declaration last fall that the Spanish Flu pandemic was over.

"Mr. Ragsdale." The mask muffled his voice. "Thank you for being on time. Have a seat."

Steve sat in one of the two chairs in front of Jellup's large desk. He laid some papers on the desk in front of him. Mr. Jellup was perusing a file lying open in front of him.

"I see here, Mr. Ragsdale, that your payment is due next month. In fact—"

"I have come to ask for an extension. I—"

"You've already had an extension, Mr. Ragsdale." He looked closer at the file in front of him. "In fact, you've had two."

"I paid off the first one last year. With the blasted War and the Spanish Flu, you know what prices are like. They've only gotten worse. I can't sell cotton at six cents and make a living, let alone pay the government their pound of flesh. It ain't because I'm a deadbeat. Things out of my control."

"I'm afraid that's not my problem, Mr. Ragsdale."

"Blood from a turnip, Mr. Jessup. 'Nuff sed."

Steve drove back to the farm from Blythe, his blood boiling from the injustice of it all. Charging him for *living on his own land*, which he bought *with his own money*, which contributes to society! How they ever got *that* scam over the American people showed how stupid the masses are. Governments were tricky, he had to admit. Promise the people it's an emergency, "we only need this money for a short time." Yet when did the government ever *end* a program that brought in money from the people?

"Ghouls and hogs," he said aloud, "will root in Hell's hottest bogs." He nodded to himself. "That's a good one. Have to write that down."

Yet Steve was a practical man. Greed was everywhere, though perhaps more so among politicians. Steve accepted the world as it was—not that he would keep quiet about it.

He arrived at the farm, turned off the Tin Lizzy and went inside. Stanley told him that Lydia was out back taking in the laundry. He went to stand on the back porch, watching her gather the clothes from the line. Shaking his head, he looked about the farmstead. He had done well. Wasn't his fault the world went to hell with a Great War and Spanish viruses.

Lydia spotted him. "Oh, you are back! I was just about to fold these and then set to making dinner. How did it go?"

"Not good."

She bit her lips. "No extension?"

"Nope. Rather rude about it, at that. Bureaucrats."

She came up on the porch and set down the basket of clothes. "But, Steve, we haven't done anything wrong. We've worked hard, these things are out of our control. Aren't they?"

"They don't care. We're here to fill up their coffers. If we can't, they just take our belongings."

"We're gonna lose the farm?" Tears brimmed in her eyes.

Steve took her by her upper arms. "Probably. Call the children together, we're going to have a family meeting. I have an idea."

Desert Center
(1921–1932)

The Chuckawalla Valley

The Chuckwalla Valley, in the Colorado Desert of Southern California, was shaped by geological forces over millions of years. The region consists of various rock formations, including ancient igneous, metamorphic, and sedimentary rock formations. The landscape features numerous mountain ranges, dry lake beds, and vast desert plains.

The ecosystem of the vast valley is typical of the Colorado Desert, characterized by arid conditions, unique flora such as creosote bush and desert ironwood, and fauna like the chuckwalla lizard (after which the valley is named), desert tortoises, bighorn sheep, and various bird species.

For thousands of years, the Chuckwalla Valley was inhabited by indigenous peoples, particularly the Cahuilla and Chemehuevi tribes. These tribes adapted to the harsh desert environment, developed complex social structures, trading networks, and spiritual practices centered around the natural landscape. Many of their petroglyphs can be found in the area of their settlements throughout the desert.

In the 18th and 19th centuries, European explorers and settlers began to enter the valley. Spanish missionaries, followed by Mexican and American settlers, explored the valley. The Gold Rush era saw increased activity as prospectors passed through searching for mineral wealth.

In 1921, there were no roads between Los Angeles and Phoenix. Passage consisted of two ruts in the sands, often obscured by the winds. As Model-T's began to traverse the trail, *called the Blythe-Mecca Road, it was eventually graded and compacted, and became part of the famous Highway 60.*

I've a Notion to Build Here a Town

~1921~

Steve reined up his horse as the path turned towards Gruendike's cabin. He took off his hat and wiped his brow. "Must be 110 out here," he said to him himself.

There was no sign of life at the little cabin. The old man might be hunting or prospecting, although perhaps not this time of day, unless his claim was a mine. Maybe he had gone to Blythe or Indio for supplies.

Tossing the reigns over the makeshift hitching post, he knocked on the door and waited. No answer. He could wait, but what if Gruendike was on an extended journey?

Back at the cabin door, he considered whether he should enter. He didn't think the man would mind—if anyone was aware of the importance of shelter in the desert, it would be Old Man Gruendike.

Of course, Steve considered he might have died. In which case, he ought to go in and check.

He entered and scanned the one room. No body, but there were recent signs of life. He went to the fire and placed his hands on the ashes. Warm.

Gruendike had been here this morning. The question was, where did he go? He stepped back outside and walked over to the well and back.

He heard a horse's whinny. Gruendike didn't have a horse—Steve cursed himself for not getting his gun, but it *was* Gruendike—on a large fine horse. Beside him was another man leading two burros—another prospector, by the looks of him. Steve stepped outside.

Gruendike peered at him through rheumy eyes and raised up straight. "Well. If it ain't the Cotton Farmer!"

"Hello, Gruendike. Pleased you remember me after three years. Hope an unannounced visitor is not a problem."

The old man dropped down off the horse. "That's the only kind I git! And it's to my liking, young man. Come in." He turned to the man next to him. "This here's my friend, Gus. We call him the Mayor of Corn Springs, though his only constituents are his eighteen burros. Sorry, Cotton Farmer, don't 'member your name."

Gus was a small man, wearing a dinghy white cotton shirt and a wide-brimmed hat. An unlit pipe stuck out of his mouth. Steve estimated he was around sixty years old, but it was difficult to tell with these weatherbeaten desert rats.

Steve reached out to shake the man's hand. "Steve Ragsdale. Your name is Gus? I think I met you in Indio years ago? Lederman? Something like—"

Gus pulled the pipe from his mouth. "Lederer. Nice to meet your acquaintance again, sir. I might have a recollection of you. I been here since '15, just mindin' my own business."

"And you know Randall Henderson, also a friend of mine."

"Ah, yes. Randall's a good man. Why for the life of me he's interested in us desert rats, I don't know. What brings you out here, Mr. Ragsdale?"

"Call me Steve. Well, I got a proposal here for Peter."

"You better make it quick. Ol' Pete just proved up."

Gruendike gave him a nasty stare. "You jumping' my news?"

Steve raised his eyebrows. "You did?"

"That I did. Dug out the major vein a fortnight ago. Tell ya 'bout it, but let's get inside. Needin' some water and whisky." He turned to Gus. "You, too, Gus."

"Naw, I need to get back. Them mountain lions been getting past my fences and traps and eating my cats. Going to catch one, skin him, hang the hide on a tree as a message to the rest."

Gruendike and Steve said farewell to Gus and went inside. As the old prospector brushed past, and Steve caught a whiff of body odor that nearly knocked him over.

"Fix up some coffee, unless you jes' wantin' water."

"Water is just fine. Thank you." Steve took a seat at the table. "Mighty fine horse ya got there."

Gruendike set two jars of water down on the table, took a seat himself, and let out a big sigh. "So what brings ya here? Yer contraption broke down again?"

Steve chuckled. "I carry all manner of repair materials in my Lizzie nowadays. Larned my lesson, I did." He took a sip of the lukewarm well water. "Where you coming' from today?"

"Indio. What's this here proposal? Got to tell you, I'm retired now." He chuckled.

"No better way than just to come out with it. Can't make a livin' with cotton, not with the government taking so much in taxes, even in tough times. Since that day I met you, I've had it in my mind there ought to be an outpost here along the road—though callin' it a road is mighty generous. I'm wanting to set up a petroleum station, a mechanic's garage, and a place for to get water and a bite to eat. Don't know how much of the land around here is yours, but wonder if you'd be willin' to sell a portion of it to me."

A big grin broke out on the man's face—treating Steve to a view of yellow and missing teeth in the sand-and-sun blasted leather visage. "Well, well. When the good Lord brings rain, it sometimes comes as a flood." He cackled.

"Beg pardon?"

Gruendike leaned over. "As I say, I proved up my claim. Now I'm getting an offer for my land. Too bad Wilbur didn't hang around. I'm feeling generous, so this is also your lucky day, Mr. Ragson—"

"—Ragsdale—"

"—mainly because it's *my* lucky day." He leaned back in his chair. "As I said, I hit a vein that paid off big. Got me a nice house in Indio, been moving my belongings there. Bought that horse you're admiring. Gettin' out of the dirt and sand and sun."

"You're leaving your claim?"

"Yes, sir." He slapped his hands on the table. "Tell you what. The Lord blessed me, I'm blessing others. Like old Abraham. Ain't that what the good book say? You give me $100, and the whole claim is yours. It's about 40 acres."

"The whole claim?" Steve was taken aback. He was prepared to offer up to $900—everything he had, except enough to get by the next couple of months.

"Cabin, well, land—yep, all of it. I'll show you the boundary. Bet that'll fix you up nice for yer plan. It's a mighty fine idee you got there. Four to six cars a day coming' through."

"That is mighty kind of you. One hundred? Is that a fair price for you?"

"Naw, it ain't fair! It's a steal!" He guffawed. "Myself paid $200 many years ago. Don't matter now, I turned that $200 into a gold mine—literally!" He cackled. "Take me up on the offer before I come to my senses."

Steve laughed. "Thank you, Gruendike. I accept your terms. You're an answer from God."

"Don't know about that. Lessin' angels drink whiskey. Which is what we need to seal the deal." He got up and started rummaged around in a cabinet, bringing out a dusty bottle, which he set on the table. "Been saving this."

"Mr. Gruendike, I don't drink alcohol. Consider it the Devil's brew. But I'll toast you with water."

The old prospectors bushy eyebrows shot up. "No? I predict maybe in a couple years living in the desert, you'll find whiskey a mighty fine necessity."

He twisted off the cork, took his cup and threw the water on the dirt floor. He filled his cup and raised it to Steve. "To proving up a claim and building a desert outpost!"

Steve raised his jar and toasted. "Amen, Gruendike! I can draw up a bill of sale here. I'll go file it back in Blythe and bring you a copy."

"Suit yourself. Didn't used to need government papers. Guess we don't want the govmint hasslin' us, though."

"Mighty right, you are. I know first hand."

Once the old prospector had moved all his belongings out, Steve enlisted the Model T, towing a buckboard, to move the contents of the family farm to Gruendike's Well. The children wanted to come with him every time—especially Thurman and Stanley, now fourteen and six years old. Steve could have used Thurman's help, but he wanted him to stay and help Lydia while Steve was gone. The boys were disappointed, but Thurman perked up when Steve told him he was the "man about the farm" when his father was gone, though Herbert and Stanley were not too happy at this pronouncement. Once the cabin was habitable for the six of them, they would all make the trip for good.

Gruendike had left many items. He had not concerned himself with orderliness or neatness. Each trip out, Steve stayed a few days to work on the Ragsdale's new home. The first task was to clean out the cabin and scrub it good. He wanted it to feel like *his* place—because it was.

He set to repairing things inside and outside the cabin. The well was in good shape, although the hand pump could be improved. The paddock would be fine for their horses. Steve was also considering buying some goats. They seemed to do well in the desert environment.

The third task, and the most time-consuming, was to add two small room additions to the little cabin. This meant hauling lumber and other supplies from the farm or Blythe. The local Tamarisk and Ironwood trees, although plentiful, were not suitable for lumber. Much too difficult to work with.

Further plans included the construction of a small shed lean-to for effecting repairs of wagons, carriages, and automobiles, and another small structure for Lydia to serve food and drink. He had already brought out a fifty-five gallon drum of fuel—he was ready to serve travelers!

Currently, he was working on the additions to the cabin. He had the two new rooms framed and was now roofing them.

"Mornin' there, Steve! How's it coming along?"

It was Gus Lederer, who lived about fourteen miles away at Corn Springs. Gus often stopped by and offered to help. Gus baked eighteen large pancakes each morning for his eighteen burros. He did some prospecting, grew vegetables (something Steve was quite interested in), and painted desert scenes. Every spring, he went to the Imperial Valley and worked in the cantaloupe fields to make money for the rest of the year.

Often accompanying him was his good friend, "Little Tommy" Jones, who had a shack at Aztec Well, just up from Corn Springs. The diminutive man was originally from Wales, and was not only a prospector, but he wrote copious amounts of poetry. He had shared some with Steve, who found it quite inspiring.

Despite their often solitary lives in harsh conditions, these "desert rats" had a unique community, and were always looking out for each other. It made sense here in the desert, and could sometimes be the difference between life and death.

"Going well. How're you two?"

"Might fine. Enjoying the hot weather before fall. Just finished feeding my burros, Tommy came by, we thought we'd come down and see if you could use some help."

"Sure, you can help me finish up the roofing, and maybe we can even get to putting up the interior walls, if'n you got the time."

"We got nothing but time!" Little Tommy exclaimed.

Steve's plan was to finish the current addition as a bedroom for Lydia and himself. The other addition would be for the boys, and Thelma would sleep in Gruendike's old bed—with a new mattress, of course! Steve had already constructed a partition to give her privacy.

"Gus, I'd love to learn vegetable gardening from you, to see if I can do some down here."

"Yep, be happy to. I've got better water supply up at Corn Springs, though."

"I tried some of that at my last place in the Borrego badlands. No luck," Tommy added.

"That's my concern," Steve replied. "Gruendike's Well—I need to think of another name—doesn't supply a lot of water. Not sure if it's the way it's dug, or blockages, or the pump, or if it's just a small aquifer."

"There's two other wells in this area," Gus said. "Man named Henry Hartman dug this one before Old Man Gruendike bought the land, and another over at Palen Dry Lake. Close enough for you to haul water, maybe even run a trough or a pipe. They's both uphill from here. I'll show 'em to you. But Hartman thought all three was from the same aquifer, so you might just need to dig this'n out a bit more."

Steve's had already moved most of his farming tools out here. He had told his Indian farm hands to go find other work. He was gonna let the cotton fields go. Was the tax collector's problem now.

As they were finishing up the last section of the roof, they heard a shout. Looking towards the dirt ruts, they saw a man approaching on foot. Farther out, they could see his automobile on the trail.

"Looks like you already got a customer, Steve."

"He ain't the first. Every day I been here working, at least one person needs something—sometimes two or three."

Steve climbed down and greeted the man. He had run out of fuel, probably because he didn't realize traversing the sand and gravel used more fuel than on town streets.

"Good day, sir. My name is Steve—owner of this little out-post. Can I help you?"

"So thankful you are here," the man said. "Don't know what I'd have done otherwise." Sweat stains were showing through his shirt. He took off his hat and wiped his face with a kerchief.

"Prob'ly kick off," Little Tommy said quietly.

"Someone might've come by with enough extra fuel to share," Steve said to the man. "But who knows how long you would've waited. I got fuel in that drum over there. We'll get you filled up and on yer way."

"You are a desert angel, sir."

Gus, having come alongside, nodded his had. "Steve here set up this outpost here to help out travelers like you. Fifty miles in either direction to civilization. You should tell people 'bout it."

"I surely will."

Using Steve's Model T, they hauled the drum out to the man's automobile and filled his tank.

"What d'ya call this outpost?" the man asked.

"Gruendike's Well, though I'd like a better name," Steve said.

Gus looked at Steve. "How 'bout Ragsdale's Well?"

Steve shook his head. "Not about the well or me. It's about service—fuel, repair, food, drink, *and* water."

"Well," the man said, "I don't care what you call it, I'm just glad you're here in the center of the desert."

Steve clapped his hands. "That's it! Desert Center."

Gus smiled. "Perfect!" he turns to the man. "Tell everyone you know!"

The man laughed as he handed payment to Steve. "Surely will! Thank you Desert Steve of Desert Center."

Gus laughed along. "And now you have a desert rat name! Desert Steve! Along with Little Tommy, Old Man Gruendike, Pegleg Smith—"

"And what's your desert rat name?" Steve asked.

Gus smiled broadly. "The Mayor of Corn Springs, of course."

One Hundred Long Miles of Damnation and Sand

~1921–1922~

A month later, Steve stood outside the finished and expanded cabin, repair lean-to, and refreshment stand. In front of him were a small collection of people. Gus and Little Tommy were there, of course, as well as Marshall South, an interesting chap from Australia. He lived in Oceanside, working as a writer, but he visited the desert often, usually with his wife, Tanya. They frequently spoke of moving to the region to live a simpler life. Randall Henderson had driven out from Blythe, along with a friend named Robert Lee. A smattered of other desert rats were there—John de la Garza from Corn Springs, sometimes referred to as the "Mayor of Corn Springs," even though that's what people called Gus as well. Steve never got a straight answer out of either of them about that. Since Corn Springs was just a little area of rough tents and shacks, it didn't really matter. There was Frank Coffey, who supposedly had worked every mine in the area, and, for some reason, referred to his burro as "Mrs. Coffey." Lydia, Thurman, Thelma, Herbert, and Stanley rounded out the group,

"I hereby designate this place as Desert Center, California!" Steve shouted. The small collection of people clapped and cheered.

"Oy, now," Tommy Jones shouted, in his Welsh accent. "Is this an *official* town? Did you tell the authorities in Sacramento what you are up to?"

"'Cause we *know* how much you love politicians," Randall added. Everyone laughed.

Steve laughed along. "Sometimes ya gotta dance with the devil to do God's work! Ain't got the paperwork back yet, but it's a done deal."

Lydia stepped up beside him. "Thank you all so much for coming. And for all your help. We couldn't have done it without you."

Steve smirked. "Well, we'd have made do and probably faster without all the talking."

"Stop it," his wife said with a little smack to his arm. "Now, everyone, we have a feast prepared. Bighorn sheep: shot, dressed, and cooked by Gus himself."

"Is that what we been smellin'?" De la Garza said. "I thought Steve hadn't taken his weekly bath yet."

Steve started to retort, but Gus broke in, "Before we eat, I got another something for this here ceremony." He stepped over to his burro and pulled a square wooden frame out of a bag and held it up.

Steve's jaw dropped. It was a beautiful painting of a Desert Toad. "It's a beaut, Gus," he said as he walked closer. He peered at it. "Wonderful work—is that Desert Center there in the distance?"

"Reckon so, my friend."

Steve clapped Gus on the back and did not stop grinning for an hour.

Steve sat on a boulder looking at a spadefoot toad that had found some water—somehow and somewhere. The toads were rarely seen unless there was rainfall in the mountains that moistened the dry stream beds.

He'd tried cooking the toads. Not bad, but Stanley was the only one who seemed to enjoy them.

"Well, Mr. Toad, what do you eat out here?"

The toad answered him with a blinking stare.

"I can't keep driving to Happy's Ranch for fruits and vegetables. Gotta be a way. I tried some Desert Fan Palm fruit, that's okay. And of course, like the Indians, we can make mesquite paste. But that don't make much of a diet."

Steve looked out beyond the arroyo where he sat. Meat was not a problem, as he had successfully hunted mule deer, bobcat, desert kangaroo rat, black-tailed jackrabbit, Gambel's quail, and rattlesnake.

"Mr. Toad, man cannot live by meat alone." He leaned forward, taking his pipe out of his mouth. "Gus grows corn up by his cabin. But it's cooler there, with more water and shade." He stared off, his mind working. "Wonder if I could rig something up—"

He heard a shout a way away and, turning, saw a man walking towards the shack and makeshift garage. Saying farewell to the toad, he approached the man.

"Can I be of help?"

"Ah, yes, sir, I hope so. You run this establishment?"

"I own it."

"I'm stuck in the sand a little ways back."

Steve smiled. "That's why I'm here. That, and fuel, water, and food."

He and the man climbed in Steve's altered Model T and drove out to find the man's automobile off the ruts, rear wheels stuck deeply in the sand from spinning at high speed. Another man was waiting by the car, sweating profusely.

"My business partner, Roberto. We're on our way to Los Angeles.

Steve nodded and got to work. He attached the chains and made quick work of pulling the other automobile back onto the tracks of the road.

The Blythe-Mecca road was more clear these days with more traffic. It came from Blythe, through Pale Valley, up the summit and across to Shaver Valley and Box Canyon, then down onto the desert floor and through Desert Center. From there it was a fairly straight path to Indio.

Steve had been exploring the land around his new place, and wondered why that route had been chosen—it had some of the heaviest sand in the flat areas, and required a lot of travel up and down canyons and hills. Perhaps the first travelers didn't know any better, and now everyone just followed it.

If two cars came from opposite directions along the road, one would have to pull off to the side to let the other pass. It didn't happen often, but when it did, one could get stuck in that heavy sand. Steve had modified his Model T to serve as a tow truck, and made it a practice to drive out once a day in both directions for several miles to check for trapped travelers.

Most days, he didn't see any. A busy day would see five or six at the most—not all stuck in the sand, though.

"We're fortunate that you were here, Mr. Ragsdale. You say you *live* out here?"

The man was sweating profusely in the desert sun as he leaned against his automobile. His fellow traveler was doing the same.

"Yup. My family and I live in the little cabin you saw beside the garage," he waved towards the slight rise. "Belonged to an old prospector. Fixed it up, built a little repair garage and shed for food and water."

"But...*how* do you live out here?" This was the second man.

"We got a well. Deer, bobcat, rabbit, snake. Produce is more difficult, but there are some edible plants."

The first man spoke. "I guess it ain't too far to Indio or Blythe if you need something,"

"Fifty miles either way. I make weekly trips into Indio and Point Happy Ranch."

"Happy Ranch? That's where we are headed. Happy Lundback is quite a character."

Steve laughed. "And a real pioneer. Saw the value of that land near the Point when everyone else ignored it."

The man looked up at the sky and squinted. "Guess we better be on our way. Thank you for your help, Mr. Ragsdale. What do I owe you?"

"This one's free. Old Man Gruendike helped me and my family when we got stranded here years back, right about in the same spot. Passing along the help. I just asked that you tell people about Desert Center, and come visit when you're by again."

"Mighty kind of you." He and the other man climbed into the Model T and thanked Steve again.

Steve nodded. "Safe travels."

He watched the vehicle crunch its way up to traveling speed and head down the ruts, watching it until it was so small it disappeared in the yellow and brown land.

Steve gazed at his land in the bright sun—cooler than usual, but still in the 90s. There hadn't been anyone by in two days. Which was fine by him—they'd had numerous travelers during the winter, and he had several projects he needed to work on.

As he was thinking, he spotted an automobile making its way towards him. From this distance, he could only see a dark shape and dust.

The automobile pulled up and stopped in front of Steve in a cloud of dust. Steve turned his head to avoid getting it in his eyes, then turned back to give the man a piece of his mind.

"Desert Steve! How have you been?"

It was Randall Henderson. "Randall! What in tarnation are you doing here. And why are you driving like a bat outta hell?"

He climbed out of the automobile and slammed the door. "When I'm not flying my plane, I fly in my automobile." Randall was an accomplished pilot, having been trained during the great war on a two-seat pilot trainer known as the Curtiss JN-4. Later, he bought a used Curtiss, and used it to travel around the desert, explore, and even take aerial photos. "Got some news for you. Well, it's news about me, but I'm here to tell you. Got some water or something?"

"We got some fine well water. And we got ice. It's a secret how I do it. Only ice within fifty miles!"

They made their way over to the café, as Lydia called it, even though it was just a shed with three walls and a counter, with a few handmade stools.

"Randall? Is that you?" Lydia called out as they drew near.

"Pleased to see you again, Mrs. Ragsdale. How is business at the Desert Center café?"

"Been slow lately. That's fine with me, gives me time to go rock houndin'."

Randall raised his eyebrows and looked over at Steve, who returned a smile.

"You bet," Steve said. "She's taken to rock hounding like a desert fox to water. Quite good at spotting finds. Even led a group of adventurous women on a trek last month."

Henderson nodded. "This is the area to do it."

"Oh, my, but where are my manners!" Lydia exclaimed. "Let me get you some water. Unless you'd like some cool tea or a sarsaparilla. The tea is homemade, the sarsaparilla is from a bottle. And we have ice!"

"I heard. The tea sounds perfect." Privately, Henderson would like a beer, but he knew alcohol was not to be found in Desert Center.

They sat at a table and Steve looked at him expectantly.

"You both know I been burning the candle at both ends at the *Blythe Herald*. Doing almost everything myself. Loved it, but it was killing me." He leaned forward. "I got an offer last month from the *Calexico Chronicle*. They need a lead editor and investigative reporter. Right up my alley. Did the interview and took the job on the spot."

Steve reached out his hand. "Congratulations, Randall. That's a good rag. I've picked up some copies in Blythe and Indio."

"They have a good staff. And they are giving me free rein to follow stories I want—especially desert stories. So I can get serious about my work on the desert rats."

"That *is* good news." Steve took a swig of tea. "Mmmm. Delicious, Lydia! So what brings you out this way? Surely you didn't drive out here just to tell me that."

"No, but that was part of the reason. I have some time between the jobs and decided to travel around the desert a bit. Not sure if you know that a lot of people are hearing about Desert Center and Desert Steve. I want to interview you for the paper."

Steve grinned. "Mighty flattered. It is an awful lot of work, be nice to have some recognition. But mostly be good for advertising."

"Good. Do you have time now?"

"All the time in the world for you."

"One other thing. I know you've written a bit yourself, I remember your letters in the *Herald*. I'd like to ask you to send me anything you have as well—as long as it has to do with desert life or desert rats."

Steve's pride welled up. He considered himself a good thinker and a good writer. "Thank you mightily, friend. I do write frequently, though I need a better place to do it. Somewhere with some solitude. Mostly been writing about politicians and their taxes, government corruption, and the evils of booze, but I enjoy writing about the desert. The desert tortoise is a particular interest of mine."

"Bring it or send it to me when it's ready. Now, if it's alright with you, I'd like to get a tour of this place and what you're doing to live out here. You altered the Model T to serve as a towing truck?"

"Yup, and more. Growing food has been failure after failure, but have some new ideas…and other ideas for growth as well. Come on, I'll show you what we've done."

Snakes With Broken Backs

~1922~

"You bought what?!"

Steve laughed at Lydia's shocked face as he held the contraption in front of her.

Thurman came in. "Is that a radio?"

"Indeed it is. While the desert life has great benefits, we do need to know what's going on in the world. No one delivers papers out here—yet."

He had just come back from Indio, and Happy Lundbeck, the owner of a large ranch there, had a radio to sell. Not only did Steve mean what he said about needing to know what's going on in the outside world, but he was also fascinated by this relatively new and freely available technology.

"Baseball?!" Herbert said, who had just come in to see what the excitement was about.

"Yes," Steve laughed. "We can listen to baseball games."

Thurman and Herbert cheered. Lydia said, "I don't know a lot about them. But don't they have to have a tall antenna? And can we receive the programs so far out here?"

"That question right there tells me that you know more than most. These signals can travel a long way. They can even bounce around the Earth during certain atmospheric conditions."

"Turn it on! Turn it on!" Herbert shouted.

"What's there to listen to?" Lydia said. "It must be something appropriate for the children."

"I understand there are two radio stations in Los Angeles that we should be able to pick up. Both just started about six months ago: KFI and KNX. I don't know what the letters mean yet, but I wrote down the frequencies so we can tune them in."

Lydia looked doubtful, and started to speak when Stanley came rushing in.

"Father! There's a customer!"

"Ah, well, it appears that the radio will have to wait. Duty calls. Come on Thurman."

The two stepped out to see a Model T parked in front of the repair garage. It was quite new, although covered with dust from the desert. That it was a Model T was no surprise, since well over half the automobiles in the United States were Model T's. This one was black, with the tapered, curved top, and folding hinges located where the flat side met the curve top. Ford has been producing these since 1917, and the only color available was black. Steve had laughed when he read that Ford told his employees, "our customers can have their Model T's in any color they want, as long as that color is black."

A young man, dressed foppishly and not for the heat, was standing beside the automobile, mopping his brow with a handkerchief. A young woman was visible in the passenger seat. Blonde, with a stylish hat. She was fanning herself furiously with a printed fan.

Steve shook his head. Did these people not understand what "desert" meant?

He approached. "Good afternoon, sir. I'm Desert Steve, owner of this town. What can I do for you?"

The man looked around curiously, as if wondering how a well and three structures constituted a town. Steve didn't care. It was a town to him. His town.

"Thank you, Desert Steve. I need some fuel. And some water if you have any. Not for the auto, for us."

"Of course. It's why we're here. I'll get your fine vehicle filled right up. And right over there—" He pointed to the newly constructed structure which housed Lydia's refreshments counter. "My wife can help you out with water, as well as other drinks and some bites to eat, if you so desire."

"Excellent, thank you."

He went around to the passenger side of the automobile and opened the door, extending his hand to the young lady. "My dear Doris, let us get some drink and a bite to eat if you'd like."

"What I'd like is to be out of this damned desert."

"Now, dear, there's no need for that sort of language. This is the only way to Palm Springs. And this gentleman's wife is waiting to serve us."

Steve watched as Doris allowed the man to take her hand. They headed over to Lydia, with Doris chattering the whole way.

Steve looked at Thurman. "Some people should never leave their towns."

"Just what I was thinking."

Steve walked over to the fifty-five-gallon drum, which had a glass tube attached, with markings In units of a gallon, and a hose with a hand pump. He grabbed the edges of the barrel.

"Thurman, give me a hand."

Stanley, who had followed unnoticed, said, "I wanna help!"

"You can't, you're only six." Thurman had been helping Steve with fueling and even some repairs and towing.

Steve looked at his youngest. "Someday. Come watch and learn."

Stanley came closer, offering a sneer to Thurman.

"Thurman, help me move this barrel closer to the automobile. Need to build some sort of wheeled platform for the barrels. We'll do that next week. You can help, Stanley."

They both maneuvered the drum, which was about three quarters full, closer to the Model T. Steve motioned Stanley over, showing him how to read the glass tube markings. Then he showed him how to check the paper log in a leather cover hanging from the drum.

"You're learning to read, Stanley. Can you see here how we make sure the last indicator setting—that's the glass tube—matches what we wrote down last time?"

Stanley frowned. "Why check it if no fuel—" (he pronounced it "fool") "—is used since last time?"

"Could be we forgot to write it down. But also, out here in the desert, some of the fuel can evaporate."

"What's that mean?"

"That's when some of the fuel escapes as vapor. Do you know what vapor is?"

"It's like when mom's soup boils and steam goes up."

"Yes. Good. Quite similar."

Thurman pulled the stop on the top of the gas tank and put the tube from the drum inside. Steve worked the hand pump.

"Put your ear against the tank, Stanley." The boy did so. "Hear that gurgling sound when I pump? Mean fuel is going in."

"I hear it!"

"Good. If you are pumping by yourself you gotta check that every once in a while. You keep the hose about an inch or two inside the tank. When you hear it stop making noise, you know it's near full."

"Yes, sir." He checked with his ear three times. After the third time, he shouted, "It stopped!"

Thurman pulled the hose out and peered inside. "Yup. Full up."

"I wanna see!" Stanley said. Thurman braced his brother as he stood on the running board to look inside.

Steve took the hose and looped it around the pump handle on the drum, then checked the current price of fuel, written on the side of the drum with a grease pencil. He did that whenever he refilled the drums in Blythe.

"Nine and a half gallons, Thurman. At thirty-six cents a gallon. What's the total?"

Thurman looked up, thinking, then used his fingers to tally. "That's $3.42."

"Good." Thurman and Stanley were both smart, but Steve wanted them to have proper schooling. The closest was in Thermal, which was about sixty miles away, but Steve didn't care. Education was important.

They maneuvered the barrel back to its original location just as Thelma came out of the refreshment stand with four empty buckets. "Thurman! Mother says help me fill these up from the well."

Steve retrieved some rags from the garage, and handed one to Stanley. "Help me dust off the automobile." Steve knew he probably wouldn't do a thorough job because couldn't reach the top, but it was important for him to start working. The automobile would be just as dirty in another twenty minutes, but he had found that the customers appreciated and remembered the extra touch.

The shiny black finish was sparkling by the time the man and Doris returned.

"My good man, what have you done? This looks as good as it did when I bought it two months ago." Even Doris was smiling. "Hope I don't owe extra for that," he laughed.

"No, sir, on the house, courtesy of Desert Steve and Desert Center." It struck him that he needed to fashion a sign for his outpost."

"Mighty kind of you. Desert Center?"

"That's right. Fifty miles in any direction to civilization."

"I'm glad you're here. What do I owe you?"

Steve gave him the amount. As the man fished in his money purse for coins, Doris spoke to Steve for the first time.

"How far to Palm Springs?"

Of course they are going to Palm Springs, Steve thought. "About seventy-five miles. You're almost halfway from Blythe. It's a pretty straight shot from here."

She looked around. "I hear there are rattlesnakes."

"Well, ma'am, we used to have *lots* of rattlesnakes. Desert was crawling with 'em. Scooted around in groups and ate everything in their path. Lotta people died back in those days from rattlesnake bites."

Her eyes grew wide.

"But they are all gone now," he continued. "I ain't seen a one for years."

"Oh, that's good. What became of them?"

"Henry Ford. When he got to making all these automobiles a few years ago, this road across the Chuckawalla Valley became so crooked that a cow pony couldn't follow it. Nothing but Fords ever tried to cross this way. They zig-zagged along through the sand and when the rattlers would start chasing them, them damn snakes would break their backs making the turns. They're all dead now."

She searched his face to see if he was joking. Steve remained impassive.

"So no reason to fear, ma'am."

"Oh...ok—" she looked at her companion. "We should be going."

They got into the automobile and shut the doors. The man leaned out the window. "Mighty fine to meet you, Desert Steve. We'll see you on the return trip."

And *that* is what Steve liked to hear. He wanted people to remember this place. And he had a lot more plans for Desert Center.

Can't Agree with Themselves or the Rest of the World

~1922-1925~

Steve was in the garage working when he heard the braying of a burro. He stepped out into the sun to see Gus and one of his eighteen animals.

"Morning, Gus! What brings you down here?"

"Fine morning to you, Steve. I'm on my way to Indio for supplies. You be needing anything?"

"No, I'm set. Thanks for asking. Good weather for a trip," he said, looking up at the clear, cool sky.

"Yep, nice cool winter. Say, would you mind doing me a favor? I'll be back Tuesday morning. Could you go check on Tommy? I saw him yesterday, and he wasn't doing well. He has those spells sometimes, I'd feel better someone checked up."

"Be happy. Matter-of-fact, I was headed up into them hills to do some hunting. Not too much farther to his cabin."

"Much obliged. I'll come back by in the morning."

Steve had been hunting all morning when he tracked and shot a small deer up in a nearby canyon. After dressing it, he tied it over the back of his burro. It was only a couple of miles from there to Corn Springs, and then a short distance up to Aztec Well.

All was quiet as he approached Tommy's little cabin. No smoke from a fireplace. It was just a bit after noon, so the diminutive Welshman could be up at his mine or hunting.

"Tommy! You here?!" he shouted as he approached the cabin. He knocked on the door. As he started to turn away, he saw that both of Tommy's burros were in the pen.

Frowning, he pushed open the door and waited for his eyes to adjust to the dim light coming through a small, high window.

Tommy lay on his back on his bunk. Mouth open. Gray pallor.

Gus was going to be devastated. They had been friends for a long time here in the desert.

He stripped back the bedsheets, and saw that he was shirtless. He found a relatively clean shirt and put it on him, arranged the body, then stood before him and said a prayer.

Turning, he looked around the cabin. Tommy had posted a lot of his own poetry on the walls. One of them was framed and set over the fireplace. He moved closer and read:

> *I am the desert, I give peace...I give strength, I give power. I give peace for every hour. I am the desert giving giving giving. Come to me, you who are weary of living.*

Steve nodded to himself, and said aloud, "Right ye are, Little Tommy. Rest in peace."

He would rather not do anything until he could return with Gus, but he did take the meager amount of food there so that it would not spoil. He checked through the cabin one more time, then left, making the sure the door was latched. Back outside, he fed and watered the burros.

It was a melancholy trip back down and over to Desert Center.

Gus arrived back at Desert Center the next day. As Steve expected, he took the news badly. Steve sat with him in the café and let him talk about his friend. His eyes frequently welled up with tears. Finally, exhausted with emotion, he turned practical, asking Steve if he had materials to make a grave marker. Steve found a rectangular piece of sheet metal and some paint. While Lydia prepared lunch for them, Gus worked on the marker.

After eating, they both headed up to Aztec Well. Once the grave was dug, they wrapped Tommy's body and laid it to rest. After filling it with dirt and sand, they used nearby rocks to make a burial mound.

Back at the little Welshman's cabin, they went through his belongings. There wasn't a lot: cooking and eating utensils, tools, a gun, and his prospecting equipment. A few clothes. The rest was a number of books and papers of poetry—both Tommy's verse as well as other poets.

"How old was Little Tommy?" Steve asked.

Gus paused from folding Tommy's clothes and blankets in a neat pile. "Seventy...seventy-two, I think. He always used to joke he was wiser than me because he had a couple decades on me."

Steve chuckled. "He didn't appear that old. I thought maybe he was around sixty."

"Yep. Well-preserved. He said it was that moonshine he brewed up."

"I didn't know he had a still."

"He knew your thoughts on alcohol—he wouldn't have said anything. I tried some once. I'd rather drink out of one of your fuel drums."

They both chuckled lightly, and then became somber again. They worked in silence for another hour, then loaded up the burros and went back out to the grave.

"Shall we put up the marker?"

After mixing up some cement, they set the metal in the ground at the foot of the grave. They both stood back and examined their work.

> *Thomas "Tommy" Jones*
> *Born: 1850, Wales, England.*
> *Died: Nov 8, 1922*
> *Miner*
> *Poet*
> *"May He Strike It Rich In the Great Beyond."*

"Amen." Steve said.

Three years later, in the winter of 1925, Steve burst into the cabin one evening, startling Thelma and Lydia, who were preparing dinner. He was covered in sand and dirt, which was not unusual at the end of a day. But his face was red with anger.

Thurman and Stanley came rushing in from their room.

"Father! You're back! Did you—" Stanley shouted, stopping abruptly when he saw his Father's expression. Herbert appeared in the bedroom doorway and stopped, eyes wide. It didn't happen often, but when Steve got angry, it could be frightening.

"What is it?" Lydia said, wiping her hands on her apron and walking to him.

"Government *bastards!* A group of people who can't agree with themselves or the rest of the world. It's as if they follow us around trying to make trouble!"

"What happened?"

"Our road. The Mecca-Blythe Road. Those ruts out there." He pointed roughly towards the road.

"What about it?"

"They're gonna make it a proper road."

Lydia frowned. "That…sounds like good news."

"They are moving it ten miles to the south."

She looked at him in stunned silence.

"Our life blood is gone."

Faith is Believing Everything Is Well...

~1925-1926~

"How can they just move a road?"

"Because the government thinks they own everything. They want to expand Highway 60 from the Arizona border all the way to Los Angeles. They'll grade the road and pack it down, and have plans to eventually pave it. But the engineers, with their heads up their asses, decided the road needed to go through here farther south."

"How will people get here? Don't they know the service we provide?"

Steve sat down heavily in a chair at the table. "They don't care. They gonna do whatever they want. Not many travelers are going to drive six miles out of the way on sand. Not when the road is smoother and faster." He shook his head. "First they tax me out of farming, now they take my road."

Lydia sat down beside him and put her hand on his arm. "How did you hear this? Maybe it won't really happen."

He took a deep at the beginning to calm down. "It's in the *Herald* and the *Sun*. They decided that with increased traffic between Los Angeles and Phoenix, it's needed. Which is true."

lled a crumpled page out of his worn trousers and read

The old highway there will be abandoned when the new work is completed,' said Mr. E.Q. Sullivan, division engineer for the California Highway Commission, 'and we will later surface such stretches of the new road as are necessary.'

ey both sat silently. The four children had taken seats on the or, sitting quietly, watching their parents.

All that work. The rebuilding and extension of the cabin. The an-to garage. The drums of petrol with the hand pumps. Upating the well. The ill-fated farming attempts (which he still ad not given up on). Modifying the Model T to act as a tow ruck.

"Steve, you have said for years that this road is in the wrong place. Sand is too heavy, some vehicles have trouble with the inclines—"

"I know what I said, Lydia." He didn't appreciate being reminded. "The one time the government does something right, and it's still wrong."

Lydia, chastened, sat for a moment, waiting. She knew this is how Steve worked through difficulties. Explode in anger or frustration. Then logic took over as he weighed the situation. Eventually, a plan would emerge.

He shook his head. "They're doing the right thing." Steve took off his hat and wiped his brow, and stared off far away look in his eyes. Lydia waited. She knew that look. He was calculating, assessing, and planning.

He stood suddenly. "We'll move."

"Move?"

He looked at her. "Yes, *move*. Move the entire damn town six miles."

"Steve, how can we move—"

"We can and we will. Boys are all old enough to help. 'Nuff sed."

But he grimaced at the work involved. He just recently felt like that place was in order. Of course, there was always improvement to be made, but he had the place running well. And they were making money.

To have to start all over again...

He looked at the children. "What do you think, children? Ready for another move? Not so far this time. Still gonna be a lot of work. Faith is believing everything is well, if we work like hell."

"I'm ready!" Stanley shouted. "We'll make a better town!"

"We did it once," Thelma added. "We can do it again."

Thurman and Herbert nodded, although Herbert seemed less than enthused.

Steve patted Stanley on the shoulder, smiling now. "Better than better. I'll build a proper garage. And get some real metro pumps instead of these hand pumps." He turned to Lydia. "And I'm gonna build you a real café. Tables and chairs. A kitchen."

Lydia shook her head. "I can't believe this."

"And here's what else. F. C. Payton is the contractor handling the grading work. I'm gonna get in contact with them and offer my services to their surveyors. I know this area better than anyone. I can make some money at that while we're moving our town."

He plopped his hat back on his head. "We'll take a disaster and turn it into an opportunity."

Later that night, after the children were asleep, Steve and Lydia sat out in front of their cabin. At night in the desert, the stars shone like 10,000 candles in the sky.

"I can't believe it," Lydia said, her eyes brimming with tears. She had become quite attached to their little personal town, even though calling it a town was generous. "How did this happen?"

"Eh, it was bound to happen. I just didn't think it would happen this quickly. But the Mecca-Blythe Road—such as it is—is the only route connecting the Palo Verde Valley with the Coachella Valley and points beyond. The government commission took over the route on January 1st last year. They want to make it an extension of Highway 60 from the East Coast, a sort of 'Atlantic and Pacific highway.' Makes sense, really."

"And we're going to move the whole outpost?"

"Yep. You can't fight City Hall, as they say in New York."

"The buildings?"

"Been pondering that," Steve said. "They're only sitting on concrete slabs. I intended them to get us up and running, not as permanent structures. Always planned on building more substantial buildings. We take these apart and use the materials. But I'm gonna build solid, permanent structures this time. Highway 60 will be there forever, and so will Desert Center! A proper fuel station, repair garage, offices, and a café. To start."

"We should build a market. People are always asking if we have any goods for sale."

Steve raised his eyebrows. "Excellent idea!" He put his hand on his wife's shoulder. "With a graded road, more people will be driving out, which means more money. When we have enough, I am going to build us a proper house. With a screen porch on top, for the hot nights."

Lydia smiled. "That does sound nice."

"We gotta see this as the next step in our growth, not a set-back. Tomorrow I'll head out first thing to Riverside, meet with the officials and tell them I can help with surveying. You and the children can start making lists of everything—you and Thelma inside the house and café, the boys in the garage and outside." He looked at her. "This will be much easier and faster than our move out here."

"No use waiting, I suppose."

He smiled at her. "Good thing I married a pioneer woman."

"When you first started courting me, I told you I wanted to get out of Coffeyville, and maybe even go to California. Just didn't think I'd have to move twice."

He turned away to leave and then stopped. "One more thing. Thurman drives the children to school in Thermal five days a week. Fifty-two miles each way!"

"They've never been late once, dear."

"Only because I threatened to skin them alive. But that's fuel we could be selling instead of using. And a lot of traveling time that they could be helping out around here."

"But you've said they need a proper education with a school-teacher."

"Agreed. The new Desert Center is going to need a school."

...If We Work Like Hell
~1926~

"Damn it!" Steve cursed as he stared at the outlet pipe. Thurman had been operating the hand windlass for twenty minutes. "Nothing. Again!"

"What about over there?" Herbert said, pointing to a low depression about five hundred yards away. Herbert wasn't much for physical work, but he was observant and clever.

Steve stared for a moment, then shook his head. "Nope. If there was anything at the third hole we dug, it would have been there, too."

He stepped back a few feet, sand sat down on the fender of the Model T. It did not rain often enough for a collector—he'd be lucky to get ten gallons during an entire year. He had to have a well like Old Man Gruendike had up at the old place. Steve had never surveyed and dug a well before, but he'd read as much as he could find, and talked to plenty of people in Blythe and Indio. He'd explored the other wells up by their old home, noting the lay of the land and the geology. There was nothing fancy about the well at Old Man Gruendike's. He was sure he could do it—unless the aquifer was too deep. Or worse, there was no aquifer under the new place.

He wasn't prepared to believe that yet.

He'd begun by exploring the land within a mile radius of their new property. Noting where there seemed to be signs of runoff, or particular clumps of flora, or tell-tale depressions in the land. He marked it all on a rough, hand-drawn map. Next, he went out on multiple days and evenings, watching for wildlife, marking where any might go to find water. But those were merely dew collections or other surface water in shadowed areas. He marked the places on the map, anyway.

The boys and Steve had been exploring the area for a week, digging holes based on his map. Thurman and even eleven-year-old Stanley were quite helpful. Herbert less so, as they always had to drag him along, complaining.

This was the ninth hole they had drilled. As dry as the other eight.

Finally, he went south and trudged up the Chuckawalla Mountains. The Model T got him a good ways up, but he had to hike the last few miles. He located a peak where he could view the land all around Desert Center.

It was a beautiful view of the entire area for many, many miles north, east, and west. He could see the new road snaking through the desert to the east. He spotted both the new and old Desert Center. To the north and northwest were the mountains on either side of the Pinto Wash.

He could see the folds and washes where water might flow, though he knew much of them were ancient and had been dry for centuries. From his map and explorations, he knew the areas that still had some water. But depending on water flow from the mountains would not be enough. Looking at the geology of the land, and what he had learned about geologic processes, gave him some idea where the aquifer should be.

He was sure there was water down there. Some explorers and miners had told him there was an aquifer that ran the entire length of the valley. He had been drilling in all the right places. The fact that he was coming up dry meant that the aquifer was too deep for him to reach. He was going to have to hire some-one with the proper drilling machinery and knowhow.

He didn't like it. He preferred doing things by himself, and would sometimes rather do without if he couldn't.

But his town had to have a good supply of water. It was a basic necessity, and he had no choice.

The drilling company finally found water at 423 feet. There was no way he could've drilled that deeply his own. However, it cost him $12,000—far more than he was planning. More than he had paid for his cotton farm back in '08. He told the fore-man that he thought he was overcharging him because he knew he had no choice. The man countered by pointing out that sur-veying, drilling over four hundred feet, out here in the middle of nowhere, was a high-cost endeavor, and he was not charging him any more than he would anyone else.

Steve wasn't so sure.

Meanwhile, Steve had set proper foundations for a café and a garage, and had begun framing. Gus came one day, not long after the well was working, to help him with the foundation of the market, across the new road from the café and garage.

"How in blazes did you come up with $12,000, Steve? Did you strike it rich and not tell the rest of us?"

"I had to get creative, and there are some tales to tell."

"Pray tell?"

"First thing was to go to Happy Point and talk to the Indians. I told them if they would make jewelry, clothing, knacks, and other items, I would take them on consignment and sell them to visitors. People are always asking for artifacts."

"You made $12,000 selling Indian baubles?"

"'Course not. But I made a lot. Indians didn't want a lot of money for their stuff. Travelers, especially from the east, coming through the desert for the first time, are willing to pay a lot for Indian goods. They sell themselves. Easy."

"Ok. What else?"

"Started doing desert tours for visitors. Took them up to Corn Springs and showed all the old Indian petroglyphs. Or out to Palen Dry Lake to hunt for quartz."

"People paid you to show them rocks?"

"Yep. Too bad you didn't think of it. I also organized some more strenuous rock hunting trips, which are very popular with the people who come up from Calexico or Mexico, and out from Palm Springs. Especially the rich ones. Seems they like feeling like they're roughing it. They'll pay a lot for a day to collect rocks, with the possibility of finding gold."

"You ain't gonna find gold on the surface."

"They don't know that. Besides, it's not impossible, just unlikely. They're paying for the experience. And the government paid me for helping them survey the road, plus some other odd jobs here and there."

Gus regarded his strange friend. "Sometimes I don't know how you find enough hours in the day to do everything you do."

"Rights now I gotta finish up building a town. Appreciate your help, friend. Let's get this finished so we can start framing once it's set. Which happens astonishingly fast out here. Where are the boys?"

"Thought I heard them over behind the garage."

Steve yelled out, and the three of them appeared.

"Got a new job for you, boys. Come on over by the café."

The garage and offices were already framed and the outer walls almost complete. Even though it wasn't finished, he had set up the equipment so that he could offer fuel and services before finishing the detail work. The café was taking longer because he wanted to build it adobe style, with a full kitchen, and either build or buy tables, chairs, and booths.

Steve led the boys to the east side of the café.

"Gather around, boys. You're gonna love this."

He pointed to piles of building scraps, where they had been throwing unused materials.

"I need you to move all this back about a hundred yards. Then—"

He was interrupted by a cry from Herbert. "All of it?"

Steve fixed him with a steely eye. "I ain't got to the good part yet. Once you get that pile moved, I need you to dig."

"Dig?" Stanley said, who was the hardest working one of the three, although Thurman was a close second. "Thought we had all the water we need."

"It's not to find water. It's to *hold* water."

The three looked confused. Then Stanley's eyes lit up. "A swimming pool?!"

"A plunge pool. Can you imagine how many people from May through September would pay a few cents to take a little dip? And if they stop, they'll buy fuel, they'll buy food, they'll buy goods at the market."

"How deep does it need to be?" Stanley asked.

"You dig, I'll tell you when to stop. Make that end deeper than this end, so people can wade in. Soon as you start, the sooner you finish."

"A pool!" Stanley shouted. "Let's go!"

Thurman, driving the Model T with Stanley riding shotgun and Herbert in the back, pulled up beside the concrete pad that

Steve and Gus had poured days before. Gus, John de la Garza, and Frank Coffey had come out to help. The four men were preparing to wall the market, while the boys moved everything from the Gruendike location.

Steve stood up, stretched, and walked over to the wagon being pulled by the automobile.

"Dammit, Thurman. You were supposed to bring the wallboards and sheets, not this!"

"I told him!" Stanley said.

"Shut your pie-hole," Thurman said as he got out of the truck, wiping his brow. "I thought we were bringing everything that's left."

Steve sighed. "No matter, it's gotta all get here anyway. Unload all this and then go back and get the boards and sheets."

It had been a lot of work the past month. Sunup to sundown, every day. After Steve had located the proper site, cleared the land, and poured the concrete pads, they began disassembling the buildings at the original site. Steve put the women to work packing up and taking everything apart. The boys loaded and hauled the materials to the new site. Every few days, Steve would drive into Indio or Blythe for new materials and supplies. While he was gone, the boys used a couple of burros to haul the wagon. They were not happy during these trips, because the burros took much longer.

The seven of them were able to unload the wagon quickly. They placed everything beside another large stack of supplies and materials. The boys got back in the Model T and drove off in a cloud of dust.

"I'm surprised at the amount of progress that you've made since the last time I was here," John said. "I can't believe the garage and the café are already completed."

"There is still a lot to do inside. But it's ready to serve guests. We ain't gonna miss a single day of fuel, repair, or food and drink service. Once this new part of the road is open, we'll shut down the old place for good." He pointed to the east. "Going to build us a proper house over there. Then we're gonna do a long building here, beside the market, that can hold some offices or businesses. Including a post office."

"A post office? You can't just build a post office, the government has to do that."

"Already contacted them. They agreed to install a post office if I'll build the building."

"That mean we can get mail here?" Frank asked.

"You bet. And down there, beyond the plunge pond, I'm going to build some cabins. Some travelers don't want to drive ninety miles across the desert in one go. I'll offer a place to stay, at a good price, in beautiful Desert Center, where Desert Steve is open every day unless the sun don't shine."

"The sun always..." Gus shook his head. "Never mind."

We Lost Our Keys, We Can't Close!

~1926~

Steve strode along Highway 60—now "Main Street" of Desert Center—surveying his work, as he did each morning on the way to his office.

He always arrived at 6am, ready if someone needed fuel or repairs. The boys were also available, if not at school. Since it was summer, someone was always here, twenty-four hours a day. All three boys worked shifts at the garage or the café. Herbert always chose the café—Stanley was happy to take his shift at the garage. He liked pumping gas from the "real" pumping machines. Steve discovered that, occasionally, Stanley even paid Thurman some of his wages to let him take his shifts. Thurman didn't mind the work, but being nineteen, he appreciated the money more. Steve didn't say anything. He admired a clever work ethic.

Lydia was the queen of her café. Not only did she have Thelma helping her, but they had hired two other women—Ruby and Bea. Sometimes twenty cars could pass by in a day, and most stopped for gasoline, food, or just a grateful plunge in the pool. Steve insisted the café be open twenty-four hours a day because many people chose to drive the desert at night instead of during the hot days.

He looked at the market on the other side of the street. He had an employee there, as well, and possibly another soon—perhaps as manager, so Steve could be relieved of minor business matters such as stock and inventory. At first, he just sold sundry goods that any traveller might need. But he soon added camping and exploration supplies, as more and more visitors wanted to explore the desert—hikers, rockhounds, those interested in the Indian artifacts, and, of course, those looking for gold and iron nuggets.

Next to the market was a line of shops. Most were empty at the moment. The post office was up and running—he was quite proud that he got the state to agree there were enough businesses and people in the area (including the prospectors in outlying areas) to warrant a post office with a single postal worker.

He went inside and retrieved the day's mail. As he left and walked across to the garage and café, he admired the sign he had Gus paint. Large enough to be seen from far away, it said "Desert Center" in the middle, followed by "CAFE" in large letters underneath.

Beside the café was the garage, now owned by Ragsdale Desert Service & Supply, Inc., sold for a dollar by Steve. Of course, he was still the owner, but his lawyer suggested he form a company to protect his assets. He had plans to buy more of the surrounding land. Forty acres was not even close to what he needed for his ideas.

He strode to the café and smiled at the sign beside the door:

We Lost Our Keys - We Can't Close!

"Good morning, Mr. Ragsdale," Ruby said, the thirty-three-year-old. She had one small child. Her husband had been killed while out hunting bighorn sheep near Thermal. An unusual occurrence, but Steve felt sorry for her when he heard about it, and offered her the job. She had done well helping Lydia with cooking and serving. Steve allowed her to live in one of the little cabins he had built, for a small pittance out of her paycheck.

"Doin' well, Ruby. How are things here?"

"Going well. Only those two so far today." She nodded to a couple siting at a table eating breakfast. Steve frowned. They looked familiar.

"Good morning, I'm Steve Ragsdale, owner of this town. I think we've met before?"

"Desert Steve. Good morning," the man replied. "We met a year or so ago. We're both writers who love the desert. Name's Marshall South. This is my wife, Tanya."

Tanya dimpled. She was quite beautiful, Steve noticed her Russian accent, along with a thick crop of long, curly, brown hair.

"Ah, yes. I remember. You've been published nationally."

"Articles and essays, but having trouble finding publishers for my novels."

"I read something you wrote in the *Saturday Evening Post*. Something about not wanting to write as slaves for money? I can—"

Lydia came out from the kitchen. "Sorry to interrupt. Steve. Can I ask you something when you get a chance?"

Steve frowned at her, took his leave of the Souths, and followed Lydia to the kitchen, where Ruby and Bea were working. Bea was an older woman, perhaps 55, who answered an ad for a cook that Steve had advertised.

"When do you think you or one of the boys can get that gas line fixed?" Lydia said. "It leaves us with only one stove, which is fine when it's slow. But busy season is coming. Bea and I will need to be cooking at the same time."

Ruby spoke up. "Will we need to hire another server when it gets busy?" This was her first year—she had not experienced the traffic in October through April. "The children will all be in school when September rolls around and Thurman will be driving them. Less workers."

"Woah, slow down, women, I can't answer everything at once." He stepped up to the counter and took a seat. Ruby placed a cup of coffee in front of him. He gazed around the dining area. A long counter with plenty of seating. Tables throughout. Against the far wall, padded booths—he made them himself with materials from Blythe.

"I'm fixing the gas line today. I contacted the state to send us a school marm, like I mentioned. We'll save fuel, wear and tear on the auto, and Thurman will be happy to retire as the 'school bus driver.' Plus, he'll be available for work." Steve had purchased a used Model T just for that purpose, although they used it for business, too.

"So we *will* have our own school?" Ruby said. She didn't like her little girl going so far for schooling, even if she was with the Ragsdale boys and Thelma.

"If'n the government doesn't prove intractably stupid, which is a distinct possibility." He looked over at the wall clock. "I been expecting a response from them for days, and I'm hoping it's in this stack of mail." He held up the mail bundle for them to see, picked up his cup, and retreated to his office.

A few moments later, he threw the letter down on his desk and sat back heavily. "In order for a school to be established," said the State, "there must be a minimum of eight students."

Desert Center had five.

Apparently the State doesn't care that children have to drive 104 miles a day, five days a week, to go to a less-than-stellar school in Thermal. Once, they got stuck coming back. Steve was surprised it was only once. When an hour had passed after they should have been home, Steve drove out with the towing truck to find them. He assumed they were stuck, but of course, their mother was worried sick it was something worse.

He blew out a long breath. Had to be something he could do.

Eight. They need eight. He stood up. "I need three more children!"

He ran back into the café, startling everyone inside. "Going to Blythe! Be back late afternoon!" And with that, he was out the door.

"How does this look, Mr. Ragsdale?" The printer pulled the paper out of the typewriter and slid it across to him. Steve perused the text.

> *Needed post-haste. A mechanic with a desire to live where God rested—Desert Center. Adventure, helping stranded motorists, and the best town in the desert. Apply to Mr. Steve Ragsdale at the address below, or visit him in Desert Center—where the sun always shines!*
>
> *Must have at least 5 years of experience and three children.*

"Yep. Looks mighty fine."

The editor nodded and shook his head. *Strangest advert I ever ran.*

"Now, I want to make sure this will not only run in the *Herald*, but also the *Calexico Chronicle* and the *Los Angeles Times*? How about Palm Springs?"

"There's no paper in Palm Springs. Yes, will run in all three, starting next week."

"Then thank you very much, sir. What do I owe you?"

They settled up and Steve left the office with a lighter step.

"Yes, exactly right, Stanley, hold it like that while I nail 'er in." Steve was more impressed with Stanley's work every day, even though he was only eleven years old. He was smart—so were the other children—but he had Steve's energy and desire to build, accomplish, learn, and work hard.

"Steve, is this where you want the door framed?" That was Daniel, the new mechanic.

"Yes, correct. But we ain't hangin' the door yet. We'll put a canvas flap that can be tied up all around if need be. We'll worry about a door when the schoolmarm gets here next month."

Steve had designed a little schoolhouse for the eight children to be enrolled in Desert Center School. The newspaper ad had produced just one applicant. Steve hired him on the spot. Daniel, and his wife Catherine, and three elementary-school-aged children. Daniel was a good mechanic, down on his luck because of the economic troubles, and the family was grateful and happy to move to the desert. They were fitting in quite well in Steve's little community.

The building was simple. A concrete foundation, but not a pad—faster and cheaper for a single-use building. He designed it to hold about twenty children. Steve had no doubt they'd eventually have that many—at least.

They were using leftover lumber from the other buildings, and the walls were thick paperboard. That's what Stanley was helping with—he would hold a flimsy board up against the framing, and Steve would work around the perimeter, nailing it to the framing. Meanwhile, Stanley and Herbert were doing the same on the opposite side, and Daniel was framing out the door and windows.

Steve had poured the concrete himself a couple of days ago, after framing it. He had the boys remove the wood frame while he was on an errand to Indio, then they went to work. The roof —also paperboard, was already in place.

By sundown, they would have a schoolhouse. Not permanent, not fancy—but serviceable.

"Father, father, come quick! Come quick!"

Steve was behind the café, working on building a small shed for storage. He had arrived before sunup.

"What is it, Stanley? Good lord, you'd think something was on fire."

"Goats, father! It's our goats! Come on!" And he took off running again.

Steve shook his head and followed, running as well. What could've happened to the goats? He could not image what would rile the boy up so.

As he came around the front of the café and out onto the road, he saw the townspeople—most of them—gathered around the schoolhouse.

He slowed his run to a quick walk. Nothing was important enough for these people to leave their posts. Guests could show up at any moment!

"What the hell is going on here, people? Why aren't you working—"

He stopped dead in his tracks. The town had about eight goats, four owned by Steve. They allowed them to roam free during the day, but put them in pens at night to protect them from predators—animal and human.

All eight goats were milling about the schoolhouse. They had eaten the paper walls up as high as they could reach.

Every head turned to watch Steve. His temper was well-known. They waited.

Steve walked to the schoolhouse, lifted a hand and felt the scraps of paperboard, dangling like rags. He turned back and place a hand on the nearest goats and patted him. He looked up at the crowd.

"Guess our goats ain't gonna be hungry for some time. Apparently, they got their fill of fine schoolhouse." He laughed.

The relief was palpable. Everyone laughed.

"But now what?!" Herbert cried out. "We have no school!"

"Well, I reckon the goats are telling me I shoulda just built a proper schoolhouse in the first place. No faith, no glory. So that is what we shall do. If we can't finish it by the time Ms Petry-Smith arrives, they'll use one of the cabins, and if we have lodgers, they'll have to double up.

"We begin tomorrow, after I've drawn up some plans. Now, you people with jobs get back to work! Ain't running' a resort here."

The Alligator
~1927–1928~

A year later, Desert Center had continued to grow steadily. More businesses, more residents, and more guests.

Steve began periodically holding meetings with the entire population, excluding anyone under twelve (though they were welcome as long as they behaved). It only totaled nineteen adults right now, but that was just the start. Steve had big plans.

"Ladies and gentlemen of Desert Center, I call this meeting to order. The first order of business is this: we now have a sheriff for our town."

There were some surprised exclamations and clapping.

"Who is it?" Ruby asked.

"You're looking at him." He laughed at their confused looks. "You know I've been talking to the county about it. They said that with Prohibition in place, they could use a sheriff. So they deputized me. Mind yourself!" he said, with a twinkle in his eye.

"Now, to the main business. More and more travelers are coming through here—I envision the day when we have fifty or sixty a day." He saw doubt in some eyes, but he knew they did not have the vision he did. "We're going to need more housing and shops. You may have heard that Coleman wants our market here to be a Coleman retailer. We might even need another fuel station."

"That requires land. Right now, Ragsdale Desert Service & Supply owns about forty acres on each side of the road. That ain't close to what we need. Here is my proposal:

"For each one of you who files for a Desert Entry Lands Deed while employed by me, for land surrounding our town, I will buy it back from you, with a five percent commission for your trouble. You make money, our town grows."

"Are there any taxes or other things for our purchase?" Daniel asked.

Steve nodded. "A smart question. There are not. If you kept the land, then yes, you would owe taxes after the first year. But since I'm going to buy it from you, you will incur nothing more than your initial outlay of money which you will get back within a short time, plus the five percent."

Ruby raised her hand. "Mr. Steve, why can't you just buy it yourself? I'm not saying it's not a fair and reasonable idea. Just curious."

Steve sighed. "There are two reasons. The first is because the State won't allow me to buy that much at one time. The second is, I would rather not do it all at once—I can't afford to pay you all off at the same time. So, we'll set up a schedule, over a couple of years. As we grow, we'll have more money pay anyone who wishes to take advantage of this great deal. You make money, the town grows, we all do well."

He was satisfied to see many nodding their heads in approval. Five percent of a land claim would be a nice return for these people, and the time frame made it possible for Steve to do it.

As long as they kept growing.

Gus was at the meeting, though not a resident. "Pretty clever idea. Just how much land you wantin', Steve? I'm curious."

"Eventually? Five hundred acres."

Steve enjoyed the shocked look on their faces.

"'Nuff sed. I called this meeting adjourned!'"

Not only did Steve's plan work, but the next year saw Desert Center grow, and even allowed expansion beyond his town. He also had enough employees that he could spend more time writing articles and poetry.

He took off his hat and wiped his brow with the back of his hand, turning to look up at the summit of the ridge above. Turning again, he could gaze across the flat land at Desert Center. A broad smile appeared on his face.

He looked west, to his left. About thirty-five miles down Highway 60 to the west was Cactus City: his second outpost. It was just a small stop to the north of the highway, with a single fuel pump and a little shack for sundries and food. It amused him to call it Cactus *City*.

To the east, about another thirty miles, he had plans to build another little town, to mirror Cactus City on the opposite side of Desert Center. He had surveyed it a couple of weeks ago and filed a claim for the land. The day he did so, it was so blazing hot—even for the desert—that he decided to call this outpost "Hell." Lydia and others took him to task for it. She said there was no need for vulgarity. He told her it wasn't vulgarity—it was the truth!

He'd never felt better in his life. But with all the busyness of running his growing kingdom, he was finding the need for a place to retreat. He had been eyeing this ridge south of Desert Center. It was a long ridge, rising about two hundred feet above the desert floor, and about a mile long. It looked like an old alligator laying in the middle of the desert, so he had named it "The Alligator."

Continuing his exploration, just below the highest point, he spotted some Indian hieroglyphics on the rocks. A bit of rummaging around revealed a few Indian artifacts as well. Probably the Cahuilla. But he didn't want his writing spot to be this high up the ridge. The winds could get strong during the season. He made his way back down to a nice flat spot not too far up the slope. He'd pour a concrete foundation, about fifteen or twenty feet square, with simple wooden walls and roof.

He sat on a nearby rock, thinking about his ideas for writing. The first project was a series of pamphlets that he would distribute to travelers, with information about travel, the do's and don't of the desert, advertisements about Desert Center, and perhaps some of his poetry. Next, some articles about the desert or politics for the *Blythe Herald* and the *Calexico Chronicle*. It would be was his chance to write exactly what he thought, no matter what others might think. He would touch on several topics: his criticisms of politicians and government, the increasing rise of vandalism, and the celebration of vices such as drinking and prostitution. Maybe nobody would ever publish it, but he didn't care—he would publish it himself and hand copies out for free if need be.

He had already begun writing the first pamphlet. The informational material was easy, but he wanted to include some poetry. He had an idea to write about the founding of Desert Center, in a series of stanzas, which he would call "Spasm #1," "Spasm #2," and so on.

As he sat on the rock, in the bright sun, near where his writing shack would soon be, he decided to write down the first "Spasm," which he had been composing in his head for weeks now. He pulled out his notebook and pencil and begin scribbling.

SPASM No. 1
Away out on the desert one hot summer day,
Old Desert Rat Steve's car broke down,
Just Fifty miles East, or Fifty miles West
Says Steve, is the closest town.

SPASM No. 2
Steve needed water, gas, oil and food,
A tire and some other small things,
Says he I've a notion to build here a town,
All I lack is some money and brains.

He read over what he wrote. *That's a good start*, he thought. And it gave him another idea. He should start advertising Desert Center in the papers of nearby towns. He knew all the editors, of course: he visited them whenever he was in their towns.

Next time he was in Blythe, he needed to buy a hand press. The world was going to hear about Desert Steve—and especially Desert Center.

The truck bounced along the dirt road, kicking up dust behind him. Steve was coming back from Corn Springs, and it was about noon—hot in this December of 1928.

As he approached Highway 60, he could see in both directions for quite some way. Desert Center lay to the left. To the right was an expanse, not a car in sight. Only the ribbon of the road.

Wait a minute. Steve slowed down and squinted. Something *was* on the side of the road—an automobile.

Rather than turning left towards Desert Center, he turned right. As he pulled up behind the vehicle, a man exited the driver's side.

"Howdy, sir," Steve said as he got out. "Do you need some help?"

The man was large, and wearing a nice suit. He doffed his hat. "Yer a sight for sore eyes! I ain't seen a person come by here for over an hour. Got stuck off the side here. Not quite sure how it happened, it's a pretty straight narrow road."

Steve stuck out his hand. "I'm Steve Ragsdale, known as Desert Steve. I own the town down that way, and I can pull you out. If there's any damage, we got a garage with a fine mechanic."

"Well, you're an angel in disguise then, aren't you? Don't think there's any damage."

Steve went back to his Model T and pulled out the cables. He attached them to the frame at the front of the man's vehicle, and then to the hooks on the back of his.

"Get in and do your best to keep the wheel straight as I pull her out."

Soon the truck was back up on the road. He got out and unhooked the cable from both vehicles and stored them back in the truck.

"I ain't got any money to pay you, sir, but I got something else you might want—especially out here in the desert."

"Naw, don't worry about it. Just bein' a Good Samaritan, like the Good Lord said."

"I insist. I prefer to pay my debts." The man motioned Steve to his boot and opened it, rummaged around in a bag and pulled out an unlabeled bottle. "Some of the best hooch you find anywhere these days."

Steve kept any emotion from his face. A bootlegger, and a reckless one, at that. If he was gonna barter with illegal goods, he should be more careful. But Steve didn't have his badge or his handcuffs with him. He cursed his lack of forethought.

"Mighty friendly of you. I know some people in town that might be interested. And seeing as it's close to suppertime, we got a fantastic café."

"I appreciate that. I'm famished and thirsty sitting out here for a couple hours."

"Finest café in a fifty-mile radius. My wife runs it."

"Mighty fine, mighty fine. I'll just follow you in."

Steve got back in his truck, watching in his rearview mirror as the man followed him. They picked up speed down the road and soon arrived in Desert Center. Steve pulled into a spot before the café. The man pulled in beside him.

"Come on inside, let's see if my wife is working. Either way, we'll get you some food and drink."

Steve set him down at a booth. He walked to the counter and leaned over to Ruby. "Go take an order from him. If he tries to leave, find some way to stop him. Offer free slice of cake or a dip in the pool or something."

Inside his office, he made a quick radio call to the police. He grabbed his badge and stuck his pistol in his waistband, then went back into the café. Walking up to the man's table, he held out his badge. "You are under arrest. Please stand up and turn around."

The man slowly placed the coffee cup down and swore. He started to stand and stopped. "I wasn't selling it. I was giving it away!"

Steve knew that was a lie. "Possession is illegal."

"Confiscate and let me off with a warning?" He leaned In conspiratorially. "There's quite a bit more in my automobile."

Steve moved his duster so the man could see the pistol. "You trying to bribe an officer of the law?"

The man stood and turned around. Steve handcuffed him and led him back into the office. "Sit down in that chair. We got about an hour before the deputy from Indio gets here to take you away. I'll read you some of my poetry to pass the time."

The man's brow furrowed as Steve pulled some papers from his desk.

"I call this one 'Automogitis.' Seems appropriate.

> *In nineteen hundred and thirteen,*
> *My Lizzie friend and me*
> *Traveled over the sun-kissed trail;*
> *O'er'snake tracks toward the sea.*
> *I promised her I'd trade her for a brand-new model 'T,'*
> *If she'd keep put-put-putting, and take me to L.A.*

He looked up at his prisoner, who was staring at the far wall. He muttered something under his breath.

"What was that?" Steve asked.

The man shook his head. Steve continued.

> *Wal, poor old Liz went loco*
> *As she jumps a cactus clump;*
> *She threw me out on a diamond back,*
> *And I kicked her in the Roly-coaster.*
> *Sez I, 'I've kicked a lady for the first time in my life,*
> *But you had it coming to you; you act just like my wife.'*

He went on, reading the entire 54-line poem. He came, finally, to the last stanza:

The greatest curse or grand reward that God or man can give,
Is the prefix "un" or desirable citizen to our names while here we live.
Nuff Sed.

"That's one of my longer poems. Quite proud of that one. Here's another I'm working on right now, about how we founded Desert Center."

This one was even longer, although unfinished. He then regaled the poor bootlegger with another piece he was working on about Highway 60.

When Ruby knocked on the door and let in the Indio deputy, the prisoner jumped out of his seat to greet the officer.

"Never thought I'd be so happy for a deputy to take me away."

Desert Steve laughed.

No Time to Bellyache and Whine About Depressions

~1929~

"What do they mean, 'economic turmoil'?" Herbert asked.

Steve looked up from the newspaper he was reading. The family—except for Thurman—were sitting together after dinner. Thurman was out with Wanda, a girl he had been courting for a few months. Lydia told Steve it was serious.

Lydia and Thelma were knitting, Stanley and Herbert were sitting on the floor playing a game. A news program was playing on the radio, which had come on after a baseball game they had been following.

"That means things ain't so good with buying and selling," Stanley answered Herbert. "Makes things pricier. Sometimes businesses close, and people can't find jobs."

"Is that gonna happen to us?" Herbert looked worried.

Steve laughed. "No. But some of our supplies are already more expensive, and we might need to cut down a bit on a few things. Some of what's going on doesn't affect us, like the stock market. Do you know what that is, Stanley?" Steve liked testing his fourteen-year-old.

"Something to do with people buying parts of a company so that the company can operate, but then they make money back if the company does well."

"Close enough. If it goes well, they make a lot of money. If the stock market goes bad, then some of those people can lose a lot of money. Sometimes it's the company's fault. But sometimes the economy of the state, country, or world goes bad."

He watched as Stanley contemplated his words. He waited. Finally, spoke.

"Seems like money should always buy the same amount of things it always has. Though I reckon that if a lot of people want something, and there's not much of it, maybe makes it more expensive? Or if there's a lot, prices go down."

Steve smiled. "That is certainly part of it. It's a very complex system with many—"

A knock sounded at the door. Steve folded his paper and set it down on the chair behind him. He opened the door to see Marshall South and a small, dirty, wizened-looking man.

"Marshall! What a nice surprise." Marshall and his wife, Tanya, had finally moved out to the desert for good. The economic difficulties were part of the reason. But Marshall had always been fond of writers such as Emerson, Thoreau, and Hesse, and their interest in finding peace and solitude in nature to write. So the Souths bought a place on a peak in Anza-Borrego, and named it Ghost Mountain. He was building a unique adobe home, all by hand, using local resources, naming it "Yaquitepec" after a local Indian tribe. It was primitive—more so than Gruendike's Well. They made as much as they could with their own hands—clay pots, weaving their own clothes, and making rope, shoes, candles, and soap.

"Evening, Steve. I'm sorry to bother you and yours at night, but I want to introduce you to a new acquaintance, Justus Smith."

Mr. Smith took off his hat with a cloud of dust, and nodded his head at Steve. "Pleased to meet you, sir."

Steve nodded. "Pleasure's mine." He looked at Marshall with a cocked eyebrow.

"Justus here, he's a prospector up in the mountains near Ghost Mountain. Been out here for a long time."

Obviously, Steve thought.

"His eyesight isn't good these days, so I was thinking it'd be better for him to be around people instead of alone. Wondering if you've got a place he could stay, and maybe some work he could do?"

Steve's heart went out to the man. A prospector—a desert rat—losing his eyesight. Not only difficult to dig or pan, but to find food.

"I reckon I do. I know prospectors are good with their hands, and so he could work in our garage. And I'm founding another town, a fuel stop, near Skyway. Could use some help clearing the land and construction."

Marshall turned to Justus, and said, "I told you. Steve is the busiest man in this desert, and he always has something going on."

"As for lodging," Steve continued, "I do have a small cabin that almost never gets rented—it's just a one-person hut, really. You can set up there for now, Justus, no charge. When you start working, we'll figure out what a fair rent would be."

Marshall nodded at the short man. "This is a good deal, Justus. Time for a change."

Justus looked down at the ground. "Don't much care for change. I like my little cabin."

"I understand." Steve said. "I've left places I enjoyed. But you know what I've found? Change keeps coming along, whether we want it or not, like a boxer who won't let up. Might be the weather, might be the job market, might be losing our eyesight or just getting older. Can't stop it. So we gotta figure out how to bend that change to our own good.

Justus nodded. "Them's some wise words, Desert Steve."

"Let's walk on over, and I'll show you the cabin. You got belongings with you?"

"Jest a few things. Blanket, my tools, few other things."

"Alright." He turned to Lydia. "Could you round up some extra sheets and a blanket? Stanley, would you go get a bucket of hot water and bring it over to the cabin?" He turned back to the two men. "Follow me."

The men stepped away as Steve came out of his house, and he led them towards the collection of cabins that Steve had built for guests. Justus trailed behind the other two.

Marshall placed his hand on Steve's shoulder and leaned in. "Really do appreciate this, Steve. Justus is a good man, but he shouldn't be living alone, isolated. And I think his eyesight is worse than he lets on."

"No need to thank me, Marshall. Desert rats look out for each other."

"It's gettin' bad, my friends."

Steve, Thurman, Stanley, Gus, and Marshall, were sitting at a table in the café, eating lunch. Randall had joined them, on a research trip, having flown into the little runway Steve had graded and marked.

"Well, I can't see how some big-city stock market problem's gonna affect us," Gus said.

"Not as much as those who invest or depend on it. But everything's gonna get more scarce and expensive," Steve replied.

"They are saying it's America's fault," Marshall said. "That crash in March was because investors got spooked, and they pulled back, or sold off, and that has a cascading effect. Fortunately, they were able to stabilize it, and—"

"Who's 'they'?" Thurman asked.

"Some economic professors. Don't think it was the President who said it."

"Hoover. What a moron." Steve said. "Thinks way too much about his own power. Usually better to leave well enough alone."

Randall shook his head. "Perhaps, but if they had done nothing, it could have gotten worse. Maybe a bigger crash. Maybe a depression, as they are calling it. Then it would be rough on everyone." He looked at Steve. "How many towns you got now?"

"DC, Cactus City, Hell, Skyway are running now. Got an idea to buy some land around Shaver's Well. I'm not worried about those. They are small potatoes compared to DC. I could shut them down in a minute if need be."

"I did hear that a couple of Senators are working on a tariff act to protect us from any future issues," Marshall said.

"Bah," Steve replied. "When did the government ever do anything that didn't have unintended consequences?"

Thurman spoke again. "The roads? That's helped us a *lot*."

Steve gave him a frown. "Ok. Roads. Railroads. War. The big stuff that must be done. But they should stay out of meddling in our money and wages and trade."

Gus took this opportunity to stand up from the table. "Enough o' this talk for me, men. I'm a poor prospector, and I don't need to worry myself about such stuff. I'm gonna head back."

Marshall stood as well. "And I. Building a fancy fireplace for Tanya. Need to get back on it."

The rest continued their discussions, turning to other issues closer to home. About ten minutes later, Daniel stepped into the café, looked around, and then came over to Steve.

"Justus didn't show today. I checked his cabin. No answer."

"Did you go in?"

Justus was pretty old, after all.

"Yeah. Not there. Asked around, too. No one has seen him."

"I have an idea. You get back to work.

Steve drove east, parked his Model T, and began trudging up the trail to Chuckwalla Springs. He was only about halfway up when he saw Justus trudging slowly up the trail ahead. He caught up with him.

"Justus?"

"Oh! Desert Steve?"

"Yes, it's me. What are you doing? You didn't go to work."

Justus hung his head. "It ain't that I'm not grateful, sir. And I'm a hard worker. I just ain't cut out for regular life. People and buildings and work schedules. Guess I been prospecting too long. I just wanna pan for gold. It's all I know. Makes me happy."

Steve looked upon the old man with compassion. And he certainly understood feeling like a place is not for you. Isn't that why he left the pulpit? He'd found what he loved doing and where to do it. Shouldn't an old desert rat like Justus be allowed to do what he wants?

"I understand, my friend." He thought for a moment. There had to be a solution.

He clapped his hands together. "Tell you what. Come on back with me tonight. Tomorrow, you and I will pack up your belonging, along with some vittles, and tomorrow, you and I will come up here. We'll repair and renovate your cabin. You can continue to pan for gold and live in Chuckwalla Springs. I'll bring you groceries—or someone will—every couple of weeks."

Justus eyes lit up. "You'd do that for ol' Justus?"

"We desert rats gotta stick together."

"Thank you mightily, Desert Steve. You are an angel." The man seemed overcome by Steve's gesture.

"Not sure everyone would agree with that assessment," Steve laughed. "Come on, let's head down."

A few months later, a group sat in the diner, listening to the radio. All the employees who were not working at the moment, and some of their families. The tinny voice came out of the radio was reporting from New York.

Widespread reports of men jumping out of windows from high stories in New York. Some have lost millions. Some have lost everything they have.

Despite the measures the government took after the crash on March 25, which helped for a short time, a sell-off began in September. On Oct 24th, the market crashed 11%. Further government actions did not help, and it crashed again—12%. Another 11% drop followed, and caused a panic. Though it recovered 12% the next day, the damage was done.

Reports say that thousands of investors lost everything, some stocks just cannot be sold for even a penny.

It is estimated that over a billion dollars have been lost
The President this morning—

"A *billion?!* What is a billion?" Gus exclaimed.

"A thousand million. A one with nine zeros," Stanley said. Gus looked like he was trying to understand and failing.

Lydia looked at Steve. "Why are you looking so smug?"

Steve shook his head. "Not smug. A lot of suffering, and more to come. It's just that I knew something like this was coming. Government should not mess with the economy. Dumbest people running the country, 'cause they don't know how to run a business. All they know is power, money, and elections."

Bea had been standing in the doorway of the kitchen for a while, listening. "What's gonna happen to us, Mr. Steve?"

"Well," Steve said, sitting back in his chair, "it ain't gonna be as bad as for rich investors and people who live in big cities. But I read this morning that prices will keep going up, and many jobs will be lost. Then goods will become scarce. Our costs will go up. Might not be able to afford things, might have to let people go."

"Surely the government will do something to help out?" Ruby said.

"Are you not listening?" Steve said. "The government *caused* this problem—or, at *best*, made it worse."

Lydia frowned at Steve.

He nodded and grimaced. "Yes, Ruby, I am sure they will try. Doubt they'll do anything that will actually work. Or if it does, cause problems down the road."

The radio was still going.

—and some economists are forecasting that these is-
sues could last years. For more, we turn to—"

Steve leaned over and snapped off the radio. "Enough. More information will come out over the next weeks. My big concern for us is two things. Fuel prices and whether people will keep traveling as much as now. They certainly won't in the same numbers. We gotta start cutting back."

His employees looked worried.

"What about Skyway and Shaver's Well stations?" Stanley asked. "We stop working on those?"

"I'm gonna hold off buying the land around Shaver's Well. Let's keep going with Skyway, see what happens." He looked around at each of them. "Everybody get back to work. Crash or no crash, we still got things to do. Something will turn up."

No Drunks, No Dogs...
We Prefer Dogs
~1931–1932~

Steve walked into the kitchen where Lydia was sitting at the table with the financial books, bills, and receipts, in front of her. She took care of all the bookkeeping for the café, as well as serving, cooking, and anything else that needed done. Now that she had help, she could take time to lead groups of women rockhounding.

"Lydia, I'm going up to take some groceries to Justus."

She sighed and looked up at him. "We didn't talk about Thurman and Herbert."

Steve shrugged. "Not much to say."

"But they are *leaving*."

"Yup, they are. I had hoped they'd both want to continue my work here. Want there always to be a Ragsdale running Desert Center." He sat down across from her. "But they have to find their own way. My father hated the idea of me pursuing the ministry. And it made all of us miserable. I won't do that to my sons. A man's gotta follow his conscience."

"I think it's Wanda's influence."

"Wanda is a good woman for Thurman, Lydia. If they think it best to live in San Bernardino, so be it. It ain't that far. As for Herbert...it was his first chance to get out. I think he's wanted out since he was a child. At least he's going to work with his brother."

Lydia looked up from the books and papers. "I don't like it. I wish you'd make them stay."

Steve stood up and pushed his chair in. "Ain't gonna tell grown men where they can live and what they can do. *You* left *your* family."

"Fine. Go help Justus."

Steve shook his head. He knew that when she got irritated, there was no point in talking any further.

As he made his way out of the café, he heard his name called and saw John Hilton beckoning him from the counter. Steve had met him a few months ago when he moved out to Twenty-Nine Palms. He had been working for a gem company and making jewelry for Hollywood stars, but they closed down due to the depression, and he could not find work.

"Hello, John."

"I've got a question for you. Have you ever considered having someone play music here at the café?"

Steve scratched his beard. "It's never crossed my mind. Why do you ask?"

"I'm trying to find some ways to make money. I'm a pretty decent guitarist and singer, I've been playing here and there to make a little bit."

"Did you open that curio shop in Indio you were talking about?"

"Just getting ready to open. Got a good collection of stones, gems, geodes, some Indian artifacts, and more. Hope that'll bring in some steady money, but these days, who knows."

"Good. Well, I'll give music some thought, but I'm not sure. This is a place where most people stop as they're traveling somewhere else, and they don't stay long. Besides, if people are listening to music, they usually want to drink, and I ain't never allowing alcohol in Desert Center."

"I understand." He took a sip of his coffee.

"You know, with your knowledge of rocks and gems, you should get in touch with the Sierra Club. They're always looking for guides and speakers for some of their treks in the desert."

"That's a good idea. I'll look into that."

Steve took his leave of Hilton and put a sack of groceries from the market in the back seat of his auto, as well as some soap and rags. He took food and supplies up to Justus every couple weeks or so. He drove up as far as he could, then hiked the rest of the way to Chuckawalla Springs.

As Steve drew close to Justus' tiny cabin, he yelled out. Justus appeared, blinking in the sun. "Desert Steve? That you?"

"It's me, Justus. Any luck this week?"

"Naw. Just a few little flakes. I'll strike it big someday. Come on in."

Steve unloaded the groceries onto his little table. He watched as Justin ran his hands over the cans, bags, and containers.

"I was just about to make me some food. Can you tell me which one of these cans is pork and beans?"

Steve knew Justus couldn't see well, but he didn't know how bad. He looked through the cans on the shelf and took down one labeled "Pork and Beans," handing it to the old prospector. "You can't read the labels?"

"Sometimes. Mostly not. It's okay, makes every meal a surprise," he cackled.

"But you can find your way to prospecting?"

"Yep. Long as I leave after the sun is up, and make sure to come back before dusk. Though I've done it so many times, I could probably find my way in the dark. And then little flakes of gold still sparkle in the pan."

"Promise me you'll be careful, and if your eyes get worse you'll tell me."

"Sure, Desert Steve, whatever you say. Do you want some of this?" He opened the can and dumped it into a pot.

"I got to get back to town. I'll see you in a couple of weeks."

Justus reached out and grabbed Steve's arm. "Thank you, Steve. I do appreciate your help. I'm happy here."

"My pleasure. And if you ever need it, you got a place in Desert Center."

Steve walked towards the café. It was a warm evening in October, with the sun setting. He spotted at least five automobiles out front. He could hear the buzz inside before he arrived. A sound that made him happy.

Stepping inside, the place was more full than he had guessed. Some were residents, but the cars must have been full of families or other groups. Lydia gave him a wave from behind the counter, then stuck her head through the kitchen door and yelled, "Need table four order *now!*"

Steve went over and found a seat at the counter as his wife came back. He gave her a smile. "Busy night? Think your boss might let you off early?" He laughed.

"Comical," she replied humorlessly. "It's good, but exhausting."

A commotion caused both of them to turn toward the back corner booth, where two men and a woman were arguing. As Steve watched, he saw that man and the woman were trying to calm the other man down. Loud and rude, he was haranguing the them in a slurred voice. "Hussy" and "bastard" sounded out for all to hear.

Lydia leaned over. "He was drunk when he walked in."

Steve got up and went behind the counter and into the kitchen to the back storage, and pulled out a sturdy stick about the size of a baseball bat. He strode back out into the café and over to the table.

As he arrived, the man stopped yelling at the two and all three looked up at him.

"Sir," Steve said, "You are drunk. You must've missed the sign outside. Please leave."

The man laughed. "What are you, a goody-two-shoes? Prohibition ain't no more."

"First, I'm the owner of this café and this town as well as its sheriff. Second, you're misinformed. The Nineteenth Amendment still stands, the Cullen–Harrison Act merely allowed beer or wine under 3%. But I don't care whether you got drunk on legal or illegal alcohol. You're drunk in my town, and I'm telling you to leave."

"And I'm telling you, I ain't ready to go back to my cabin yet."

"I am not telling you to leave the café. I am telling you to leave Desert Center."

The man laughed. "Don't think so, podner. This here's a public place, and mebee I been drinking, but I ain't causing any—"

The room had become dead quiet as the other diners watched. The other man broke in. "William. Stop. Maybe if we leave now, he'll let us stay the night, and we leave in the morning." He looked at Steve questioningly.

"I ain't going nowhere," the drunk man continued. "Public place, I ain't breakin' no laws, and no desert hick gonna tell me otherwise."

Steve hefted the stick. "You are wrong on all counts. I may be a desert hick, but I am the law here. And we don't tolerate drunks. Out. Now."

Steve grabbed the man's arm and yanked him up out of the booth, bending one arm behind, and propelled him towards the door. He could tell the man was surprised by his wiry strength.

The man turned and tried to throw a punch, but Steve easily ducked out of the way. He whirled and cracked the man on the side with the stick. The man yelped and tried to swing again. Once again, Steve avoided the blow and delivered one of his own to the man's head, causing him to reel backwards.

Steve said loudly but calmly, "Someone open the door."

Lydia ran over from behind the counter and held the door open. She gave the man a shove as Steve forced him out. "Don't come causing trouble in my café—ever!" She yelled.

Steve turned the man around and pushed away from the door, raining down blows. The man, fending off the blows with up-raised arms, fell down in the dirt. Steve stood over him.

"Now. *William*. Because your friend—who has bad taste in friends—offered a compromise, I ain't gonna run you out of town. Go back to your cabin and sleep it off. Leave before sunrise tomorrow, and we'll have no more trouble. But if I see you again in this town anywhere after sunrise, you'll be arrested. Or maybe you'll just feel buckshot next time and not a stick."

The man grunted and rolled up on all fours. "You a crazy man!"

"Many say so. But it's my town. Now git."

There was no answer, but he lurched unsteadily to his feet and stumbled towards the cabin, muttering to himself. Steve followed at a distance until he saw him enter the cabin he was renting. Back at the café, he confronted William's acquaintances.

"Your friend is no longer welcome in my town. You two did nothing wrong, and tried to get him to be reasonable. I have no problem with you. But I better not see him outside that cabin, and he better be gone by sunrise."

"Yes…sir. I'm sorry for the kerfuffle. We'll do as you say."

"See that you do."

Steve went back into the kitchen and put away his stick. As he walked back out—noting that everyone was now chattering away—Gus burst in the front door. He was breathing heavily and covered in dirt and soot. Part of his duster was burned along the bottom.

"Gus?! What in tarnation…"

"My—my cabin exploded."

"Gus! I *told* you not to keep your dynamite inside. Keep it at the mine! Or at least away from your cabin."

"I know. But there's been stealing going on—we got an idea who, but—"

"What happened?"

"Well, near as I can tell, a spark from either my lantern or fireplace must've hopped over to the box where I keep the sticks. Fuse got lit, and they all went up. I woke up to smoke and a sizzling sound. Sussed it out pretty quick and grabbed my cloak and ran before the whole thing went up—blooey!"

Steve shook his head. "And they call me crazy. Your burros?"

"Spooked, but fine. Checked on them first thing."

"Alright. Well, look, all the cabins are full, so you can bunk down in our summer porch for the night. Tomorrow we'll go up and see the damage. We can rebuild with a *concrete* floor this time, Gus. Not wood." He leaned in. "And no dynamite inside."

And Layed Me Down
~1932~

Steve lumbered up the trail towards Corn Springs. The last few years had been rough, but not as bad as other towns. He'd been able to keep his satellite outposts up and running, although Shaver's Well and Skyway had not become profitable enough to be worth it, and considered cutting his losses in both places.

The newspaper pictures and radio descriptions of the suffering in the big cities was sobering. No work, long lines to get government bread and cheese—no one had seen anything like it here in America. Steve felt vindicated, though it was no comfort to be right. Even the Smoot-Hawley Tariff Act, which was supposed to help, made things worse.

"World's gettin' too big and complex. Little guys always suffer," he said to an Indian petroglyph as he passed by. He nodded to himself. "Desert is the place to be."

His expenses had risen, and the scarcity of supplies was affecting him like everyone else. The depression also meant fewer travelers through the town. More troubling were the number of employees he had to let go, plus others that just moved away seeking employment elsewhere. Many who stayed were willing to work for room and board, which Steve was happy to provide.

It wouldn't last forever. Some said things would begin to turn positive within the next year.

At the moment, though, his concern was Gus. He hadn't been in town for five or six days, and that was unusual. They had rebuilt his cabin, and he promised not to store explosives inside, so surely he hadn't blown himself up.

He knocked on the door. "Gus?"

"Yes," a weary voice said, not sounding much like Gus. "Come on in."

Steve stepped inside to a bit of a mess. He wrinkled his nose. The odor of vomit. Food and cans on the table, leftover dishes and food on the table. His eyes adjusted, and he saw Gus lying on the bunk, looking pallid and feverish.

"Hey, Steve. Got bit by a big ol' black widow a few days ago. Cleaned out the bite with alcohol and a firestick. Thought it helped, but took a turn for the worse yesterday." He paused, seemingly confused. "Or maybe the day before…"

"Gus, you should've come into town soon as you got bit. They can be deadly. Lemme see."

Gus moved wearily and pulled up a sleeve. Steve noticed his breathing was labored, and he was sweating.

There was a large red area on his upper arm. The flesh was bubbled up in the middle, like a boil, but it was dead-looking: gray, black, and yellow.

"What symptoms do you have?"

"Fever, headache. Vomiting. Muscles hurt. And I am *so* tired."

"We need to get you help. When's the last time you cleaned it?"

"I…I don't remember."

"I'm gonna clean it. It's gonna hurt like hell."

Gus nodded. As Steve cleaned, Gus moaned and rocked, but did not say anything.

Steve raised up. "Can you get on a burro? Gotta get you the closest doctor."

"I can try."

But the poor prospector was so weak, he could hardly stand. Steve doubted he could even sit on a burro, let alone make a trip to Indio or Blythe.

"All right, new plan. I'm gonna go draw some water and leave a couple of buckets here beside you. Try to clean that thing every couple hours. Drink lots of water. I'm going to come back in the morning with Ruby, who has some first aid training. If you don't start to improve, we'll find a way to get you to a doctor."

He cursed himself for not having a doctor in Desert Center, which he had been wanting for several years.

Gus nodded. Steve went and got the water and set it beside him, along with some clean rags. He tidied up the cabin a bit, then headed back down. Gus was already asleep when he left.

The next morning, Steve drove his automobile up as close to Corn Springs as it could get. Ruby came with him. Gus could lay in the back seat on the way to a doctor, with Ruby to care for him.

Steve knocked and went in without waiting for a response. Gus was asleep in the bunk.

Steve moved close and started to put his hand on his friend when he stopped. Gray pallor. Mouth hanging open.

"Oh, no."

Ruby went over to Gus and took his wrist, and then placed her hand on his chest. She laid her ear over his mouth for a few moments.

She sat up and shook her head. "I'm sorry, sir."

Steve set his mouth. "Stupid stubborn prospector. Damn him!" He turned and stepped outside.

After a while, he came back in. Ruby had cleaned and arranged the body and was wrapping him up.

"Thank you." He started to tear up, but choked it back. "Let's secure the cabin, and I'll come back up later with tools to bury him."

Steve returned the next morning and hauled Gus's body up to Aztec Well. Gus and Tommy had been friends for decades. It seemed proper to bury Gus next to his friend.

The other residents of Corn Springs, few as they were, came out and helped him bury their "mayor." Steve recalled almost ten years ago when he and Gus had buried Tommy.

Harry Oliver was also present, a recent resident of the area who had homesteaded over near Borrega Springs. He was an artist and an art director of Hollywood films. He also wrote humorous articles and had been published. Also in attendance were John de la Garza, and Susie and Lulu, two of the longtime female residents of Corn Springs, both photographers.

When they finished digging the grave, a few of them helped Steve lower the body into the pit. Steve touched his friend's forehead in farewell, then climbed out, and they made quick work of filling it. He then directed everyone to gather rocks to make a mound, just like Tommy's. Twin graves for two desert rats.

They all stood silently for a few minutes, then, then one of the women, Susie, asked Steve to speak a prayer.

"Our Father in Heaven, thank you for Gus. He worked hard, helped everyone, and cared for your creatures. Bless him in his eternal rest. I hope you'll allow him to have a street of gold in front of his heavenly mansion. In the Name of the Father, the Son, and the Holy Ghost, Amen."

Steve then affixed a plaque at the foot of Gus's grave, nearly identical to Tommy's. He stood back and read aloud.

Augustus "Gus" Lederer
Birth: November 10, 1868
Death: December 16, 1932
Prospector, Burro Fancier, Flapjack Maker, Vegetable
Gardener
"Mayor of Corn Springs"

After a few moments of silence, the group began to disperse. They promised Steve they would divide up Gus's eighteen burros among themselves, and bring any unclaimed creatures to Desert Center.

Harry Oliver approached. "I'm sorry for the loss of your friend. I only met him once, but he seemed like a good man."

"One of the best," Steve said, not taking his eyes off the mound of stones. Sensing that Steve did not want to talk, Harry took his leave.

Steve sat on a nearby rock beside the twin grave. When the sun began casting shadows across them, he bid farewell to his friend and headed back to the valley.

Steve sat at a booth in the far corner of the café. Everyone, including Lydia, was allowing him space. Eyes occasionally darted quick looks at him. "Let him be," Lydia said to anyone who asked.

Death comes to all. But this one brought more grief to Steve than he expected. Was it because Gus was his earliest and dearest friend in the desert? Was it because Gus was always willing to help anyone, even his burros? Or because he was such an encouraging friend to Steve?

It was all of that and more, of course. Steve was angry that a mere spider bite did him in. All those years living and prospecting and working in the desert, and a tiny spider ended him. If Gus had gotten help earlier, he probably wouldn't be dead. If Steve had found a way to drag him down the mountain and gotten him to Indio or Blythe, he might not be dead. Steve's logic told him that the trip alone might've killed him. But it didn't make him feel any better.

He picked up his third cup of coffee and downed the rest of it in an angry gulp. He knew that it was okay to mourn—proper, even. But then a man had to get up and get back to work.

There was a lot going on. While authorities kept saying the country was coming out of the depression, he could see no sign of it. They had started calling it the "Great Depression"—the worst in the country's history. So much suffering and death and loss.

Since 1925, his town had grown steadily—rapidly, at times. Now the population was a third of what it had been. He had let go so many good employees. Closed down two of his outposts. Thurman and Herbert had moved to Redlands. Thelma was leaving soon—her husband, Arthur, a military man, had been reassigned to Temescal. Steve didn't suffer the loss emotionally as much as Lydia, but it still had an effect. Now it was just Steve and Stanley, with Lydia running the café. Not that he had any complaints about Stanley: his youngest was diligent, responsible, and smart. But they were only two men instead of four. He needed to find a competent secretary.

And Gus was dead.

He took a deep sigh and looked around the café. There were just few patrons this afternoon. So different from a few years ago, when it would've been full at this time. He glanced over at the counter. Ruby caught his eye and indicated the coffee pot with a questioning look. Steve shook his head.

As critical and demanding as he was, Steve was also an optimist. He believed there were always options, he just needed to use his brain and come up with a solution. But he was at a loss. He had wracked his brain for months with no fruitful ideas. He and Lydia argued a lot. His employees avoided him when they could. He refused to believe that this would end like preaching or the cotton farm. Still, it was difficult not to think that—

The door opened and Daniel walked in from the garage next door, where he had been working on a customer's automobile—the first repair work in two weeks. He came over to Steve's table and slid into the seat across.

"Did you finish the repair?" Steve asked, ready to lay into him if he was just taking a break.

"Yeah. Pretty easy fix. Lot of sand up in the engine compartment. Blew it out, drained the oil and fuel, cleaned all the fittings and gears and then refilled. Purred like a kitten."

"Good." Steve looked down at the paper that was laying beside him and picked it up. "I prefer being alone right now."

"I know. I just heard some news that might affect us."

Steve took a sip of his coffee. "What's that?"

"There's a man named Joe Chiriaco who just bought some of the land along the freeway about twenty-five west of here. Just beyond Cactus City."

"And?"

"Rumors are he gonna open a station, and a store, and perhaps a café."

Steve didn't say anything.

After a while, Daniel started to fidget. "I just thought… maybe you'd want to know…we gonna have competition."

Steve scratched his beard. "It ain't competition. Some green new upstart trying to imitate me. Sincerest form of flattery. We'll see. Do you know anything else about him?"

"He's from Alabama, though been living in Los Angeles the last few years. Apparently he came across that land, and how cheap it was, and with the roads continuing to improve, thought it was a good idea."

"He came to the same conclusion I did—but fifteen years later. Where's the land?"

"Shaver Summit. The high section of Box Canyon Road."

"That's only gravel right now. But I did hear talk they're going to pave it. It runs parallel to the Bradshaw Trail. I was going to buy that land and open an outpost at Shaver's Well."

"You're not worried?"

Yes, Steve was worried. Just another bit of bad news. Maybe this young man knew something he didn't know. Maybe Steve, now fifty years old, had used up all his ideas.

"No," Steve lied. "Everyone knows about Desert Steve and Desert Center. Nobody knows this Joe Chicory, or whatever his name is."

"Chiriaco."

"What kind of name is that?"

"Indian, I think."

"Well, thanks for the bad news, there's been a paucity," he said, with no little bitterness.

Daniel flinched. "Sorry, boss, I just heard it myself and felt like I oughta tell you."

"Government idiocy, the depression, fuel prices going through the roof—"

"Father!" Stanley burst through the café door and came straight to the table.

Steve looked up. "Thought you went to Riverside?"
"Just got back and I have some news! We're saved!"

Saved By Water
(1933–1941)

The Colorado Aqueduct Project

In the 1920s and 1930s, the rapid population growth and agricultural development in Southern California created an urgent need for a water supply, as much of the southern part of the state is desert. In 1928, the Boulder Canyon Project Act authorized the construction of the Hoover Dam and other related infrastructure, including the Colorado River Aqueduct. The Metropolitan Water District of Southern California was established in 1928 to build and operate the aqueduct, to bring water from the Colorado River to the Los Angeles area.

Construction began in 1933, and when completed in 1941, it ran for 242 miles from Lake Havasu on the Colorado River to Lake Matthew's in Riverside County. It consisted of open canals, pipelines, and tunnels, with five pumping stations, and provided water to millions of residents in Southern California, including Los Angeles, Orange, Riverside, San Bernardino, and San Diego counties.

At the height of construction, there were 30,000 men employed. Not only did they construct canals, install equipment, and dig tunnels, but they paved roads, dugs wells, and ran power lines, which benefited the desert communities as well.

Hell Has Frozen Over

~1933–1935~

Steve looked sideways at Daniel, then back at his son. "Go on."

"They're going to build an aqueduct!"

"What?"

"An aqueduct! It's used to supply water long distances."

"I know what an aqueduct is, boy. Why don't you calm down, take a seat, and talk."

Daniel slid over and Stanley sat down. "You know in the last couple years, they formed the Metropolitan Water District? Trying to get better water through the desert. Los Angeles is growing and needs more."

"I know that. So what?"

"Well," Stanley said dramatically, "President Roosevelt has decided that there needs to be an aqueduct across the desert. It will solve the water problems in Los Angeles, and give employment to *thousands* of men as they build it. And it's gonna run through the mountains north of here!"

Steve looked at Daniel then back to his son, then up at the ceiling. Daniel and Stanley could see his mind working.

"Assuming this is true, it—"

"Oh, it's true! I heard it first from some friends, but I went to the government office in Riverside and asked around. The project has already been approved and being surveyed."

"Assuming the government don't screw it up, it'll be bigger than that for us. They'll need infrastructure, which will help us —roads, electricity, and so on. It won't only be the men—many of them will bring families with them. They will need places to live for a few years." He smacked the table. "We need more cabins! Expand our workforce at the café, garage, and the general store. This will be the end of our economic problems, and we'll be ahead of the recovery."

Stanley beamed. Steve reached over and clapped him on the shoulder. "Excellent news!"

He jumped up and hurried into the kitchen, startling Lydia and Ruby at the stoves.

"Lydia, Hell has frozen over! The president has done something smart for once."

Steve and Stanley sat in Steve's office with a rough map of Desert Center and vicinity on the desk between them.

"This red line marks the seven hundred acres that I own. My thinking is that we build new cabins here—" Steve pointed to an empty area. "We can probably house between forty and fifty families there."

"Gonna take a while to build that many houses," Stanley said. "What about bringing in trailers?"

"Good idea. We also need to think about water."

"There's a gully that runs through there from the mountains, but I don't remember water ever being in it. Could there be water below ground?"

"You're too young to remember this, but I dug all over the place before I found water. We just need to pump more from the aquifer."

"Install more pumps?" Stanley thought for a minute. "We're gonna need an average of twenty-five gallons a day per person."

Steve nodded. "The aquifer can handle that with ease if I trust what the the drillers said about the aquifer. You learning that stuff in school?"

Stanley made a face. He didn't like high school, and couldn't wait to graduate so he could work full-time in Desert Center, though Steve kept pushing for him to attend college. He changed the subject. "Do you know about this Kaiser company?"

"Contracted by the Metropolitan Water District. Owner Henry Kaiser is a genius. Builds river dams, some of the largest ever. Also has companies that build ships, cars, railroads. He sees a need and figures out how to do it, cheaper than others, and gets the contracts. A pioneer, up there with Henry Ford. Anyway, we need to get to work right away so it's ready when the workers start showing up. Can you get together a list—"

"Excuse me, Steve?" His new secretary, Terry, stuck her head in. He had hired her recently and she was proving to be one of the best hires he'd made.

"James Pomeroy is here for your meeting, sir. From Simpson and Klein."

"Thank you, Terry. Send him in." Steve turned to Stanley. "Some proposal for the town, I don't know what it entails. Why don't you go and find out about trailer costs?"

Stanley left and Terry ushered in the visitor.

"Have a seat, Mr. Pomeroy," Steve said, indicating the seat vacated by Stanley. He sized him up. Large man, friendly face. "How was your trip from Blythe?"

"Quite well, thank you. Much better now with the new road."

Steve nodded. "Don't I know it. Better for business, too."

"Yes, Mr. Ragsdale, and that's why I'm here. I have an excellent business opportunity for you that will cost you almost nothing, but will reap big profits."

Steve laughed. "I'm always up for a good business opportunity. But when something sounds too good to be true, it usually is."

"But sometimes they *do* come along. Especially in the right environment. And that's what we got here." He shifted a bit in the wooden chair, and his large body spilled over the edges and armrests.

"And what is that environment?"

Pomeroy leaned forward. "The aqueduct. There will be thousands and thousands of men moving into the area. I am sure you have already foreseen the traffic your town will see. A great thing for everyone, especially in these days coming out of the Depression."

"No doubt. We've already had an uptick in visitors."

"I have a proposal that will make you even more money. All those men, when they're not working, are gonna want to be relaxing. My company, Simpson and Klein Distributing, is prepared to offer you a distribution contract. No charge to you, we take a percentage of sales—a very fair percentage for you. Your customers will love the fresh, from-the-tap refreshments, and the variety of products we can offer. I'm talking about beer, Mr. Ragsdale. With the Twenty-First Amendment now passed, they're going to be thirsty for it, if you'll pardon the pun."

Steve's face darkened. "You're offering a beer concession for my café?"

Pomeroy failed to pick up the negative tone. "Indeed, we are! Imagine all those thirsty workers, out in the hundred-degree sun. You're gonna sell hundreds of thousands of gallons every year."

Steve sat back in his chair and regarded the salesman. "I'm sure they'll want to drink a lot. And I *would* make a lot of money." He leaned forward, with his arms on the desk. "But alcohol comes with a price beyond the mighty dollar. Drunkenness, fights, prostitution, and even death. Alcohol takes advantage of weak men to make a profit. I won't be part of it."

Pomeroy seemed confused. "I...I don't understand. It's just beer. Everyone sells it and drinks it."

"Not everyone."

"But...do you know how much money you could make? I'll tell you something I probably shouldn't. My bosses deeply desire this concession. To sweeten the deal, they are prepared to offer *you* $5,000 for the right to sell our beers. We take 25% of your sales. You have nothing to lose!"

"Mr. Pomeroy. If I ignore my conscience for the sake of money, I would be a hypocrite and a sinner. There will never be alcohol sold in Desert Center."

He held Pomeroy's eyes for a few moments. "'Nuf sed."

The aqueduct workers and their families descended on the desert like the biblical locusts of Egypt. Steve was thrilled and overworked. It was a booming time for Desert Center. Even Joe Chiriaco's new Sierra Summit outpost was doing well. There was plenty to go around.

Steve hired more workers for the café and the garage, and expanded the market. He had dirt roads plowed to the east of the town, laying out a neighborhood grid and hiring men set up new trailers and houses, north of where he had built his own house.

The chief engineer of the project, Frank E. Weymouth, occasionally came into the café to get away from the bustling tent city to eat and to work at one of the tables. Steve found him to be an interesting man, and he learned a good bit from him about major construction projects.

"Tell you a story, Mr. Ragsdale, that you might truly appreciate, being one of the 'desert rats,' which, as I understand, is a compliment."

"It *is* a compliment. We love the desert and cherish it," Steve replied.

"We were digging one of the portal tunnels through the San Jacinto Mountains near here, and we came across an old Spaniard's grave. It was right in our path. So we had a meeting. What do you think we did?"

Steve shook his head. "I suppose, being a government job, just plow through it. Doubt that's why you're telling me the story, though."

"Astute of you. We approached the executives and told them that this was an important historical find. We suggested we bring in archaeologists and historians and then re-engineer the path to avoid the site."

"I'm impressed. But I suspect the executives were not all that concerned about history and desert archaeology."

"Some were. Some weren't. Their primary concern was delay and overrun costs, of course. But we assured them we'd only lose a small amount of time, and the cost would be minimal. They agreed. We re-engineered the path and moved it one hundred feet, so as not to disturb the grave. After the archaeologists did their work, we put up a historical marker. You should visit it sometime."

"I'll do that. And on behalf of all the desert rats, thank you."

During one of their discussions, Steve asked him about the conditions and difficulties.

"You might think the greatest obstacle out here is temperature," Frank said. Or water and the other infrastructure. Or supplies. But it isn't. It's *temper*."

"Temper?"

"Temper. Of the men working. Jobs like this—far away from larger cities, little or no entertainment, no new people to meet—well, it attract drifters, down-and-outs, outcasts. Men who would not do the job if they had other options. We'll hire a rock miner, he'll work hard for a nine-day shift, take his four-day break, and then disappear. Found a better job, can't take the work, don't like the foreman, whatever. And if they do come back, many come back beat up and ragged from enjoying themselves *too* much on their off days."

"How do you handle such men?"

"How would you?"

Steve scrunched his face up and thought. "I'd have sound, mature foremen, in key positions, paid well. I'd allow no slack—one instance, and they are fired. Or two, rather. I believe in second chances."

"Correct enough, though we have often found it difficult to find a good foreman, even at an excellent salary. Don't get me wrong—" he rushed to say. "Only about twenty-five to thirty percent create problems. And most of those straighten up after the first incident. If it's something particularly destructive, we fire them immediately."

"Do you have many such incidents?"

"Not so far. I was on a dam project up north before this, and we had two murders. Alcohol was involved, as you might imagine."

"Of course. One of the reasons I forbid alcohol here."

Frank raised his eyebrows. "You don't sell alcohol at the café?"

"Nowhere in Desert Center. Never have. Never will."

Frank sat back in his seat. "Now I understand why so many of the single men go to Summit or Blythe on days off."

"Desert Center is good for families. No alcohol, no gambling, no prostitution."

"You a man of God, Mr. Ragsdale?"

"I am. Was actually in the pulpit for a few years as a young man."

"I consider religion a stabilizing force for good," Frank said. "Wish more of the men who worked for me were religious. But they're a rough crowd."

"The two ain't incompatible. People say I am rough."

"Fair point. I understand you founded Desert Center when there were no roads."

"That's right. Nothing for fifty miles in either direction. Honesty, industry, sobriety. That's my belief and I expect all my employees to follow suit."

"Good characteristics for any venture, even building an aqueduct." He pushed his seat back. "And speaking of that, I must get back. I enjoy your company, Mr. Ragsdale."

"Likewise. Come back any time, Mr. Weymouth. We're always open."

Eighth Heaven
~1934~

"Arthur Knightingale?"

Standing in the doorway of the Palm Springs home was an elderly man, with a bit of a stoop to his posture. He was leaning on a cane.

"Yes. Who might I have the pleasure?"

"Steve Ragsdale. Owner of Desert Center."

The man nodded. "I've heard of you. Desert Steve. A fellow pioneer. What do I owe the pleasure, sir?"

"I'd like to buy your property up on Santa Rosa Mountain."

"Indeed?"

"Been up there. Saw the signs. Beautiful place."

"It is. But since you have been there, you know there is no road. Or no road to speak of."

"Yes."

"And you want to buy it anyway?"

"I do."

The man nodded. "Come on in and let's talk."

Ensconced in Knightingale's sitting room, Steve spoke. "How did you come by the land, Mr. Knightingale? I have a strong interest in desert history, and I learned that you used to work for Southern Pacific Railway, and that land originally belonged to the company."

Knightingale nodded. "Yes, interesting story. I was a pioneer in these lands when I was a young man. Did all sorts of things to get by. For a while, I worked for S.P. laying track. Government had granted that land on Santa Rosa to the company to encourage construction of a transcontinental railroad back, oh, thirty or forty years ago. Eventually, they decide to run the line elsewhere. I saw my chance and bought the land cheap from them. Used it to camp, lived up there for a while, and hunted for my food when times were tough."

"Did you ever think of building?"

"I did, but the only access was that small trail with switchbacks and narrow places. No way to get material up to build anything bigger than an outhouse, unless you wanted to make thousands of trips up and back."

"I understand. Building Desert Center, I had to haul materials from Blythe and Indio. Didn't have a big wagon, didn't wanna pay for a transport. And that wasn't up a mountain."

The old man nodded. "You gonna use it for hunting?"

"I'm going to build a cabin retreat for me and my wife. And a place for me to write."

Knightingale shot him a confused look. "With no road?"

Steve smiled. "I have an idea for that."

"I'm curious. Not that it matters. If I sell it to you, none of my business what you do with it."

"I'll pay you the asking price."

Knightingale spluttered his coffee. "You don't want to haggle? I'll have you know that's five times what I paid for it."

"Right there is the reason. You're an honest man. A fellow pioneer. And you're a smart man, snapping it up on the cheap when you saw the chance. And it's still a good price, at that."

"You are an unusual man, Mr. Ragsdale. Tell you what: pay me four times when I paid for it, and it's yours."

Steve stood at the summit, turning around and looking at his new land. Two-hundred and eighty acres. Santa Rosa Peak was second tallest of this mountain range at about eight thousand feet. Mr. Knightgale had the place up for sale for many years, with no buyers. It was remote and not easy to access. Exactly what Steve wanted.

Things were going well for Desert Steve's empire. The Colorado Aqueduct project had brought thousands into the area, and the Ragsdales had prospered. He had been able to hire employees, and more importantly, managers. Stanley was only twenty, but mature and responsible as a second in command. Steve had insisted he go to college, but allowed him to take less than a full load so he could continue working.

Steve walked around the area, appreciating the cool mountain air. Beautiful, majestic Pinyon pine trees, through which he could view of the valley far below and the towns of Palm Springs and Indio. On the south side of the peak, the Anza-Borrego wilderness spread out far below.

He gazed up at a particularly tall tree. "If I build a tower up there, I'll bet I could see Mexico to the south. Maybe even the Pacific Ocean to the west," he said aloud.

He scrambled to the top of a boulder the size of a house, the highest point he could find without climbing a tree. He took a deep breath, turning around and looking at the view from his new purchase.

Steve smiled. Just few short years ago, he was worried that Desert Center might not survive. Today, things were better than even he predicted. He was in seventh heaven.

"That's it!" He exclaimed aloud. "I name this place 'Eighth Heaven'!"

An officer of the US Forestry Service and Civilian Corps appeared in the doorway of the waiting room.

"Mr. Ragsdale? I'm Jamison Crawford. Come on back to my office."

He offered him a seat, and rather than sitting behind his desk, he took a second chair next to the first. Steve made a mental note. The man was down to earth, and didn't put on airs, like most government workers.

"I must ask, Mr. Ragsdale. Are you the 'Desert Steve' Ragsdale of Desert Center?"

Steve nodded with a tight smile. "That's me."

"You've done quite a service for the State when we needed help with roads. Not to mention your town itself. You have a keen eye for future needs."

"Thank you, sir. I like to think so. In fact, that's why I'm here. I think you and I can work together to solve a need we both have. You see, I own almost three hundred acres on top of Santa Rosa Peak."

Crawford cocked his head. "You bought the Knightgale land?"

Steve was impressed. Not only was he down-to-earth, but he knew the goings-on in his jurisdiction. "I did. And as we both know, fires are quite a problem up in that area."

"Indeed they are. About every two to four years. They are difficult to fight."

"And that is what leads me to my proposal. I'd like for you and the Corps to build a dirt road to the peak, just large enough for a vehicle. I'll provide transportation for the men and materials to build it, using my vehicles from Ragsdale Desert Service and Supply. My son Stanley is a hard worker and a good driver. He'll do the hauling."

"Interesting proposal. Why should we do this for you?"

"Having a road up through that area will give you better access to fight the fires, better access to the forests. I get a road to my land where I plan to build a small cabin. You pay for materials and labor; I provide the transport for it all."

Crawford smiled. "I see why you have done so well in Desert Center, Mr. Ragsdale." He sat for a moment, considering something. "A number of us have been urging the Service to build a road up into those mountains for years. For exactly the reasons you state. The hesitation is because of the cost."

"Then we're a match made in heaven."

"Perhaps so," Crawford laughed. "It's good argument for my superiors. Construction costs are only going to keep going up, and the likelihood of anyone else offering to help out is slim to none."

Steve nodded. Crawford tapped his fingers on the armrest of the chair, thinking.

"We have our monthly meeting next week. I will present this idea. They will probably want more specific details, and you and I can talk more after that."

Steve nodded. "I appreciate that, sir. I need to make a trip back here next week, I'll come on Friday and check in with you, if that's suitable."

Steve left the forest services offices in Riverside, chuckling to himself that he'd worked out a deal with the government. Sometimes you gotta dance with the devil.

"No, not there. *Here.*" Steve outlined an area in the dirt, among the sticks in the ground and ribbon connecting them. "It's going to be a large fireplace—about eight feet wide and six feet tall. All stone. So what I wanna do is build a set of tracks from the woodshed to the cabin, with a trap door just big enough for a small tram car to go through. Easy to load big logs right into the fire."

Stanley nodded. "That's clever. What else?"

Steve spun around and pointed at the tallest pine tree right at the peak. "Gonna build a little treehouse up there. Just a platform with half walls and a canvas roof to keep out rain and snow. 'Bout forty up: see those three large branches? Top of the world. Beautiful view, and maybe best place to sleep and write during the hotter days."

Stanley straightened up from where they had been squatting, looking at Steve's scratched drawing in the dirt. "So I'm gonna be driving the truck with materials and men to build the road?"

"Yep. I'll pay you the regular wage."

Stanley nodded. He loved this sort of thing almost as much as his father. "One room cabin? Log walls?"

"Log cabin. Stone fireplace, of course. One large room, one smaller room for bedroom, fireplace at the one end. Stone will be from around here. We'll haul local logs up, from as close as we can."

"What about water?"

Steve shook his head. "Closest source is down at the spring. Been collecting metal milk containers to lug water. Easy to transport with my automobile once the road is finished. Also thinking that when I come up here for a spell, I'll bring a couple of goats. If I take the backseat out I think I can fit two of them in there."

The sight of his father driving with two goats in the backseat amused Stanley. Although he was pretty sure the people who knew Desert Steve wouldn't even bat an eye.

"How much land around here do you own now?"

"Five hundred and sixty acres."

Stanley whistled. "You own land, cities, business, and now a mountain retreat."

Steve smiled. "A desert rat who got lucky." But Steve didn't really believe that. Everything was turning out just how he envisioned. Explore, then find a way to create something meaningful out of what he found.

And he knew he was quite good at it. With more time to write, the world was going to know, too.

Steve stepped backward from the café, looking up at the new sign he had commissioned. He'd had the idea years ago while looking at an old Albers flapjack flour package at Gus's cabin. He loved the silhouette of the old prospector sitting on a stump, holding a frying pan over a fire, a coffee pot nearby, with his burro in the background. Not only did he like the picture, but the sign served as an homage to his old friend. He'd had the painter retouch a few things to get it exactly like Steve wanted it. Below the prospector, in large white letters, it read, "Desert Center Cafe."

It fit perfectly with the desert and the adobe style café and garage. He nodded to himself, smiling. Turning, he gazed in admiration at the post office, general store, gas station, repair garage, and camping store. Route 60 running right through his town. To the right were the small cabins he'd built first. Beyond that, to the north of the highway, was the schoolhouse—a large, proper building, with room for growth. On the north, new housing built for all the aqueduct workers and their families—completely full. Everything he planned and more.

"Steve! Will you come in here and help me deal with our son?!" It was Lydia sticking her head out of the café.

The café was empty at the moment, being mid-morning. They'd have a few travelers throughout the day, and often some of the family members of the aqueduct workers came in for lunch, coffee.

He saw Stanley and Lydia sitting in the booth in the corner, opposite one another. Both looked irritated.

He slid in beside Lydia. "What kinda holy hell you giving your mother now, Stanley?"

Stanley sulked, unbecoming of a young man of twenty years. "I hate college."

Steve laughed. "That's it? Come on, son, you know that good things—worthwhile things—are not always easy or fun. Can't be as hard as when you hauled people and materials up to Eighth Heaven. Or, worse, digging for water when you were eleven."

"It ain't that it's *hard*. Hard work don't bother me none. I just don't see the point. I don't need all that stuff to work in Desert Center. I'm gonna run it some day!"

"Hold your tongue, boy," Lydia said. "Your father ain't even close to expiring, and you know he'll never retire."

"I didn't mean *that*," Stanley replied. "I just mean all I wanna do is work here, and college ain't that."

Lydia looked at Steve with an expression that said, *See? He's your son and this is your fault.*

Steve rested his elbows on the table and steepled his fingers. "Stanley, *all* education is worthwhile. You never know what knowledge might be helpful someday. Even if you never use what you learned in a class, the *discipline* of learning makes your mind sharper. Can't tell you how many times I've used my learning about cotton farming or seminary to build up my empire."

"Our," Lydia said.

Stanley continued to sulk. "I ain't going back this fall. I just turned twenty. You can't make me. I'm an adult."

"You live with us and eat our food!" Lydia said. "You wanna be out on your own? What are you going to do? No school drop-out's going to work for me."

"Now, no call for that, Lydia," Steve remonstrated. He turned to look at Stanley. "However, she has a point. The one prerequisite for you working for me is that you must get a college degree. We agreed upon it."

Stanley glanced up at his father. "I want to renegotiate. Why don't *you* try going to college?"

Steve paused for a moment.

Finally, he learned forward. "Yes. That's it. You're going to go back to college this fall. And your mother and I are going to go with you."

"What?!" Stanley and Lydia said at the same time. "No," Stanley replied. "What would that look like, my *parents* taking me to school?"

"We ain't *taking* you to school. We're going to enroll."

There was a moment of shocked silence.

"Have you finally lost your mind?" Lydia said, as Stanley said, "What?!"

Steve basked in the reaction for a moment.

"I could use some more formal education in some areas, and so could you, Lydia. Can only help us. Not full-time. Just two classes a week."

"Steve, I am *not* going to college at my age! Who will run the café?"

"Poppycock. The café can be run by Ruby and Bea. Terry can help with administrative work. We're at the point where we can afford to take time away. We've gone away for a week to Eighth Heaven, and nothing fell apart. It's perfect timing." He pointed at Stanley. "And if your mother and I are going to college, you have no excuse."

Lydia sat quietly, her jaw working. Stanley stared at the table. They knew better to argue with Steve once he set his mind to something. Lydia pursed her lips. Stanley shrugged.

Steve smiled. "It's settled then. I'll contact the school, get course lists, and we'll all get registered. We'll choose classes at times so we can drive together." He stood to leave and clapped his hands. "This is gonna be fun."

The café was packed with families and children, employees, aqueduct workers, and some relatives and friends from out of town. Steve had brought in extra chairs to line the walls, and placed chairs in between all the tables and booths. Lydia and the others had decorated the inside with twinkling lights, pine boughs (from Eighth Heaven), and mistletoe (gathered nearby), adding to the festive Christmas atmosphere.

Lydia provided punch and coffee for anyone who wanted it, and Bea had baked Christmas cookies. Others brought cookies and candy to share.

The aqueduct had been completed last month, although it would still be many years before water ran. Pumps, gates, and runoff culverts had to be installed and tested. Which meant that most of the families who had lived in the trailers and the cabins were leaving. A few hundred would stay for the final tasks of the aqueduct project in the area.

Losing thousands of area residents weighed on Steve's mind. Traffic through the area had picked up steadily, and Steve did not expect that to change—it had nothing to do with the aqueduct. But it wouldn't make up for the loss. He had been pondering this for a year, and still had no solution.

But it was Christmas Eve, and he was not going to dampen the celebration. Or his role in it, which had become a tradition.

Lydia stood on a chair behind her counter and banged on a pot with a wooden spoon. When it was quiet, she spoke.

"Merry Christmas, everyone! This is the busiest Christmas we have ever had here, over ten years in this café—fifteen years in the desert!"

Cheers and claps broke out, with shouts of "Best town in the desert!" and "Merry Christmas!"

"We'll be sad to see so many of you leave in the coming year. We pray that God goes with you in your next adventure. And may you never forget our little oasis!" That caused raucous cheers to break out again. She waited.

"We're happy to have this Christmas with you. And, of course, Christmas Eve in Desert Center would not be complete without a visit from that jolly old man." She held out her arm to the door of Steve's office. It slowly opened, and Steve burst forth, wearing a red hat with white fur around the rim, red pants, a red shirt, a big belly (extra café towels), and black boots. The long beard was not so much white as it was gray and black, and perhaps not as long as that of Saint Nick.

He hefted a large canvas sack, lumpy with packages, and shouted "Ho, ho, ho! Merry Christmas, everyone!"

There was more cheering and clapping, especially from the children. Everyone who had been here fore more than a year had experienced Santa's visit to Desert Center.

Lydia sat down in the chair behind the counter. Randall Henderson and Edmund Jaegar had joined them tonight, and Lydia had invited them to sit with her behind the counter. Jaegar was the biology teacher at Occidental College in Los Angeles that Steve had met and gotten to know. He lived in a cabin in Palm Springs most of the time, but took frequent desert trips to explore its fauna and flora. Jaegar was a widely published scientist.

Edmund leaned over to Lydia. "Steve's been doing this since you founded the town?"

"He started it the first Christmas we were at Old Man Gruendike's location. It was just our family, and it had been a rough few months, moving from our farm on the border. He said he did it for our children, a gift for dragging them out into the middle of the desert. Honestly, though, I think he does it because he enjoys it."

"Presents for everyone!" Santa said, his jolliest voice. He began working his way through the crowd, handing out small bags of candy and nuts. Once everyone who wanted a treat had gotten one, he made his way to the corner where a large wooden throne sat, made by Steve a few years ago.

He took the seat. "Santa has special presents for all the children. Santa knows all, has determined that they have been good boys and girls this year." He cocked his head at a few murmurs from the parents. "Perhaps there have been a few naughty incidents. But in the spirit of Christmas, those are forgiven," he said with a chuckle. "When I call your name, come on up!"

Terry stood beside him with a clipboard, dressed as Santa's helper. She pulled a wrapped present out of the bag and handed it to Steve. He looked at the name and called out.

"Jane Forsyth!"

A little blonde girl of around six years made her way through the crowd to Santa, and took the present from him. "Thank you, Santa," she said politely (under instructions from her parents).

"Go ahead and open it, dear," Terry said. Steve took her shoulders and turned towards the crowd. She ripped open in the paper enthusiastically, and then jumped up and down at seeing the contents. "The blonde doll I wanted! Look, mom, its eyes move!" She ran back to her parents.

Next was Thomas Pendo, who received a Buck Rogers rocket pistol, which had just come out last year. The gift distribution went on for some time, with Terry moving it along as quickly as she could—there were about thirty-two children.

Jaegar whispered to Lydia, "Does he buy the presents himself?"

Lydia snorted. "Are you kidding? Steve's too cheap for that. Though he does buy all the candy and nuts. No, the parents get the presents and wrap them and then give them to him beforehand."

"It's a lovely tradition. I'm sure these children will remember it for the rest of their lives." He looked around the room at all the people.

Randall said, "Steve can be rough, as we all know, but he has a heart of gold. Lydia, what are you going to do when all these people leave?"

"We've been talking about it for a while. We'll have to let some of our employees go. But we're hoping with the economy booming now, and travel becoming easier, it won't be desperate like before." She looked at her staff, standing behind the counter at the far end. "Don't know how I would choose between the five of them. I just don't…" Tears came to her eyes.

"My apologies," he said. "I shouldn't have brought it up at this festive time."

Lydia wiped her eyes. "No need for apologies. Everyone knows what's going to happen. Steve always comes up with something. No matter how hare-brained."

As if on cue, Santa shouted, "Timothy, come on up! Have I got an answer to your wishes!"

Desert Magazine
~1936~

Steve heard an automobile pull up outside the cabin. He took his dishes from lunch and put them in the metal bin, beside one of the water buckets. He went to the window and peeked out. It was a Model A Coupe, parked next to his old jalopy. He threw open the door.

"Randall, my friend, it is so good to see you. But what in the world possessed you to drive all the way up here?" He noticed a younger man getting out of the passenger side.

Randall grabbed Steve hand and shook it. "It's been too long since I've seen you. We stopped in Desert Center and Stanley told me you were here. So we decided to make the trip." He indicated the young man beside him. "Let me introduce you to one of my partners and a good friend at the *Chronicle*, J. Wilson McKinney."

Steve shook the young man's hand. "Are you even old enough to hold a steady job?" he said.

"It's a pleasure to meet you, Steve. And I am twenty years old," he laughed.

"If'n you're a friend of Randall, then you are most welcome to Eighth Heaven—my humble abode. Or one of them. How long you been working at the paper?"

"Since I was seventeen."

Steve opened the door wider. "Come on in, gentlemen, and have a seat. I don't have much, but there's a little food, some water, and goat milk. And coffee."

The two men came inside, placed their hats on a hat rack, and took seats where Steve indicated by the fireplace. McKinney looked around at the small cabin. The massive fireplace with smoldering logs, a small table that would seat perhaps four, and a table against a window where food might be prepared, but there was no sink nor stove. Beside the fireplace were three chairs. At the other end of the cabin was a desk filled with papers and books. A doorway led into what looked like a small bedroom.

"Some coffee would be nice," Randall said.

"Same for me," McKinney said.

"I should warn you about Steve's coffee," Randall said. "It's *quite* strong."

"True," Steve said as he grabbed three cups and filled them from the pot hanging over the fireplace. "It'll keep you up for three days and destroy any illness you might have."

He handed the cups to the two men and sat down next to them. McKinney took a tentative sip. "I'm amazed at how much cooler it is up here than on the desert floor."

"Can be fifty degrees difference or more," Steve said. "You can be in shorts and no shirt, and a few miles uphill you're suddenly wanting a parka and snowshoes." He turned to Randall. "It has been a while. Tell me how things have been going."

Randall talked about the *Calexico Chronicle*, his book on the desert rats, and living in Calexico. McKinney occasionally interjected with a remark about the paper or life in the border town.

"But we didn't just come to see you because it had been a long time, although that was a big part of it," Randall said. "I want your thoughts on an idea that McKinney and I have. We have been taking a lot of trips, exploring the desert and its communities. We just saw my brother in Indio, and we're headed over the mountain to Anza-Borrega, and then down to San Diego, where we have a meeting. Hoping we could trouble you for a floor to sleep on."

"Of course. You're always welcome here, even if I'm not present. It's pretty nice here in June, you can slap down your sleeping blankets here, or outside, but you can also sleep up in the tree platform I built."

"I saw that. Must be quite a view from up there."

"Top of the world." Steve leaned forward. "How's your brother doing?" Steve had met him once, a few years ago. He was a famous real estate developer in the area.

"Doing quite well. He's got some ideas for a new town between Palm Springs and Indio."

"Sounds interesting. Now, tell me about this idea you got."

"We're thinking about selling the *Calexico Chronicle*. If we can get enough capital, we want to start a magazine exclusively about the desert."

Steve raised his eyebrows. "Indeed? Bold and risky. And needed, in my opinion."

"We think so. We would like to have articles about all things desert-related. People, places, things. History, trails, rock hunts, wildlife, the dangers, and the joys. We want to capture the vision and beauty of our desert."

Steve sat back in his chair. "We've had a few little rags here and there, as I am sure you know. None of them lived up to anything. I know you'd do it right."

"We've been discussing and throwing around ideas this entire trip," McKinney said. "The more we talk, the more enthusiastic we are. But we're aware of the difficult issues: selling advertising, should we have a poetry page, can we do—"

"Yes, do a poetry page," Steve interrupted. "I write poetry, as Randall knows. May not be the best, but I know plenty of the desert rats who are also fine poets. And you know I'll advertise Desert Center."

"Was hoping so," Randall said. "When we get back, we'll explore selling the present newspaper and see how much we can get. From there, if it's viable, we'll start mapping it out. I want to publish the first issue next year."

"Be happy to help, if there's anything I can do."

"Thank you, Steve. Hope you'll write some articles as well."

Steve smiled. "Love to. In fact, I got an idea for an article about the desert tortoises. Think I've mentioned it to you before. People mistreat them often, and now I don't see as many around." He stood and took their empty cups. "Another cup? If not, I usually take a walk after lunch. Join me if you like, I'll show you around."

The two visitors were delighted at the offer. Steve filled and lit his pipe before leading them out. "The road you came up on is called the Santa Rosa Mountain Truck Trail. Bit of a mouthful, but that's the government for you. I helped them build the road for fire safety. Let's head on down this trail over here."

They walked a few hundred feet into the quiet forest. Reddish dirt and old pine needles covered the path. They stopped at a fork in the trail. Steve pointed down the right-hand branch. "Down that way is an old abandoned mine, called the Garnet Queen Mine. Someone dug it back in 1905, don't know when they abandoned it."

"Have you explored it?" Ask McKinney.

"Just the first few hundred feet. Didn't find so much as a single flake. Explains why it's abandoned."

They took the left-hand trail, walked a bit further, and then Steve indicated a rough wooden bench he had he cut from an old dead log. "Often sit here and contemplate things I want to write about." He pointed out beyond the trees. "You can see Indio and the east end of Palm Springs."

The men looked where he was pointing. McKinney whistled. "What a view."

"Tell us more about this tortoise issue you were talking about," Randall asked.

"It's been bothering me for some time. Been thinking of writing it up as a pamphlet to hand out to travelers at the café. But being published in a magazine would be better. The desert land tortoises—terrapin—are the most magnificent creatures! Truly God's most wise creatures."

"A turtle?" McKinney said.

"No doubt, my young friend. These wonderful, kind creatures, always in their homes, protected from most things, are not protected from evil men. Can't tell you how many times I've found them along the road, dead with bullet holes, or crushed because people try to drive over them—for sport!"

"That's terrible!"

"Not too long back I had a man come to me. Wanted to do turtle races in Desert Center. Said if I'd gather up the stock, he'd split the profits with me, and we'd make a lot of money. I got right up in his face and said, 'No, dammit, no!' Wanted to give him a good swift kick in the pants, too. Said, 'If I was down on my luck starving, I'd sooner rob a bank then take advantage of these poor creatures!'"

Henderson glanced over at McKinney and nodded. "Exactly the type of article we'd like to have."

Steve smiled again, nodding, and took a long draw from his pipe. "If you do publish it, tell ya what. I'll also put a notice in there that if anyone gives me sure proof of someone abusing one of them within 100 miles of Desert Center, I'll give them $100."

"You would?" McKinney said.

"Sure as I'm sitting here. We got to protect the desert." He stood up and fiddled with his pipe. "Lemme show you the tower. You might wanna sleep up there tonight. Gets pretty warm inside this time of year.

The three men stood looking up at the massive tree and the treehouse nestled in its thick branches. McKinney, shading his eyes, asked how high it was.

"'Bout forty feet, I reckon."

Randall was over by the stairs. "Interesting that you built sloped stairs rather than a ladder. Must've been quite a job."

"'Twas, but necessary because it's easier to carry stuff up. I often write there when it's not too cold, and as I said, sleep up there when it's hot."

Randall bent down to look at the first step. "What are these carvings?"

"The Ten Commandments. One on each of the first 10 steps. That and the Sermon on the Mount are the best guides for life I know of. Let's go up."

Once at the top, the three men stood silently, taking in the panorama. The platform was about eight feet square, with short wooden walls about three feet high all around, with a canvas roof.

Steve pointed. "The farthest area you can see there is old Mexico. Over there is the Panamint mountain range near Death Valley. Finally, in that direction, when it's clear, you can see many of the southern California cities on the coast."

"This is quite something. You are a blessed man, Steve," Randall said.

Steve nodded. "That I am, my friend."

"So what's your next big project?"

Steve tapped his pipe against the outside of the wall to clear it. "Nothing major at the moment. Biggest concern right now is promoting the town. Now that all the aqueduct people are leaving, or most of them, we've had a huge decline in revenues."

"How are your outposts doing?"

"About the same as Usual. Which helps. Now that they're paving the road between Blythe and Indio, I think there'll be more travelers."

"We travelled a good bit of that paved section on the way to Desert Center," Randall said. "People who wouldn't venture out on a dirt road, even if graded and packed, can traverse that easily. That should bring you more customers."

"True. But it won't make up for the numbers we had. We need something big."

"Like what?"

Steve smiled. "I have no idea. But faith is believing everything is well if we work like hell. And that's what I'm gonna do."

That Half-Baked Quadruped Called Man

~1937–1939~

"Terry, send Williams in as soon as he shows up."

"Yes, Mr. Ragsdale."

Steve saw lawyers as a necessary evil. He preferred to write contracts himself, or better yet, agree on the details with a gentlemanly handshake. After all, if a man's word isn't enough, what good is paper?

"It's proof of the agreement, in case you have to go to court," the lawyers told him. *Fair enough*, Steve thought, *considering that I have to deal with that half-baked quadruped called man.*

Navigating the rules of business, government regulations, and commerce—most were unnecessary, and as far as he could tell, every one of them had unintended and detrimental consequences. Usually, they benefited the government more than the people they were ostensibly serving.

Today, however, he needed a lawyer's help. More people were traveling through the desert, which helped, but it did not replace the aqueduct workers and their families. The last of them had left in January when water began to flow for the first time. He and Stanley came up with the idea to subdivide some of his seven hundred acres to the north and set up a housing tract. Perhaps some decent housing would lure people to move here, not just cabins and trailers. But these days, a subdivision required for meeting a number of state regulations and filling out forms, applications, and reports.

Steve looked over his notes and the plot plans he and Stanley had sketched out. He was hoping Stanley would be here, but he and Crystal were out of town visiting her parents. They were getting married in six months, and decided it was time he met her parents. Steve didn't disagree, but he missed the help.

These plans could really put Desert Center on the map in a larger way. He envisioned competing with Blythe and even San Bernardino someday, but without the negatives of a big city. For Steve, a big city was where some humans exist in smoke, filth, and mist. The desert was pristine.

A knock sounded as the door opened. "Mr. Williams is here, sir," Terry announced.

Williams stepped in and greeted Steve. The attorney had helped set up Ragsdale Desert Repair and Supply a many years ago, and also assisted in getting the proper permits and other necessary tasks when Steve built the extra housing for the aqueduct workers.

"Good to see you, Steve," Williams said as he sat down. He opened a briefcase and pulled out some papers and a notepad. "I did some research on the necessary permits and applications. I do have some questions in order to finalize them." He settled a pair of spectacles on his nose.

"Good. Want to get on this right away." Once Steve decided on a plan, he was ready to jump in.

"We'll need to write to both Riverside and Sacramento for other paperwork. I need some details: how much of the land, how many houses, characteristics of those houses, plans for infrastructure, and so on."

Steve spun the map around so that Williams could see it. "I want about forty homes, two bedrooms each, kitchen, bathroom, living room. Each on a third of an acre of land. Will pipe water, sewage, electricity. Do that all ourselves."

Williams was writing furiously. Without looking up, he said, "Those will require inspection and approval by power and water people. So will the homes, at some point. Go on."

"Roads, obviously, but again, we'll do that ourselves."

"Paved?"

"Haven't decided. Maybe."

"Okay, we'll hold off on that for now. State will have to authorize that as well. Sale or rent?"

"Both."

Williams sat back. "Alright. Pretty standard. How about resident restrictions?"

"Standard, mostly. Only domiciles, no businesses."

"Age or race restrictions?"

"Don't care about age or race. Good people are good people. Just want to keep out lowlifes and no-goods."

"Well, that isn't one of the possible restrictions you're allowed because it's not legally definable. Deal with it on a case-by-case basis."

"I'm aware of that. And I do. With a stick, if necessary."

Williams looked up at him across his spectacles. "Should be careful about that. Someone might press charges."

"Eh. It's my land, my town, my buildings. Used to, a man could defend his land and the government appreciated it."

Williams was used to Steve's rants, and usually ignored them. "Other restrictions?"

"No alcohol allowed."

"You already said no businesses."

" I mean the residents. Desert Center is alcohol-free. Sometimes guests sneak it into the cabins when they stay here. Hard time stopping that unless I catch them. So there will be no alcohol in the homes, autos, wagons, whatever."

Williams sat back and took off his spectacles. "You can't do that."

"The hell I can't. It's my land."

"It *is* your land. But a homeowner has the freedom to drink what they want, as long as it is not illegal."

"I want to make it illegal *here*."

"Only governments can pass criminal statutes. You can refuse to serve it at your businesses. In a town you own. But you can't tell private citizens they can't have alcohol in their own homes."

"Well, that takes the cake. When I want to build on my own land—which helps mankind—I gotta fill out all sorts of forms and follow all their restrictions. Then, when I wanna have my own restriction on my own land—for the good of mankind—they won't let me. If residents wanna drive to Joe's ridiculous little stop down the road to drink the devil's brew, I ain't stopping them. Just don't bring it to Desert Center."

"The governments—county and state—will never give you the necessary permits if that is one of the restrictions. And if you tried to do it later, the residents could sue, and I guarantee you they would win."

Steve sat chewing on his lip, shaking his head. "Don't know what this country is coming to when a man—"

"Steve." Williams leaned forward. "I understand. Most people would even agree with you about the problems alcohol can cause. But people have freedom in their own homes. Besides," he sat back, "you're arguing out of both sides of your mouth. You criticize the government for taking away your freedom to do as you please on your land, but you are taking away homeowners' freedom to do as they wish in their own homes."

"'Cause I know better. You're a lawyer. Isn't it your job to figure out a way?"

"It's my job to make sure we do everything properly and legally. If there was a way to do it, I'd tell you. There isn't."

"Hmph." Steve sat back, arms folded, staring at the map on his desk.

"Okay," Williams said. "Let's move on. There's just a couple more issues that—"

"No."

"No what?"

Steve stood up. "We're done. Ain't ever having alcohol in Desert Center. If I can't have a subdivision with no alcohol, then I ain't having a subdivision. 'Nuff sed."

Two years later, Steve sat in his little writing shack at The Alligator. He was gazing at a piece of paper, where he had written out an advertisement he planned to run in the newspapers and magazines of the larger surrounding area.

> *(my picture on left). (On right.) "Desert Steve" Ragsdale invites you to visit him at . . .*
> ### Desert Center
> *California*
> *On U.S. Highway 60-70-93*
> *Hotel service, cabins, café, store, garage, free swimming pool and showers, the largest landing field between Los Angeles and Phoenix, lighted all night. Good mechanic, tow car service. Everything for you and your car day and night.*
> ### WE HAVE LOST OUR KEYS—WE CAN'T CLOSE

"The sky is our limit, hell is our depth
We have sunshine the whole year round
If you wish to get fat, or wish to be lean
D.C. is the best place to be found"
   *

50 miles west of Blythe
50 miles east of Indio

A knock came at the open door. "Steve?"

Steve looked up to see Randall Henderson.

"Randall!" He stood up. "Just the man I need to see,"

"Likewise." Randall tossed a copy of Desert Magazine on the table. Steve glanced down. A large desert tortoise graced the cover. It was dated June 1939.

"There it is." Randall said, beaming.

Steve picked up the magazine. "My article?"

"You bet. It's a big hit."

Steve flipped to the table of contents. There it was, about halfway down, and three entries below an article on desert gems by John Hilton.

WILD LIFE. *My Friend, the Tortoise*
  By Desert Steve Ragsdale *21*

He flipped to page 21, where another picture of a turtle graced the top of the page. Superimposed over it, on the left, was a picture of Steve, with his hat, beard, and pipe.

"Thank you. A true joy to see my writing in print." He couldn't wait to get back to town and show everyone. "And there's my reward notice. Mighty fine."

In a small, set-off box, were the words

I will pay One Hundred ($100.00) reward for conclu-
sive proof of deliberate torture, crushing, or killing of
a Desert Tortoise within a radius of 100 miles of

Desert Center, California. If accompanied by indis-
putable proof of the identity of the guilty party, provid-
ed he is of legal age.
(Signed) DESERT STEVE RAGSDALE.

He sat back down with a broad smile and placed the magazine
back on the table.

"Maybe this'll lessen the deaths of the poor creatures by
man. Did you hear that the measure to protect the desert tortoises, sponsored by Assemblyman Paul Ritchie, was enacted
by the legislature? Nine out of ten of the bills offered in either
the state or the national capitals are hogwash, but I'll give due
where due is earned."

Randall looked around the little shack. "I hear you're out
here at your shack a lot. Or up on Santa Rosa. Getting away
from the hustle and bustle?"

"It's a good little retreat. Love Eighth Heaven, of course—
more of a home than this little shack. But this is a quick get-to.
Unless it's too cold or too windy, I live out here sometimes.
Cook out in the open, do my writing and thinking outside."

Randall nodded. "Sounds like a good life."

"I gotta tell you, my friend," he leaned forward. "For the first
time in my life, I'm doing whatever I want. And it pleases me
to think and write in solitude. Away from radio, autos, and
noise. And the gossip and criticism of my good wife, God bless
her."

"How is Lydia?"

Steve shrugged. "Eh. She accompanies me to Eighth Heaven
sometimes, but she always complains about the drive. She's
been quite negative lately. Only thing that seems to make her
happy is our new grandson."

"Stanley and Crystal's?"

"Yup. Three months old."

Randall waved at the papers on the table. "What are you writing?"

"Anything and everything I please. I never considered any of it would be published—and thank you for that again—" he tapped the magazine "—but mostly about politics, the scourge of man, and, of course, the desert. And I'm working on a little book called *The Philosophy and Sayings of Desert Steve*. I want to hand it out to customers."

"When you get it ready, let me know, I can put you in touch with some printers in Blythe." He stood up. "Need to get on my way, going to visit the Souths up on Ghost Mountain."

"Ah, yes. Give Marshall and Tanya my best."

"I've heard there's some friction between them. I think she's fed up with trying to live off the wild. Anyway, do you have the advertisement you want us to run?"

Steve found the paper he had been working on and handed it to him.

Randall reviewed it and said, "Looks good. Next issue?"

"Yes. And beyond. Might change it up a bit each time, if that's possible."

"Not a problem. We can have this typeset easily. We'll use the same pic as the article."

"Same price as before?"

"Of course." Randall retrieved his hat and looked around the tiny shack. "Any plans to expand this place?"

"Nope. It's perfect for me. Got all I need. I can stand outside and look over at my creation." A worried look came over his face. "Which is still dwindling, slowly. Trying to figure something out, but nothing so far."

Randall donned his hat. "You will."

They stepped outside into the bright sun.

"You know, there is one thing I might add here," Steve said. "See that level spot over there, with the flat boulder behind it?"

"Yes."

"I'm gonna dig my grave there, and put a plaque on that rock. I want to be planted in the desert."

Randall laughed. "That sounds perfect, but not sure the county will let you do it."

"Already done. Ben White, the county coroner, has been a friend ever since I got him out of a tough fix with his broken-down car between here and Riverside. Said he'd give permission." He took a puff of his pipe. "Can't believe we're in a day and age where you need the government permission to bury yourself on your own land."

"Well, if anyone should be 'planted' in this desert, it's you."

We Have Rattlesnakes, Cactus, and Some Sandstorms

~1940~

David, Lydia's father, had moved in with them from Coffeyville after his wife passed away. Thelma was also living with them while her husband was on duty, along with their four-year-old son, Stephen. It made for a household that did not have much peace and quiet for Steve, but he felt it was duty to help out family.

However, all three of them had travelled to Coffeyville to see relatives. With a break from family, he invited John Hilton and his son over for lunch. John had told him that his young son, Phillip, was fascinated with rock hounding, and John thought he would enjoy meeting Steve. This afternoon, the three sat at the table, eating a simple lunch that Steve had brought from the café.

"Did you see Marshall South's article in *Desert Magazine*?" John asked.

"Randall told me they contracted him to write twelve articles about their 'experiment' on Ghost Mountain."

"It's interesting, but they've got two children now, and a third on the way. I hear Tanya's not as happy with the primitive living now."

"I heard that. She lived in Oceanside while pregnant until each baby was born."

"The desert is rough enough as it is. Why settle in a place with no water nearby?" He slashed his hand dismissively. "But enough gossip—except about rocks! Did you hear the report that Jackson Hill found Peg Leg's lost mine?" John asked.

"No." Steve replied. "Seems like someone claims they found it every year or so."

"True. He said it was marked on a map he got decades ago in Alaska. Finally made it out here and found it. I don't believe it, of course. No one's found it in 100 years or more."

"It's a great desert legend, but I doubt the mine existed. What else did Jackson say?"

"He said that inside the mine he found a vein of thousands of tons of quick ore, five feet wide and five thousand feet long. If true, that could yield a $1,000 per ton or more."

"I never heard of a vein like that."

"I went to check it out. He said it was in the Chuckawalla Mountains about fifteen miles southwest. I needed to go out there anyway because I was writing an article for *Desert Magazine* that mapped out the rose quartz field in the same area."

"Read that article. Quite interesting."

"Much obliged. I didn't find the mine, of course, though I did discover an old tourmaline mine. Don't know if that's what Jackson found and lied about it, or just didn't know what he had."

"Why don't you just go ask him?"

"I've been looking, but he's nowhere to be found, and nobody's seen him."

"That just gives credence to a hoax."

Young Philip had been listening to the two men, turning his head back-and-forth as each spoke. Steve turned to him.

"You know about the legend of Peg Leg's mine?"

The boy shrugged. "A little. Some man in the 1800s found a massive mine of gold. Sold maps to it but could never find it again."

"Pretty much. People been looking for it ever since. Some think it's real, some think it was a hoax to make money. He was quite a character throughout his life. But enough of legends. What interests you about the desert, Phillip?"

The ten-year-old smiled self-consciously. "I think it's beautiful. People think it's empty, but it's not! There are so many animals, insects, plants, and especially rocks and gems. It's like a treasure hunt!"

Steve laughed. "Appreciate your enthusiasm for the desert, boy. Don't ever lose that. I remember the first time I came out this way. Had a cotton farm south of Blythe, broke down right around here. Back then, the road was only ruts in the desert through the sand. Nearly starved, ate rattlesnakes to stay alive. Decided to build an outpost right there so it didn't happen to anyone else."

Phillip's eyes shone. "You made this town when there were no roads?"

"You betcha. It was rough going, but what an adventure! Everything you see around here was once just sand."

"What about the heat? What did you do for water?"

"There's water five hundred feet below the surface, tough to get to. Had to drill nine holes before finding it. Even with our well, it's quite dry here. In fact, last year we had a funeral for one of our older residents, and we had to prime the mourners so they could cry."

Phillip giggled. "How many people are there in Desert Center?"

"Used to be thousands when they were building the aqueduct. Less than 100 now. Pretty rough, but something good about to happen. I can feel it in my bones, and the terrapins tell me."

"The turtles talk to you?"

"Tortoises. All tortoises are turtles, but not all turtles are tortoises. Tortoises live on land, don't go in water. There's physical differences, too. Our desert tortoises are the smartest creatures around. They know the score."

John Hilton smiled at his son, seeing how he enjoyed listening to Steve's stories—which John knew were often embellished and perhaps fictional on occasion.

"I wrote an article about them for *Desert Magazine*," Steve continued. "Probably have a copy around here somewhere if you want to read it."

"I have all the issues at home, I'll find it for him," John said. "You know, it would be a good adventure sometime if you'd take us out to show us some of your favorite rock-hunting places."

"That be mighty fine. Aqueduct really did rockhounds a favor, there's now dirt roads all around. I know a place where we can find some rose quartz, blue quartz, amethyst, and even some chalcedony."

Phillip squirmed with delight. "I've never found any chalcedony!"

"Well then, young sir, we'll just have to find you some. Unless you want more helpings, I'll clean up, and we'll get on our way."

John started. "I didn't mean now."

"A chance to get out in the desert, do some rock hunting and exploration? Always time for that. Unless you got somewhere to be?"

John laughed and shook his head. "Let's do it."

Philip clapped his hands. "Thank you, Mr. Ragsdale!"

Steve slowed the auto as he turned off Highway 60 onto the old aqueduct road, heading towards Rice Road. John had allowed his son to sit in the front while he squeezed into the rear seat.

"It smells like goats back here," John said.

Steve ignored him. "I'll tell ya, Phillip, when I first got here, there were no roads. Before Henry Ford invented these contraptions, it was horses, mules, and wagons. Not many people took the challenge to drive between Phoenix and Los Angeles. But the Model-T. What an invention! Everyone knows how it changed our lives, but few know how it changed the desert."

"Did *you* ever make the trip with horses and wagons?"

"Indeed I did! Didn't wanna leave my wife and children without the Model-T, just in case there was an emergency on the farm while I was hauling stuff out to build Desert Center."

They bounced along the rough road, an ancillary aqueduct, about ten feet across, to their left. There was no water in it this time of year, and the concrete shone bright in the blazing sun. Steve peered ahead, looking for signs of the quartz field.

"You built that café and garage?"

"First, built a little place at Old Man Gruendike's well. Was a good spot. Rebuilt his cabin, built a lean-to as a garage, built a little shack for Lydia to serve drinks and refreshments. Four years there, steady stream of travelers, enough to get by. Then the government, in all its wisdom, decided to make a proper road, but ten miles to the south!"

"You told me it was three miles south," John said.

"Don't interrupt. Did I tell you one year it was so hot and dry in Desert Center that we had to staple stamps to envelopes? Ah! There it is!"

He slowed the automobile to a crawl and turned away from the aqueduct. After another fifteen or twenty minutes across unmarked sand, he stopped. "This looks promising."

Out of the auto, he led them to a small dry gully, and they began exploring. Phillip found some small pieces of quartz—fairly common. Then Steve cried out, "Here ya go, Phillip!"

Phillip ran over and Steve handed him a stone. "Crack that open with your hammer, and we'll find a nice, large piece of quartz."

Phillip squatted down on the sand and laid the rock upon another, larger rock. He positioned it like his father had taught him, then gave it two large whacks. It fell apart in two pieces, revealing a pale pink glassy surface.

"Yup," Steve said. "Rose quartz. Lots of it here. Pretty picked over, since this is an easy spot to get to."

Phillip examined the crystal, using some spit to clean the surface. "Is there a vein under the ground here?"

"Probably washed down from the hills by runoff over the centuries, even thousands, of years."

Phlllip showed his father the quartz, then offered it back to Steve.

"Naw, that's yours. I got plenty."

After a bit more exploring, they boarded the auto again and headed back toward the ancillary aqueduct. Turning right, he continued along their previous route, away from the highway. Soon they came to a siphon gap and Steve stopped again.

"Everyone out. Need to cross the auto over, and it can be dangerous. I done it many times, I'm good at it. But never take it for granted."

John and Philip stood at the edge of the concrete as Steve, leaning out of the auto with the door open, positioned the front two tires on two of the siphon rods. He slowly inched the auto forward, head out the window to watch the position of the tires. It was about an eight-foot drop to the concrete below. If Steve miscalculated, the auto wouldn't fall to the bottom, of course; the tires would fall into the gap between the thick rods and the auto would be stuck, its undercarriage resting directly on the siphon rods.

The other two watched in awe as he manipulated the wheel, acceleration pedal, and brake, all while leaning out and swiveling his head back and forth watching the tires, front and rear.

Once he had crept the vehicle across, he waved them over, and they crossed, walking on the bars, wide enough for human feet, as long as one watched the footing.

With all aboard, Steve accelerated down a faint trail towards the mountains.

"Have you ever fallen through the siphon gate?" Phillip asked.

"Just once. Didn't have time to walk back to my town before dark."

"What did you do?"

"I slept in the auto, had cactus juice for breakfast, used some rope, a tree, a boulder, and the spare tire to make a small crane. But the auto was too heavy. First thought about walking back and getting another auto or a burro. Finally took everything out of the auto, including the seats, to make it light enough to work. Got it wedged up, held each tire in place with various sized rocks as I worked on each wheel. Finally got it back up on the siphon rods. Took me all day. Pair of tortoises and a desert fox watched me the whole time from the bank. Probably taking bets when I'd fall through. But I made it, so they wandered off, disappointed."

Phillip grinned, looked back at his father, who smiled and shrugged.

About forty-five minutes later, they were in the foothills, with larger boulders and some bushes. He stopped the automobile and led them up between the boulders. "We just crossed the Palen Wilderness, on what's called Palen Lake, but there hadn't been water there in ages. That over there, to the west, is the Coxcomb Mountains and south of that, Eagle Mountain where the Colorado Aqueduct runs." He turned back to the foothills in front of them, and the mountains beyond. "This here's the Granite Mountains. There's a place...haven't been in a while...I think..." He scanned the ground, then looked up at the mountains, checking where they came from. "Yes...just up here..."

Soon they came to a large boulder—the size of a house—cracked right down the middle. "Dig right here," he said, pointing to a place nearby. Phillip jumped forward and began digging on the surface. Steve and John joined him.

"Why is the ground softer here?" Phillip asked.

John responded. "Because some of the runoff from the mountain comes right through here. If you look closely, you can see we are in a little valley."

Steve joined in. "Water ran down here a lot, thousands of years ago. Carve out this little valley. Then the earth changed, and surface water disappeared. Over the years, the wind, and time, and heat filled it in a bit, eroded the sides. Hard to tell it was once a stream."

John straightened up. "You know, Steve, I been working with the Sierra Club for a while. We should lead some treks together. I know the group in the Palm Springs. They would enjoy this sort of thing."

"Let's do it. With my knowledge of the land, and your knowledge of minerals and rocks and geology, it'd be good fun."

"I'll get working on it. Maybe next year. We can—"

"Bonkers! Look at this!" Philip yelled from about fifty feet away. He ran over and displayed four grapefruit sized pieces he had broken open.

Steve took one and looked it over. "More quartz. This one is blue quartz, and this is white quartz—well, might be rose, actually. But these..." He brushed it off and cleaned it with a bit of water from his canteen. "Ah! You hit the jackpot, Phillip!"

He handed it to the boy, who examined the sky-blue gem. "What is it? Is it chalcedony?"

Steve smiled. "Amethyst—pretty rare. Good work. But this one—" he held it up into the sun, "is chalcedony! Just what you wanted!"

Phillip did not stop smiling. The rest of the trip.

The Sierra Club
~1941~

Steve banged a ladle against a pot to get everyone's attention. Sixty-eight people were gathered around a large campfire, finishing up the several pots of stew they had cooked over smaller fires. John Hilton was beside his automobile, hooking up a six-volt Kodachrome projector to the battery so he could display some photographic slides of one of his trips. He had brought along some wood to make a little frame to hang a sheet as a screen.

Steve was surprised at how many people had signed up for the Sierra Club trek. John said there had been a surge of interest in mineral and rock hunting. He also thought people wanted to get away from all the disturbing news coming out of Europe and arguments as to whether the United States should get involved in the war.

The group had all arrived Saturday night at Box Canyon, about ten miles from Mecca. It was late November, but still warm. After some songs and entertainment (John played the guitar and sang), they ate a camp dinner.

"Attention, everyone!"

He waited for them to settle down. "I'm Desert Steve, founder of Desert Center. Come visit us if you haven't been there. Come visit us if you *have* been there!" He waited for the few chuckles to die out. "Thanks for coming to this trek. John here, who you all know, is gonna show us some slide pictures from his Mexican coast trip this year—he describes it as 'the worst trip I have ever taken.' When he's not painting, he's taking trips. You'll be entertained."

"Here's a little background before we head out in the morning. Back in '05, George Wharton James found an old Indian trail that he followed to a group of palms. Not an easy trail. He wrote about the oasis he discovered at the end of that trail in his book, *The Wonders of the Colorado Desert*. When the book came out, no one knew where the place was, and many tried to find it. No one did."

"Until Desert Steve came along!" John shouted, who was now setting up the screen.

"True!" Steve said. "But I warn't looking for it, though I knew of it. 'Bout fifteen years ago, I was prospecting in the hills for water that I might be able to pipe down to Desert Center. Came across an old trail, so I followed it and realized that it was a barren and desolate trail to the top of the ridges—just like James had described. So I kept going. After scrambling over some boulders and following a concealed tunnel through some rocks, I came out into the most beautiful oasis I have ever seen out here. Full of green trees and palms.

"Most of the trail is fairly simple. But the last part is a challenge. This was advertised for experienced hikers. So look out for each other, take care, and we'll see the prize at the end without incident."

He looked over at John and raised his eyebrows. John gave the thumbs up that he was ready.

"I'll let John take over now. Someone keep that fire burning over there—I reckon we'll want some coffee before this is over!"

Early the next morning, they set out, with Steve leading the way. After a while of hiking, he stopped at the top of a rise and looked back down the old trail towards their campsite. The group were strung out down the way, and he could see some of them had still not left the camp.

John came up beside him. "Are they coming along?"

"Some of them are taking their sweet time, examining every bush and shrub, insect and bird, along the way."

"That's the botanists and photographers. They always straggle on treks."

Steve pulled off has knapsack and set it down. He pulled out a thin white cloth and began tearing strips. "We'll tie this along the route, so they know which way to go. But when we get to the tunnel, we'll have to wait for everyone."

Soon they were on their way again. The trail was mostly clear, bur rockslides had fallen over some places, and the trail was quite faded, with so few hikers.

"Look at that deep coating of green lichen on these ironwood trees!" exclaimed one young man, Herbie, who had been keeping close to Steve and John.

"Indeed," John replied. "You'll see a lot more, and more variety, when we get closer to the water."

About an hour later, Steve informed the group that they had reached Grotto Canyon. From here, they would follow the dry water course. Someone pointed out that there had been water in it recently.

"Most of the water comes after January and until about March, but there is a bit of runoff in November or December sometimes," Steve explained.

They stopped for a rest, then continued on, climbing up to a ridge. Soon, they came to be a vertical rock wall—a seeming dead end.

"We'll wait until the rest catch up."

"This looks like a dead end," one of the few women in the group said. She was short, stocky, and knew a lot about rock formations. Steve learned that she taught classes on rudimentary geology in Palm Springs.

Steve smiled. "It does, doesn't it?" She laughed.

Once the rest of the group was accounted for, Steve climbed atop a short rock. "This is the most difficult part of the trip. A narrow passageway. Get out your flashlights. You'll need them. There's some tight spots, and a drop-off we'll have to rappel down, a drop of about ten feet. Follow one at a time. Keep an eye on each other."

He scrambled over a few large boulders, behind which was a narrow crack in the vertical rock wall. It was just enough for them to squeeze through. One man had to back out and try again—he said he had a bit of claustrophobia, but he was determined. A little ways in, it opened up to about five feet wide.

True to Steve's words, it became quite dark. Every once in a while, a dim light would appear from above, filtered down through an opening. One spot required them to squeeze through between the rock walls sideways. Steve worried about some of the larger members, but they all eventually made it to the ledge.

"This is the drop I spoke of. Looks about twelve feet." He leaned over to John. "Don't recall it being that far down last time I was here."

He pulled a rope from his knapsack, affixed it to a vertical column of a rock by looping it around and tying a bowline knot, backed up by a stopper knot, to be safe. He tossed the standing end over the edge.

"John, you want to go down and help them while I stay up here to direct? Or other way 'round?"

"I'll go down. You giving directions up here is probably best since you've done this." John, practiced through his many explorations of the desert, rappelled easily and quickly. Steve reminded those with less experience how to loop the rope and grasp the rope inside it, hand wrapped in a cloth, and how to pay it out using the other hand, and how to use one's feet to slowly and safely make the way down the face of the rock.

It took about forty minutes for all sixty-eight to get down, with relatively few problems. One man slipped and fell about six feet to the ground, but was not injured except for his pride.

Steve gave the word, and they continued down a dim trail, walls of rock and sandstone on either side. About 100 yards along, they turned a corner around a massive boulder to behold the oasis. Steve moved aside and let them pass—he enjoyed watching their expressions as they saw the lush hideaway.

In the middle middle was a large pond, circled by green fronds. Tall palms and about forty Washington Firs—full, vibrant green, growing all around the pond and up the slopes.

Many of the trekkers went straight to the water to refresh themselves. The water was quite cool, and even the surrounding air was cooler than the trail back beyond the tunnel. The humidity was higher here than normal for the desert.

"Look here," John said, tracing a spot along a rock wall. "You can see here that the water comes right up to the fault line here and here."

"I also noticed that there must've been a fire not too long ago. You can still see some burned-out wood."

"Campfire?" Herbie asked.

"Probably not. Not sure anyone else even been here since James, except me. Lightning."

They all found places to sit, either reclining on the ground or atop small boulders. Steve climbed a larger rock that had relatively a flat top. They took sandwiches and other food out of their packs and began to eat, enjoying the coolness and the quiet.

Once everyone was about finished, John asked if there were any questions for Steve or himself.

A man sitting on the ground near the pond spoke up. "Desert Steve, can you tell us some about the prospectors you have known in your time in the desert?"

Steve nodded and stood. This was a topic he loved to talk about.

"When I came here over twenty years ago, there were no settlements, outposts, or roads. But several prospectors were here, long before me, and some still today, though not as many."

"Why is that?" someone shouted.

"Mostly 'cause all the accessible areas have been picked over. There is still a lot of gold and gemstones underground, but difficult for a lone prospector to get to without machinery. Supposedly there's a big iron deposit under the Eagle Mountains, discovered by the aqueduct miners." He looked at John.

John stood. "In the old days, there was plenty for the taking, as Steve says. Some dug mines until the vein played out. Others just panned in the washes—even the dry ones. All sort of gems were found: iron ingots, and varieties of quartz, chalcedony, and gold."

"If you're interested in the history of this desert," Steve added, "make a trip to Corn Springs and talk to the people who live up there in shacks, cabins, and tents. Gus Lederer, God rest his soul, was one of the early settlers in that area. Attracted people who loved the desert. They got a lot of knowledge about the history of the desert that most people don't. John de la Garza lived there most of his life, came on foot from Nevada and never left. He worked the Morning Star Mine. And if you go to Corn Springs, you've gotta meet Susie and Lulu! Came about the same time I did, from the Salton Sea. They once told me that there's a Spanish galleon sunk there—came up from the Gulf of Mexico when the water went all the way south."

John picked up there. "A contemporary of de la Garza, Martin Augustine, is one of the few who struck gold in these parts. Moved somewhere back east with a fortune. Of course, the most famous gold mine is that of Thomas Long Smith."

Some Sierra club members nodded in recognition, others looked confused. "Better known as Peg Leg Smith." This elicited more nods. "We know a good bit about him—except where his mine is located!"

"Was it true that he was a kidnapper?!" This was the geology teacher.

"That and more! A fur trapper, a New Mexico scout, a horse thief. Got shot by an Indian arrow and lost his leg, earning his nickname. Said to have cleaned up his act and became a guide for expeditions out here in the Colorado Desert. Around 1850, he showed up in towns, saying he discovered a considerable vein of gold-bearing quartz. He sold maps to the mine, but no one's ever found it."

"And people are still showing up," Steve interjected, "a hundred years later, saying they found the mine. Nothing has ever come of these findings, most believe they are either lying or mistaken."

"Our next trek should be to find the mine!" shouted a young man in the middle of the group.

"That'd be quite a trek. Rumors of its location are all over, from here into Arizona, south to the border, and as far north as the Mojave."

John spoke up again. "Hank Wilson believes Peg Leg *did* find a mine, though he exaggerated the size. But others think he was just a huckster and a fraud. Steve here, for instance."

Steve laughed. "It's true. Met a lot of hucksters and snake oil salesmen in my life, and these Peg Leg stories have all the earmarks. Harry Oliver, another Desert Rat, has probably done more research on Peg Leg than anyone. If you wanna know anything about the legend, go ask him."

The group sat pondering this famous one legged man and his gold for a time, then John stood up and clapped his hands. "We need to head back to camp, we don't want to be out when the sun sets."

"Make sure and pack everything out!" Steve shouted.

It was a little quicker getting back, except for having to scale the little cliff. As they walked back down the trail, John came alongside.

"You know, those stories of Peg Leg are deeply embedded in the history of our land. I think it exemplifies many things about the Desert: hope, gold, shady dealings...do you think if we all put our heads together with everything we know, we might be able to figure it out?"

"I have my doubts. Oliver has collected so much about the old boy. Randall Henderson has been researching the story for years. He wanted to write a book or a series of articles about him."

"I didn't know he wanted to write a book about him. I'll have to ask him about it the next time I see him."

They walked along in silence for a bit, ruminating about desert legends.

John turned serious. "How are things in Desert Center?"

Steve shook his head. "Not good. We had to lay off almost everyone. Went from a population of hundreds to just nineteen. And that includes me, Lydia, Thelma, and her son."

"I heard Lydia's father died in November."

"Yes, and she's been inconsolable. You know he lived with us after his wife died?"

"I remember. Has Thelma heard from Robert?"

"Not in a few weeks. He's still in Alabama. Thelma is worried that if we enter the war, he'll be called over to Europe."

"Doesn't sound like Congress or the president have the stomach for it. Not after the Great War."

"The War is what caused me to leave my cotton farm and come out here, so guess that worked out well for me in hindsight. Still. Spend. Fight. Kill. A damned hellish mill is war. I'm fine if we just stay out of it."

Fight and Go to War

~1941~

Rosa came into the café all aflutter, on her day off, announcing something about Hawaii being attacked. Lydia sat her down at the counter, trying to calm her. Steve came out of the office and, upon hearing her, turned on the radio.

The café went silent as the somber voice of a reporter crackling through the speaker.

Hello, NBC. Hello, NBC. This is KTU in Honolulu, Hawaii. I am speaking from the roof of the Advertiser Publishing Company Building. We have witnessed this morning in the distant view a brief full battle of Pearl Harbor and the severe bombing of Pearl Harbor by enemy planes, undoubtedly Japanese. The city of Honolulu has also been attacked and considerable damage done. This battle has been going on for nearly three hours. One of the bombs dropped within fifty feet of KTU tower. It is no joke. It is a real war. The public of Honolulu has been advised to keep in their homes and away from the Army and Navy. There has been serious fighting going on in the air and in the sea. The heavy shooting seems to be...a little interruption. We cannot estimate just how much damage has been done, but it has been a very severe attack. The Navy and Army appear now to have the air and the sea under control.

Lydia reached over and took Steve's hand. "What does this mean?"

"It ain't good," Steve said. "We'll go to war for sure now."

"Oh, no. Poor Thelma. Her husband will be sent for sure."

Everyone sat in stunned silence. It was difficult to conceive that the Japanese had attacked the United States, who had been sitting out the war.

Steve stared at his coffee cup. Another world war? As if things weren't bad enough. He'd read about Hitler's actions and speeches, and they were atrocious. A megalomaniac with Russia on his side—for their own purposes, of course. And perhaps Italy.

A war economy was good in many ways, but at what human cost? And things like fuel and everything involved in maintaining, running, and repairing military machinery could become scarce. Until the country ramped up production (which is what helped the economy). But everything Steve needed to run his businesses would become more scarce and expensive until then.

And people would surely travel less.

A month later, Steve's fears were recognized. The US immediately declared war and ramped up its war machine quickly, isolationist politics forgotten in the collect outrage at the attack. Steve was amazed at how quickly a government could move fast and efficiently when it decided to. He remembered hearing Don McNeil, on his NBC radio show, saying, "…sometimes you can strike a giant who is dozing momentarily…when the giant is awakened, look out." His words were prescient.

On this day, Steve entered the café and immediately noticed a group of soldiers—army officers by the look of their uniforms—crowded around a table near the far window. As he headed over to greet them and offer his hospitality, he saw that John Hilton was among them. A map was spread out on the table and John was pointing to a spot.

Steve drew close and John looked up. "Steve, glad you're here. Let me introduce you to these men."

There were five, all looking in their forties or fifties. "Sirs, this is Desert Steve Ragsdale, and he knows as much about this area as anybody. Been here since 1921. He owns this town and a lot of the surrounding land."

Each one introduced themselves by rank and name. Indeed, they were all officers, and rather high up in the chain. Why were they in his café in the desert of California?

"Welcome to Desert Center, and if you need anything, just let me know. Hospitality is our hallmark, especially to our men in uniform." Despite Steve's distrust of the government, he had respect for the men who fought on behalf of the country.

A colonel, by the name of Patterson, spoke up. "We've been looking for a place to build a training airfield. John here has been quite helpful in offering his services."

"John knows the area pretty well himself," Steve said. "He's an excellent guide. But he should have told you that we *do* have an airfield." Steve had built it many years ago, at the suggestion of Randall, who was a pilot.

"He did. We need something quite a bit larger and secure for training."

Steve's mind went into full gear. Were they going to build a base? A few hundred men would go a long way to helping out his town. He glanced over at John and saw he was watching Steve and smiling.

John pointed to a spot on the map, still looking at Steve. "I suggested here."

Steve bent down and looked that John had circled. It was west and north of old Gruendike's well.

"It's a good spot. Near the first spot I founded this town. Secluded enough. There's a well there, so you know there's an aquifer. And not far from the highway or the aqueduct."

The colonel looked at Steve and then at John. "Our commander wants us to locate three or four amenable spots in the Colorado Desert, and then he'll come out and assess and choose. We have three suitable spots including this one. Would you be interested in accompanying us on our reconnaissance mission when he arrives? We'll pay you for your help, of course."

Steve and John exchanged a glance and both answered in the affirmative.

The Colonel nodded. "He'll be happy to have a couple of local guides."

"Desert Center's hospitality is famous in these parts," Steve said, "and you can tell your commander that we will be at his service. I don't know how many men you're talking about, but we do have empty trailers and cabins."

One of the other officers smiled. "Hospitality is appreciated, but we will be building our own barracks. We have a lot of men to train for the deserts of Africa."

Now it made sense. Train in the desert to fight in the desert.

"I see," Steve said. "How many men are we talking about?"

"The General oversees quite a large number of companies of men."

"The General?"

"The Commander of the Second Armored Division. Major General George S. Patton."

Saved by War
(1942–1944)

Desert Training Center

When the U.S. entered World War II after the bombing of Pearl Harbor, the military needed a training ground that could simulate the harsh desert conditions troops would face in North Africa. In 1942, General George S. Patton, known for his skill at armored warfare, was chosen for the task of training a million men to endure the harsh conditions of the Sahara Desert in Northern Africa. He determined that the Colorado Desert was the ideal place, and the area around Desert Center was perfect, as it resembled the North African deserts.

Camp Young, covering 18,000 square miles, became the command hub for the Desert Training Center/California-Arizona Maneuver Area, named after Lieutenant General S.B.M. Young, a notable figure in U.S. military history.

The camp included essential facilities such as barracks, mess halls, administrative buildings, and training areas. The massive infrastructure was built quickly, and was rudimentary, with soldiers living in tents and using makeshift facilities. The training regimen at Camp Young and other associated camps was rigorous, focusing on desert survival, navigation, and combat tactics.

Troops practiced large-scale maneuvers, including tank, infantry, and artillery operations. Soldiers were trained to cope with extreme heat, limited water supply, and difficult terrain, which were critical skills for the North African Campaign, and included live-fire exercises to simulate real combat conditions. Numerous U.S. Army divisions, including armored and infantry *units, underwent training at Camp Young. This included the 1st, 3rd, and 9th Armored Divisions, and the 2nd and 9th Infantry Divisions, among others.*

Spend, Fight, Kill—A Damned Hellish Mill

~1942-1943~

Six months later, the construction of the base infrastructure was at full throttle, and Desert Center was quite busy with the population of men, some of them with families. The café was a favorite among the latter, and the Ragsdales adopted some of the men who were away from their families. Steve had offered the military help in the infrastructure constructions, although Stanley did most of the work, using the vehicles and equipment from Ragsdale Desert Supply and Repair.

Able to hire new employees, Steve now had more time for his own pursuits. He called Stanley into his office one morning.

"How is it out at Camp Young?" Steve asked.

"Them military guys are efficient and fast! Not like when we helped out the Forest Service with the highways and the road up to Santa Rosa."

"Breath of fresh air. Military doesn't seem to have governmentitus like the rest. Have you encountered General Patton?"

"Not yet. He's not here often. The soldiers say he'll be here, once the base is finished, to begin the training. I've heard stories he's quite a character."

"He is. Tough old bird. John and I and his officers went out with him to survey the three locations we suggested. We were at the first location in Arizona, and the General liked it. John, looking out for us, warned him that there were lots of sidewinders in the area, so it was not the best. Patton said snakes didn't scare him, and we made camp. During the night, sitting around a campfire, Patton is telling a story. Suddenly, he draws one of his revolvers and shoots a snake that had slithered up just outside the camp circle, drawn by the fire. Blew his head right off."

Stanley laughed. "I was told that once, he—"

A knock on the door was Ruby, bringing them lunch. Stanley furrowed his brow. Why was she serving them lunch? Usually, his father just walked out to the counter.

"How's the building coming along here?" Steve asked.

Ruby sat plates of food in front of them each, then utensils from her apron, and left.

"We got all the cabins and trailers ready—cleaned and checked out the last of them yesterday. Be nice to have them all full again."

"Good. We will. This is a giant operation, as you know."

"At full operation, they say there will be over a million men."

Steve whistled. "I didn't know it was that many. Will be good for business. Until they all ship out to Africa to face Rommel. You know," he leaned forward conspiratorially, "that same out-fit had the gall to come in and offer me the beer concessions again. I practically kicked 'em out this time."

Stanley nodded. Alcohol would change the character of Desert Center. People always talked about progress. But what was progress?

"We'll be growing and prospering for at least the next couple of years. Even better than the aqueduct. That's why I called you in here."

Here it comes, Stanley thought. *I knew something was up.*

"I want you to manage Utopia and be in charge here in DC when I am away."

Stanley sat up with a jerk. "What? Where are you going?"

Steve laughed. "I'm not going anywhere. But I have been running this place for over twenty years. I want to do more exploring the desert. More writing. Finish my book. I want to spend more time at Eighth Heaven. I'll still be here, but I want you to run Utopia and take my place for day to day management when I'm not here. You think like I do about this place, and you've always loved it like I do."

Stanley smiled. His father was a tough old bird, like Patton. When he gave compliments, he meant every word. "Thank you, Father. I'm honored. And I won't let you down."

"I know you won't. And also," he lowered his head, fixing him with his eyes, "I'll be watching you."

In April of the next year, the military began using their new 570-acre airport, and the troops began arriving for training. Desert Center was a hub of activity like it had not seen, even during the aqueduct construction days.

Stanley stuck his head into the office where Steve sat writing some poetry. "Father?"

"Yes, come on in."

Stanley took a seat.

"How's the day-to-day, son?"

Stanley nodded and took a seat. "Busy as foxes with a herd of dead deer, now that the base is up and running at full capacity."

"Good. Everyone seems pleased."

"Yes." he paused. "Need to ask you about something."

"Sure."

"I just overheard some men talking. Appears they are working up a scheme to get Joe Chiriaco in trouble."

"What do you mean, a scheme? And why do we care?"

"'Cause I think what they are doing is wrong. I don't care for Joe, but that don't mean I think he should get jailed for no reason."

"Jailed? What's he done?"

Stanley shifted his bulk in the chair. "That's the thing. I don't think he's done anything wrong. You know he accepted the Schlitz beer concession we turned down, but he does not have a license for alcohol—only beer. Apparently General Patton was going to help him get one, but hasn't and probably won't. More important duties."

"Rudy Heimark offered me that same concession."

"I remember. Anyway, I overheard these three men talking in our café, about how it's illegal to sell beer to Indians, even if they're enlisted men. They've heard Joe say, 'It's wrong not to sell to them—if they can fight for the country, they ought to be able to buy beer.'"

"Well, he has an argument. I don't know Joe well, not happy about the way he goes about some things, but he don't strike me as a lawbreaker."

"Exactly. As far as I know, he's not selling it to them, he just thinks he should be able to. And he has a sign saying he cannot serve alcohol to Indians. These men said they found an Indian soldier—who apparently doesn't look much like an Indian—and they paid him to go buy beer from Joe's place. They took a photo of it and are going to turn it over to the police."

"Why would they do that?"

"They don't like Joe."

"I don't like Joe either. He doesn't respect the desert, only cares about his business. That don't mean I wish him ill will.

Certainly wouldn't want any desert resident being framed. Who are these men?"

"Not soldiers, I think they might have been former employees of Joe's. Seemed pretty upset with him."

Steve sat back in his seat. "So some disgruntled ex-employees are trying to set up Joe. What do you want to do?"

"I don't know. Guess it isn't our business. But…it don't matter if it's a competitor or my own wife—it ain't right."

"Looks like I raised you right." Steve nodded slowly, thinking as he blew some smoke out of his pipe. "You wanna tell Joe what you overheard?"

Stanley shifted uncomfortably. "Not sure that's a good idea. Joe and I have had some…words. Back when he was trying to build those homes on our land. He said it was a misunderstanding, but I wasn't too kind."

"I remember. Emotions sometimes get the best of us, and then we have to pay the piper. But I can't talk to him—I know for a fact he despises me, even though I've never done anything to him. Do we have someone else who could go talk to him?"

Stanley thought for a moment. "Harley—used to work here at our service station—now works for Joe. He needed a better job, and we had no openings back then. We're still friends, and Joe would trust him, I think."

"All right. Do it. Let me know what happens."

"General, sir. Good day!" Steve had arrived at the café from his writing shack to find General Patton working at a booth. He frequently came here to work, and he could use the phone booths Steve had installed against the back wall.

The large man was shuffling through papers. A map was spread on the table. Africa, Steve noticed. Of course.

The general looked up and took his unlit pipe out of his mouth. "Good day, Steve."

"Are they treating you well here, sir?"

"Affirmative. Excellent place to get away from the base to work." The general relaxed into the seat of the booth. "Closer and quieter than Chiriaco's café. Off-duty soldiers are as loud as a tank battery."

Steve nodded. "I am sure they are. Especially with alcohol in them."

He grunted and motioned to the seat across. "I understand you don't sell alcohol here. Did old Indian Joe beat you to the concession?"

Steve sat down across from the General. "They came to me first. I told them I'd never sell alcohol in Desert Center."

Patton's eyebrows went up. "Why is that?"

Steve shrugged. "I ain't never seen anything good come of drinking. Fights, divorces, even death. The Good Lord may have drunk wine, but he didn't visit honky-tonks, and I won't have them in my town. They even offered me $5,000 to take the concession."

The general studied Steve for a moment, then nodded. "Principled. I like that in a man, even if I disagree. Many men would give up principles for money." He picked up a lighter and lit the pipe, puffing until the bowl was glowing amber. "I don't mind my men blowing off some steam by drinking, as long as they're off-duty, and it doesn't affect them when they're on. Enjoy a bourbon myself occasionally. Especially with the fine cigar. But you are correct, alcohol can create problems when undisciplined men imbibe."

"Saw plenty of what it can do in Coffeyville, growing up. And had some incidents here when people brought it in, unbeknownst to me."

"My men are disciplined, and know not to get out of control. But with this many men, there's always a few that can't handle it. I'll tell you a story."

Patton loved to tell stories, especially of his own exploits, some of which were bold and out of the ordinary. Steve enjoyed hearing them.

"About a month ago, a couple of the men got drunk out in Indio. Didn't do anything, but they were walking through town being loud and, according to the local sheriff, 'disturbing the peace.' He arrested them. So I sent one of my envoys to retrieve my men, along with a report of their crimes from the sheriff. Told the envoy to tell the sheriff I'd personally ensure they received appropriate military discipline." He took a puff of his pipe. "Sheriff refused."

Steve raised his eyebrows. "What did you do?"

"Talked to him myself. Told him those men were United States soldiers, under my command. They are not regular citizens. I gave him my guarantee that proper justice would be administered. He still refused. Know what I did?"

"What's that, sir?"

"I drove my half-track to the jail in Indio, trained the guns on it, and demanded he turn my men over to me for punishment."

Steve laughed. He liked General Patton's style. "And did he?"

"Half-track guns can be persuasive."

"And what of the men?"

"They'd never been in trouble before. Had them spend a week in the brig. One is actually officer material—the other is training to be a chaplain." Steve frowned at that. "Like I said, don't mind them drinking. But a real man knows how to handle it and avoid any issues."

"Perhaps, but there are not a lot of those."

"More than you might think. But as I said, I respect your principles. Still wish someone around this desert had a real liquor license, and not just beer. However," he looked over at the counter and held up his coffee cup to Rosy, who rushed to get the pot, "this is some of the best coffee I've found, and coffee is the proper drink for working."

"On that we agree, General. And speaking of that, I'm gonna get me a cup and get to work myself."

"I've learned some about the history of this place. You've done a bang-up job. Tells me you're a smart man who can think beyond the normal ways. I seek those characteristics in men under my command."

Steve laughed. "Well, I did just get my draft registration in April."

"Eh, we're gonna put an end to this war within the next year. Mark my words."

"I have no doubt, sir."

The Greatest Magazine on Earth

~1944~

Steve was quite happy that the base was heavily active over the next couple of years, although Patton was not often there once everything was running smoothly. Recently, he had returned briefly as the training near its end, but had left again to meet his men at the staging base in Africa.

One of Patton's concerns had been moving the massive number of men when it was time to go to Africa. To remedy that problem, he had his men construct rails from the base to Indio, Rice, Blythe, Wiley's Well, and the Shaver Summit airport (such as it was). Steve figured the rail lines would probably be useless once the base was shut down, seeing as they had no other destinations.

Steve sat on the peak of The Alligator, watching one of the troop trains chugging away in the distance. This particular train, Steve knew, was filled with soldiers headed to Blythe and then to transport planes bound for North Africa. Major General Alvin Gillam took command of the Desert Center base, which would continue as a training center, though with a much smaller complement of men. Steve didn't know Gillam, and had not really tried to get to know him. There was nothing wrong with the man—he was a solid military leader. But Steve enjoyed

Patton's colorfulness, his ability to cut through noise to get to the point of a matter, and to think beyond normal ways of doing things. Results were what mattered to Patton—and Steve operated under the same guidelines. If an unusual path worked best, then that's the way it should be done.

In the flat, quiet desert, he could hear the train cars clacking even from this distance. Turning his head, he looked to Desert Center. Once again, business would drop off and even many of the non-military residents would leave. Not as many as when the aqueduct workers left, but it would be quieter in Desert Center.

The good news was that the first "freeway," constructed in Los Angeles, was being extended east. It would turn route 60 and 70 into "Interstate 10." Steve wasn't sure the difference between a freeway and a highway, but one difference seemed to be that highways run through towns and have stop signs and traffic lights, whereas freeways were only accessible via on "on-ramps"—no stopping on the road. What this meant is that the road would again be moved south—but this time, only about fifty or a hundred yards. Desert Center would become an exit off Freeway Interstate 10.

Unlike the last relocation of roads, Steve thought this would be an improvement. A freeway was easier to travel, faster, and the offramp would have a sign announcing Desert Center. A wider road and a better surface would probably result in more travelers. Furthermore, he expected it would increase safety for his town. With the highway as his Main Street, there were sometimes issues with drivers speeding through. No fatal accidents had occurred, but the resident parents were always worried for their children children.

He hated to see Patton and his men leave. But he wasn't worried. He had come out of cotton farming with a great new life. Highway 60 moved south, so he moved the town, and it worked out well. After the boom of the aqueduct, things seemed dire, but then Patton came along, creating another boom. Perhaps this newfangled freeway would have a similar effect.

Steve watched the landscape fly by on Highway 10 as he rode in the passenger seat of Randall's truck. He rarely rode with anyone, so this was an interesting treat.

"I sincerely appreciate you helping us move, Steve."

Randall glanced in his rearview mirror to make sure that McKinney and Dartmouth were still following in their respective trucks. It had been a long drive from El Centro to Desert Center, and now to Palm Desert, all three vehicles pulling trailers loaded with equipment and office supplies.

Steve pulled his pipe from his mouth. "Happy to help. A historic moment."

"I don't know how historic it is," Randall said, "but I think moving *Desert Magazine* to Palm Desert will be much better for us. El Centro is too far south and east. This new town of Palm Desert is perfect."

He maneuvered the vehicle into the right lane, soon coming to the offramp labelled "Palm Desert."

"It's also quite fortunate that your brother is a big time developer who took a liking to this area, and not a journalist like you."

Randall laughed. "True. We are close, but our paths have been very different." He made a couple of turns. "Up ahead is a new street called El Paseo. That's the street where Carl said he constructed the building for the magazine. You might remember that Patton stored many tanks along here when there were hardly any buildings."

"Was this even called Palm Desert then?"

"I don't know. Cliff would."

Soon they turned onto El Paseo and Steve spotted a new adobe building, single story, but with an architecture that looked like several square buildings of varying sizes collected into one. Finished, square posts of dark wood stuck out at the top of each wall, about six feet apart—joists that supported the flat roof. Fist-sized rocks, shaped and set in cement, provided framing around windows and doors, It was the largest building around.

As Randall turned into the parking lot, with McKinney and Dartmouth following, they saw a man standing outside the building, near the corner, smoking a cigarette.

"That's my brother," Randall said. "I don't think you've ever met him, have you?"

"Briefly, when you and he were traveling through Desert Center."

"Ah, yes. I recall. He had just begun doing his developments out here. Ever seen the Shadow Mountain Country Club?"

"Just from outside it. Pretty fancy."

Randall parked and as they exited, Randall's brother approached and the two hugged. Randall turned to Steve, with his hand on his brother's shoulder.

"Clifford, this is Desert Steve. He just reminded me that you two met a while back when we passed through his town. And coming up now are Wilson McKinney and John Dartmouth, who you know."

The men shook hands all around and exchanged pleasantries. "I remember you, Steve, and now we both have something in common. You founded Desert Center, and I founded Palm Desert. I think I had an easier time of it!"

Steve laughed. "Probably so, Cliff, but Palm Desert is far beyond anything in Desert Center. I was flying by the seat of my pants. You're a true developer."

"Thank you. I lived in Pacific Palisades before I moved out here, and wanted to bring some of that sense to the desert: plenty of palm trees, custom homes on large lots. I've been working on commercial developments for years, too, so I know how to do this. But I can't imagine starting a town with just an old prospector's well in the middle of the desert with no roads."

"If you two are finished with this mutual admiration," Randall interrupted, "I'd like to start unloading. I have an issue to publish next month."

Cliff took his brother's arm and said, "Come around to the front, first, I want you to see something."

He led the other two around the corner to the front of the building, taking a path out into the rest of the parking lot. He stopped and turned to the front of the building. Beaming, he pointed to the large letters fixed above the large, wood, double doors.

Desert Magazine Building

"I didn't know you were going to put the magazine's name on the building! That's fantastic!"

Steve nodded. "Got yourself a real big-city office here. Makes your old place in El Centro look like one of my old cabins."

Randall feigned hurt. "It wasn't that bad."

"No, it was worse." They all laughed. Randall directed them back to the vehicles to begin unloading the equipment.

Rocks Won't Burn, But Trees Will

~1944-1945~

The fire had come within a few hundred yards of his cabin. Fortunately, he was there at the time, and helped the firefighters establish a downslope break. This was the second fire since Steve had built Eighth Heaven, but this one was more extensive and damaging. The Forest Service determined it had started by a campfire that had not been put out properly. No one knew who had been so careless, and it was unlikely they would be identified. They were lucky that Steve didn't know who they were.

"Thank you, Captain," Steve said, as they stood outside the cabin, exhausted and covered in soot. "Sure glad we have that road. Would've been a lot worse."

The fire captain nodded. "We wouldn't have been able to save much up here, including your cabin." He hoisted himself up into the firetruck. "Thanks for your help, Steve."

Steve nodded went back up to his cabin. He sat on the porch, on a crate he had turned on its long side, pulled his pipe and tobacco pouch out of his vest. After packing the bowl and lighting it, he took a long draw, then blew out smoke slowly.

This pipe, he thought, *and my fireplace, should be the only smoke that's ever seen up here.*

Of course, lightning could start a fire, as it had in the past. But that was rare. And more importantly, it was natural: part of God's creation and plan. Incompetent or stupid men were another story. "Damn bastards," he muttered to himself.

He sat for a time, smoking and thinking. After a while, he pulled the pipe out of his mouth, nodded to himself, and smiled. He knocked the pipe against the porch post to clear it, put it in his pocket, and headed to his storage shed.

Steve stood at the edge of the dirt road, staring at the slope before him. Burned trees and blackened rocks stretched out, laying naked on black, ashy ground. How many trees had died? How many animals? All because of man.

He turned away and looked at the slope above the road. Some of the trees had burned there, but not as bad. The road acted as a bit of a fire break. Where the fire was too large, the road enabled the firefighters to get to it and stop it from jumping the road towards his cabin.

He picked up three small buckets by their handles and walked until he found what he was looking for: a large outcropping of rock on the upper side of the trail. A flat surface. As if nature had set up a blank billboard for him.

He put down the green and red paint buckets, and climbed up with the white. He balanced the bucket on a rock and began painting, making the letters wide and large. No one could miss them if they came up this road, whether by auto, horse, or foot.

He made quick work of it, then carefully backed down. He retrieved the other buckets and walked about twenty feet to turn and examine his handiwork.

NO! ROCKS
WONT BURN
BUT TREES AND
MEN
WILL!

He continued up the road, finding a tree hollowed out by the fire, the top broken off. A thirty-foot-high trunk, like a sentinel made from an eviscerated corpse.

For this one, he had written a short poem. He first painted the interior white, as a backdrop, so the letters would stand out in contrast. Then, using black, red paint (red for the word "fire") he painted the words:

TO
MAN
AND
TREE
I SAY TO
THEE
BEWARE
OF
FIRE
IT'S
KILLING
ME

"Good," he said to himself. "One more should do it."

Along the slope, he located a tall, beautiful tree, about four feet in diameter at the ground. All the lower branches had been burned off, and the bark was gone. Steve knew this tree, he admired it whenever he came by. He lamented its death, shook his head, and got to work. Another colorful one: black, red, green, and white.

LIKE WAR
TO U
FIRE
TO ME
A TREE
IS
DEATH

Perhaps that will make the reckless people who intrude his mountain peak think a little bit. He didn't understand why people did not treat God's creation with more reverence. It was one thing to use trees for something constructive: buildings, homes, and so on. For them to merely burn without meaning, in Steve's mind, was a slap in the face of God.

Steve stepped up the three concrete steps to the front door of his house, knocking the dirt and sand off his boots. As he opened the door, Lydia called out.

"Steve? That you?"

"Yeah."

"Been wondering when you were getting back. Thelma called. I have bad news." Her tone perked up his ears as she came out of the bedroom.

"What kind of bad news can they have? Her husband is—."

"Your father passed."

He sat down on the couch. His eyes squeezed shut.

"She said he died in his sleep. He'd been going downhill rapidly since Melissa died a few years ago." Melissa was his second wife.

He breathed deeply. "It was expected."

"Are you okay?"

"He was ninety-one—" he flicked his hand, "—and he did not suffer. That's the way to go."

"I know you hardly talked to him after he remarried. And you didn't like Melissa, but she died a few years ago. I don't know why you didn't talk to him more."

He stood up and took a deep breath. "And that makes me realize I need to get our graves dug. I want to be buried at The Alligator, near my writing. But I need to get up to Corn Springs first and—"

Lydia stared at him. "Steve, your father just died! And you're just going to go about your business? We should go, at least to be with Thelma. He was her grandfather you know, living with her for four years. It's an easy trip these days."

Steve shook his head. "We ain't going to Taft. Thelma's there with Larry and Sharri, they have their church, they got friends. We'll go eventually. There's no urgency."

Lydia set her mouth in a thin line. "You can be so cold-hearted sometimes."

"What the hell's wrong with you? It's my father, I can handle his death however I want."

"I know he hardly spoke to you, either, after he remarried. That's no reason—"

"Lydia! He is with the Lord. He is no longer suffering. Nothing I do changes that. Truth is, he would want me to just keep working."

Lydia huffed. "You're probably right about that. Both of you think work is more important than anything."

"I'll thank you to keep your thoughts to yourself about my father." He stood up. "I'll call this afternoon. Gonna wash up and change clothes first. Then to Corn Springs."

"I need to get back to the café." She turned and left.

After the fire, Steve spent most of his time at Eighth Heaven, cleaning up debris on the road and surrounding trails, both on his own land and State land. He travelled to Desert Center at least once a week to check in with Stanley and take care of anything that needed his attention. Stanley was doing a fine job, in Steve's opinion—but he didn't have Steve's experience.

In his office on this day, he was, looking over some financial reports Stanley had left for him. Things had begun to slow down more than he had hoped. There were still soldiers and staff at Camp Young, but only a couple hundred now. Few came into Desert Center except for an occasional meal at the café. They had everything else they required at the base: mail, entertainment, mess hall, and fuel. If they wanted alcohol, they went to Joe's. The new freeway, the Interstate 10, saw more traffic than the old Highway 60 through town, but not in the numbers Steve had hoped. At least not yet.

Sitting back in his chair, he blew an exasperated sigh. He needed to think of something else. Maybe it was as time to start founding some new outposts along Interstate 10? He wasn't sure that would help—the desert was not the same as back in the old days, when travel was slower and more difficult.

He decided he'd go over to The Alligator and get his head clear. Do some brainstorming. He stood and picked up the un-read newspaper that he had retrieved this morning. As he started to walk out, a headline caught his eye. He sat back down and began reading.

A broad smile came to his face.

Saved By Iron Ore
(1945–1949)

The Eagle Mountain Mine

The iron ore deposits in the Eagle Mountain area were first discovered in the late 19th century, but it was not until after the Colorado Aqueduct was built that it was known just how large the iron field was. .

Kaiser Steel Corporation, a major steel producer founded by industrialist Henry J. Kaiser, was established during World War II to supply shipyards and support the war effort. It acquired the rights to the iron ore deposits at Eagle Mountain in the 1940s.

Extensive infrastructure was required to support the mining operations, including the construction of a company town (also named Eagle Mountain) which contained housing, schools, medical facilities, and recreational amenities for workers and their families. At its peak, it housed several thousand residents. Kaiser built a more upscale community for the executives and their families, with a golf course and a large pond, named Lake Tamarisk, just up the road from Desert Center.

Kaiser also constructed a fifty-one-mile railroad to the company's steel mill in Fontana. The mine began operations in 1948.

Eagle Mountain was an open-pit mine which extracted millions of tones of ore, making it one of the largest iron mines in the Western United States. It also brought extensive employ-

ment opportunities and contributed to the economic develop-
ment of the region.

You Find the Lizards Talking to You

~1945~

"Steve, I'd like your advice on a project, and maybe some help."

"A new project?" Steve asked. Harry Oliver was always coming up with new ideas.

"A magazine for the desert."

Steve looked up from the paper he was reading. "We got *Desert Magazine, The Gold Miner, Todo.*"

"And I've been published by all of them. And more. But I think there's room for one more."

"So have you given up all your Hollywood work? Didn't you do a film recently?"

"Few years ago. *The Outlaw,* in 1941. I feel like I've done what I set out to do over the last twenty or so years. Even got nominated for an Academy Award for a couple of films as art director."

"I didn't know that!"

Harry shrugged. "That was back when they started the Awards in the late '20s. I want to focus more on my paintings and drawings, architectural designs, and writings."

"I read your *99 Days in the Desert*. A good work. And that reminds me about a book I hope to write that I'd like some of your thoughts. But go on about this new magazine."

Harry leaned over, growing animated, as he often did when discussing a new project. "You know I've been out here a long time. Homesteaded in Borrego in 1929, then in Thousand Palms during the War. I've spent so much time out here, and when you do that, you find yourself talking to yourself. After a few more years, you find yourself talking to the lizards—"

"Or tortoises." Steve said.

"—then, in another couple of years you find the lizards talking to you! When you find yourself stealing their amazing tales, you are about ready to start a desert paper, in my opinion. Now that the War's officially over, it seems like time."

Steve regarded his friend with no small amount of envy. "That's some wise words, Harry. Whatcha gonna call it?"

"I'm thinking the *Desert Rat Scrap Book*. It won't be a normal rag. Mostly humor about the desert. Anything goes. I'm going to print it on one seventeen by twenty-two heavy stock, folded so you get five pages. I'll advertise it that way—'the only five-page paper in the world, and the only newspaper you can open in the wind!' The front page will have one of my woodcuts or drawings."

"Articles?"

"Short articles, but all stories, or lore, or legends, about desert rats and desert stories." He reached into his bag on the seat beside him and pulled out a large paper. "Here's the cover for the first issue I drew yesterday, with some potential content."

Steve took the paper. Hand-drawn graphics, almost cartoon-like, with typeset articles and other boilerplate text. The art around the page mimicked a leather-bound notebook with string binding the pages. Below the season and date, in big bold letters, red on yellow, was the masthead.

Harry Oliver's
Desert Rat
Scrap Book
A Pocket Sized Newspaper
Covering the Great Southwest.

Three article titles sat underneath the heading. "LEM...The Desert Efficiency Expert," "No burro, no gold," and "Whiskers."

Steve looked up. "You already have articles?"

"Just a few I have written or got from other places. The one on efficiency is from my book *Desert Rough Cuts*. The one on Captain Catnip Ashby is from Robert Wagner's *Script*. I'm also gonna add a page of 'argument starters'—a collection of desert sayings that people can argue over. Updates on Peg Leg's lost mine—"

"—I'd be disappointed otherwise—" Harry was well known for his obsession with the legend of Peg Leg.

"—and then just tidbits here and there. John Hilton said he'd be happy to contribute regularly. So—will you write for me?"

Steve beamed. "If John agreed to it, then I'm in. Anything in particular?"

"Long as it has to do with the desert and has some humor, your choice. But if you want to run some ideas past me, that's fine. I would definitely like to include some of your sayings, if that's ok, but will ask first—"

"Sayings? Like what?" Whether Steve admitted it or not, this conversation was pleasantly feeding his ego.

"Like one you say a lot: 'even the woodpecker owes its success to the fact that he uses his head.' And definitely want to run your notice of reward for the wanton killing of tortoises."

Steve nodded. "I appreciate that, Harry. I'll give it some thought. I like the idea of something with a bit of humor. When do you plan to publish the first issue?"

"I'm hoping for next March or April. I don't expect to have a steady publication schedule. When I've gathered enough material, I'll publish an issue. I'm thinking four times a year would be ideal."

"Sound about right. I'd like to see a lot more articles about the old prospectors people don't know much about. If it hadn't been for Old Man Gruendike in 1915, my family and I might be skeletons baking in the desert."

"You should write about that—how you got the idea of Desert Center."

Steve removed his pipe from his mouth, and tamped it down. "Funny you say that. I been working on a series of poems about it. Just about done. Here…" He rummaged around on the table beside him and pulled out a notebook. Flipping open to a marked page, he read out loud.

N.Y. and LA, and London, don't you know,
Are small towns compared with D.C.
They boast of their wonders, all in a row,
But our rest room's a million square miles, don't you see!

The sky is our limit, hell is our depth,
We have sunshine the whole year round,
If you wish to get fat, or wish to be lean,
D.C. is the best place to be found.

"That's the last part, but I think I need a better."

Harry laughed. "That's precisely the sort of the thing I'd love to see in the *Scrap Book*. Down home, simple, to the point—and capturing the character of the desert rats."

Steve crossed the street, holding his left arm wrapped in a bloody rag. Wincing, he pulled open the door to the medical clinic and shivered in the cool air. This was the only air-conditioned building between Riverside and Phoenix.

No one was inside the waiting room. He tapped the bell on the desk.

Steve had met Dr. Sydney Garfield a decade earlier, when he had a successful practice in Indio. In 1933, the doctor saw an opportunity to serve as medical support for the Colorado Aqueduct project. He closed the Indio practice and opened a clinic in Desert Center, which he named Contractors General Hospital. It contained a four-bed clinic, a surgery, and offices, cooled by a new ammonia air-conditioning system. Steve had been happy to welcome him, of course, especially after the death of Gus—any significant town needed a doctor. Garfield confirmed that he did not move his practice *just* for the aqueduct workers—he wanted to serve the entire surrounding community.

Dr. Garfield stepped out of a back room, white medical shirt a bit disheveled, stethoscope stuffed in a side pocket. "Steve! What brings you—" Noticing the arm, he said, "Ah. Come on back to the surgery. How did it happen?"

Steve followed the doctor down the hall. "Being distracted. I was welding some railings over at the cabins, and I set the welding machine up on some rocks, so the gun could reach the spot I was working on. Accidentally pulled it over, and it fell on me, gashing my arm. Don't think I broke anything, but it's pretty deep."

Dr. Garfield indicated a chair for Steve. He unwound the rag and whistled. "Yep, that's pretty ugly." He rummaged around in his storage drawers and brought out supplies to clean the wound. He then began examining it closely, poking and prodding and pulling. Steve scrunched his face in pain but made no sound.

"Doesn't appear to be as deep as it originally looked. But you do need a few stitches. I don't think it's broken, but there could be a fracture. It'll need to be bound up and immobilized anyway."

He gathered the supplies for stitching, and then took a seat on a rolling chair and slid over to Steve. He motioned for him to place his arm on the wide arm of the patient chair.

Looking at Steve, he said, "Want some Novocain?"

Steve shook his head. "Don't want a dead arm the rest of the day."

"You can't use the arm—it needs to be in a sling a few days so you don't pull the stitches."

"Sure, doc, whatever you say. But no Novocain."

Doctor Garfield gave a "harumpf," knowing Steve would do as he damn well pleased and would probably be back soon with the stitches pulled. He leaned down with the needle and sutures and began working.

Steve looked out the window to the right. "How's it going with the iron mine workers?"

"Funny you ask. Had a few interesting weeks. I've had a problem with payments—especially the single men. They get paid once a month, and immediately spend most of it on alcohol in Chiriaco Summit or Blythe. Then, when they need medical care, they can't pay. I can't refuse them, of course. They promise to pay later. Sometimes they do, sometimes they don't."

"Not surprised. That's why Desert Center will always be alcohol-free."

"Other places will never do that because it is so lucrative."

"Did I tell you I was offered $5,000 for the beer concession back in—"

"Yes, many times. You turned it down. Anyway—" the doctor hurried on before Steve could launch into the story of the concessions, "—news of this apparently got all the way up to Henry J. Kaiser himself, and he came out here personally to talk to me—"

"The big boss himself?!"

"Yes. He said he had an idea: I should charge a nickel a month, taken directly out of the worker's paycheck. Three cents for wives, and two cents for each child. He said he'd set it up with his payroll people if I wanted to give it a shot."

Steve's brow furrowed. "That's quite clever. Guess the man who has successfully built ships and dams and aqueducts has to be pretty smart. You agreed?"

"I saw no downside. I get paid, even if they don't need the care, but when they do, they can come in as often as they need. I ran numbers on it. It'll provide steady income for my practice. I plan to expand the beds—perhaps eight more—and bring in more equipment and a nurse or two. We're going to be busy for a while with this iron mine."

"From what I hear about the mine, it will be operating for many decades."

"Seems like it. Largest iron field in the U.S., I heard. Okay—" Garfield tied off the last stitch, cut the excess, checked his work, then cleaned the area with alcohol.

After putting a sling on the arm, he accompanied Steve back outside. "Now, Steve, please move that arm as little as possible. That'll be ten dollars."

"Well. Doctors cure a little belly-ache, bills you a big headache. Should've done it myself. The cost of staying healthy keeps going up."

"That's only because you keep living."

"Well, the cost of dying is getting out of hand, too. I got an idea for that…

Garfield held up his hand. "I'd like to hear, but not today. Prepaid healthcare does mean a lot of paperwork."

Steve doffed his hat and pulled his pipe out of his jacket. "See what I mean?"

"Pull the stitches out, it won't heal correctly. And you'll have to come back for me to restitch it."

"Sure thing, doc." Steve left with a wave as Garfield rolled his eyes.

Steve looked up from the café booth where he was sitting as the door opened to reveal Harry Oliver, blinking from the bright sun outside. Steve watched as his friend's eyes adjusted.

"Hello, Steve!" Harry shouted, once he spotted him.

"Harry, good to see you. I see you've copied my whiskers?" he said, as he stroked his own beard.

Harry scratched his wiry beard. "Yes. And no. They are mine, they just happen to look like yours. Funny story: the *Desert Sun* ran a story about Desert Center, and they put my picture instead of yours."

"I didn't see that. Which one of us should be insulted?"

"Both."

"Agreed."

Harry slid into the opposite bench seat and set a black nugget down on the table between them. Steve looked at it, picked it up, rubbed it, spit on his fingers, and rubbed again. He raised his eyebrows.

"Gold?"

"Yep. Eighteen karat."

Steve rolled his eyes. "Don't tell me. You found Peg Leg's mine? Harry, we can go to my office and I'll show you many similar nuggets from the 'lost mine' that people have brought me over the years."

Everyone who knew Harry knew of his fascination with the legend of Peg Leg's "lost mine."

Harry smiled broadly. "I didn't find the mine, but this is from the mine."

"Of course it is." Steve took a deep breath and looked at the nugget again. He pulled out his pocket knife, opened the blade and scraped at the nugget.

"This is a replica of a gold nugget, made with plaster of paris and lacquered with a few coats of gold paint."

"Maybe. Or perhaps it's really from the lost mine. Depends on who's looking at it."

"Are you sure you aren't related to ol' Peg Leg?" Steve tossed the nugget back to Harry. "Why are you wasting my time again with this obsession? You've been on this since the 1920s, so I guess you're not gonna give up?"

"No, because it's so much fun! What a great legend of the desert. All the elements are there. A man with a peg leg, shot by an Indian arrow, cut off his own leg, saved by Indian women, wandered the desert as a prospector, finds a massive mine, and spends the rest of his life trying to find it again."

"It's a great legend. 'Legend' being the key word."

"Now, you *know* Peg Leg was a real. Thomas Smith, brother of the famous Jedediah Smith. Born in Kentucky in 1801—"

"I know Peg Leg Smith was real. It's the mine that's the scam."

"Maybe. Maybe not. But I have a great idea for me and you."

"Ah. Should've known."

"You've had some crazy ideas of your own from time to time. Let me finish my story."

Steve nodded reluctantly. "Fair enough. Go ahead."

"So this is the story: man born in 1850, runs away from home at fifteen, worked on the Mississippi, became a fur trader, and Indian scout, got shot by an arrow in the leg, and amputated it himself, worked as a kidnapper in Mexico and a horse thief in California, and then finds the biggest gold mine in history."

"Everyone knows this."

"Would you *please* stop interrupting? He escaped into the Santa Rosa mountains and down into the Badlands. *That* is where he found the massive gold-bearing quartz mine. So he gathered a bunch of the nuggets and left the area to sell them. When he came back, he couldn't remember where the mine was. He knew *about* where it was, so he started selling maps and the nuggets he did have. He did this for fifteen or twenty years."

He stopped and sat looking at Steve expectantly.

"Are you done?"

"Almost."

"Doesn't that sound like a rotten pail of fish? He found a gigantic mother lode that no one else has been able to locate in almost a hundred years. Instead of continuing to look for it, he sold maps and a few nuggets. All the earmarks of a fraudster."

Harry leaned back and considered Steve for a moment. "Perhaps. Or perhaps it's all true. Either way, this leads to my idea."

Steve took a sip of his coffee. "Finally."

"You know about the annual Peg Leg trek I've been leading?"

"Harry, why do you keep telling me things I know?"

"It's how storytelling works. I was in the film industry, remember?"

Steve laughed. "Touché. Yes, I know about your trek, every April 1 since 1900. Nice choice of a date, by the way."

"Nineteen oh six. But I've been leading it earlier in the year because of the lack of tourists in April, when it starts to get hot."

"I didn't know that."

"You don't know because you've never been, despite all the times I've invited you. But now I've got an idea that I think you might want to be part of. Instead of the trek—or maybe we keep the trek, too—starting next January 1, we hold a Peg Leg Smith liars' contest every year."

Steve raised his eyebrows. "A liar's contest?"

"We hold it in the Borrega wilderness somewhere, have a big fire, perhaps a chuckwagon, everybody pays a small fee to enter. No fee to come and listen. Five-minute stories, and they must mention or relate to Peg Leg or his mine. You and I judge the stories and hand out some sort of cheap trophy."

Steve chuckled. "You are something. Even though you live in the desert, your mind is still in Hollywood, isn't it?"

"It's a great idea, yes?"

Steve smiled. "I admit it is. Get people learning about the desert, focus on some desert lore, have some fun. Yep, that's some good stuff. I'm intrigued. Why hold it in the Borrego wilderness?"

"Because I am fairly certain that the mine was within 100 miles of there. It's also close to my ranch."

"I think the last one is the only one that matters to you."

"You're a spoil sport. Need to fill in the details. You love desert lore as much as I do. I'm also going to contact Ray Herrington. Do you know him?"

"The man who runs the rock shop at Knott's Berry Farm?"

"Yes."

"Never met him. Know who he is."

"I know him pretty well, and he has a good relationship with Walter Knott, and I want him to ask Mr. Knott if he might want to sponsor the contest and provide some prizes. He's a big supporter of western pioneer history."

Steve nodded, thinking. "The more we can bring people to the desert and teach them about it, the better. They'll learn to respect it. In a fun way."

Harry smiled again. "So you're in?"

Steve looked at him for a moment then pounded the table with his right fist.

"Let's do it!"

Steve threw open the door to the Forest Service main office. The man behind the desk jumped at the sudden intrusion.

"I need a gate," Steve said. "Before deer season starts."

The officer set down his pencil. "Excuse me? Do I know you?"

"You should. I'm Desert Steve Ragsdale, I own Desert Center. I have land and a cabin on Santa Rosa Peak. You must be new, I haven't seen you before."

Powell sat back and nodded. "Ah, yes." He smiled, not necessarily friendly. "Desert Steve. I'm Officer Powell."

"So you *have* heard of me. I helped build all your fire roads in the forests. Now I need you to return the favor and build me a gate."

"I didn't know that you helped build the fire roads. Thank you for your assistance. Now, what is this about a gate?"

Steve, noting that the officer did not offer, pulled a chair in front of the desk with a scrape and sat down.

"The Santa Rosa Truck Road—which I helped build—is also the road to my cabin. Deer season is almost upon us. Hunters come up that road all the way to my land, thinking it's public land. I'm not fond of bullets flying around my cabin, especially if I am outside working. I'd like you to build a gate, with a lock, where the road enters my land."

"We don't usually build gates, or anything, for private land. Just on government land."

"Then put the gate three feet outside my land on government land. It can't be that complicated, just put a gate there, with a lock, like you've got at the bottom of the Santa Rosa Truck Road at Highway 74."

Officer Powell shrugged, pulled a pad of paper in front of him, and began scribbling. "I can place a request, and we'll see what the higher-ups say. But I wouldn't get your hopes up. There's no reason for us to build a gate."

"There are other locked gates outside other private properties in the mountains. What do you have against me?"

"Not a thing, sir. *Those* gates were put in during World War II because they were worried about sabotage to the forests. There is no danger of that now."

"Well that was moronic because the Krauts weren't gonna attack empty mountaintops. However, the danger of me being shot by a wayward hunter is quite high."

"Be that at as it may, we don't build structures for private use. But I will send your request. You have my word."

Steve stood up and regarded the man. "A man's word used to mean something, even if he did work for the government. So I'll take your word for it. But the forest service was much more efficient and amenable in the old days. Give me the name of your superior, and where I can contact him."

"As you wish." Officer Powell wrote on a piece of paper and handed it to Steve. "Good luck. We'll be in touch. Nice to meet you, Mr. Ragsdale."

Steve turned and left without a word.

He Dug His Own Grave
~1947–1948~

Steve took a puff from his pipe as he leaned against a boulder, watching the four men dig.

"Hey! Quinn! You guys make sure it's eight feet deep, vertical on the sides, like I said."

Quinn looked up from above the hole where two other men were down inside the small pit, digging. He and another employee, Robert, stood outside the hole, shoveling the dirt from the hole into wheelbarrows, to be moved away down the slope.

"I know. They're about six feet now. You want me and Robert to go get the posts and the walls?"

"Sure thing."

Quinn tossed his shovel down and nodded at Robert. They both hiked down the slope, below Steve's shack, where a truck held four by fours, four wooden walls, and a sheet metal liner that Steve had fashioned at the garage in Desert Center.

Steve stood and gazed around. It was the perfect spot. His writing shack was near the foot of the slope. Beyond and around, desert and scrub, and further out, Interstate 10. Just beyond that was Desert Center and Palen Dry Lake, with the Eagle Mountains in the distance.

He walked over to the pit and looked in.

"That's good, men. Just make sure the corners are square and the floor is flat. We'll put the posts in the corners first."

The two younger men, Benny and Armitage, nodded their assent.

Once they had finished, Steve directed them as they drove the four posts into the corners of the pit. Next, they maneuvered the four wooden retaining walls into place, nailing them to the posts.

Once finished, the men went back down to the truck. It took all five of them to maneuver the sheet metal box, open on the top, up the slope. With some swearing, they were able to drop it into the pit, just inside the wooden walls.

They all stepped back, sweating from the heat and the exertion.

"Now, where's the lid I made?"

"Still in the truck."

"Well, go get it. Doesn't do us any good there."

The "lid" that Steve had constructed was a hinged coverer the pit. Two of the men lined it up at one of the long sides, while Quinn affixed the hinges to the top of the wooden wall. Once finished, Steve motioned them all away and stepped back.

"Good job, men. Quinn, get the camera, and we'll memorialize the moment. Go up the slope there. Open the lid back up boys."

Steve found his pipe he left in a little crevice on top of a rock, and struck a pose. Quinn asked him to hold still as he snapped the picture.

"A good morning's work. Thank you, men. Let's head on back to town."

As the men gathered the pickaxes and shovels, placing them in the wheelbarrow, Steve stepped up the slope a way and gazed around one more time. He smiled. Life was grand for Desert Steve. Just a poor, simple man who created his own little empire out of nothing. A good life, well spent. As his eyes lifted to look at Desert Center, he said to himself, "And my remains will lie here forever, on The Alligator, overlooking my legacy."

With that, he closed the lid to his grave and followed the rest of the man down the slope to the truck.

Steve finished chopping the last log and loaded it onto the cart. As he began pushing it towards the cabin on its track, he heard a vehicle coming up the dirt road. He stopped and looked towards the trail, waiting.

A Forest Service truck came into view and pulled up next to his jalopy. They often stopped by to say hello as they did their scheduled rounds through the fire roads.

The ranger got out, a young man that Steve did not recognize. Steve waited rather than going to meet him.

"Mr. Ragsdale?" He said as he approached.

"You're looking at him."

"I'm Ranger J.B. Holland. I understand you're a reserve forest ranger?"

"That's right. I help protect the desert *and* the mountains."

"We appreciate your service." He looked down and at the envelope he was carrying. "I'm assigned to these roads today, and Officer Powell at headquarters asked me to deliver this to you."

Steve, holding the man's eye, took the paper and held it in front of him. Handwritten on the outside was

Mr Steve Ragsdale
Santa Rosa Peak

Steve looked up. "How'd you know I was here? 'Bout half the time I'm in Desert Center."

"They told me to tack it to your door if you weren't here. Said it wasn't urgent."

Steve opened the envelope and read the short letter. He looked up.

"You're denying my request for a gate? Despite the danger to public safety? Namely, keeping me from being shot by a hunter trespassing on my land?"

The man looked uncomfortable. "I'm just delivering it. I had nothing to do with the decision."

Steve regarded him for a few moments. He took off his hat and turned around for a moment, wiping his brow. "That's the thanks I get for helping you out all these decades. They send me a lackey," he muttered.

"Excuse me, sir?"

Steve turned back around. "Never mind."

"You know, sir, nothing keeps you from building your own gate on your land."

Steve rolled his eyes. "Of course I know that. But it's *your* road that allows the hunters—eh, never mind." He stuffed the letter back in the envelope. "Thanks for acting as a postal man. Take a message back to your superiors. I resign as a reserve forest service firefighter. I'll protect my own land, and that's it. 'Nuff sed."

"When will you be back?"

Steve loaded his rucksack into the car. "Few days. Gonna run over to the Coleman store for some gear first."

"And what is this again?" Lydia seemed put out again, and Steve didn't know why. She had been that way a lot lately.

"Peg Leg. The contest Harry and I have been planning. Told you about it countless times. The Peg Leg Smith Liar's Contest."

Lydia didn't respond, but he could feel her eyes burning into his back. He shut the trunk and turned around.

"It's not that long, Lydia. And Stanley does a good job of running my town."

"*Your* town?"

He shrugged. "Our town."

"I think I had a lot to do with it. And the children. Do you recall the move from the cotton ranch? The first spot at Gruendike's? My café is the center of the town."

Steve threw up his hands. "All true, Lydia. I'm merely talking about whose name is on it. It don't diminish you or anyone." He shook his head. "Damn, woman, it seems like you just want to argue sometimes."

"And I think you been gettin' too big for your own britches. Acting like some overlord!"

Steve stuck his hand through the open window of the auto and pulled up a copy of *Desert Magazine*. He flipped to a page, folded it open, and slapped it down on the hood.

"Who is that?!"

Lydia glanced at the ad, which she had seen hundreds of times. A picture of Steve at the top. Below that, it read

DESERT STEVE
invites you to
DESERT CENTER
S.A. "Desert Steve" Ragsdale
owner and operator
Stanley Ragsdale

Manager

"My picture, my name as owner and operator. That means if something goes wrong, I get the blame. If there's problems, people are going to come to me. Doesn't mean other people haven't contributed. But it's my name on the line."

Lydia gave a harrumph. "Pride goes before a fall, husband."

"Don't quote scripture to me, *wife!*"

But Lydia had already stomped off. Steve shook his head and got into his vehicle.

Steve walked into the Coleman store on the Main Street, just down from the market. He strode directly to the aisle he needed, picking up several propane canisters. He took them to the cashier.

"What's wrong?" She asked, observing his frown. "Thought you was off to the liars contest."

"I am," Steve replied. "Just needed these canisters." He shook his head. "I'm fine. Just a forgotten bloke. Wears a yoke. Works all day. Nothing to say."

She tilted her head. "No one forgets you. And never will."

He paused as he laid his payment on the counter between them. He gave a wry grin. "Not sure *everyone* believes that."

She nodded knowingly, and placed the canisters in a sack. As she handed it to him, she patted his hand. "You have fun up there, you and Mr. Hilton. It sounds wonderful."

Steve paused, started to say something, then nodded. "Sure will."

Who the Hell Named Me a Judge?

~1948~

John Hilton, Ray Hetherington, Harry Oliver, and Steve stood before the crowd assembled around a large fire. John nodded at Steve that everyone was ready. He stepped up on a crate and banged on a metal pot with his pistol.

"Thank you all for coming to this annual Peg Leg's Liar's Contest!" There was some cheering, and to Steve's dismay, he could see a couple of people were already drunk. They served no alcohol, so these people had brought flasks. "Of course, this is not technically the first. Harry Oliver founded the Peg Leg Trek in 1916, and has led treks almost every year since. Last year, Harry came to me, and we decided that the old deceiver—that's Peg Leg I speak of, not the Devil—needed an annual event."

There was cheering at this as well, and Steve waited for them to calm down.

"Tonight, the contestants will stand before us and tell us a tale. When all are heard, we'll judge the best three for first, second, and third place. The judges are myself, Desert Steve, the owner of Desert Center, open 24/7 because we can't close —we lost our keys! The second judge is Harry Oliver, ex-Hollywood art director, humorist, and editor of the *Desert Rat*

Scrap Book. Joe Wright, of Knott's Berry Farm, is the third judge. Ray Hetherington, also from Knott's Berry Farm, will make the presentation of the prizes."

There was more whooping and hollering. "Before we begin with the first contestant, Harry is going to tell us about the man we're celebrating. Harry, as many of you know, is an expert on old Peg Leg."

Steve stepped down and Harry took his place to much applause.

"Thank you, Steve, and welcome everyone. All the best to our contestants. The most creative—but still believable—will win.

"Thomas L. Smith was born in Kentucky in 1801, and ran away from home at age fifteen. Worked on boats on the Mississippi River. Perhaps he ran into another great storyteller, Mark Twain. Thereafter, he worked with John Jacob Astor as a fur trader beyond the Mississippi, and later as part of the LeGrande expedition into Mexico because he could speak several Indian languages. During one scouting expedition, he took an arrow to the right knee, which resulted in a deadly infection. Since there were no doctors, he amputated his own leg with his skinning knife, passing out from blood loss and shock. Some Indian women found him nearly dead. They took him in and used chewed roots and berries to help him recover. He carved a wooden leg for himself, earning the moniker 'Peg Leg' for the rest of his life. It was said that during fights, he learned how to remove the leg quickly to use as a weapon.

"After 1840, Smith began kidnapping Indian children to sell as servants to wealthy Mexican households. Eventually, on the run from the local tribes, he came to California and operated as a horse thief as part of the largest horse stealing operation in California and Arizona.

"Once again running from authorities, he came up into these very mountains and the Barga Badlands. It was during this time that he said he found a massive gold-bearing quartz mine. Taking a bag of the best nuggets, he travelled around California, showing people the nuggets and telling them his story about the mine. He went back many times trying to find the spot, but could never locate it. So he kept selling a nugget here and there, and sold maps to the area where he thought it was located.

"He never found the mine. After a saloon fight in San Francisco in 1866, he died. Since then, many others have tried to find the lost mine. Occasionally, someone will appear with nuggets and say they found it, only to turn out to be mistaken, or, more often, a scam.

"Some don't believe there ever was a mine, and that Smith merely hit on a scheme to make himself money without doing anything illegal. Others believe the mine exists, and still others think the truth lies somewhere in the middle.

"I will leave those ponderings to you, for tonight we are here to honor this legend of the desert, whether he be a huckster or just a forgetful man. But I have no doubt that people will keep looking for Peg Leg Smith's lost mine for another hundred years, and another after that. Who know? Maybe some adventurer will get lucky."

Harry paused dramatically for a moment to let all that sink in. "Let's hear from Ray."

He relinquished his spot, and Ray took over. "Welcome, all you liars! As you may know or not know, I run the Rock Shop at Knott's Berry Farm. So I am interested in everything that has to do with quartz, gold, amethyst, iron nuggets, and more. There are many legends out there about fabulous finds that have been lost. But this is the most famous of all.

"As Harry said, there is much debate about whether the mine existed. No one knows what Harry thinks. Desert Steve thinks Peg Leg was just an old fraudster who got the gold by stealing it from other miners. Hank Wilson believes the story is true, pointing to the evidence that Peg Leg *did* come out of the desert with several black and gold nuggets that he found near three small buttes. I say, either way, it's a great story and a good reason for us to gather, celebrate the prospectors of this land, and see who can tell the best whoppers! As I mentioned, I run the Rock Shop at Knott's Berry Farm. Come visit us!"

Steve leaned over to Harry. "By all that's holy, every time you talk to Ray, he mentions Knott's Berry Farm three or four times."

Harry chuckled. "Yes, some people just can't stop advertising." He offered a smirk at Steve, who either didn't get his point or just ignored him.

"My boss," Ray was saying, "Walter Knott, loves the idea of this contest. As prizes, he has sent a number of cases of our berry preserves, as well as some old phonographic records that came from the ghost town section of Knott's Berry Farm. Best of luck to the contestants!" He waved and stepped down.

More applause as Harry got back up. "Without further ado, let's begin!" He looked down at a paper in his hand. "Our first contestant is Homer George. Come on up, Homer!"

Homer was a rather large man with a large belly, a thick white beard, and was wearing cowboy boots and a duster over jeans and a flannel shirt. He was chewing on an unlit cigar.

"My name is Kelligrew Smith, but people call me Kelly Green. I'm the nephew of Peg Leg Smith, and have been my entire life. This distinction meant nothing to me until my parents passed away after trying to smoke some Pinyon Pine needles in imitation of the local Indians. Apparently they did not clean and prepare the pine needles properly, and some sort of poison got into their lungs. They died quite painfully, crying out, 'Pinyon! Pinyon! Pinyon!' with dry cracked lips. But that's a story for another time.

"When I went through their belongings, I came across a letter that was signed 'Peg Leg.' It was written to my mother, Peg Leg's sister." Kelly Green held up an old, yellowed piece of paper. "I was excited that it might be the location of the mine, but alas, it was not. It did, however, tell my dear old mother that he left some treasure for her in the Ironwood Mountains, buried under a pile of rocks where the Aguirre Wash makes a hairpin turn halfway up the mountain. He included a drawing.

"I knew that she had never gone to get the treasure—she didn't expect to die from smoking pine needles! More's the pity because I grew up in a fifteen-by-fifteen-foot shack with my parents and five brothers and sisters. We had to take turns sleeping every three hours during the night because we didn't have enough space for all of us to lay down at once.

"I set out immediately to find the treasure. It was fairly easy to get near, but getting up to the pile of rocks he had marked on the map was difficult, and it took me three months to find the location. I knew I had found it because there was a small sign about fifty yards down slope that said, 'this is what you are looking for.'

"As I drew near, I saw a most curious sight. The entire area was circled by hundreds of turtles, as if they were protecting the rocks. Behind the turtles was a ring of wolves, circling the turtles.

"Curious, I drew closer. When I got about twenty feet away, the turtles stuck their heads out of their shells and made a terrible hissing sound. Then the wolves raised their snouts and began howling. They set up such a racket that other animals and birds begin to chatter and move all through the forest—scrambling, flying, climbing, crawling."

"I took out my rifle, but there were too many of them. I had never been attacked by turtles, and I was pretty sure I could outrun them, but fifty wolves would have a distinct advantage.

"As I stood, wondering what to do, one of the wolves trotted to the pile of rocks and rummaged around. The rest of the animals fell silent. The wolf then came straight at me, slowly, through the circle of turtles and then the circle of wolves. I wasn't sure whether to run or shoot, when I noticed he was carrying a little bag in his mouth. When he was about ten feet from me, he dropped the bag, backed up five feet or so, sat down on his haunches, and looked at me expectantly.

"I moved forward slowly, one step at a time, keeping my eyes on the wolf. He didn't move. I reached down, eyes still forward, and picked up the bag, slowly backing up. The wolf stood up and growled loudly, but did not advance.

"I kept backing up until I was far enough away to turn around and run. When I felt like I had run far enough and didn't hear any pursuit, I stopped and opened the bag. Inside were two golden nuggets, five acorns, and the lower jawbone of a rabbit.

"Not quite the treasure I was hoping for. I went back a year later, with more guns, dynamite, and traps. But a landslide had covered the entire area with rocks, dirt, and uprooted trees. It had utterly changed the landscape. I'm sure there's more treasure up there, but we'll never know. The lost treasure of Peg Leg is lost again!"

There was some applause, and someone shouted, "What did you do with the stuff in the bag?"

Homer, aka Kelly Green, said, "I et the acorns, bought a round of beer for everyone at my favorite saloon, and gave the jawbone to my nephew."

Everyone laughed and applauded. Once it was quiet again, the rest of the contestants went up one by one. Some recited poetry, some sang songs, but all included Peg Leg or his mine, or both, in some direct or indirect way.

One story included a Spanish army made up entirely of elderly men who were sharpshooters but could not move quickly. Two were about finding Peg Leg's mine, but stories such as these were common and not considered the best, as it was a rather obvious way to tell a Peg Leg Smith story. Another claimed that Peg Leg was still alive because he had found not only gold, but also a tributary of the Fountain of Youth, which was a deep aquifer under the desert that ran all the way into Mexico. Interestingly, about half of the storytellers also mentioned finding a peg leg on the way to the contest

The final contestant offered a story about finding a time machine, and going back and marrying Peg Leg's future mother, thus claiming that he was Peg Leg's father and therefore heir-in-reverse. (This contestant had *also* found a wooden leg on his way to the contest.)

Steve leaned over to Harry. "Seems mighty peculiar that seven people in this group have found wooden peg legs on their way here. Over a pretty widespread area. You wouldn't know anything about that, would you?"

Harry held his eyes for a moment, then smiled and said, "I have no idea what you're talking about."

"Uh huh."

The judges awarded first, second, and third place, all of which involved a handmade trophy (which they were required to return for the next year's contest), a free dinner (normally a dollar per person), and, of course, bragging rights, along with some phonograph records and a case of Knott's Berry Farm's fruit preserves.

The next morning, as they were all packing up their tents, sleeping bags, and other belongings, Harry asked Steve for his assessment of the first official Liar's Contest.

"I think it was a smashing success. But we should charge up-front for the food, so we have some operating expenses."

"Excellent idea. I say we do it every January first. It makes for a great tradition, part of the lore of the desert rats. Speaking of desert rats, did you hear Joe Chiriaco got acquitted?"

"Joe is not a desert rat."

"No, but he wishes he were. The judge ruled in his favor."

"Of the beer charge? That still going on?" Steve had forgotten about it until Harry mentioned it.

"Not anymore. Since Joe had been a soldier, the army stood up for him, and the judge threw it out because the whole thing was fishy—why did someone happen to be there to take a picture, and why was the Indian soldier in disguise?"

"I knew about the scheme because Stanley overheard it and warned Joe. Least I think he did. Glad the law worked this time."

"Well, he shouldn't have been selling beer to Indians, if he was."

"Wonder if there is anything illegal about leaving wooden legs all over the place, so people will think they found something historical? Sounds like some chicanery to me." Steve looked sideways at Harry.

"I told you I don't know anything about that."

Never Having Stretched the Truth in my Life…

~1948-1950~

Almost a year later, Steve sat at his desk in Eighth Heaven during a cold December, a fire roaring in the massive fireplace. Puffing away at his pipe, he reviewed a letter he had just drafted. He was hoping that Randall would publish it in *Desert Magazine*

Harry Oliver had again asked him to be a judge at the Peg Leg Liar's Contest—the second official contest, to be held January 1, 1949—just a few weeks. In the interest of the contest's jocularity, he thought he would write this letter protesting the appointment as judge. It could also be good publicity for Desert Center.

Being an honest man, and never having stretched the truth in my life, I am puzzled to know who the hell named me as one of the judges in the Liar's Contest that precedes the Pegleg Smith lost gold trek in Borrego valley New Year's Day.

My personal opinion is that the biggest liar of all is now dead. I refer to Ol' Pegleg Smith. The only thing that he knew about gold was the nuggets he hi-graded from some working mine dump, or stole off an Indian or honest prospector. He would pull out that pocket-worn nugget he carried around and tell a fabulous yarn about where it came from. The reason there are so many different versions of the Pegleg yarn is because he told a different story each time.

But we think it is okay if a lot of folks wish to gather around an open campfire in Borrego Valley New Year's Eve and swap lies, which everybody knowing to be good-natured lies, cannot do any harm.

Maybe after all Ol' Pegleg did not live in vain, if he causes folks to get out in the clean desert hills, while pretending to hunt for a lost mine.

DESERT STEVE RAGSDALE

He nodded his head and smiled, folded it up, and put it in an envelope.

The cabin door opened, and he jumped a bit in surprise. He had forgotten she was coming. A rather long trek from Desert Center. *Can't remember the last time Lydia made the trip with me.*

"Good morning," she said, as she took off her coat and hat. "How is your writing coming along?"

"Just finished my letter about the Peg Leg contest. I'm gonna take it down to the *Desert Magazine* offices after I finish cleaning up breakfast."

"Did you hear Marshall South died?"

"Tragic. I think the divorce did him in."

She nodded. "He made his sons lie in court, saying he beat them because the court wouldn't grant her a divorce without good cause."

"He was a good man. Tanya and the children didn't even attend the funeral."

He collected his papers and began cleaning up the dishes.

She poured herself a cup of coffee from his pot. "Go ahead on down to Palm Desert. I'll clean up for you. You'll be back up after?"

He paused. "Maybe. I should go check on Cactus City, then see how things are going with Stanley."

She frowned. "I'll be here if you decide to come back. I can make dinner. I don't have to be back at work until tomorrow after lunch."

Steve nodded. He donned his coat and hat, said an awkward goodbye, and stepped out into the snow.

He shivered.

Four months after the second annual official Peg Leg Liar's Contest, Steve and John stood in the same area near Borrego Springs. Before them were two structures, built by Steve, about six feet high and six feet wide, both covered by canvas.

"John, you remember at the Liar's Contest, I made a New Year's resolution that I would build a monument to Peg Leg. So I came up with a couple ideas."

"That's why you asked me to meet you here? You built a Peg Leg monument without checking with me?"

"I always keep my resolutions! Don't need to check with anyone to keep my word."

"Good point. Let's see it."

"Slow your horses, I got some things to say first."

"As usual," John muttered, laughing. "Should I make myself comfortable?"

Steve ignored him. "I thought to myself after I made the resolution, that a monument to such a colossal liar should have a few characteristics. One—"

"We don't know he was a liar."

"—don't interrupt. One, there should be a permanent sign memorializing the shyster."

"We don't know he was a—"

"Will you *stop* interrupting? There should be a way to memorialize all the people who come here for the contest and the trek." Steve moved over to the structure on the left and pulled off the canvas. It was a metal sign with painted letters, black on white, which read

PEGLEG SMITH
MONUMENT REGISTER
ERECTED BY
DESERT STEVE
FEB 12. 49

Below the sign, on a little shelf, was a metal mailbox. Steve pulled the door and pulled out a notebook, displaying it for John.

"Everyone who visits here can sign this. A monument to Peg Leg, and a monument to all the people who pay him tribute. Fulfilling my New Year's Eve resolution."

John nodded. "I like it!"

Steve pointed. "You see that space right over there?"

Harry looked. Behind the sign was a circular area, with stakes driven into the ground around it and a rope marking it off. In the middle was a pile of rocks. "Yes?"

"From now on, everyone who attends must bring ten rocks and add them to that pile. I know we did that last year, but I'm making it official. And this—" he stepped over and pulled the canvas off the second structure "—commemorates *that*."

This sign was smaller, and made of wood, with the letters burned into it.

LET THOSE WHO SEEK PEGLEG'S
GOLD ADD TEN ROCKS TO THIS PILE
HARRY OLIVER — 1948

"Why is my name there? You built it."

"Yes, but it was you who started the rock pile. I made the monument."

"Fair enough. And it also publicizes both of our names. You're never one to pass up an opportunity."

Steve laughed. "It's good for business. How do you think I was so successful out here in the desert?"

"Leave it to Desert Steve to make a monument that is not like other monuments. However, you've given me an idea. I'm going to talk to the Borrego Springs Chamber of Commerce, and ask them to register this area as an *official* California historical landmark."

"It should be. Think they'll listen to you? Government bureaucrats never see the value of things as they should."

"I'm currently the mayor, so I might be able to influence them."

Steve turned and looked at his friend. "You're the mayor of Borrego Springs? I didn't know that."

"It pays nothing, there's almost nothing to do, and it comes with no perks. It's mostly listening to complaints and ignoring them. As the founders would have preferred, I suppose. So I don't advertise."

"Clever chap." Steve turned back towards the car. "Let's go get some lunch."

Steve entered the post office and greeted postmaster Johnson. "Did they arrive?"

"I don't know. Let me check."

"Damn it, man, I asked you to be on the lookout for it and let me know!"

The postmaster frowned at him. "Mr. Ragsdale, I do have other duties. If everyone asked me to notify them when they received a package, I could never sort all the mail."

"But everyone doesn't ask you, just me. Do I need to remind you who owns this town?"

"You may own this town, sir, but the Federal government owns the post office. *They* pay me, not you." Before Steve could launch off on a rant, he squatted down to the floor and lifted a large box and set it on the counter. "Here you go. Blythe Printing Company."

"That's it." Steve pulled his knife from his belt and slit open the top of the box, opening the flaps. He smiled as he looked at the stack of books inside, then pulled one off the top and handed it to Johnson. "Here. You get the first copy, you need it. I wrote about how incompetent and useless the government bureaucrats are."

He tossed the little book across the counter to the postmaster. The cover had an American flag with a picture of Steve. In bold letters at the top was the title, *We American Voters Demand True Americanism*. He then picked up the box and left, loading it into the back seat of his new Chevrolet sedan (his second). As he shut the door a voice came from behind him.

"You didn't show last night."

He opened the door to the driver side and started to get in. "No, I didn't."

She flung up her hands. "What the hell, Steve?"

He sighed turned back to her, the open door between them. "I'm sorry. Busy."

She set her jaw and stared at him with a steely look. "You're a damn bastard."

"Yeah. You're not the only one who thinks so."

She turned and stormed off.

"Nuff sed," he said, to no one.

He slid into the seat and dropped his head. "Without women, there would be no bad men. Women are the best. And the worst in the Universe," he mumbled. He raised his eyebrows, grabbed a notebook on the seat beside him, and scribbled down the words he had just spoken. "Not bad."

He strode into the offices of *Desert Magazine*, said hello to the secretary, and walked into Randall's office. McKinney was there, too. In a period they were going over a spread for the new issue.

"Steve," Randall said. "To what do we owe the pleasure?"

"First, the pleasantries. How is married life?"

Randall smiled broadly. "Wonderful."

"Good, Cyria seems like a fine woman. And the wedding was beautiful. Was a good trip to Phoenix, although Lydia complained the whole time."

"Thank you for being there, my friend. What can I do for you today?"

"Got my book from the printer. Wanted to bring you copies." He handed a copy to each.

Randall smiled as he took the book and examined the cover, then flipped open to the table of contents. "This is the one you've been telling me about? Been working on it for a year?"

"Yup. All the main points of what's so wrong with these New Dealers and how it destroys this country. *Desert Sun* said they'd run a notice on it."

McKinney was looking at the table of contents. "Social Security Bushwah. Bootleg Booze Today. Cause and Cure of the

Dirty Deal." He looked up at Steve. "You sure know how to turn a phrase."

"Not sure either of you agree with my thoughts, but it don't matter. It's out there for those who have ears to hear. Or eyes to read."

"I'll look forward to reading it," Randall replied. "Though I am sure I've heard all of your thoughts on the matters. What else are you working on these days?"

"Well now, that's tough to answer in less than an hour. With Stanley running the towns, and Terry's help, I got a lot more time to write. Got a couple new articles for your rag, if you'll have them. Oliver asked me to write some little bits for the *Desert Rats Scrap Book*. Trying to get an article into the *Calexico Chronicle* and *Blythe Herald* newspapers, and another one I hope the *Los Angeles Times* will accept."

"That's great, Steve."

"And, of course, I'm still adding to my book, *Philosophy and Sayings of Desert Steve*. Just came up with a new poem right before I drove here. In fact—"

A secretary stuck her head in. "Sorry to interrupt you gentlemen, but there's a call. For Mr. Ragsdale."

They all frowned, including Desert Steve. "For me?"

Handle pointed to the phone on his desk. "You can take it here unless you want privacy."

"Nah, this is fine."

He took the receiver. "Hello?"

It was Stanley. "Father. Glad I caught you."

"How'd you know I was here?"

"Johnson told me you took your books to Palm Desert, so I figured you were going to see Randall."

"What's wrong?"

"I thought you might want to hear this news before you left Palm Desert. I found out who splashed all that tar and oil on the market building. It was Peterson's kid. I confronted his father, his friends confessed, and he's at the dentist right now. In Palm Desert."

"I thought it might be that little bastard! Thanks son, I'll take care of it right now."

Steve slammed the receiver down. "How many dentists are there in town?"

Both men frowned. McKinney said, "Just the one, over on Portolo. Grimsby."

"Thanks."

With that, Steve rushed out of the office, leaving the two editors perplexed.

Steve pounded on the door. He waited a few seconds, then pounded again. It finally opened to a frowning and irritated Dr. Jack Grimsby, DDS.

"What in tarnation?! Why are you pounding on my office? I got a patient in the chair!"

"Does that patient go by the name of Jackson Peterson?" Steve held up his sheriffs badge to Dr. Grimsby's face.

"What's this…" He seemed to notice the rifle in Steve's other hand for the first time. "What's going on?"

"I'm Steve Ragsdale, I own Desert Center, and I'm the sheriff. Is he in there are or not, doctor? Impeding an officer of the law carrying out his duty is—"

"Yes, yes, he's here. He's in the chair. I just gave him Novocaine."

"That young man vandalized my market building, and I think he's also the one that vandalized the service station last month. I'm arresting the little bastard."

The doctor examined the badge. "Officer Ragsdale, do you have a warrant for his arrest?"

"My warrant is this badge and his crime. His friends Pinky and Julianne 'fessed up to being with him when he did it. Hand him over."

The doctor sighed. "This is not your jurisdiction. Can't you wait until he gets back to Desert Center?"

"No can do. Been trying to find the culprit for a month. Ain't nobody gonna treat my town like that."

"See here. What if I promise to call the police right now and have them come over and talk to you and let *them* arrest him, will that be okay?"

Steve considered for a moment. It was true, he had no jurisdiction to arrest anyone here without a warrant. Damn. Getting harder and harder to dispense justice in this country, even when you have them dead to rights.

"Very well. But only because I assume you're a man of your word. Call them now. And don't say a word to Jackson, I don't want him lighting out. I'll wait in my car."

The doctor relaxed. "Thank you."

"But if that rat leaves before they get here, I'm gonna have you arrested, too, for interfering with police action."

"I'll make the call. Please wait in your car."

The doctor closed the door, and Steve heard the lock click. Whether it was to keep him out or the boy in, Steve was unsure.

One good thing about progress: with the new paved road, one didn't have to pay so much attention to the road. Left a lot of time for thinking.

The new roads brought more traffic, too—an average of five hundred cars a day drove by Desert Center. Not all of them stopped, of course, but many did. Steve's little town was worth about half a million dollars now, and going strong. He was no longer dependent on aqueducts, wars, or iron mines. With excellent employees like Stanley and Terry, he had far more time to think, read, and write. And the roads made it easier for him to get to Eighth Heaven.

With things going so well, he had bought some property in Pinyon Pines, a beautiful little valley in the mountains above Palm Desert, on the way up to Eighth Heaven. He had begun building a small house there. Maybe it would make Lydia happier, since she didn't like the road up to Eighth Heaven.

Back in Desert Center, Steve stepped into the office and stopped at the sight of Stanley sitting behind the desk.

"I didn't arrest the bastard, but I did get the local police to arrest—"

Stanley hadn't even acknowledged his father's entrance, but was staring at the blank wall across from him.

"What is it, Stanley?"

Not changing his gaze, he said, "You better get home to Mother."

Steve's heart skipped a beat. "Is she okay?"

Finally, Stanley turned and looked at his father, but his face was still blank. "No. You need to go."

Steve turned and fled out of the office, running down the street towards their house, forgetting his car. What could've happened? He knew she hadn't been herself for a while, hardly talking to him. Was she sick? Or—

He took the steps in two leaps and threw open the door. As he started back to their bedroom he saw Lydia was sitting on the couch.

"Lydia? Are you okay?"

She had obviously been crying. Not looking at him, she pointed to a letter sitting on the coffee table before her. Frowning in concern, Steve picked it up and read the short, scribbled paragraph.

"Oh, no," he said, and dropped to his knees.

Betwixt-and-Between
(1950-1971)

Whom the Gods Would Destroy...

~1950~

"Please, Lydia, I beg your forgiveness." Steve was on his knees before her as she sat on the couch with her head in her hands, sobbing.

"Lydia, you are the love of my life. I do not know why I—"

Lydia jerked up. "That's a *lie*! Bastard. If you loved me, you would never have carried on with that woman. You—"

"No, my dear, no, it isn't true. I did sin, but it was temptation and weakness. It's not the man I am."

Her face became steely. "Yes, it is. You are an arrogant, selfish, putrid man. As I have been telling you for some time."

A rush of thoughts came over him. *Whom the gods would destroy, they first make famous.*

No, cried part of his mind. *I didn't mean to do any harm. I just had so much to do, so many people to deal with and...*

He started to get angry. How dare she criticize him for one sin, when he had done was so many good things, when he had cared for her, when he had done things that no one else could've accomplished. For months—no, *years*—she had been critical and distant and irritable.

Yet, Steve was too logical for such rationalizations. Those things might all be true, but it didn't make wrongdoing right.

Certainly not an ill-advised dalliance. There were reasons perhaps—but no excuses.

He, Steve Albert Ragsdale, a man of God, who preached discipline and hard work, had acted the hypocrite.

Steve's head dropped, "I...I confess it. Like King David, I was given much and I stopped paying attention. Confession is good for the soul, and I confess all to you now. I *am* a despicable man, an arrogant hypocrite. Please forgive me."

Lydia put her face back into her hands, elbows on the table. She was no longer crying. It had been replaced with a cold distance.

"I've heard all your sermons, Steve. And I was naïve enough to think you believed them."

"I did! And do! That does not mean I am not susceptible to the temptations."

"You." She looked at him through her hands. "You, of all people. You berated everyone in Coffeyville who touched liquor or visited a brothel. You condemned Poppy for his bar business *from the pulpit*. You trash poor sweet Joe Chiriaco for simply trying to *imitate you* in building a desert town. You ran people out of town because they didn't do exactly like you wanted. You set yourself up as a desert god, dispensing your own brand of justice. And then a...a...*this*. With one of your employees! Why should I believe *anything* you say?!"

Steve fell back on his haunches, then forward on his face, like a child.

The morning was still, except for the occasionally neighing of a horse and bleating of a goat. The sunlight fell through the front window, making dust mites visible. They drifted slowly across the sunbeams.

He sighed. "I am deeply sorry, Lydia. We have grown apart. I have been too busy, you have been distance and critic—you won't hardly even go with me to Eighth Heaven when I ask, and—"

"Stop!" She stood, her eyes red and face blotchy. Steve sat up, alarmed. "Don't you *dare* blame this on me. I want you out of here by nightfall. I cannot kick you out of your precious town, but I can kick you out of this house. Go live with your partner in sin. Or under a rock. I don't care." She stood, looking down at him with a fierceness he had never seen from her.

"What about the house I'm building on Pinyon Flats for us? What about the 29th anniversary party at the café on September 24? The chef is going to bake 129 cakes for it. We got speakers scheduled, advertised it, we—"

"See? All you care about is your business! I'm going to visit my brother in Fresno for a few weeks. Do whatever you want. I want you out of this house before I get back."

Steve nodded, looked around the room, then slowly stood and bowed his head. He took a deep breath.

She waited, jaw clenched.

He nodded. "Perhaps *you* cannot kick me out of my own town. But I can. I'll exile myself. My punishment is to be cast out, like Adam and Eve out of the Garden."

They stood six feet apart, staring at each other. Steve's eyes, pleading for mercy. In Lydia's eyes, only hatred.

Finally, she shook her head in disgust and left the room. Steve collapsed into a chair as the front screen door slammed shut.

He stood back and looked at his handiwork. A nice painted wooden sign, white background with black letters. He didn't need a metal sign here, like down in the desert, where the sun would quickly bake and peel the paint. He nailed the sign to the post that he had planted in the ground in front of the little house.

He stood back and looked with approval. The home was nothing fancy, more like a cabin. But unlike Eighth Heaven, this one had a living area, a kitchen, and a bedroom. A small fireplace. Quite small, yes, but it would've been a perfect little getaway for him and Lydia.

Now, it was one of the two places he would live, since he had nowhere in Desert Center now.

Of course, he still had the shack on The Alligator. But it was quite small, and had no fireplace. Nothing but a roof over his head, a table, and a chair. A great place for writing and reading, when it wasn't scorching hot.

This place would be perfect, and if he would rather not drive all the way up to Santa Rosa Peak, he could live here. Easier to get to Cactus City, Skyway, and Utopia.

He looked over his property. He needed a shed for his goats. He had built one out of sheet metal up at Eighth Heaven, and would do the same here, even though there was water readily available. He had become used to goat milk, and he was fairly certain the goats enjoyed the rides back and forth.

"Hey, neighbor!"

Steve turned around to see a man and woman approaching.

"Good afternoon."

"This your place? We live up on the other side, been here for a few years. I'm Hector and this is my wife, Betty."

Steve wiped his hand off on his shirt and stuck out his hand. "Steve Ragsdale."

Hector shook his hand. "Desert Steve Ragsdale?"

Steve doffed his hat. "One and the same."

"A pleasure to meet you! Didn't know we had a celebrity here. Thought you were from Desert Center?"

"Oh, I am. But I have a place up on Santa Rosa Peak, and I bought this one earlier last year. My son Stanley runs the day-to-day businesses."

"Betty and I have stopped many times at your café. Wonderful place."

"Thank you."

"May I ask you, Mr. Ragsdale? What is the sign mean?"

"I got a writing shack in Desert Center called 'The Alligator.' My cabin up on the peak is 'Eighth Heaven.' I didn't want this place to feel left out, so I've given it a name as well."

All three turn to look at the sign:

Betwixt-and-Between

A Courageous Pioneer and the World's Worst Poet

~1951-1952~

At the knock, Steve went to the door and opened it. Stanley was standing outside, shuffling his feet.

"Hello, Stanley, thank you for making the trip here."

"Sure, father. I've been wanting to see your new house here, anyway."

Since his dalliance had become public, Herbert, Thelma, and Thurman had not spoken to him. He had tried to call, but if anyone answered they hung up immediately when he announced himself. Stanley seemed mostly normal. He'd always been Steve's right-hand man. But there was a slight distance that had not been there before. Perhaps a bit more formality.

"Looks good," Stanley said, looking around. He then turned back to his father. "You said it was quite important."

"I'll get right to it." He motioned for Stanley to sit down, and he sat across from him. "I ain't getting any younger, and running Desert Center and the other towns, plus my writing, I can't do it all anymore. You've been doing a fine job with Utopia and continuing to help out in DC and the others."

"Thank you."

Steve knew that Stanley cherished what they had. More importantly, Stanley believed in the same things that Steve did. The things that made Desert Center successful.

"It's time to semi-retire. I'll still oversee Desert Center and others, but more like a chairman. I own it, but I want you to take over. And at some point I'll sell it to you for a dollar. How does that sound?"

If Stanley was surprised, he hid it. "Father, you're as spry as ever. Is this necessary? Is there something else going on?" He seemed genuinely concerned.

He shrugged. "Only the obvious. Although I am getting slower, maybe you haven't seen it. But, I am, in general, exiling myself."

Stanley raised his eyebrows. "From Desert Center?"

Steve hesitated. "For the moment, at least. I cannot live at home, and your mother wants nothing to do with me. Obviously, I cannot abandon Desert Center. I will check in with you frequently. I'll visit the other towns so you can focus on DC. And if we need to meet we can do it at one of those towns, or here, or even over at The Alligator. Maybe eventually I can be back in town."

Stanley stared off into space for a moment, a variety of emotions playing across his face.

"You know how much I love DC. Ain't going anywhere. Though Crystal and I are looking at moving out to Lake Tamarisk into a nicer house with the children. And I got some great ideas—I think we need another service station, and I'd like to put up a hamburger stand."

Steve nodded. Stanley was definitely his son in his thoughts and desires. He'd do an outstanding job at keeping a Ragsdale in charge of Desert Center for a long time. And then perhaps his children, and so on. "All of that sounds good, I don't see a problem living in Lake Tamarisk. I'd appreciate it if you run ideas by me for anything major, but the daily running is up to you. 'Course, I am always here to advise or help in any way. I do still own the thousand acres."

"Thank you. It's quite an honor and I am happy to do so. Thrilled, really."

Steve asked him about Crystal and the boys, they talked a bit about the desert and a few other things. He offered him lunch, but Stanley said he needed to get back. Not only did he want to let Crystal know, but he had a town to run!

After he left, Steve made a pot of coffee and sat in his favorite chair that he'd brought down from the Santa Rosa cabin. He lifted the latest issue of *Desert Magazine* from the table beside him. Randall had written an article about Steve, and he was flattered when Randall told him. And a bit surprised. The magazine didn't usually do biographies unless someone was dead. (Steve asked Randall if he knew something he didn't know.)

Randall's response was that Desert Steve had impacted the area more than anyone else in the past thirty years, and it needed to be documented. Steve suspected his old friend was also trying to rehabilitate his status. Randall, after all, had been divorced as well before he married Celia. Steve had gotten a lot of criticism—deserved—although not much to his face. People don't care much for hypocrites, especially religious ones. As if they aren't as susceptible to weaknesses as any human.

Randall had asked if he wanted to see the piece before it went to press, but Steve declined. Steve trusted him. He would rather not influence him in any way, but was curious what he had written.

He flipped to the table of contents, but did not see anything with Randall's byline. He flipped to the Randall's regular piece, "Just Between You and Me, by the Editor." Nothing there, either, just a call for people to take better care as they

travel among the date gardens along Highway 111 between Indio and Palm Springs, and some updates and history of the
magazine.

Maybe it didn't make the issue. He went back and flipped
through, page by page. And there it was. Right after an article
by Jean McElrath about Marty Hess, a prospector looking for
uranium, entitled "He Tells 'Em How to Find Uranium." *How
times have changed,* Steve thought. *Used to be, they only
looked for gold or iron.*

"A Courageous Pioneer and the World's Worst Poet" was the
title. Steve laughed—Randall always told him how bad his poetry was. (He was not the only one.) Steve didn't care, he
thought it was good and it said what he wanted, in his style.

He began reading. It described how he left Blythe and bought
Gruendike's Well, and everyone thought he was crazy. How
Desert Center had just celebrated its twenty-ninth year, becoming "one of the best known and patronized service stations in
the California Desert," worth half a million dollars now. Randall even quoted Steve's motto, "Honesty, Industry, and Sobriety," which was posted at all of his businesses. That's right—
being a responsible citizen means being honest with your employees and customers, working hard, and not giving in to the
Devil's Brew.

Steve felt a pang of guilt at the word "honesty." He had surely failed at that—but it was the first time in his life with any
significance. Pretty good record at age sixty-eight, if you asked
him. And he had learned a lesson in humility.

The story closed with a description of the twenty-ninth anniversary celebration. Steve had the chef bake 129 cakes, and
served each slice with ice cream—for free—to all who stopped
by. Steve also had several speakers come out and present talks
about the history of the desert, including Randall, along with
Harry Oliver, John Hilton, Edmund Jaeger, and others.

Steve smiled. Short, but to the point, capturing the most important things about him (except the poetry, but that was humorous, and no one could say Steve didn't have a sense of humor).

He laid the magazine aside. It reminded him of a piece of poetry he'd been working on last night, about hospitality. He wanted to post it at Eighth Heaven. He read it over, then made a few edits.

> *If hungry, then come to our house made of logs,*
> *we will share our beans and also our hog,*
> *but don't shoot a deer or birds, my friend,*
> *if I catch you at it, I'll kick your rear end.*

Or maybe he'd take it down to Randall at the magazine's offices when he headed back east. Perhaps he'd see fit to publish some of his "bad poetry" and let the people decide, in the spirit of true democracy.

Steve laughed and went to get another cup of coffee.

A year and a half later, Steve had a good system in place. His complete exile did not last long, although his presence in town was never the same. Stanley had long been involved in the workings of Desert Center, so he did a good job taking over the day-to-day operations. He didn't have the experience or knowledge that Steve had, but much of that could come with time. Steve began to focus more on the other little towns and outposts that he owned, while mostly just checking in at Desert Center.

After the first few months, Steve approached Lydia and asked her if she could forgive him. She told him that was God's job, not hers. He took exception to that, and recited the part of the Lord's Prayers where it says, "and forgive us of ours sins, *as we forgive those who sin against us*." She slammed the door in his face.

The second time he tried to talk to her, she was a bit kinder. But she told him, in no uncertain terms would they ever be husband and wife again.

They developed a détente. Steve spent most of his time at Betwixt-and-Between or Eighth Heaven, or visiting Cactus City and Utopia, but would come into Desert Center once a week or so to check on things and take care of anything that was needed from him. He told her he would always let Stanley know when he would be there, and Stanley would let her know. If he had to stay overnight, he would sleep at The Alligator, although he had a plan to use one of the cabins on the opposite side of town from Lydia's house once it was vacant.

Stanley was becoming the same towards him as he used to be, but his boys would have nothing to do with their grandfather. He was pretty sure it was their grandmother's influence, and not Stanley.

Today was one of his days in Desert Center, and as he walked in the café, he was surprised to see a crowd of people around a table where sat Frank Hines, one of the mechanics.

Steve pushed his way past everyone.

Frank looked up. "Mr. Ragsdale! Did you hear?"

"Hear what?"

"I nearly got nabbed by a flying saucer."

Steve gave him a steely look. "Didn't know you was fond of the bottle, Frank."

"You know I don't drink except on weekends! And only a beer or two." Someone snickered. "And never in Desert Center!" he added quickly. "No. This was real."

"Suppose you tell me?" Steve took a seat across from Frank. He gave some nasty looks to the people crowded around his chair, to which they muttered some apologies and back up a little.

"I was driving up along 60 last night, when out in front of me, way up in the sky, was a dim light. Just standing there."

"How high?"

"I don't know. Way up, maybe. But it just *hovered* there."

"You was traveling east, weren't you?"

"Yeah. How'd you know?"

"Because planes flying into Palm Spring would be flying right at you, and look like they're standing still. That's what it was."

Frank shook his head. "No, because it *moved*. It dropped way down, almost in front of me, then sped up—right at me!"

"That ain't no plane," someone said behind Steve.

"I started slowing down, and then this big...gray, huge, like the size of this café, buzzed right over my head."

Steve shook his head. "Still coulda been a plane. Trying to scare you. Playing around."

"It had no wings. No windows. No landing gear. No props, and no jet exhaust. And get this—"

"Thought you said it was last night. How'd you see all that in the dark?"

"Because it was all lit up. Like nothing I ever seen. I'm telling you, it was a UFO."

The same voice behind Steve spoke again. "There was another sighting a couple of weeks ago in Borrego Springs. And a few months ago, same thing you just described, between here and Blythe. Definitely UFOs. They're checking us out."

Steve stood up. "Well, you can spread that tomfoolery if you wish. Maybe it was a military project, some secret plane they're working on."

Someone on the other side of the table said, "Tell him what happened after that!"

Frank nodded. "It went off to the side, then swerved back and hovered right over my truck! Stayed there about a mile or two, then shot off into the sky. I was scared to death!"

"Well, then it was probably a helicopter," Steve said. "But more likely it was your addled brains."

He stood up and made his way through the throng of people, as all of them began talking at once. Heading to the counter, he asked Ruby if the latest issue of the *Blythe Herald* had arrived. She retrieved it from behind the counter. "Here you go—I put it aside as you asked."

"Thank you. Everything okay?"

She nodded. "It's fine. 'Cept for that crazy crew." She rolled her head towards the UFO table.

"As long as they keep buying coffee or food, consider it a business opportunity. Otherwise, if they're just loitering, kick 'em out."

He took the paper and sat down at the far booth in the corner. Flipping to the "letters to the editor" section, he scanned the content, then slammed it down.

"Damned papers." He had written an article about the dangers of welfare in creating a lazy class. Pay people to do nothing, and they'll keep doing nothing. If the government types wanted to get into helping people—the church's job!—they should at least make them work for it. Work on roads, telephone lines—something.

Steve often helped people out. He considered it a duty of all Christians. If they were elderly or incapacitated, it was free. But if they could work, he gave them a job to do, and paid them properly for it. In fact, some of his current employees in the town had been down on their luck when they were first hired, and that's how they found gainful employment. The country would be better off if they'd listen to Steve.

Or at least print his letters.

Bugs in His Head
~1952~

On Mondays, Steve drove to Desert Center and checked in with Stanley, then spent time with Terry going over the businesses, new projects, any issues that needed his input or decision. After that, he would drive to Cactus City to check on it.

Then he'd head back to Desert Center and stay the night. Two years after his exile, he had a little cabin on the west end of town—the opposite end from where Lydia lived. Ruby told him that she was at the café two or three days a week, checking on things and keeping the books. When Steve was in town, she stayed home.

On Tuesdays and Wednesdays, he would visit Skyway, Box Canyon, Utopia, and Shaver's Well. All little stops modeled after Desert Center on a smaller scale. Fuel, minor repair facilities (more sophisticated work would be towed to DC), and a place to get something to eat and drink. All were doing well, although Hell was the most problematic because it was between Cactus City and Desert Center, and probably not necessary with the modern roads.

Today, however, he had a different task. Hitching a ride with a local desert rat, One-Eye Dustin, to Mecca. He'd gotten a call from the Riverside Sheriff's department that there was a man with a warrant out for his arrest, staying at a flop house in Mecca. Since there was no sheriff in Mecca, they asked him to make the arrest, being the closest. He didn't do much police work anymore. There was an officer in Desert Center, but he was happy to help when needed.

He stood outside the cheap hotel, having checked out the property from a distance, making sure the man couldn't run if he got wind of an officer of the law outside.

He went to the front desk and flashed his badge. "Officer Ragsdale. I got a warrant here for the arrest of one of your guests, Jimmy Padilla. Tell me what room is in."

The poor boy behind the counter didn't even ask to see the warrant, as he should have. He looked scared. Steve didn't bother to tell him that there was no danger: the man had been robbing houses in the area and was wanted in Riverside for several other burglaries of businesses. He targeted them at night when no one was around, but in two encounters with security guards, from which he escaped, he did not have any weapons.

Steve walked back to the room and knocked on the door. He waited thirty seconds, then knocked harder.

"Police. Open up, Jimmy."

He heard some commotion from the inside and a voice. Was there someone with him? Steve pulled his pistol from the holster at his side and cocked the trigger.

"Open the door, Jimmy, and this will go a lot easier for you. I know you're in there, and I don't wanna have to break down the door."

After a couple of seconds, he heard the chain of the door lock being slid aside and the door opened slowly. Steve shoved fast and hard on the door with one hand, the other pointing the gun at Jimmy's head. His eyes darted around the room. Empty.

Jimmy's hands flew up. "Okay, okay, I'm here, don't shoot!"

"Anybody else in here?"

"My friend, Delia."

"Tell her to come out, her hands up."

Jimmy raised his head slightly and said, "Come on out Delia! It's the cops, they got us good. They won't hurt us if we cooperate."

Steve waited. There were no sounds from the bathroom.

"I guess she's not coming out." Steve said. "I'm gonna cuff you to this bed and go get her."

Jimmy's eyes bulged. "Are you blind? She's right there," he said, nodding to his right.

"Where?"

"Right beside me!"

"You playing with me, pal? Give me your wrist."

"I ain't playing no games. I'm going along. So is she!" He complied and Steve cuffed one hand, pushed him down to the floor, and attached the other to the leg of the bed.

He opened the small closet. Empty, with just a few unused hangers dangling haphazardly.

Going to the bathroom door, he knocked. "Delia? Come on out or things are going to get a lot worse for you."

Nothing. Gun at ready, he checked the door knob. Unlocked. He threw it open, canvassing the small bathroom.

It was empty.

A simple sink, toilet, and bathtub with a shower curtain which was drawn open. The window high above was intact, too small for any human. He went back to Jimmy.

"Apparently she escaped through the toilet."

Jimmy, sitting on the bed looking down, shook his head. "I don't know what's wrong with you, man. She been sitting across from me the whole time."

Steve looked at the other bed, then back at Jimmy. "Okay, let's go. We're gonna take a train ride. Tell Dalia to follow along." He released the cuff and fastened it on Jimmy's other wrist, behind his back. He pushed him in front, towards the door.

"Come on, Delia," Jimmy said. "This man is going to take us on a train ride."

The train station was less than half a mile away, so they trudged along, Jimmy chattering away to the invisible woman. Steve showed his badge at the small office. The man behind the counter waved them through.

When the train arrived in Thermal, an old prospector got on board. Steve did not recognize him. He took a seat across from Steve and his prisoner.

"Hey, you're Desert Steve!"

Steve nodded. "I am."

"Met you a couple years ago at the Peg Leg Liar's Contest. Name's Dillon. Dillon Thompson. You're a sheriff?"

"Sheriff, proprietor, founder, and owner of Desert Center, among other things. Pleasure to meet you again, Dylan."

Dylan nodded at Steve's prisoner. "What's he done, Steve?"

"Bugs." Steve pointed to his head. "Wanted for robberies."

"Bugs in his head and his hands tied! No wonder he's crazy!" The man cackled.

Steve shook his head and wondered how many other tetched people he would see today. The world was truly falling apart.

Steve enjoyed living at Betwixt-and-Between. The neighbors were friendly and it was a respite from the heat. It was also closer to Palm Desert, so he was able to see Randall more often.

He still went up to Eighth Heaven, but not as often—especially not in the winter. He had gotten to know a man who lived nearby on the other slope—Charles Kaplan, who kept an eye on his cabin when Steve was gone.

His travels to Desert Center and the others became less frequent. They ran smoothly, with Stanley running things and hiring responsible managers. The proliferation of the telephone had made running the businesses easier, too.

Today, however, he had gone to visit Skyway, merely because he had not been there in over a month. On his way back to Desert Center, about five miles out, he spotted the three cars on the side of the road. Peering ahead through the windshield, it looked as if they were occupied.

There had been a string of armed robberies in the area. Reports were that it was three or four middle-aged men. He reached over into the back seat and pulled his rifle out as he slowed and came to a stop behind the cars. Keeping an eye on them, he took his sheriff's badge out of the glove compartment and clipped it on his vest.

Two people in the first car, three in the second, and he could not see the front car. He got out, leaving the door open, and walked slowly towards the last car, rifle down but ready. A man stuck his head out of the driver's side as Steve approached.

"Hello! We're not broken down, just stopped a bit." Two middle-aged men, younger than the reports of the robbers. "Officer," he added, as he saw the badge and the rifle.

Steve looked up at the other two cars. There was no one in the front car. Five men total. The car door of the second car opened.

"Stay in the car!" Steve shouted. The figure slid back in and shut the door. He turned back to the driver. "Identification, please. Both of you. Keep your hands where I can see 'em."

"Sure, officer, no problem."

Steve watched them carefully, glancing periodically at the other car, as the two men took out wallets and handed him their drivers licenses. Steve looked them over. They did not fit the profile of the burglars.

"You Adamski or Peterson?"

"Adamski, sir."

"Thank you, Adamski. Those three with you?" He nodded to the car ahead.

"Yes, sir. We're all friends, traveling from Phoenix."

"That's fine. Stopped you because we've had some burglaries in the area recently. Do you mind telling me what you are doing stopped here?"

"Sure, but you ain't gonna believe it. See, we was driving through, and we saw a UFO hovering right over there." He pointed to the south.

Oh no, Steve thought. *Not again.* "That so?"

"Yup. Was shaped like a huge thick cigar, all silver—"

"—thought we decided it was like a flying submarine—" This was his passenger, a large man with longish curly hair.

"Whatever," Adamski continued. "I was pretty sure they was looking for me, so I set out—"

"Stop," Steve interrupted. "They were looking for you?"

"Yes, I believe so. I been contacted by aliens a few times, and they told me they would come back for me."

Oh, Lord, why didn't I just drive on past. My damned sense of duty... "And your friends?"

"They stayed behind. I went—"

"—yeah, we don't wanna be abducted like Adamski here—"

"—right up below the ship. A little scout ship came out of the bigger ship and landed beside me. And the alien who I met before—Orthon is his name, near as I can tell—and his pilot got out. They're from Venus."

"Are they?" Steve replied. "And how do you know that?"

Adamski looked baffled. "They told me."

Steve nodded, then leaned further in and looked at the passenger. "Did you see this meeting?"

"Yessir. We were all standing out here by the cars. We didn't see nothin' land, but we saw him talking to someone. Too far away to see anything else."

"Yup, they were afraid, but not me. They been looking for someone on Earth like me."

Steve wanted to end this as quickly as possible, but his curiosity about this crazy story getting the best of him. "What happened?"

"Nothing. They just told me they were still doing research, and would contact me later. Told me to wait nearby. So we're getting ready to drive on down the road and see if we can find a place to stay. Saw a sign for Desert Center. Do you know if it has lodgings?"

Steve decided against telling them it was his town. "Yes. Cabins, trailers, and such. Go to the café and they'll help you out."

"Very obliged, officer. This is big stuff, and I'm gonna write a book about what I learn. They are clever and loving."

"That's good. Wouldn't want trouble from aliens." He almost let them go at that point, but felt like he should do his due diligence as an officer of the law. "You stay put, I'm gonna go talk to these three, then you can be on your way."

The three other men had the same story. They were not burglars—just crazy. They seemed harmless, and their money would be as good as anyone else's in Desert Center.

Back at Adamski's vehicle, he returned their licenses. "Men, you aren't doing anything dangerous or illegal. Follow the speed limit, don't cause no trouble."

"Yes, officer! Of course."

Steve got back in his car, shaking his head. The desert was a great place, but it did attract crazies.

The High Cost of Dying
~1958~

"I've decided to sell *Desert Magazine*."

Steve looked up from his coffee. "You're selling? Randall, you founded it and have been running it for twenty years."

Randall sat back and sighed. "I don't want to. But I'm getting old, my friend. It's time for me to slow down a bit."

"I understand." He sighed. "It's getting harder for me to get up to Eighth Heaven, let alone do all the work that it needs. Especially in the winter. I've even considered selling it and living at Betwixt-and-Between and Desert Center."

"That might be even sadder than me selling the magazine."

The two men sat silently for a while.

"Who you gonna sell it too? And when?"

"Charles Shelton."

"Your assistant editor? Seems like a good choice."

"He's been with me for years. Going to sign it over on my 70th birthday this April. I'll keep working there some, doing some writing and editing. I just can't run it any longer. More time to work on my books, anyway."

"That's quite some news. I'm not sure what to say."

"You can say, 'congratulations for the great run.' All good things must come to an end."

"I suppose. Except for the things eternal. Well, Randall," Steve lifted his coffee cup, "here's to being part of desert history and the next chapter in your life."

The two old desert rats clinked their mugs together and took sips of the bold coffee.

"This is the happiest moment of my life," Harry Oliver told the crowd gathered for the dedication. "I have a lump in my throat so big it will take at least four bourbons to wash it down."

The crowd laughed appreciably. Steve kept his face impassive. He loved Harry, despite his cavalier attitude towards alcohol.

"We all know the story of Peg Leg—or at least some of it. And many of the conflicting stories. We know he was a prospector, an Indian scout, a fur-trader, a mountain man, and a teller of tall tales—and especially the story of his gold mine. Every few years, someone says they found it. But it always turns out to be either a hoax, a lie, or a mistake. So far.

"In honor of this great adventurer, storyteller, and legend of the desert, Desert Steve and I started the official Peg Leg's Liar's Contest and Trek, held every January first, right here."

"Tell 'em about the peg legs all over the desert!" someone shouted from the crowd. Steve could not see who it was, but it sounded like John Hilton.

"Ah, yes, well…" Harry smiled. "Many wooden peg legs have been found in the desert, purportedly belonging to Smith —who often used his leg as a weapon. How those peg legs have ended up there, and whether they really belonged to old Peg Leg, who knows?"

"You do!" Shouted someone else, to more laughter. This was Edmund Jaegar.

Harry smiled. "And now, without further ado, here is Officer Underwood from the California State Park Commission." Harry gave way and made his way into the crowd to stand beside Steve.

Steve patted him on the back. "About time they did this."

An older man in the uniform of the State Park took Oliver's place and cleared his throat.

"We are pleased to have worked with the Borrego Springs Chamber of Commerce to erect this monument. While we do not know the truth of the mine, we know that Mr. Smith was a historical person who has had quite an effect on the lore and the legends of the deserts of California. It is only fitting that we unveil this monument to him and that legacy. We thank Harry Oliver for his decades of work in keeping the legend alive, and many others who have done so as well."

He nodded to two young men nearby, who took up spots on either side of the canvas-covered monument.

"On behalf of the State of California, I hereby dedicate this monument, Marker Number 750, located at 33° 17.773′ N, 116° 17.884′ W, to Thomas Long 'Peg Leg' Smith, here in the Anza-Borrego Desert State Park."

With another nod, the men pulled the tarp away to reveal a squat stone column, with a metal plaque, inscribed

PEG LEG SMITH
Thomas L. Smith, better known as Peg Leg Smith, 1801–1866, was a mountain man, prospector, and spinner of tall tales. Legends regarding his lost mine have grown through the years. Countless people have searched the desert looking for its fabulous wealth. The

gold mine possibly could be within a few miles of this monument.

CALIFORNIA REGISTERED HISTORICAL LAND-MARK NO. 750

The crowd applauded and a few gave cheers. Someone yelled, "Now let's go find that mine!" The officer thanked everyone for coming and dismissed the crowd.

Steve walked to the monument and stood in front, reading. Harry joined him.

"Well, Harry, I will say that these words on this here plaque do not sound like the normal boring State Park Historical Markers. 'The gold mine could possibly be within a few miles...?'"

Harry looked at Steve. "It could be."

Steve pursed his lips. "Do you have something you'd like to tell me?"

"I suppose I did have a hand in writing the text."

"Had a hand?" Steve raised his eyebrows.

Harry smiled. "I might have talked them into letting me write the inscription. But they approved it!"

Randall, John, and Edmund joined them.

"Excellent work, Harry. I'm glad you finally got them to do this," Jaegar said.

"It took years of bothering them about it. I think ten years of the Liar's Contest helped. So Steve is part of this, as well."

"I would say that the four of you," Randall said, "have done more for the desert and its lore than any other four men still living."

"You're included in that, without question." The others joined in with agreement. Steve turning to John. "Was that you that yelled out from the crowd, John? About the peg legs?"

372

"To quote our famous friend here, 'who knows?'" he said with a grin.

Steve sat in a chair in Stanley's office. He had just come from Pinyon Flats after getting a call from Mecca. Terry had moved to Pinyon Flats to better help him out, but today, he needed to be with someone in the family.

It couldn't be Lydia, even if he wished it so. Besides, he knew she got the same call. For a few years, on occasion, he would walk down to Lydia's house and knock on the door. She always answered. He would ask to come in, and she would seem put out, but would invite him into the dark paneled living room. She would offer him some coffee, and after some brief chatting about their health, their children, and other news, he would wish her the best and take his leave.

He always left feeling worse than he did before. So after a few years, he stopped.

The office door opened and Stanley lumbered in. Steve thought he had gained even more weight than the last time he saw him. The damage to his face from the sun could not hide that he was a man of the desert.

"Father! Didn't know you were in town." He stopped abruptly, seeing the look on his father's face. "What's wrong?"

"You haven't talked to your mother?"

Stanley frowned. "No. I just got in from Calexico."

"I got a call from Thelma. Your brother Herbert is dead."

Stanley sat down slowly. "What? How?"

"Don't know. Said they found him in the morning, in his bed."

"Have you talked to mother? Or the others?"

"No. I drove right here. I'm sure they called her already."

"I can't believe it." Stanley moved about the room aimlessly. "He was…what, fifty?"

"Forty-nine last May."

Stanley sat down in a chair across from Steve. "I just saw him a few months ago. He was passing through between Redlands and Mecca. He seemed to be doing well."

Steve didn't respond.

"Thurman found him?"

"Yes. They were all in Mecca."

"I guess I should go see Mother. And call Thelma."

Steve stood up. "Good. I'm going to go to The Alligator. I'll call Thurman and Thelma first." He paused. "Need to find out about funeral arrangements."

"I'll take care of it and let you know."

Stanley nodded. The two desert men, father and son, stood for a moment, then hugged briefly.

Steve flipped the welder's mask back down over his face and continued working on the metal plaque. He'd been needing to do this for a long time. With all the deaths lately, if he put it off much longer, it would be too late.

Always strong and spry, he felt himself slowing down. Doc was worried about his heart. If he was honest with himself, his breathing did not seem like what it used to be, either. He only noticed it when he was climbing steep slopes. When he lit up his pipe, he coughed more than he used to.

He started to light the torch again to weld the last line in place, when he caught a motion to his left. A boy was standing in the garage entrance, watching.

Steve straightened and flipped the mask up. "What are you doing there, Dan?"

Dan was one of the children of the local employees at the Eagle Mountain Mine. Steve had seen him hanging around the Desert Center garage often, sometimes even helping out pumping gas for customers just for the fun of it. Steve guessed he was about ten years old.

"Nuthin'. Just watching."

"You interested in welding?"

"I don't know. Maybe. It looks interesting."

Steve put down the torch and picked up a second welding helmet. "Safety is always first when working with machinery of any kind. Come over here and put this on, and these here gloves, and you can stand next to me. I'll show you."

The boy's face lit up. "Thank you, Mr. Ragsdale!" the helmet was too big for him and looked a bit comical. Steve smothered a laugh.

"Do know what this is I'm working on?"

"A sign?"

"Of sorts. It's a metal plaque that's going to go over my grave when I die."

The boy's eyes got big. "Are you going to die?"

Steve laughed. "We all die. I'm a lot closer than you are, so I figured I oughta do it."

Steve showed him how he ran the bead of solder along the edge of the metal letters, holding them down against the plate with a gloved hand as it cooled. He did a few more, and noticed the boy watching closely.

"Why don't you try one, Dan? I'll hold it in place."

"Really?"

Steve took the next letter and placed it, putting a spot weld to hold it. He guided the boy's hand as he worked around the letter with the solder.

He straightened up, clicked off the torch, and raised the visor. "Good job. Maybe someday you could work in the garage here."

"That would be fun."

Steve considered the boy for a moment. "Dan, how come you aren't afraid of me? Some kids are, it seems." Which still included Stanley's boys, unfortunately.

"Well, sir, I know Sid and them say to stay away. But my dad told me there was nothing to be afraid of, that you wouldn't hurt anyone who didn't have it coming. Said if I ever saw you I should talk to you because I could learn a lot."

Steve nodded. "You tell your dad I appreciate that, and he is right. I enjoy teaching, and I never hurt anyone unless I had to protect property or person. Did you know I was the sheriff here for a long time ?"

"No sir. Was it dangerous?"

"Sometimes. But a man does what he has to do. And he should always consider what the right thing is, and do that. Regardless of the cost. God blesses the diligent, responsible, and compassionate."

Steve flipped the visor back down. "Now, let's finish up this line, and I'll show you how we make a period after the 'C.'"

Farewells and Peg Legs
~1962~

"You what?!" Charles Kaplan stared at Steve. His Eighth Heaven neighbor seemed genuinely shocked.

Steve and Charles were sitting at the corner of Highway 73 and Pinyon Road, just across from Pinyon Flats. Steve often sat there, on a chair he had brought from home, ready to converse with anyone who wished. The topics were wide-ranging: the Santa Rosa mountain communities, desert history, desert rats, desert flora and fauna, politics, writings, books—anything was game. Charles frequently stopped by to chat.

"I know you've always loved my cabin. I'd like to sell it to you, if you want it," Steve said.

"But...why? You've owned that for what, almost thirty years? You love that place. Why do you want to sell it?"

"I don't *want* to. It's the perfect location for solitude, peace, and enjoying the wonderful things that God has created." He settled back a little more in his chair, slumping slightly. "My health is not what it has been. My heart's not well, and I have trouble breathing. Doctor says I'm gonna have to start carrying oxygen around soon. Tough to hike in the mountains with a metal canister. The trip up the dirt roads, the switchbacks, and the elevation..." He paused for a moment, his thoughts drifting. "Like I said, I know how much you admire it, so I'm offering it to you first."

"Steve, I am stunned and flattered. It would be an honor. You're one of the most famous men around here, and that cabin is your most famous residence. I read that lengthy article about you in *Desert Magazine*, I think it was the last issue."

"I saw it." Randall had written it. Though he was no longer the owner or editor, the magazine staff were happy to publish anything he wrote. This one was more lengthy than the little notice he wrote ten years ago. Steve thought it was well-written and that it captured him quite well.

But it also read like an obituary.

"Thanks, but I ain't one for flattery. Being successful means you don't get a big head when you get flattered. I've done what I've done, and now it's time to do something different."

Charles regarded him for a moment. He'd always seen Desert Steve as larger than life. But sitting with him now, he noticed the frailty. A bit of slowness.

"None of my children are interested. Has to be someone who will appreciate it. Take care of it, keep it up. Enjoy it as much as I have." He took a puff of his pipe. "That person is you."

"Thank you."

Steve shrugged. "There's no hurry or deadline. Whenever you're ready, I'm ready."

"Give me a few days to figure out some funding, and we can draw up the paperwork." He leaned forward. "But if you change your mind before then, you let me know, and we will end it."

"In my mind, it's already sold. Shake." He held out his hand.

The two men shook solemnly. Charles noticed that Steve's handshake was still as strong as ever.

Steve pushed his way into Randall's house as soon as the host opened the door.

"Uh, come on in," Randall said, amused at his friend.

"You seen this?" Steve handed him the latest copy of *Desert Magazine*. March 1965, folded open to page twenty.

"Of course I've seen it. Just because I sold the magazine doesn't mean I don't keep up. I still—"

"Have you read it?"

"Scanned the part written by Choral. Another hoax, right?"

"Read the letter."

Randall frowned playfully and took the magazine from him. "Dear Choral Pepper, although the enclosed story has no by-line, I believe—"

"Not the whole thing. Just the part where it talks about the nuggets."

"Okay…let's see…

More important, I am also enclosing two of the Peg Leg nuggets. One is still black, exactly as found and the other has the black copper oxides removed by the process mentioned in the story and is now native 'gold' in color. You will have these nuggets to show one and all who have doubted the story of peg leg black nuggets. You may keep them with my compliments for the desert magazines collection of desert artifacts – – – in this case you can start a new collection of items from the mine that have been found.

He looked up at Steve. "So. Another hoax."

"This one is different." He looked around the room, as if seeing it for the first time. "Is Cyria here?"

"No, she went into town to—"

"Sit down and read the entire article. I'll go make some coffee."

Randall smiled, knowing that once Steve got ahold of something he was passionate about, he would plow ahead, with blinders on for anything else.

The article began with a note from the editor, Choral Peppers, saying that the letter and the article were sent anonymously to the magazine, and they did not have time to fully vet it, but believed there was enough truth in it that it should be printed. Apparently, the anonymous author had also sent some gold nuggets along with the letter.

The letter was short, but the article was fairly long. By the time Randall had finished, Steve had brewed the coffee, poured two cups, and sat quietly, waiting.

"Quite well-written. This is no uneducated man," Randall said.

"He says he's not a scientist, but his detailed explanations, with scientific terms, descriptions of where gold comes from, how it gets found, and why Peg Leg's gold is high in content, how it oxidized—black gold."

"Anyone would know that if they asked around and did a little research."

"True," Steve said. "But his writing skills are excellent. Most prospectors I know can't write worth a damn."

"So now you think Peg Leg's mine is real and this gentleman found it?"

"No! I still think Peg Leg was an old reprobate who stole the nuggets from other prospectors or unattended mines. I might be open to the idea that he found a few nuggets here and there and decided to make up a story. But there's no mine."

"Fair enough. It says right here that he didn't tell anybody about for ten years because he knew everybody would descend on his discovery. Says he spent a few days every year removing every trace of gold he could find on the surface or slightly below it," Randall said, glancing down at the article.

"Sounds reasonable, doesn't it? Except that ain't how geology works. You don't find that much gold just sitting on the sand. Also, if he's taken all the gold, why won't he tell anyone where it is? He says he's not gonna buy the claim or try to do any excavation himself."

"Okay. But he says he made $314,650 from all the nuggets he found over the last ten years. That's a lot of money, but it's far less than the legend and what others have said. It's always been rumored it's in the millions. Why would he make up a number so much smaller, if he's pretending he found the mine? *That* would cause people to question whether it is Peg Leg's."

"Because he is smart, and he knows that people like you, who know the legend well, would be more inclined to believe him if he *didn't* exaggerate."

Randall frowned. "You're assuming that he's a con man. What if he really found it and that's the actual amount? It wouldn't be surprising that Peg Leg exaggerated his find, then this gentleman finds it and is just being honest as to what was there."

"That's the *only* reason I doubt it. I'm saying when you put all the questions together, he didn't find Peg Leg's mine. He's a new sort of fraudster—a smart one. Take the legend to a whole new level. *That's* what he wants. Not just another easily dismissed huckster. But it's fake."

"Then why are you so interested?" Randall asked.

"Because I enjoy desert lore and legend. For someone to come along and mislead the poor readers of *Desert Magazine* who don't know better is troubling."

"Well," Randall said. "If I didn't know better, I'd think you were jealous. Even if it *is* fake, it's a good one, as you say. Best ever."

Steve fixed him with a stare. "It's fake. 'Nuf sed."

They both were quiet for a moment.

"Maybe I do wish I'd thought of it," Steve said. "But I'm gonna write a letter to the magazine taking it all apart. Do you think they'll publish it?"

"I'm sure they would if it was a letter to the editor. I don't know if they'd publish a full article rebutting it, but maybe. You know we've published a lot of material about Peg Leg, including many where it was claimed to be 'found.'"

"And every one of them, fake."

"So far. But by your own admission, this one is different. Plenty of details, he sent samples, a timeline that fits. The only real question is why is he keeping the location hidden after he removed all the gold. But people are quirky." He looked over his glasses at his friend. "Desert Steve."

Steve cackled. "Fair enough. But I've been thinking. This is why I'm here talking to you. If it is another hoax, then who is this man? Who would do this for fun? Who is smart enough?"

Steve continued looking at Randall, waiting.

Randalls head snapped up. "Oh!"

"Harry Oliver," they both said at the same time.

"Let's go pay him a visit," Steve said.

"It wasn't me, my friends, although I wish it had been. This is an excellent job. Nice touch to send some genuine black nuggets."

Steve and Randall looked at each other and then looked back at Harry.

"Are you saying it wasn't you? Just like you are not the one who carved wooded peg legs and put them all over the desert?"

"I don't know anything about that. But that would be more my style. And I do know how to carve wood." He smiled as the two other men shook their heads. "But, no, my friends, hand on the Bible, swear to God in heaven, I am not behind this." He paused for a moment. "Wish he'd sent that letter to my *Scrapbook*. Could use the article and publicity. We've scarcely been able to put out the last two issues. I have been running a lot of older material again."

"I been writing a bit about how we need better laws to protect the desert wildlife," Steve said. "I could get you something if it would help."

Both men turned to look at Steve. "*You* want more government regulations?"

"My fine fellows, I never said I was against *all* laws. Just the preponderance of them into areas where they're unnecessary."

"We should go search for this. The map he included covers a large area, but with his details, we might be able to narrow it down," Harry said.

"You're crazy," Randall said. "You and I are both seventy-seven, and Steve is older than that!"

"That's right," Steve replied. "I'm your elder, and I'm telling you that none of us is strong to go traipsing around the desert for something that doesn't exist." He brushed off his legs and stood up. "More's the pity. And speaking of that, I need to get back to Betwixt and Between. You ready, Randall?"

Randall nodded stood as well. "Sorry for bursting in, Harry, and thanks for your hospitality."

"Always good to see you, old friends."

They went to the door and opened it. Steve turned back.

"I still ain't convinced you're not behind this."

Harry shrugged and smiled.

What All Men Get in Time

~1965–1970~

Several months later, Steve sat on his front porch, smoking his pipe, looking out at the hills and mountains from Betwixt and Between. There were four or five sheets of paper sitting on his lap. Other sheets were scattered on the wooden deck. Desert magazines lay on a nearby table, along with a couple of old books.

The sound of a vehicle stirred him from his reverie. It was Harry Oliver's brown sedan. The old artist, director, publisher, and desert rat carefully got out of the car and paused, hands on his hips, looking at Steve.

"Hello, Steve, my friend. How are you this afternoon?"

"You're a sight for sore eyes. It's been a while."

"My apologies, it's getting harder to get around. Went to Palm Springs to talk to my lawyer about some things I'm doing. Can't come this close without seeing you. Mind if I join you?"

"Harry Oliver is always welcome."

Harry trudged slowly up the short path and climbed the steps with care. He sat down heavily in the chair next to Steve.

"How are you doing?"

Steve took a couple of puffs of his pipe, then removed the stem from his mouth and sighed. "Just got a letter from my niece, Ruth. My sister, Minnie, passed away."

"My condolences. Are you going to the funeral?"

"Don't think I can make the trip. Minnie lives...lived...in Taft. Maybe, if Stanley would go. Her husband Robert died a while back. I was at their wedding in Taft in...well, must've been about 1912. I was farming cotton in Blythe."

"Did she have other children?"

"Has another daughter named Marion. Only met her a few times. Last time I talked to Minnie, she had just had a new grandchild. The sixth, I believe."

They sat quietly for a while, basking in the comfort of a long friendship and beautiful scenery.

"Minnie was five years younger than me. We got along pretty well growing up."

"How many brothers and sisters you have? A lot, as I recall."

Steve nodded. "Six. My youngest brother Daniel ran away from home when he was sixteen, but I was long gone by then and really didn't know him. No one knows what happened to him. Next youngest was William—he was just a small boy when I left. Alice, the oldest, and Charlie, the next oldest, live in Oklahoma with their families. Rosa lives in Van Nuys. Just saw her a few weeks ago. My mother died in '28, and my dad died seventeen years later. Never heard from him much after he remarried." He took a puff. "Minnie is the first to pass."

"That must be a shock. Being younger."

"Going to start happening more often." He looked at his friend. "Before you drove up, I was sitting here contemplating that the end is coming."

"What do you mean?"

"My death."

"That's a bit morbid and premature."

"No reason to get maudlin. 'What all men get in time, who, fool-like try to rhyme.'"

"Who wrote that?"

Steve took the pipe out of his mouth and grinned. "Me."

They both laughed.

"Already got my grave ready for me. Across from Desert Center. Right where I want to be planted."

Harry chuckled. "I'm envious. I checked on doing the same for myself on my property in Borrega Springs, but the county told me, in no uncertain terms, that bodies could not be buried there."

"Bastards. Governments wants to license our birth, tax our property, tell us how and when and where we can build on our own land, how we die, and everything in between. Soon they'll pass laws telling us we can't even smoke a pipe."

The two men sat together, watching the sun creep towards the mountain line.

"Heard you sold Eighth Heaven."

"Couple years ago. My health just wouldn't let me get up that way anymore. Doc says my breathing and heart will only get worse. But I'm fine for now with my oxygen tank. Don't need it too often."

"Speaking of health, I'm going to cease publication of *Desert Rat Scrap Book*. You know I could never publish on a steady schedule because money was always scarce. Subscriptions have dropped off a lot."

Steve nodded. "No one that can take it over?"

"Trying to find someone, but no luck so far. There's an ex-merchant seaman who lives near me, he's expressed some interest. We'll see."

Fifteen minutes passed. Harry stirred.

"I suppose I should head back out before it gets much darker."

Steve picked up the papers on his lap, tapped them together on his leg, and set them beside him on the table. "You're welcome to stay the night. Get a start after breakfast."

"I was hoping you'd offer. I've missed our talks about the desert, politics, art, and writing."

Steve looked over at his old friend and smiled. "Agreed. Talking with my desert brothers is one of the few pleasures left for me."

The door to the café burst open and Riley, one of the mechanics, came rushing in. He scanned the room and saw Steve eating breakfast, at his usual corner table.

"Mr. Ragsdale! Tommy's dead! Murdered!"

Steve stared at him with a fork halfway to his mouth.

Stanley came out of the office. "Riley! What's the ruckus?"

"Tommy was murdered last night, boss! They found his body off Eagle Mountain Road."

"Where? Who did it?" Steve said.

"Supposedly the station was robbed, and he went a-chasin' them in his pickup! Body was found between Phone Line Road and the mine."

"Alright. I need to get out there." He stood up.

Stanley put his hand on his father's shoulder. "Dad. You aren't a police officer any longer. And your oxygen. Remember?"

Steve glared at him. "I know that. I *was* one. And this is my town. I got oxygen in the car."

"Well, technically, you don't own the town, I—"

"Listen, boy—" Steve's glare intensified.

"Father. I understand. But it happened last night. The police have already been there—right, Riley?" He glanced at the young man but did not wait for an answer. "There's nothing you can do. Let them handle it." He gently helped his father sit back down. "Get back to work, Riley."

As if on cue, the café doors opened and two officers entered. Steve recognized them: Jonathan Margrave and Terry Rose. Rose was a detective. Stanley motioned the two men over.

"Steve, Stanley. How are you gentleman?" Margrave said with a nod to each.

"We're fine, officers. You here about Tommy's murder?" Stanley said.

Rose spoke. "You heard?"

"Riley here was just telling us. Do you need me?" Steve said.

"Just informing you of the crime, and ask some questions. You don't own the East Side Service Station on Rice Road, do you?"

"No," Stanley spoke before his father had a chance. "Have a seat, gentleman. We own the land, but Tommy Shorter owns the station." He paused. "Owned."

"We have other officers with his family."

"Can you tell us what happened?"

Rose took a small notebook out. "About 6:00pm last night, two young men stopped for gas at the Eastside station. Tommy filled up their car and gave them the bill. They drove off without paying, and Tommy went after them in his pickup."

"Just what I'd have done..." Steve muttered. "If I'd been alerted last night—"

Thurman put a hand on his father's arm. "Let him finish."

"Near as we've pieced it together, the boys tried to get off the road to escape Shorter and got stuck in the sand. Shorter arrived and they shot him dead on the spot. Then they took his pickup truck. We're out looking."

"What kind of gun did they use?" Steve asked.

Rose looked down at his notebook. "A .25 caliber pistol. Don't know the make and model yet. Did any of you see or notice anything last night?"

Thurman called the hostess over, who had worked last night. She had nothing to report, but said she'd talk to the rest of the staff and let the officers know if she heard anything.

After a few more questions, the officers stood to leave.

"You sure you don't need me?" Steve said. I know this land better than anyone. I was the sheriff here for decades."

Margrave nodded. "I know. And appreciate the offer. At the moment, we've got the men on it. But we'll surely let you know if and when we need some help."

They nodded and took their leave of the Ragsdales.

They two men sat silently for a while.

Steve shook his head, staring into his cold coffee cup. "Murder in Desert Center. Who'd have thought it? Nothing like that used to happen."

"Different times. And there were not as many people here then. The more people you got, the higher the number of bad ones. Harder to control."

"Suppose that's true." Steve sighed heavily. "Success creates more problems than failure, sometimes." He looked up at the ceiling. "'Success brings problems, failure brings opportunities.' Might have something there. Gotta make it rhyme—" He stopped suddenly and looked down at the table. Stanley thought he saw tears in his father's eyes.

He had never seen his father cry.

He looked at old man. The creased lines were deep. His hair was all white now, the beard around his mouth colored yellow from tobacco smoke. But it was his eyes that caught Stanley's attention. They were dull. Staring. Unfocused.

"Father?"

Steve didn't answer. Then he picked up the cup and drained it. He grimaced.

"I'm fine. I'm always fine. Just…just a lot lately. Minnie died years ago. Sarah died in '67—I have no sisters. And did you hear that Kaplan turned over my cabin to the Forest Service a few months ago?"

"I did hear. Guess he was getting too old and the Forest Service didn't want anyone living up there."

"Bastards. All of them. Kaplan told me he'd take care of it and then he gives it to the *government*?"

Stanley nodded. "At least it's the Forest Service. You appreciate them. They'll keep it safe."

"What the hell, son? Lookin' on the bright side?"

Stanley frowned. "What I said is true."

Steve got up. "I need more coffee." He turned back to his son. "And they should have called me in last night. I was *here*, for God's sake. I know the desert better than anyone. Hell, I created this place."

He shuffled to the counter, muttering to himself.

Steve took his leave of Terry and wound his way through the crowd to the front of the church. He stood quietly as Cyria spoke with someone, then briefly hugged her and said, "My condolences."

She smiled through her tears and patted his hand. "You were so special to him," she said. "I know you will miss him."

Steve nodded and turned away. He made his way to the casket, glad that it was closed. He would rather remember his friend alive. He placed his hand on the casket.

"The desert will never be the same without you. Godspeed, Randall."

A voice beside him said, "I can't believe it. A heart attack. On July 4."

Steve glanced over to see Harry Oliver.

"I know he was working on a history of Palm Desert," continued Harry. "It would've been a great book."

"Yes," Steve said. "Wonder if he finished enough for it to be published. Or for someone to finish it up."

"Good question. Probably should ask Cyria. It would be a great memorial." Harry looked back down the aisle of the church. "There's John and Dr. Jaegar. Go say hello?"

The two made their way back up the aisle. The four men greeted each other.

"He's going to be missed in so many ways, by so many people," Edmund said.

The others nodded .

"What are you doing these days, Steve?" John asked.

"Mostly reading and writing at Betwixt and Between. Desert Center every once in a while. Can't travel as easily these days. You?"

"My health isn't so great these days, either. I'm mostly out at my place in Twenty-Nine Palms, painting."

"You still have your curio shop in Indio?" Harry asked.

John nodded. "My son runs it." He turned to Jaegar. "What are you up to?"

"Same as always. Living in Palm Springs, taking trips into the desert exploring the ecology." He turned to Steve. "When was the last time you saw Randall? I know you were quite close."

Steve nodded. "About a month ago. Didn't know it would be the last."

They turned to discussing some of their favorite memories of Randall. "Remember in the 20s when he used to fly those little planes all over California and Arizona?"

"I think that's why he got drafted in World War I."

"But his legacy is certainly the desert newspapers, and especially *Desert Magazine*, along with his books about the desert," Steve interjected.

"I see why you two were good friends," Edmund said. "You changed the desert by creating towns, he changed the desert by creating magazines."

Steve smiled. "I never thought about it that way." He sobered. "Must take your leave, gentlemen. Need to go get some oxygen from my car. Gotta find Terry. She drove me down."

They all said goodbye, each wondering how long it would be before they stood like this again, one less in number.

Steve looked around, but did not see Terry among the thinning crowd. He made his way outside, and found her waiting beside the car.

"Are you alright?" she asked.

"I'm fine." He stepped to the passenger side. "Thank you again for driving."

"No problem." She put a hand on his arm. "I'm not sure you are alright."

"I'll miss him, as will all the Colorado Desert." He pursed his lips, nodding. "And I'll join him sooner rather than later."

She helped him into the passenger seat, where he put on his oxygen mask and breathed deeply.

Terry went around and got in beside him and started the car. "You worried about dying?"

"Nah. No one ever really ever dies, for he or she lives in the mind of others who have known them, for the principles they lived by, and what they have done. I have lived a long life;

made many errors, but have always tried to do more good than harm."

She smiled. "I suppose that's all anyone can ask of us."

May 1, 1971
~Desert Center, California~

"Hey. What are you doing out here?"

Steve looked back at the entrance to the café. Stanley was standing in the doorway, holding the door open.

"Hello, son. Just looking."

Stanley let the door shut and came to stand beside his father. "You've been out here a long time. What are you looking at?"

Steve looked down the street to his right. Old Highway 60. Now Ragsdale Road. The café, the garage, a Greyhound Station. Across the street, the market, post office, camping store, jewelry and crystal store, and others. Cabins and trailers for rent. Down at the intersection with Rice Road, a StanCo service station. Stanley had also added a hamburger stand, and one of the more enterprising residents had set up a fried mushroom stand (Steve still had not tried one.) Housing developments on both sides of town and to the northeast.

He smiled. "Desert Center."

The two men stood silently for a while, father and son, in the warm afternoon of the desert.

"We've come quite a ways." Stanley said.

"From an old dilapidated cabin and a hand dug well? To this."

"You should be proud, Father. You set the course of history for this part of the desert."

"Certainly had a part in it. Successes, mistakes, joy, failure, triumphs. And sins."

"Feeling melancholy today?"

"It's the prerogative of the aged."

Stanley chuckled. "I suppose it is. Are you staying here tonight or headed back to Betwixt-and-Between?"

"Heading back. Oxygen tank is near empty." He turned to his car and opened the door. "I'm gonna go over and take a look at my old shack on The Alligator first."

"You haven't been there in a while. You looking at your grave as well?"

"Sure am. Keeps a man humble."

"Want me to go with you?"

"Naw. Prefer to be alone." He looked at Stanley. "Thank you."

"Okay. Be careful climbing the slope."

"Will do."

Steve considered walking down Ragsdale Road to Rice, then under the freeway to Aztec road (a dirt path) to The Alligator. But his oxygen issue settled it.

He drove his old Chevy sedan slowly on the dirt road to the end of the outcropping. His little shed stood there as always, but the door was standing open and one of the windows was broken. He had never put a lock on it. Probably some kids playing around. Never happened before.

He made his way carefully up the little slope to the two con-crete steps that he had poured so many decades ago. Inside, things were much the same as he had left them. He hadn't any belongings here to speak of, although there was some garbage laying on the floor—some food wrappers and beer bottles. Yeah. Kids.

So much of his early writing was done in this room. It has served him quite well until he built Eighth Heaven and then

Betwixt-and-Between. He tipped his hat to the place that had been so good to him for so long.

The dirt path up to the gravesite was steeper and longer than he remembered. By the time he reached it, he was gasping for air. He stood for a moment, beside the grave, catching his breath. Someone had lifted the wooden cover, and there was scrap wood and a large tree branch down inside the metal box. Looked like they'd tried to start a fire inside.

A motion up the slope caught his eye, and he glanced over to see a desert tortoise moving between one shaded rock to another.

"Hey, buddy. Should I crawl down and clean out my future resting place?"

The tortoise stopped at the sound of the voice, gazing around and fixing on Steve. They both stood for a moment, looking at one another. Then the turtle turned his head back and continued on his way.

"You're right. No need. We'll leave it for the people who bury me. I won't go in there until I ain't coming out. I've finished the race, done the best I could to keep the faith."

He walked up a little further to the large boulder with the metal epitaph. Now his breathing was quite labored, so he lowered his stiff body and sat down, leaning against a rock, catching his breath.

It was a beautiful day. *May 1, 1971. Goodness, how did I get here?* It didn't seem that long ago that he drove out here in a Model T with Lydia and the children to buy Old Man Gruendike's place. From here, higher up the slope, he could see I-10 and his town.

He turned his attention to the plaque he had made.

Founded D.C. Sept. 21, 1921.
Worked like hell to be an honest American citizen.

Loved his fellow men and served them.
Hated booze guzzling, hated war, hated dirty deal
damn fool politicians.
Hopes a guy named Ragsdale will ever serve humanity
at Desert Center.
He dug his own grave. Here are his bones.
- Desert Steve.

Steve smiled and closed his eyes. "'Nuff sed."

Afterword

Desert Steve passed away on May 2, 1971, at his home in Pinyon Flats (now called Pinyon Pines). Although Steve had made a gentleman's agreement with Ben White, the head of the Riverside County Health Department, to allow his burial at The Alligator, White had retired. The new authority refused to honor the agreement. Even some of Steves' family did not want him buried there, so he was buried at the Coachella Public Cemetery, fifty miles from Desert Center. The same words appear above his occupied grave as the unoccupied one. You can still visit the foundations of Desert Steve's writing shed, the grave, and the plaque. (The latter was moved up higher to a larger boulder.)

Steve's wish that a Ragsdale would forever serve humanity in Desert Center was not to be. Stanley operated it until he died in 1999, though he refused to do anything that smacked of modernization. Riverside County once required him to make Desert Center more attractive, so he had several hundred palm trees planted in circles along the frontage of Interstate 10. When asked about it, he said that he had always wanted a "tree ring circus." After he passed away, palms died and fell over.

Lydia passed away in January 1980. The house that she lived in after Steve left in 1950 still stands, although it appears to have been abandoned after her death. It has been thoroughly ransacked, but there is still furniture, belongings, food jars and cans, clothing and bedding, and stacks of magazines, papers, and bills and letters, some dating back to the 1940s.

When Stanley died, no one in the family wanted to take over. A few grandchildren and others tried to keep it up, but to no avail. Some family and other residents continued to live there as the town fell apart. The café finally closed in 2012, after ninety-one years of being open twenty-four hours a day.

Desert Center was used in several films in later years: *Tough Guys* (1986); *Terminator 2: Judgment Day* (1991); *H. G. Wells' War of the Worlds* (2005); *Desert Road End* (2006); *Falling Objects* (2006); *Unknown* (2006); *Battle of Los Angeles* (Eagle Mountain Mine site) (2011).

After the café closed, the rest of the businesses followed. Residents left. The plunge pool, dry now, is filled with old equipment. The housing and trailers to the east of town are now abandoned, ransacked, and falling apart. The market's roof caved in. The gas stations closed, and finally, all the businesses left except the post office. The family fought over the estate for many years, finally ending in a probate sale of a thousand acres in 2019. In May 2022, the court approved the sale of the area to Riverside resident Balwinder S. Wraich for $6.25 million. His plans include service stations, food establishments, a market, and a hotel. He said if he could keep anything of historical significant, he would.

As of my last visit in July 2024, Desert Center was still a decaying ghost town, except for the post office. Skyway, Utopia, and Shaver's Well are lost. Cactus City exists as a rest stop along Interstate 10, with no services except bathrooms. Hell was paved over with a new routing of the I-10, leaving only a few foundations beside the road. Gruendike's Well, or at least where I think it is, is now in the middle of the desert sands, out beyond acres of solar panels, marked by a few concrete foundations and a 10-inch iron pipe, sealed at the top.

The Colorado Aqueduct still provides much of Southern California's water, and has been expanded and updated in the years since.

General Patton's base was eventually packed up and everything taken away, although the foundations from some old buildings and pieces of discarded equipment remain among the sands.

The airfield was purchased by Chuckwalla Valley Associates, LLC, and became the Chuckwalla Valley Raceway in 2010. It is considered by many to be Southern California's premier road course, holding events year-round.

The Eagle Mountain Mine closed operations in 1982. The town that was built for the miners and their families—with four thousand residents at its largest—is now the largest ghost town of the approximately three hundred in California. However, Lake Tamarisk, built for the executives and managers, is still a functioning community with its golf course and small lakes.

Acknowledgements

This is a work of fiction, although I used Desert Steve and many other historical characters for inspiration, after conducting about four years of research. The flow of events is historical, although I moved a few scenes to serve the interests of the narrative. I learned a lot about the historical people mentioned herein, but any resemblance to those real people would be co-incidental, as I have never met any of them. My goal is to entertain, teach some history of the American West in the 1900s, and offer some exploration of the human condition.

If you are interested in history, and how some of the historical elements fit in with this novel, as well as some background material that does not appear in the novel, I have a series of ongoing posts about each chapter, which you can find here:

https://markusmcdowell.com/books-fiction/desert-steve-novel/

The idea for this novel came to me in November 2019. I had used the Desert Center Café for a scene in a previous novel, _To and Fro Upon the Earth_, even though I had never visited the town (thank you, online satellite maps). Once, driving from Phoenix to Los Angeles (just as Steve and his family did in 1915), I stopped there to check out the ghost town. I sent some pictures and videos from my phone to friend, Keith Johnson, who had read the earlier novel. He asked about the history of Desert Center. I didn't know, so I began researching. I discovered Desert Steve, his unique life, and the fascinating lives of desert rats and desert culture. The more I read, the more I thought, *this is great material for a historical fiction novel.*

This novel took longer to research than any other I have written. The first reason for this was because there are no definitive works on the life of Steve Ragsdale or the history of Desert Center. There are plenty of journal articles, essays, mentions in books, and a plethora of anecdotes, summaries, and recollections all over the internet. Researching and finding this material was a considerable task, and I was constantly coming across new bits and pieces, even as I worked on the final drafts. I am sure I have missed much, but I did my best to find as much as possible.

The second reason is that I have a tendency to over-research everything I do. When I was working on my PhD dissertation, at one point, my DoktorVater said to me, "You could research this topic for the rest of your life. At some point, you have to stop, and start writing." Sound advice, and is almost as hard for me to do now as it was back then.

There are many people I would like to thank for their help and encouragement in writing this book.

Jackie, the best sister anyone could hope for, and my clever and talented niece Sarah (both from the great state of Texas), for reading final drafts and offering input.

Tom Fuller (the California coast), my best friend and handyman extraordinaire, for his knowledge of building, fixing, repairing, renovating, and just about anything you can imagine along those lines.(In that way, he's a lot like Desert Steve. But he rarely swears.) He read a late draft and offered ideas.

Nelya Rose Ake (Hollywood), a wonderful friend, kindred soul, and an incredible singer. Look her up!

The Marciniak family (New York): Kristie, Brenda, Frank and Linda, for their constant encouragement.

Keith Johnson and Rodney Smith (the great state of Texas), my steady and faithful friends from college, who are a constant encouragement to me and can always make me laugh.

Fellow authors Suzanne Perry (Arizona) and Angela Jikia in (Suffolk County, England) for their frequent encouragement and keeping me on track.

Milagros Yamira Viel Fernández (Florida and Cuba), my steady friend and reader of fine literature, for her love, encouragements, and Cuban cigars.

Sam (Palm Desert) for reaching out to tell me that she had explored a lot of Desert Center and knew which was Lydia's house. She guided me through that house and other buildings, sharing what she knew about Desert Steve and Lydia.

The Palm Desert Historical Society and staff.

Thanks also to the staff at Brophy Brothers' Clam Bar and Restaurant (Ventura) and the Aquifer64 bar at the JW Marriott Desert Springs Resort and Spa (Palm Desert) for providing me a spot to relax after writing, imbibe their concoctions, and for patiently listening to me drone on about my "Desert Steve novel."

Jeep, for constructing a solid and comfortable vehicle that allowed me to get up to Eighth Heaven, cross the desert sands to find Gruendike's Well, Patton's old airfield, the area around Eagle Mountain Mine, The Alligator, and much more.

'Nuff sed.

About the Author

If you enjoyed from this book, please consider posting an on-line review. It makes a big difference to the author. Thank you in advance.

Markus McDowell is an author and editor of fiction and non-fiction in multiple genres. He is the author of *To and Fro Upon the Earth: A Novel, Mortals As They Walk, Onesimus: A Novel of Christianity in the Roman Empire*, and two short story collections, *The Sky Over Chaos* and *So Deep in Shadow*, as well as several nonfiction books in law, theology, and literature in the ancient world. He lives in California on a boat and travels extensively.

Visit the author's website at
https://markusmcdowell.com/

Become a Patron
https://www.patreon.com/AuthorMarkusMcDowell

Follow on social media:
Instagram: https://www.instagram.com/doctormarkus_author/
Facebook: https://www.facebook.com/MarkusMcDowellAuthor/
X: https://x.com/markusmcdowell
Goodreads: http://goodreads.com/author/show/
8404913.Markus_McDowell

About the Publisher

Sulis International Press publishes select fiction and nonfiction in a variety of genres under four imprints:

- Riversong Books (fiction)

- Sulis Press (general nonfiction)

- Keledei Publications (spirituality)

- Sulis Academic Press (academic works)

For more, visit the website at
https://sulisinternational.com

Subscribe to the newsletter at
https://sulisinternational.com/subscribe/

Follow on social media
https://www.facebook.com/SulisInternational
https://twitter.com/Sulis_Intl
https://www.pinterest.com/Sulis_Intl/
https://www.instagram.com/sulis_international/